"UNTHINKING BOY, THAT SACRILEGIOUS FOOT TREADS ON THY MOTHER'S GRAVE."—PAGE 296.

LIONEL LINCOLN

OR

THE LEAGUER OF BOSTON

JAMES FENIMORE COOPER

Fredonia Books
Amsterdam, The Netherlands

Lionel Lincoln:
The Leaguer of Boston

by
James Fenimore Cooper

ISBN: 1-4101-0400-1

Reprinted from the 1896 edition

Fredonia Books
Amsterdam, The Netherlands
http://www.fredoniabooks.com

In order to make original editions of historical works available to scholars at an economical price, this facsimile of the original edition of 1896 is reproduced from the best available copy and has been digitally enhanced to improve legibility, but the text remains unaltered to retain historical authenticity.

TO

WILLIAM JAY,

OF

BEDFORD, WESTCHESTER,

ESQUIRE.

———

MY DEAR JAY,

An unbroken intimacy of four-and-twenty years may justify the present use of your name. A man of readier wit than myself might, on such a subject, find an opportunity of saying something clever, concerning the exalted services of your father. No weak testimony of mine, however, can add to a fame that belongs already to posterity ; and one like myself, who has so long known the merits, and has so often experienced the friendship of the son, can find even better reasons for offering these Legends to your notice.

Very truly and constantly,

Yours,

THE AUTHOR.

PREFACE.

THE manner in which the author became possessed of the private incidents, the characters, and the descriptions contained in these tales, will, most probably, ever remain a secret between himself and his publisher. That the leading events are true, he presumes it is unnecessary to assert; for should inherent testimony, to prove that important point, be wanting, he is conscious that no anonymous declaration can establish its credibility.

But while he shrinks from directly yielding his authorities, the author has no hesitation in furnishing all the negative testimony in his power.

In the first place, then, he solemnly declares that no unknown man or woman has ever died in his vicinity, of whose effects he has become the possessor, by either fair means or foul. No dark-looking stranger, of a morbid temperament, and of inflexible silence, has ever transmitted to him a single page of illegible manuscript. Nor has any landlord furnished him with materials to be worked up into a book, in order that the profits might go to discharge the arrearages of a certain consumptive lodger, who made his exit so unceremoniously as to leave the last item in his account, his funeral charges.

He is indebted to no garrulous tale-teller for beguiling the long winter evenings; in ghosts he has no faith; he never had a vision in his life; and he sleeps too soundly to dream.

He is constrained to add, that in no " puff," " squib,"

"notice," "article," or "review," whether in daily, weekly, monthly, or quarterly publication, has he been able to find a single hint that his humble powers could improve. No one regrets this fatality more than himself; for these writers generally bring a weight of imagination to their several tasks, that, properly improved, might secure the immortality of any book, by rendering it unintelligible.

He boldly asserts that he has derived no information from any of the learned societies—and without fear of contradiction; for why should one so obscure be the exclusive object of their favors!

Notwithstanding he occasionally is seen in that erudite and abstemious association, the "Bread-and-Cheese Lunch," where he is elbowed by lawyers, doctors, jurists, poets, painters, editors, congressmen, and authors of every shade and qualification, whether metaphysical, scientific, or imaginative; he avers that he esteems the lore which is there culled, as far too sacred to be used in any work less dignified than actual history.

Of the colleges it is necessary to speak with reverence; though truth possesses claims even superior to gratitude. He shall dispose of them by simply saying, that they are entirely innocent of all his blunders; the little they bestowed having long since been forgotten.

He has stolen no images from the deep, natural poetry of Bryant; no pungency from the wit of Halleck; no felicity of expression from the richness of Percival; no satire from the caustic pen of Paulding; no periods nor humor from Irving; nor any high finish from the attainments exhibited by Verplanck.

At the "*soirées*" and "*coteries des bas blues*" he did think he had obtained a prize, in the dandies of literature who haunt them. But experience and analysis detected his error; as they proved these worthies unfit for any better purpose than that which their own instinct had already dictated.

He has made no impious attempt to rob Joe Miller of his jokes; the sentimentalists of their pathos; or the newspaper Homers of their lofty aspirations.

His presumption has not even imagined the vivacity of the Eastern States; he has not analyzed the homogeneous character of the Middle; and he has left the South in the undisturbed possession of all their saturnine wit.

In short, he has pilfered from no black-letter book, or sixpenny pamphlet; his grandmother unnaturally refused her assistance to his labors; and, to speak affirmatively, for once, he wishes to live in peace, and hopes to die in the fear of God.

LIONEL LINCOLN.

CHAPTER I.

"My weary soul they seem to soothe,
And, redolent of joy and youth,
To breathe a second spring. "

GRAY.

NO American can be ignorant of the principal events that induced the Parliament of Great Britain, in 1774, to lay those impolitic restrictions on the port of Boston which so effectually destroyed the trade of the chief town in her western colonies. Nor should it be unknown to any American how nobly, and with what devotedness to the great principles of the controversy, the inhabitants of the adjacent town of Salem refused to profit by the situation of their neighbors and fellow-subjects. In consequence of these impolitic measures of the English government, and of the laudable unanimity among the capitalists of the times, it became a rare sight to see the canvas of any other vessels than such as wore the pennants of the king, whitening the forsaken waters of Massachusetts Bay.

Towards the decline of a day in April, 1775, however, the eyes of hundreds had been fastened on a distant sail, which was seen rising from the bosom of the waves, making her way along the forbidden track, and steering directly for the mouth of the proscribed haven. With that deep solicitude in passing events which marked the period, a large group of spectators was collected on Beacon Hill, spreading from its conical summit far down the eastern declivity, all gazing intently on the object of their common interest. In so large an assemblage, however, there were those who were excited by very different feelings, and indulging in wishes directly opposite to each other. While the decent, grave, but wary citizen was endeavoring to conceal the bitterness of the sensations which soured his mind, under the appearance of a cold indifference, a few gay young men, who mingled in the throng, bearing about their persons the trappings of their martial profession, were loud in their exultations, and hearty in their congratulations on the prospect of hearing from their distant homes and absent friends. But the long, loud rolls of the drums, ascending on the evening air, from the adjacent common, soon called these idle spectators, in a body, from the spot, when the hill was left to the quiet possession of those who claimed the strongest right to its enjoyment. It was not, however, a period for open and unreserved communications. Long before the mists of evening had succeeded the shadows thrown from the setting sun, the hill was entirely deserted ; the remainder of the spectators having descended from the eminence, and held their several courses, singly, silent, and thoughtful, towards the rows of dusky roofs that covered the lowland, along the eastern side of the peninsula. Notwithstanding this appearance of apathy, rumor—which, in times of great excitement, ever finds means to convey its whisperings, when it dare not bruit its information aloud—was busy in circulating the unwelcome intelligence, that the stranger was the first of a fleet, bringing stores and reinforcements to an army already too numerous, and too confident of its power, to respect the law. No tumult or noise succeeded this unpleasant annunciation, but the doors of the houses were sullenly closed, and the windows darkened, as if the people intended to express their dissatisfaction, alone, by these silent testimonials of their disgust.

In the meantime the ship had gained the rocky entrance to the harbor, where, deserted by the breeze, and met by an adverse tide, she lay inactive, as if conscious of the unwelcome reception she must receive. The fears of the inhabitants of Boston had, however, exaggerated the danger ; for the vessel, instead of exhibiting the confused and disorderly throng of licentious soldiery which would have crowded a transport, was but thinly peopled, and her orderly decks were cleared of every incumbrance that could interfere with the comfort of those she did contain. There was an appearance in the arrangements of her external accommodations which would have indicated to an observant eye that she carried those who claimed the rank or possessed the means of making others contribute largely to their comforts. The few seamen who navigated the ship lay extended on different portions of the vessel, watching the lazy sails as they flapped against the masts, or indolently bending their looks on the placid waters of the bay ; while several menials, in livery, crowded around a young man who was putting his eager inquiries to the pilot, that had just boarded the vessel off the Graves. The dress of this youth was studiously neat, and from the excessive pains bestowed on its adjustment, it was obviously deemed, by its wearer, to be in the height of the prevailing customs. From the place where this inquisitive party stood, nigh the main-mast, a wide sweep of the quarter-deck was untenanted ; but nearer to the spot where the listless seaman hung idly over the tiller of the ship, stood a being of altogether different mould and fashion. He was a man who would have seemed in the very extremity of age, had not his quick, vigorous steps, and the glowing, rapid glances from his eyes, as he occasionally paced the deck, appeared to deny the usual indications of many years. His form was bowed, and attenuated nearly to emaciation. His hair, which fluttered a little wildly around his temples, was thin, and silvered to the whiteness of at least eighty winters. Deep furrows, like the lines of great age and long endured cares united, wrinkled his hollow cheeks, and rendered the bold, haughty outline of his prominent features still more remarkable. He was clad in a simple and somewhat tarnished suit of modest gray, which bore about it the ill-concealed marks of long and neglected use. Whenever he turned his piercing look from the shores, he moved swiftly

along the deserted quarter-deck, and seemed entirely engrossed with the force of his own thoughts, his lips moving
rapidly, though no sounds were heard to issue from a mouth
habitually silent. He was under the influence of one of
those sudden impulses in which the body, apparently, sym-
pathized so keenly with the restless activity of the mind,
when a young man ascended from the cabin, and took his
stand among the interested and excited gazers at the land,
on the upper deck. The age of this gentleman might have
been five-and-twenty. He wore a military cloak, thrown
carelessly across his form, which in addition to such parts of
his dress as were visible through its open folds, sufficiently
announced that his profession was that of arms. There was
an air of ease and high fashion gleaming about his person,
though his speaking countenance at times seemed melancholy, if not sad. On gaining the deck, this young officer,
encountering the eyes of the aged and restless being who
trod its planks, bowed courteously before he turned away to
the view, and in his turn became deeply absorbed in studying its fading beauties.

The rounded heights of Dorchester were radiant with the
rays of the luminary that had just sunk behind their crest,
and streaks of paler light were playing along the waters, and
gilding the green summits of the islands which clustered
across the mouth of the estuary. Far in the distance were
to be seen the tall spires of the churches, rising out of the
deep shadows of the town, with their vanes glittering in the
sunbeams, while a few rays of strong light were dancing
about the black beacon, which reared itself high above the
conical peak, that took its name from the circumstance of
supporting this instrument of alarms. Several large vessels
were anchored among the islands and before the town, their
dark hulls at each moment becoming less distinct through
the haze of evening, while the summits of their long lines of
masts were yet glowing with the marks of day. From each
of these sullen ships, from the low fortification which rose
above a small island deep in the bay, and from various ele-
vations in the town itself, the broad silky folds of the flag of
England were yet waving in the currents of the passing air.

The young man was suddenly aroused from gazing at this scene by the quick reports of the evening guns, and while his eyes were yet tracing the descent of the proud symbols of the British power from their respective places of display, he felt his arm convulsively pressed by the hand of his aged fellow passenger.

"Will the day ever arrive," said a low, hollow voice at his elbow, "when those flags shall be lowered, never to rise again in this hemisphere?"

The young soldier turned his quick eyes to the countenance of the speaker, but bent them instantly in embarrassment on the deck, to avoid the keen, searching glance he encountered in the looks of the other. A long, and, on the part of the young man, a painful silence, succeeded this remark. At length the youth, pointing to the land, said,—

"Tell me, you who are of Boston, and must have known it so long, the names of all these beautiful places I see."

"And are you not of Boston, too?" asked his old companion.

"Certainly, by birth, but an Englishman by habit and education."

"Accursed be the habits, and neglected the education, which would teach a child to forget its parentage!" muttered the old man, turning suddenly, and walking away so rapidly as to be soon lost in the forward parts of the ship.

For several minutes longer the youth stood absorbed in his own musings, when, as if recollecting his previous purposes, he called aloud,—"Meriton!"

At the sounds of his voice the curious group around the pilot instantly separated, and the highly ornamented youth, before mentioned, approached the officer with a manner in which pert familiarity and fearful respect were peculiarly blended. Without regarding the air of the other, however, or indeed without even favoring him with a glance, the young soldier continued,—

"I desired you to detain the boat which boarded us, in order to convey me to the town, Mr. Meriton; see if it be in readiness."

The valet flew to execute this commission, and in an instant returned with a reply in the affirmative.

"But, sir," he continued, "you will never think of going in that boat, I feel very much assured, sir."

"Your assurance, Mr. Meriton, is not the least of your recommendations; why should I not?"

"That disagreeable old stranger has taken possession of it, with his mean, filthy bundle of rags; and—"

"And what? you must name a greater evil, to detain me here, than mentioning the fact that the only gentleman in the ship is to be my companion."

"Lord, sir!" said Meriton, glancing his eye upward in amazement: "but, sir, surely you know best as to gentility of behavior; but as to gentility of dress—"

"Enough of this," interrupted his master, a little angrily; "the company is such as I am content with; if you find it unequal to your deserts, you have my permission to remain in the ship until the morning; the presence of a coxcomb is by no means necessary to my comfort for one night."

Without regarding the mortification of his disconcerted valet, the young man passed along the deck to the place where the boat was in waiting. By the general movement among the indolent menials, and the profound respect with which he was attended by the master of the ship to the gangway, it was sufficiently apparent that, notwithstanding his youth, it was this gentleman whose presence had exacted those arrangements in the ship which have been mentioned. While all around him, however, were busy in facilitating the entrance of the officer into the boat, the aged stranger occupied its principal seat, with an air of deep abstraction, if not of cool indifference. A hint from the pliant Meriton, who had ventured to follow his master, that it would be more agreeable if he would relinquish his place, was disregarded, and the youth took a seat by the side of the old man, with a simplicity of manner that his valet inwardly pronounced abundantly degrading. As if this humiliation were not sufficient, the young man, perceiving that a general pause had succeeded his own entrance, turned to his companion, and courteously inquired if he were ready to proceed. A silent wave of the hand was the reply, when the boat shot away from the vessel, leaving the ship steering for an anchorage in Nantasket.

The measured dash of the oars was uninterrupted by any voice, while, stemming the tide, they pulled laboriously up among the islands ; but by the time they had reached the castle, the twilight had melted into the softer beams from a young moon, and, the surrounding objects becoming more distinct, the stranger commenced talking with that quick and startling vehemence which seemed his natural manner. He spoke of the localities with the vehemence and fondness of an enthusiast, and with the familiarity of one who had long known their beauties. His rapid utterance, however, ceased as they approached the naked wharves, and he sunk back gloomily in the boat, as if unwilling to trust his voice on the subject of his country's wrongs. Thus left to his own thoughts, the youth gazed with eager interest at the long ranges of buildings, which were now clearly visible to the eye, though with softer colors and more gloomy shadows. A few neglected and dismantled ships were lying at different points ; but the hum of business, the forests of masts, and the rattling of wheels, which at that early hour should have distinguished the great mart of the colonies, were wanting. In their places were to be heard, at intervals, the sudden bursts of distant, martial music, the riotous merriment of the soldiery who frequented the taverns at the water's edge, or the sullen challenges of the sentinels from the vessels of war, as they vexed the progress of the few boats which the inhabitants still used in their ordinary pursuits.

"Here, indeed, is a change !" the young officer exclaimed, as they glided swiftly along this desolate scene ; " even my recollections, young and fading as they are, recall the difference."

The stranger made no reply, but a smile of singular meaning gleamed across his wan features, imparting, by the moonlight, to their remarkable expression, a character of additional wildness. The officer was again silent, nor did either speak until the boat, having shot by the end of the long wharf, across whose naked boundaries a sentinel was pacing his measured path, inclined more to the shore, and soon reached the place of its destination.

Whatever might have been the respective feelings of the two passengers, at having thus reached in safety the object of their tiresome and protracted voyage, they were not expressed in language. The old man bared his silver locks, and, concealing his face with his hat, stood as if in deep mental thanksgiving at the termination of his toil, while his more youthful companion trod the wharf on which they landed with the air of a man whose emotions were too engrossing for the ordinary use of words.

"Here we must part, sir," the officer at length said; "but I trust the acquaintance, which has been thus accidentally formed between us, is not to be forgotten now there is an end to our common privations."

"It is not in the power of a man whose days, like mine, are numbered," returned the stranger, "to mock the liberality of his God, by any vain promises that must depend on time for their fulfilment. I am one, young gentleman, who has returned from a sad, sad pilgrimage, in the other hemisphere, to lay his bones in this, his native land; but should many hours be granted me, you will hear further of the man whom your courtesy and kindness have so greatly obliged."

The officer was sensibly affected by the softened but solemn manner of his companion, and pressed his wasted hand fervently as he answered,—

"Do; I ask it as a singular favor; I know not why, but you have obtained a command of my feelings that no other being ever yet possessed; and yet—'t is a mystery, 't is like a dream! I feel that I not only venerate, but love you."

The old man stepped back, and held the youth at the length of his arm for a moment, while he fastened on him a look of glowing interest, and then, raising his hand slowly, he pointed impressively upward, and said,—

"'T is from heaven, and for God's own purposes; smother not the sentiment, boy, but cherish it in your heart's core!"

The reply of the youth was interrupted by sudden and violent shrieks, that burst rudely on the stillness of the place, chilling the very blood of those who heard them, with their piteousness. The quick and severe blows of a lash were blended with the exclamations of the sufferer; and rude oaths, with hoarse execrations, from various voices, were united in the uproar, which appeared to be at no great distance. By a common impulse, the whole party broke away from the spot, and moved rapidly up the wharf in the direction of the sounds. As they approached the buildings, a group was seen collected around the man, who thus broke the charm of the evening by his cries, interrupting his wailings with their ribaldry, and encouraging his tormentors to proceed.

"Mercy, mercy, for the sake of the blessed God, have mercy, and don't kill Job!" again shrieked the sufferer; "Job will run your arr'nds! Job is half-witted! Mercy on poor Job! O! you make his flesh creep!"

"I'll cut the heart from the mutinous knave," interrupted a hoarse, angry voice. "To refuse to drink the health of his majesty!"

"Job does wish him good health—Job loves the king—only Job don't love rum."

The officer had approached so nigh as to perceive that the whole scene was one of disorder and abuse, and pushing aside the crowd of excited and deriding soldiers, who composed the throng, he broke at once into the centre of the circle.

CHAPTER II.

"They'll have me whipped for speaking;
Thou'lt have me whipped for lying;
And sometimes I'm whipped for holding my peace.
I had rather be any kind of a thing
Than a fool."

King Lear.

"WHAT means this outcry?" demanded the young man, arresting the arm of an infuriated soldier, who was inflicting the blows; "by what authority is this man thus abused?"

"By what authority dare you to lay hands on a British grenadier?" cried the fellow, turning in his fury, and raising his lash against the supposed townsman. But, when, as the officer stepped aside to avoid the threatened indignity, the light of the moon fell full upon his glittering dress, through the opening folds of his cloak, the arm of the brutal soldier was held suspended in air, with the surprise of the discovery.

"Answer, I bid you," continued the young officer, his frame shaking with passion; "why is this man tormented, and of what regiment are ye?"

"We belong to the grenadiers of the brave 47th, your honor," returned one of the bystanders, in a humble, deprecating tone, "and we was just polishing this 'ere natural, because as he refuses to drink the health of his majesty."

"He's a scornful sinner, that don't fear his Maker," cried the man in duress, eagerly bending his face, down which big tears were rolling, towards his protector. "Job loves the king, but Job don't love rum!"

The officer turned away from the cruel spectacle, as he bid the men untie their prisoner. Knives and fingers were instantly put in requisition, and the man was liberated, and suffered to resume his clothes. During this operation, the tumult and bustle, which had so recently distinguished the riotous scene, were succeeded by a stillness that rendered the hard breathing of the sufferer painfully audible.

"Now, sirs, you heroes of the 47th!" said the young man, when the victim of their rage was again clad, "know you this button?" The soldier to whom this question was more particularly addressed, gazed at the extended arm, and, to his vast discomfiture, he beheld the magical number of his own regiment reposing on the well-known white facings that decorated the rich scarlet of the vestment. No one presumed to answer this appeal, and after an impressive silence of a few moments, he continued,—

"You are noble supporters of the well-earned fame of 'Wolfe's own!' fit successors to the gallant men who conquered under the walls of Quebec! Away with ye! tomorrow it shall be looked to."

"I hope your honor will remember he refused his majesty's health. I'm sure, sir, that if Colonel Nesbitt was here himself—"

"Dog! do you dare to hesitate! go, while you have permission to depart."

The disconcerted soldiery, whose turbulence had thus vanished as if by enchantment before the frown of their superior, slunk away in a body, a few of the older men whispering to their comrades the name of the officer who had thus unexpectedly appeared in the midst of them. The angry eye of the young soldier followed their retiring forms, while a man of them was visible; after which, turning to an elderly citizen, who, supported on a crutch, had been a spectator of the scene, he asked,—

"Know you the cause of the cruel treatment this poor man has received; or what in any manner has led to the violence?"

"The boy is weak," returned the cripple; "quite an innocent, who knows but little good, but does no harm.

The soldiers have been carousing in yonder dram-shop, and they often get the poor lad in with them, and sport with his infirmity. If these sorts of doings ain't checked, I fear much trouble will grow out of them! Hard laws from t' other side of the water, and tarring and feathering on this, with gentlemen like Colonel Nesbitt at their head, will—"

"It is wisest for us, my friend, to pursue this subject no further," interrupted the officer. "I belong myself to 'Wolfe's own,' and will endeavor to see justice done in the matter; as you will credit when I tell you that I am a Boston boy. But, though a native, a long absence has obliterated the marks of the town from my memory; and I am at a loss to thread these crooked streets. Know you the dwelling of Mrs. Lechmere?"

"The house is well known to all in Boston," returned the cripple, in a voice sensibly altered by the information that he was speaking to a townsman. "Job, here, does but little else than run of errands, and he will show you the way, out of gratitude; won't you, Job?"

The idiot,—for the vacant eye and unmeaning, boyish countenance of the young man who had just been liberated, but too plainly indicated that he was to be included in that miserable class of human beings,—answered with a caution and reluctance that were a little remarkable, considering the recent circumstances.

"Ma'am Lechmere's! O! yes, Job knows the way, and could go there blindfolded, if—if—"

"If what, you simpleton?" exclaimed the zealous cripple.

"Why, if 't was daylight."

"Blindfolded, and daylight! do but hear the silly child! Come, Job, you must take this gentleman to Tremont Street, without further words. 'T is but just sundown, boy, and you can go there and be home in your bed before the Old South strikes eight!"

"Yes; that all depends on which way you go," returned the reluctant changeling. "Now, I know, neighbor Hopper, you could n't go to Ma'am Lechmere's in an hour, if you went along Lynn Street, and so along Prince Street, and back through Snow Hill; and especially if you should stop any time to look at the graves on Copp's."

"Pshaw! the fool is in one of his sulks now, with his Copp's Hill, and the graves!" interrupted the cripple, whose heart had warmed to his youthful townsman, and who would have volunteered to show the way himself, had his infirmities permitted the exertion. "The gentleman must call the grenadiers back, to bring the child to reason."

"'T is quite unnecessary to be harsh with the unfortunate lad," said the young soldier; "my recollections will probably aid me as I advance; and should they not, I can inquire of any passenger I meet."

"If Boston was what Boston has been, you might ask such a question of a civil inhabitant, at any corner," said the cripple; "but it's rare to see many of our people in the streets at this hour, since the massacre. Besides, it is Saturday night, you know; a fit time for these rioters to choose for their revelries! For that matter, the soldiers have grown more insolent than ever, since they have met that disappointment about the cannon down at Salem; but I need n't tell such as you what the soldiers are when they get a little savage."

"I know my comrades but indifferently well, if their conduct to-night be any specimen of their ordinary demeanor, sir," returned the officer; "but follow, Meriton; I apprehend no great difficulty in our path."

The pliant valet lifted the cloak-bag he carried, from the ground, and they were about to proceed, when the natural edged himself in a sidelong, slovenly manner, nigher to the gentleman, and looked earnestly up in his face for a moment, where he seemed to be gathering confidence to say, "Job will show the officer Ma'am Lechmere's, if the officer won't let the grannies catch Job afore he gets off the North End ag'in."

"Ah!" said the young man, laughing, "there is something of the cunning of a fool in that arrangement. Well, I accept the conditions; but beware how you take me to contemplate the graves by moonlight, or I shall deliver you not only to the grannies, but to the light infantry, artillery, and all."

With this good-natured threat, the officer followed his nimble conductor, after taking a friendly leave of the obliging cripple, who continued his admonitions to the natural, not to wander from the direct route, while the sounds of his voice were audible to the retiring party. The progress of his guide was so rapid as to require the young officer to confine his survey of the narrow and crooked streets through which they passed, to extremely hasty and imperfect glances. No very minute observation, however, was necessary to perceive that he was led along one of the most filthy and inferior sections of the town; and where, notwithstanding his efforts, he found it impossible to recall a single feature of his native place to his remembrance. The complaints of Meriton, who followed close at the heels of his master, were loud and frequent, until the gentleman, a little doubting the sincerity of his intractable conductor, exclaimed,—

"Have you nothing better than this to show a townsman, who has been absent seventeen years, on his return? Pray let us go through some better streets than this, if any there are in Boston which can be called better."

The lad stopped short, and looked up in the face of the speaker, for an instant, with an air of undisguised amazement, and then, without replying, he changed the direction of his route, and after one or two more deviations in his path, suddenly turning again, he glided up an alley, so narrow that the passenger might touch the buildings on either side of him. The officer hesitated an instant to enter this dark and crooked passage, but perceiving that his guide was already hid by a bend in the houses, he quickened his steps, and immediately regained the ground he had lost. They soon emerged from the obscurity of the place, and issued on a street of greater width.

"There!" said Job, triumphantly, when they had effected this gloomy passage, "does the king live in so crooked and narrow a street as that?"

"His majesty must yield the point in your favor," returned the officer.

"Ma'am Lechmere is a grand lady!" continued the lad, seemingly following the current of his own fanciful conceits, "and she would n't live in that alley for the world, though it is narrow, like the road to heaven, as old Nab says; I suppose they call it after the Methodies for that reason."

"I have heard the road you mention termed narrow, certainly, but it is also called *strait*," returned the officer, a little amused with the humor of the lad; "but forward, the time is slipping away, and we loiter."

Again Job turned, and moving onward, he led the way, with swift steps, along another narrow and crooked path, which, however, better deserved the name of a street, under the projecting stories of the wooden buildings which lined its sides. After following the irregular windings of their route for some distance, they entered a triangular area of a few rods in extent, where Job, disregarding the use of the narrow walk, advanced directly into the centre of the open space. Here he stopped once more, and turning his vacant face with an air of much seriousness towards a building which composed one side of the triangle, he said, with a voice that expressed his own deep admiration,—

"There—that 's the Old North did you ever see such a meetin'us' afore? does the king worship God in such a temple?"

The officer did not chide the idle liberties of the fool, for in the antiquated and quiet architecture of the wooden edifice, he recognized one of those early efforts of the simple, puritan builders, whose rude tastes have been transmitted to their posterity with so many deviations in the style of the same school, but so little of improvement. Blended with these considerations, were the dawnings of revived recollections; and he smiled, as he recalled the time when he also used to look up at the building with feelings somewhat allied to the profound admiration of the idiot. Job watched his countenance narrowly, and easily mistaking its expression, he extended his arm towards one of the narrowest of the avenues that entered the area, where stood a few houses of more than common pretension.

"And there ag'in!" he continued; "there's places for you! stingy Tommy lived in the one with the pile-axters, and the flowers hanging to their tops; and see the crowns on them, too! stingy Tommy loved crowns, they say; but Province'us' was n't good enough for him, and he lived here —now they say he lives in one of the king's cupboards!"

"And who was stingy Tommy? and what right had he to dwell in Province House, if he would?"

"What right has any governor to live in Province'us'? because it's the king's, though the people paid for it!"

"Pray, sir, excuse me," said Meriton, from behind; "but do the Americans usually call their governors stingy Tommies?"

The officer turned his head at this vapid question from his valet, and perceived that he had been accompanied thus far by the aged stranger, who stood at his elbow, leaning on his staff, studying with close attention the late dwelling of Hutchinson, while the light of the moon fell, unobstructed, on the deep lines of his haggard face. During the first surprise of this discovery he forgot to reply, and Job took the vindication of his language into his own hands.

"To be sure they do—they call people by their right names," he said. "Insygn Peck is called Insygn Peck; and you call Deacon Winslow anything but Deacon Winslow, and see what a look he'll give you! and I am Job Pray, so called; and why should n't a governor be called stingy Tommy, if he is a stingy Tommy?"

"Be careful how you speak lightly of the king's representative," said the young officer, raising his light cane with the affectation of correcting the changeling. "Forget you that I am a soldier?"

The idiot shrunk back a little, timidly, and then leering from under his sunken brow, he answered,—

"I heard you say you were a Boston boy."

The gentleman was about to make a playful reply, when the aged stranger passed swiftly before him, and took his stand at the side of the lad with a manner so remarkable for its earnestness that it entirely changed the current of his thoughts.

"The young man knows the ties of blood and country," the stranger muttered; "and I honor him!"

It might have been the sudden recollection of the danger of those allusions, which the officer so well understood, and to which his accidental association with the singular being who uttered them had begun to familiarize his ear, that induced the youth to resume his walk, silently, and in deep thought, along the street. By this movement he escaped observing the cordial grasp of the hand which the old stranger bestowed on the idiot, while he muttered a few more terms of commendation. Job took his station in front, and the whole party moved on again, though with less rapid strides. As the lad advanced deeper into the town he evidently wavered once or twice in his choice of streets, and the officer began to suspect that the changeling contemplated one of his wild circuits, to avoid the direct route to a house that he manifestly approached with great reluctance. Once or twice the young soldier looked about him, intending to inquire the direction of the first passenger he might see; but the quiet of deep night already pervaded the place, and not an individual, but those who accompanied him, appeared in the long ranges of streets they had passed. The air of the guide was becoming so dogged and hesitating that his follower had just determined to make an application at one of the doors, when they emerged from a dark, dirty, and gloomy street on an open space of much greater extent than the one they had so recently left. Passing under the walls of a blackened dwelling, Job led the way to the centre of a swinging bridge, which was thrown across an inlet from the harbor, that extended a short distance into the area, forming a shallow dock. Here he took his stand, and allowed the view of the surrounding objects to work its own effect on those he had conducted thither. The square was composed of rows of low, gloomy, and irregular houses, most of which had the appearance of being but little used. Stretching from the end of the basin, and a little on one side, a long, narrow edifice, ornamented with pilasters, perforated with arched windows, and surmounted by a humble cupola, reared its walls of brick under the light of the moon. The story which held the rows of silent, glistening windows, was supported on abutments and arches of the same material, through the narrow vista of which were to be seen the shambles of the common market-place. Heavy cornices of stone were laid above and beneath the pilasters, and something more than the unskilful architecture of the dwelling-houses they had passed was affected throughout the whole structure. While the officer gazed at this scene the idiot watched his countenance with a keenness exceeding his usual observation, until, impatient at hearing no words of pleasure or of recognition, he exclaimed,—

"If you don't know Funnel Hall, you are no Boston boy!"

"But I do know Faneuil Hall, and I am a Boston boy," returned the amused gentleman. "The place begins to freshen on my memory, and I now recall the scenes of my childhood."

"This, then," said the aged stranger, "is the spot where liberty has found so many bold advocates!"

"It would do the king's heart good to hear the people talk in old Funnel, sometimes," said Job. "I was on the cornishes, and looked into the winders, the last town-meetin'-da', and if there was soldiers on the common, there was them in the hall that did n't care for them!"

"All this is very amusing, no doubt," said the officer, gravely, "but it does not advance me a foot on my way to Mrs. Lechmere's."

"It is also instructing," exclaimed the stranger; "go on, child; I love to hear his simple feelings thus expressed; they indicate the state of the public mind."

"Why," said Job, "they were plain-spoken, that's all; and it would be better for the king to come over and hear them; it would pull down his pride, and make him pity the people, and then he would n't think of shutting up Boston harbor. Suppose he should stop the water from coming in by the Narrows, why, we should get it by Broad Sound! and if it did n't come by Broad Sound, it would by Nantasket! He need n't think that the Boston folks are so dumb as to be cheated out of God's water by acts of Parliament, while old Funnel stands in the Dock Square!"

"Sirrah!" exclaimed the officer, a little angrily, "we have already loitered until the clocks are striking eight."

The idiot lost his animation, and lowered in his looks again, as he answered,—

"Well, I told neighbor Hopper there was more ways to Ma'am Lechmere's than straight forward; but everybody knows Job's business better than Job himself. Now you make me forget the road; let us go in and ask old Nab; she knows the way too well!"

"Old Nab! you wilful dolt! who is Nab, and what have I to do with any but yourself?"

"Everybody in Boston knows Abigail Pray."

"What of her?" asked the startling voice of the stranger; "what of Abigail Pray, boy? is she not honest?"

"Yes, as poverty can make her," returned the natural, gloomily; "now the king has said there shall be no goods but tea sent to Boston, and the people won't have the bohea, it's easy living rent free. Nab keeps her huckster stuff in the old ware'us', and a good place it is, too. Job and his mother have each a room to sleep in, and they say the king and queen have n't more!"

While he was speaking, the eyes of his listeners were drawn by his gestures towards the singular edifice to which he alluded. Like most of the others adjacent to the square, it was low, old, dirty, and dark. Its shape was triangular, a street bounding it on each side, and its extremities were flanked by as many low hexagonal towers, which terminated, like the main building itself, in high pointed roofs, tiled, and capped with rude ornaments. Long ranges of small windows were to be seen in the dusky walls, through one of which the light of a solitary candle was glimmering, the only indication of the presence of life about the silent and gloomy building.

"Nab knows Ma'am Lechmere better than Job," continued the idiot, after a moment's pause, "and she will know whether Ma'am Lechmere will have Job whipped for bringing company on Saturday night, though they say she's so full of scoffery as to talk, drink tea, and laugh on that night, just the same as any other time."

"I will pledge myself to her courteous treatment," the officer replied, beginning to be weary of the fool's delay.

"Let us see this Abigail Pray," cried the aged stranger, suddenly seizing Job by the arm, and leading him, with a sort of irresistible power, towards the walls of the building, through one of the low doors of which they immediately disappeared.

Thus left on the bridge, with his valet, the young officer hesitated a single instant how to act; but yielding to the secret and powerful interest which the stranger had succeeded in throwing around all his movements and opinions, he bade Meriton await his return, and followed his guide and the old man into the cheerless habitation of the former. On passing the outer door he found himself in a spacious but rude apartment, which, from its appearance, as well as from the few articles of heavy but valueless merchandise it now contained, would seem to have been used once as a storehouse. The light drew his steps towards a room in one of the towers, where, as he approached its open door, he heard the loud, sharp tones of a woman's voice exclaiming,—

"Where have you been, graceless, this Saturday night? tagging at the heels of the soldiers, or gazing at the men-of-war, with their ungodly fashions of music and revelry at such a time, I dare to say! and you knew that a ship was in the bay, and that Madam Lechmere had desired me to send her the first notice of its arrival. Here have I been waiting for you to go up to Tremont Street since sundown, with the news, and you are out of call,—you, that know so well who it is she expects!"

"Don't be cross to Job, mother, for the grannies have been cutting his back with cords till the blood runs! Ma'am Lechmere! I do believe, mother, that Ma'am Lechmere has moved; for I've been trying to find her house this hour, because there's a gentleman who landed from the ship wanted Job to show him the way."

"What means the ignorant boy?" exclaimed his mother.

"He alludes to me," said the officer, entering the apartment; "I am the person, if any, expected by Mrs. Lechmere, and have just landed from the Avon, of Bristol; but your son has led me a circuitous path, indeed ; at one time he spoke of visiting the graves on Copp's Hill.''

''Excuse the ignorant and witless child, sir,'' exclaimed the matron, eying the young man keenly through her spectacles ; ''he knows the way as well as to his own bed, but he is wilful at times.   This will be a joyful night in Tremont Street! So handsome, and so stately, too! Excuse me, young gentleman,'' she added, raising the candle to his features with an evident unconsciousness of the act, ''he has the sweet smile of the mother, and the terrible eye of his father! God forgive us all our sins, and make us happier in another world than in this place of evil and wickedness!'' As she muttered the latter words, the woman set aside her candle with an air of singular agitation. Each syllable, notwithstanding her secret intention, was heard by the officer, across whose countenance there passed a sudden gloom that doubled its sad expression. He however said,—

''You know me and my family, then?''

''I was at your birth, young gentleman, and a joyful birth it was! but Madam Lechmere waits for the news, and my unfortunate child shall speedily conduct you to her door ; she will tell you all that it is proper to know. Job, you Job, where are you getting to, in that corner? take your hat, and show the gentleman to Tremont Street directly ; you know, my son, you love to go to Madam Lechmere's.''

''Job would never go, if Job could help it,'' muttered the sullen boy ; ''and if Nab had never gone, 'twould have been better for her soul.''

''Do you dare, disrespectful viper!'' exclaimed the angry quean, seizing, in the violence of her fury, the tongs, and threatening the head of her stubborn child.

''Woman, peace!'' said a voice behind.

The dangerous weapon fell from the nerveless hand of the vixen, and the hues of her yellow and withered countenance changed to the whiteness of death. She stood motionless for near a minute, as if riveted to the spot by a superhuman power, before she succeeded in muttering, ''Who speaks to me?''

"It is I," returned the stranger, advancing from the shadow of the door into the dim light of the candle; "a man who has numbered ages, and who knows that as God loves him, so is he bound to love the children of his loins."

The rigid limbs of the woman lost their stability in a tremor that shook every fibre in her body ; she sunk in her chair, and her eyes rolled from the face of one visitor to that of the other, while her unsuccessful efforts to utter, denoted that she had temporarily lost the command of speech. Job stole to the side of the stranger, in this short interval, and looking up in his face piteously, he said,—

"Don't hurt old Nab; read that good saying to her out of the Bible, and she 'll never strike Job with tongs ag'in ; will you, mother? See her cup, where she hid it under the towel, when you came in! Ma'am Lechmere gives her the pi'son tea to drink, and then Nab is never so good to Job as Job would be to mother, if mother was half-witted, and Job was old Nab."

The stranger considered the moving countenance of the boy, while he pleaded thus earnestly in behalf of his mother, with marked attention, and when he had done, he stroked the head of the natural compassionately, and said,—

"Poor, imbecile child! God has denied the most precious of his gifts, and yet his Spirit hovers around thee ; for thou canst distinguish between austerity and kindness, and thou hast learnt to know good from evil. Young man, see you no moral in this dispensation? nothing which says that Providence bestows no gift in vain ; while it points to the difference between the duty that is fostered by indulgence, and that which is extorted by power?"

The officer avoided the ardent looks of the stranger, and after an embarrassing pause of a moment, he expressed his readiness, to the reviving woman, to depart on his way. The matron, whose eye had never ceased to dwell on the features of the old man, since her faculties were restored, arose slowly, and in a feeble voice directed her son to show the road to Tremont Street. She had acquired, by long practice, a manner that never failed to control, when necessary, the wayward humors of her child, and on the present occasion, the unwonted solemnity imparted to her voice by deep agitation, aided in effecting her object. Job quietly arose and prepared himself to comply. The manners of the whole party wore a restraint, which implied they had touched on feelings that it would be wiser to smother, and the separation would have been silent, though courteous, on the part of the youth, had he not perceived the passage still filled by the motionless form of the stranger.

"You will precede me, sir," he said; "the hour grows late, and you, too, may need a guide to find your dwelling."

"To me the streets of Boston have long been familiar," returned the old man. "I have noted the increase of the town as the parent notes the increasing stature of his child; nor is my love for it less than paternal. It is enough that I am within its limits, where liberty is prized as the greatest good; and it matters not under what roof I lay my head; this will do as well as another."

"This!" echoed the other, glancing his eyes over the miserable furniture, and scanning the air of poverty that pervaded the place; "why, this house has even less of comfort than the ship we have left!"

"It has enough for my wants," said the stranger, seating himself with composure, and deliberately placing his bundle by his side. "Go you to your palace in Tremont Street; it shall be my care that we meet again."

The officer understood the character of his companion too well to hesitate, and bending low, he quitted the apartment, leaving the other leaning his head on his cane, in absent musing, while the amazed matron was gazing at her unexpected guest with a wonder that was not unmingled with dread.

CHAPTER III.

"From silver spouts the grateful liquors glide,
While China's earth receives the smoking tide;
At once they gratify their scent and taste,
And frequent cups prolong the rich repast."

Rape of the Lock.

THE recollection of the repeated admonitions of his mother served to keep Job to his purpose. The instant the officer appeared, he held his way across the bridge, and after proceeding for a short distance farther along the water's edge, they entered a broad and well-built avenue, which lead from the principal wharf into the upper parts of the town. Turning up this street, the lad was making his way, with great earnestness, when sounds of high merriment and conviviality, breaking from an opposite building, caught his attention, and induced him to pause.

"Remember your mother's injunction," said the officer; "what see you in that tavern to stare at?"

"'Tis the British Coffee House," said Job, shaking his head; "yes, anybody might know that by the noise they make in't on Saturday night! See! it's filled now with Lord Boot's officers, flaring afore the windows, just like so many red devils; but to-morrow, when the Old South bell rings, they'll forget their Lord and Maker, every sinner among them!"

"Fellow!" exclaimed the officer, "this is trespassing too far; proceed to Tremont Street, or leave me, that I may, at once, procure another guide."

The changeling cast a look aside at the angry eye of the

other, and then turned and proceeded, muttering so loud as to be overheard,—

"Every boy that's raised in Boston knows how to keep Saturday night; and if you're a Boston boy, you should love Boston ways."

The officer did not reply, and as they now proceeded with great diligence, they soon passed through King and Queen Streets, and entered that of Tremont. At a little distance from the turning, Job stopped, and pointing to a building near them, he said,—

"There; that house with the courtyard afore it; and the pile-axters, and the grand-looking door, that's Ma'am Lechmere's; and everybody says she's a grand lady; but I say it is a pity she is n't a better woman."

"And who are you, that ventures thus boldly to speak of a lady so much your superior?"

"I!" said the idiot, looking up simply into the face of his interrogator, "I am Job Pray, so called."

"Well, Job Pray, here is a crown for you. The next time you act as guide, keep more to your business. I tell you, lad, I offer a crown."

"Job don't love crowns; they say the king wears a crown, and it makes him flaunty and proud like."

"The disaffection must have spread itself wide indeed, if such as he refuse silver, rather than offend their principles!" muttered the officer to himself. "Here then is half a guinea, if you like gold better."

The natural continued kicking a stone about with his toes, without taking his hands from his pockets where he wore them ordinarily, with a sort of idle air, as he peered from under his slouched hat at this renewed offer, answering,—

"You would n't let the grannies whip Job, and Job won't take your money."

"Well, boy, there is more of gratitude in that than a wiser man would always feel! Come, Meriton, I shall meet the poor fellow again, and will not forget this. I commission you to see the lad better dressed, in the beginning of the week."

"Lord, sir," said the valet, "if it is your pleasure, most certainly ; but I declare I don't know in what style I should dress such a figure and countenance, to make anything of them !"

"Sir, sir !" cried the lad, running a few steps after the officer, who had already proceeded, "if you won't let the grannies beat Job any more, Job will always show you the way through Boston ; and run your arr'nds too !"

"Poor fellow ! well, I promise that you shall not be again abused by any of the soldiery. Good-night, my honest friend ; let me see you again."

The idiot appeared satisfied with this assurance, for he immediately turned, and gliding along the street with a sort of shuffling gait, he soon disappeared round the first corner. In the meantime the young officer advanced to the entrance which led into the courtyard of Mrs. Lechmere's dwelling. The house was of bricks, and of an exterior altogether more pretending than most of those in the lower parts of the town. It was heavily ornamented in wood, according to the taste of a somewhat earlier day, and presented a front of seven windows in its two upper stories, those at the extremes being much narrower than the others. The lower floor had the same arrangement, with the exception of the principal door.

Strong lights were shining in many parts of the house, which gave it, in comparison with the gloomy and darkened edifices in its vicinity, an air of peculiar gayety and life. The rap of the gentleman was answered instantly by an old black, dressed in a becoming, and what, for the colonies, was a rich livery. The inquiry for Mrs. Lechmere was successful, and the youth was conducted through a hall of some dimensions, into an apartment which opened from one of its sides. This room would be considered, at the present day, much too small to contain the fashion of a country town ; but what importance it wanted in size, was amply compensated for in the richness and labor of its decorations. The walls were divided into compartments, by raised panel-work, beautifully painted with imaginary landscapes and ruins. The glittering, varnished surfaces of these pictures were burdened with armorial bearings, which were intended to illustrate the alliances of the family. Beneath the surbase were smaller divisions of panels, painted with various architectural devices ; and above it rose, between the compartments, fluted pilasters of wood, with gilded capitals. A heavy wooden and highly ornamented cornice stretched above the whole, furnishing an appropriate outline to the walls. The use of carpets was at that time but little known in the colonies, though the wealth and station of Mrs. Lechmere would probably have introduced the luxury, had not her age, and the nature of the building, tempted her to adhere to ancient custom. The floor, which shone equally with the furniture, was tessellated with small alternate squares of red-cedar and pine, and in the centre were the "salient lions" of Lechmere, attempted by the blazonry of the joiner. On either side of the ponderous and labored mantel were arched compartments, of plainer work, denoting use, the sliding panels of one of which, being raised, displayed a buffet groaning with massive plate. The furniture was old, rich, and heavy, but in perfect preservation. In the midst of this scene of colonial splendor, which was rendered as impressive as possible by the presence of numerous waxen lights, a lady, far in the decline of life, sat, in formal propriety, on a small settee. The officer had thrown his cloak into the hands of Meriton, in the hall, and as he advanced up the apartment, his form appeared in the gay dress of a soldier, giving to its ease and fine proportions the additional charm of military garnish. The hard, severe eye of the lady sensibly softened with pleased surprise, as it dwelt on his person for an instant after she arose to receive her guest ; but the momentary silence was first broken by the youth, who said,—

"I have entered unannounced, for my impatience has exceeded my breeding, madam, while each step I have taken in this house recalls the days of my boyhood, and of my former freedom within its walls."

"My cousin Lincoln!" interrupted the lady, who was Mrs. Lechmere ; "that dark eye, that smile, nay, your very step, announces you ! I must have forgotten my poor brother, and one also who is still so dear to us, not to have known you a true Lincoln."

There was a distance in the manner of both, at meeting, which might easily have been imparted by the precise formula of the provincial school, of which the lady was so distinguished a member, but which was not sufficient to explain the sad expression that suddenly and powerfully blended with the young man's smile, as she spoke. The change, however, was but momentary, and he answered courteously to her assurances of recognition,—

"I have long been taught to expect a second home in Tremont Street, and I find by your flattering remembrance of myself and parents, dear madam, that my expectations are justified."

The lady was sensibly pleased at this remark, and she suffered a smile to unbend her rigid brow, as she answered:

"A home, certainly, though it be not such a one as the heir of the wealthy house of Lincoln may have been accustomed to dwell in. It would be strange, indeed, could any allied to that honorable family forget to entertain its representative with due respect."

The youth seemed conscious that quite as much had now been said as the occasion required, as he raised his head from bowing respectfully on her hand, with the intention of changing the subject to one less personal, when his eye caught a glimpse of the figure of another, and more youthful female, who had been concealed, hitherto, by the drapery of a window-curtain. Advancing to this young lady, he said, with the quickness that rather betrayed his willingness to suspend further compliment,—

"And here I see one also, to whom I have the honor of being related, Miss Dynevor?"

"Though it be not my grandchild," said Mrs. Lechmere, "it is one who claims an equal affinity to you, Major Lincoln; it is Agnes Danforth, the daughter of my late niece."

"'T was my eye, then, and not my feelings, that were mistaken," returned the young soldier; "I hope this lady will admit my claim to call her cousin?"

A simple inclination of the body was the only answer he received, though she did not decline the hand which he offered with his salutations. After a few more of the usual expressions of pleasure, and the ordinary inquiries that succeed such meetings, the party became seated, and a more regular discourse followed.

"I am pleased to find you remember us then, cousin Lionel," said Mrs. Lechmere; "we have so little in this remote province that will compare with the mother country, I had feared no vestiges of the place of your birth could remain on your mind."

"I find the town greatly altered, it is true, but there are many places in it which I still remember, though certainly their splendor is a little diminished, in my eyes, by absence and a familiarity with other scenes."

"Doubtless an acquaintance with the British court will have no tendency to exalt our humble customs in your imagination; neither do we possess many buildings to attract the notice of a travelled stranger. There is a tradition in our family, that your seat in Devonshire is as large as any dozen edifices in Boston, public or private; nay, we are proud of saying, that the king himself is lodged as well as the head of the Lincoln family, only when at his castle of Windsor!"

"Ravenscliffe is certainly a place of some magnitude," returned the young man, carelessly, "though you will remember his majesty affects but little state at Kew. I have, however, spent so little of my time in the country, that I hardly know its conveniences or its extent."

The old lady bowed with that sort of complacency which the dwellers in the colonies were apt to betray, whenever an allusion was made to the acknowledged importance of their connections in that country, towards which they all looked as to the fountain of honor; and then, as quickly as if the change in her ideas was but a natural transition in the subject, she observed,—

"Surely Cecil cannot know of the arrival of our kinsman; she is not apt to be so remiss in paying attention to our guests."

"She does me the more honor, that she considers me a relative, and one who requires no formality in his reception."

"You are but cousins twice removed," returned the old lady, a little gravely; "and there is surely no affinity in that degree which can justify any forgetfulness of the usual courtesies. You see, cousin Lionel, how much we value the consanguinity, when it is a subject of pride to the most remote branches of the family!"

"I am but little of a genealogist, madam; though, if I retain a true impression of what I have heard, Miss Dynevor is of too good blood, in the direct line, to value the collateral drops of an intermarriage."

"Pardon me, Major Lincoln; her father, Colonel Dynevor, was certainly an Englishman of an ancient and honorable name, but no family in the realm need scorn an alliance with our own. I say our own, cousin Lionel, for I would never have you forget that I am a Lincoln, and was the sister of your grandfather."

A little surprised at the seeming contradiction in the language of the good lady, the young man bowed his head to the compliment, and cast his eyes at his younger companion with a sort of longing to change the discourse, by addressing the reserved young women nigh him, that was very excusable in one of his sex and years. He had not time, however, to make more than one or two commonplace remarks, and receive their answers, before Mrs. Lechmere said, with some exhibition of staid displeasure against her grandchild,—

"Go, Agnes, and acquaint your cousin of this happy event. She has been sensibly alive to your safety during the whole time consumed by your voyage. We have had the prayers of the church, for a 'person gone to sea,' read each Sunday since the receipt of your letters announcing your intention to embark; and I have been exceedingly pleased to observe the deep interest with which Cecil joined in our petitions."

Lionel mumbled a few words of thanks, and leaning back in his chair, threw his eyes upward, but whether in pious gratitude or not, we conceive it is not our province to determine. During the delivery of Mrs. Lechmere's last speech and the expressive pantomime that succeeded it,

Agnes Danforth rose and left the room. The door had been some little time closed before the silence was again broken, during which Mrs. Lechmere evidently essayed in vain, once or twice to speak. Her color, pale and immovable as usually seemed her withered look, changed in its shades, and her lip trembled involuntarily. She, however, soon found her utterance, though the first tones of her voice were choked and husky.

"I may have appeared remiss, cousin Lionel," she said, "but there are subjects that can be discussed with propriety only between the nearest relatives. Sir Lionel—you left him in as good a state of bodily health, I hope, as his mental illness will allow?"

"It is so represented to me."

"You have seen him lately?"

"Not in fifteen years. My presence was said to increase his disorder, and the physicians forbade any more interviews. He continues at the private establishment near town, and, as the lucid intervals are thought to increase, both in frequency and duration, I often indulge in the pleasing hope of being restored again to my father. The belief is justified by his years, which, you know are yet under fifty."

A long and apparently a painful silence succeeded this interesting communication; at length the lady said, with a tremor in her voice, for which the young man almost reverenced her, as it so plainly bespoke her interest in her nephew, as well as the goodness of her heart,—

"I will thank you for a glass of that water in the buffet. Pardon me, cousin Lionel, but this melancholy subject always overcomes me. I will retire a few moments, with your indulgence, and hasten the appearance of my grandchild. I pine that you may meet."

Her absence, just at that moment, was too agreeable to the feelings of Lionel for him to gainsay her intention; though, instead of following Agnes Danforth, who had preceded her on the same duty, the tottering steps of Mrs. Lechmere conducted her to a door which communicated with her own apartment. For several minutes the young man trampled on the "salient lions" of Lechmere with a rapidity that seemed to emulate their own mimic speed, as he paced to and fro across the narrow apartment, his eye glancing vacantly along the labored wainscots, embracing the argent, azure, and purpure fields of the different escutcheons, as heedlessly as if they were not charged with the distinguishing symbols of so many honorable names. This mental abstraction was, however, shortly dissipated by the sudden appearance of one who had glided into the room and advanced to its centre before he became conscious of her presence. A light, rounded, and exquisitely proportioned female form, accompanied by a youthful and expressive countenance, with an air in which womanly grace blended so nicely with feminine delicacy as to cause each motion and gesture to command respect, at the same time that it was singularly insinuating, was an object to suspend even at a first glance, provided that glance were by surprise, the steps of a more absent and less courteous youth than the one we have attempted to described. Major Lincoln knew that this young lady could be no other than Cecil Dynevor, the daughter of a British officer, long since deceased, by the only child of Mrs. Lechmere, who was also in her grave; and, consequently, that she was one to whom he was so well known by character, and so nearly allied by blood, as to render it an easy task for a man accustomed to the world as he had been, to remove any little embarrassments which might have beset a less practised youth, by acting as his own usher. This he certainly attempted, and at first with a freedom which his affinity and the circumstances would seem to allow, though it was chastened by easy politeness. But the restraint visible in the manner of the lady was so marked, that, by the time his salutations were ended and he had handed her to a seat, the young man felt as much embarrassment as if he had found himself alone, for the first time, with the woman whom he had been pining, for months, to favor with a very particular communication. Whether it is that nature has provided the other sex with a tact for these occasions, or that the young lady became sensible that her deportment was not altogether such as was worthy either of herself or the guest of her grandmother, she was certainly the first to relieve the slight awkwardness that was but too apparent in the commencement of the interview.

"My grandmother has long been expecting this pleasure, Major Lincoln," she said, "and your arrival has been at a most auspicious moment. The state of the country grows each day so very alarming, that I have indeed long urged her to visit our relatives in England, until the disputes shall have terminated."

The tones of an extremely soft and melodious voice, and a pronunciation quite as exact as if the speaker had acquired the sounds in the English court, and which was entirely free from the slight vernacular peculiarity which had offended his ear in the few words that fell from Agnes Danforth, certainly aided a native attraction of manner, which it seemed impossible for the young lady to cast entirely aside.

"You who are so much of an Englishwoman, would find great pleasure in the exchange." he answered; "and if half what I have heard from a fellow-passenger, of the state of the country, be true, I shall be foremost in seconding your request. Both Ravenscliffe and the house in Soho would be greatly at the service of Mrs. Lechmere."

"It was my wish that she would accept the pressing invitations of my father's relative, Lord Cardonnel, who has long urged me to pass a few years in his own family. A separation would be painful to us both, but should my grandmother, in such an event, determine to take her residence in the dwellings of her ancestors, I could not be censured for adopting a resolution to abide under the roofs of mine."

The piercing eye of Major Lincoln fell full upon her own, as she delivered this intention, and as it dropped on the floor, the slight smile that played round his lips was produced by the passing thought, that the provincial beauty had inherited so much of her grandmother's pride of genealogy, as to be willing to impress on his mind that the niece of a viscount was superior to the heir of a baronetcy. But the quick, burning flush that instantly passed across the features of Cecil Dynevor, might have taught him that she was acting under the impulse of much deeper feelings than such an

3

unworthy purpose would indicate. The effect, however, was such as to make the young man glad to see Mrs. Lechmere re-enter the room, leaning on the arm of her niece.

"I perceive, my cousin Lionel," said the lady, as she moved with a feeble step towards the settee, "that you and Cecil have found each other out, without the necessity of any other introduction than the affinity between you. I surely do not mean the affinity of blood altogether, you know, for that cannot be said to amount to anything; but I believe there exist certain features of the mind that are transmitted through families quite as distinctly as any which belong to the countenance."

"Could I flatter myself with possessing the slightest resemblance to Miss Dynevor, in either of those particulars, I should be doubly proud of the connection," returned Lionel, while he assisted the good lady to a seat, with a coolness that sufficiently denoted how little he cared about the matter.

"But I am not disposed to have my right to claim near kindred with cousin Lionel at all disputed," cried the young lady, with sudden animation. "It has pleased our forefathers to order such—"

"Nay, nay, my child," interrupted her grandmother, "you forget that the term of cousin can only be used in cases of near consanguinity, and where familiar situations will excuse it. But Major Lincoln knows that we in the colonies are apt to make the most of the language, and count our cousins almost as far as if we were members of the Scottish clans. Speaking of the clans reminds me of the rebellion of '45. It is not thought, in England, that our infatuated colonists will ever be so foolhardy as to assume their arms in earnest?"

"There are various opinions on that subject," said Lionel. "Most military men scout the idea; though I find, occasionally, an officer that has served on this continent, who thinks not only that the appeal will be made, but that the struggle will be bloody.

"Why should they not?" said Agnes Dansforth, abruptly; "they are men, and the English are no more!"

Lionel turned his looks, in a little surprise, on the speaker, to whose countenance an almost imperceptible cast in one eye imparted a look of arch good-nature that her manner would seem to contradict, and smiled as he repeated her words,—

"Why should they not, indeed! I know no other reasons than that it would be both a mad and an unlawful act. I can assure you that I am not one of those who affect to undervalue my own countrymen; for you will remember that I too am an American."

"I have heard it said that such of our volunteers as wear uniforms at all," said Agnes, "appear in blue, and not in scarlet."

"'T is his majesty's pleasure that his 47th foot should wear this gaudy color," returned the young man, laughing; "though, for myself, I am quite willing to resign it to the use of you ladies, and to adopt another, could it well be."

"It might be done, sir."

"In what manner?"

"By resigning your commission with it."

Mrs. Lechmere had evidently permitted her niece to proceed thus far, without interruption, to serve some purpose of her own; but perceiving that her guest by no means exhibited the air of pique, which the British officers were so often weak enough to betray, when the women took into their hands the defence of their country's honor, she rang the bell, as she observed,—

"Bold language, Major Lincoln! bold language, for a young lady under twenty. But Miss Danforth is privileged to speak her mind freely, for some of her father's family are but too deeply implicated in the unlawful proceedings of these evil times. We have kept Cecil, however, more to her allegiance."

"And yet even Cecil has been known to refuse the favor of her countenance to the entertainments given by the British officers!" said Agnes, a little piquantly.

"And would you have Cecil Dynevor frequent balls and entertainments unaccompanied by a proper chaperon?" returned Mrs. Lechmere; "or it is expected that, at seventy,

I can venture in public to maintain the credit of our family? But we keep Major Lincoln from his refreshments with our idle disputes. Cato, we wait your movements."

Mrs. Lechmere delivered her concluding intimation to the black in attendance, with an air that partook somewhat of mystery. The old domestic, who, probably from long practice, understood, more by the expression of her eye than by any words she had uttered, the wishes of his mistress, proceeded to close the outer shutters of the windows, and to draw the curtains with the most exact care. When this duty was performed, he raised a small oval table from its regular position among the flowing folds of the drapery that shrouded the deep apertures for light, and placed it in front of Miss Dynevor. A salver of massive silver, containing an equipage of the finest Dresden, followed, and in a few minutes a hissing urn of the same precious metal garnished the polished surface of the mahogany. During these arrangements, Mrs. Lechmere and her guest had maintained a general discourse, touching chiefly on the welfare and condition of certain individuals of their alliance in England. Notwithstanding the demand thus made on his attention, Lionel was able to discover a certain appearance of mystery and caution in each movement of the black, as he proceeded leisurely in his duty. Miss Dynevor permitted the disposition of the tea-table to be made before her, passively, and her cousin, Agnes Danforth, threw herself back on one of the settees, with a look that indicated cool displeasure. When the usual compound was made in two little fluted cups, over whose pure white a few red and green sprigs were sparingly scattered, the black presented one containing the grateful beverage to his mistress, and the other to the stranger.

"Pardon me, Miss Danforth," said Lionel, recollecting himself after he had accepted the offering; "I have suffered my sea-breeding to obtain the advantage."

"Enjoy your error, sir, if you can find any gratification in the indulgence," returned the young lady.

"But I should enjoy it the more, could I see you participating in the luxury."

"You have termed the idle indulgence well; 't is nothing but a luxury, and such a one as can be easily dispensed with; I thank you, sir, I do not drink tea."

"Surely no lady can forswear her bohea! be persuaded."

"I know not how the subtle poison may operate on your English ladies, Major Lincoln, but it is no difficult matter for an American girl to decline the use of a detestable herb, which is one, among many others, of the causes that is likely to involve her country and kindred in danger and strife."

The young man, who had really intended no more than the common civilities due from his sex to the other, bowed in silence, though, as he turned from her, he could not forbear looking towards the table to see whether the principles of the other young American were quite as rigid. Cecil sat bending over the salver, playing idly with a curiously wrought spoon, made to represent a sprig of the plant whose fragrance had been thus put in requisition to contribute to his indulgence, while the steam from the china vessel before her was wreathing in a faint mist around her polished brow.

"You, at least, Miss Dynevor," said Lionel, "appear to have no dislike to the herb,—you breathe its vapor so freely."

Cecil cast a glance at him, which changed the demure and somewhat proud composure of her countenance into a look of sudden, joyous humor, that was infinitely more natural, as she answered, laughingly,—

"I own a woman's weakness. I must believe that it was tea that tempted our common mother in Paradise!"

"It would show that the cunning of the serpent has been transmitted to a later day, could that be proved," said Agnes, "though the instrument of temptation has lost some of its virtue."

"How know you that?" said Lionel, anxious to pursue the trifling, in order to remove the evident distance which had existed between them; "had Eve shut her ears as rigidly as you close your mouth against the offering, we might yet have enjoyed the first gift to our parents."

"Oh, sir, 't is no such stranger to me as you may imagine from the indifference I have assumed on the present occasion;

as Job Pray says, Boston harbor is nothing but a 'big tea-pot!'"

"You know Job Pray, then, Miss Danforth?" said Lionel, not a little amused by her spirit.

"Certainly; Boston is so small, and Job so useful, that everybody knows the simpleton."

"He belongs to a distinguished family, then, for I have his own assurance that everybody knows his perturbed mother, Abigail."

"You!" exclaimed Cecil, again, in that sweet natural voice that had before startled her auditor; "what can you know of poor Job and his almost equally unfortunate mother?"

"Now, young ladies, I have you in my snares!" cried Lionel; "you may possibly resist the steams of tea, but what woman can withstand the impulse of her curiosity? Not to be too cruel with my fair kinswoman on so short an acquaintance, however, I will go so far as to acknowledge that I have already had an interview with Mrs. Pray."

The reply which Agnes was about to deliver was interrupted by a slight crash, and on turning they beheld the fragments of a piece of the splendid set of Dresden lying at the feet of Mrs. Lechmere.

"My dear grandmamma is ill!" cried Cecil, springing to the assistance of the old lady. "Hasten, Cato—Major Lincoln, you are more active—for Heaven's sake, a glass of water—Agnes, your salts."

The amiable anxiety of her grandchild was not, however, so necessary as first appearances would have indicated, and Mrs. Lechmere gently put aside the salts, though she did not decline the glass which Lionel offered for the second time in so short a period.

"I believe you will mistake me for a sad invalid, cousin Lionel," said the old lady, when she had become a little composed; "but I believe it is this very tea, of which so much has been said, and which I drink to excess, from pure loyalty, that unsettles my nerves; I must refrain, like the girls, though from a very different motive. We are a people of early hours, Major Lincoln, but you are at home here, and will pursue your pleasure. I must, however, claim an indulgence for threescore-and-ten, and be permitted to wish you a good rest after your voyage. Cato has his orders to contribute all he can to your comfort."

Leaning on her two assistants, the old lady withdrew, leaving Lionel to the full possession of the apartment. As the hour was getting late, and, from the compliments they had exchanged, he did not expect the return of the younger ladies, he called for a candle, and was shown to his own room. As soon as the few indispensables which rendered a valet necessary to a gentleman of that period were observed, he dismissed Meriton, and throwing himself on his bed, courted the sweets of the pillow.

Many incidents, however, had occurred during the day, that induced a train of thoughts which for a long time prevented his attaining the natural rest he sought. After indulging in long and uneasy reflections on certain events, too closely connected with his personal feelings to be lightly remembered, the young man began to muse on his reception, and on the individuals who had been, as it were, for the first time, introduced to him.

It was quite apparent that both Mrs. Lechmere and her granddaughter were acting their several parts, though whether in concert or not, remained to be discovered. But in Agnes Danforth, with all his subtlety, he could perceive nothing but the plain and direct, though a little blunt, peculiarities of her nature and education. Like most very young men, who had just been made acquainted with two youthful females, both of them much superior to the generality of their sex in personal charms, he fell asleep musing on their characters. Nor, considering the circumstances, will it be at all surprising, when we add, before morning, he was dreaming of the Avon of Bristol, on board which stout vessel he even thought that he was discussing a chowder on the Banks of Newfoundland, which had been unaccountably prepared by the fair hands of Miss Danforth, and which was strangely flavored with tea ; while the Hebe-looking countenance of Cecil Dynevor was laughing at his perplexities with undisguised good-humor, and with all the vivacity of girlish merriment.

CHAPTER IV.

"A good portly man, i' faith, and a corpulent."
King Henry IV.

THE sun was just stirring the heavy bank of fog, which had rested on the waters during the night, as Lionel toiled his way up the side of Beacon Hill, anxious to catch a glimpse of his native scenery while it was yet glowing with the first touch of day. The islands raised their green heads above the mist, and the wide amphitheatre of hills that encircled the bay was still visible, though the vapor was creeping in places along the valleys,—now concealing the entrance to some beautiful glen, and now wreathing itself fantastically around a tall spire that told the site of a suburban village. Though the people of the town were awake and up, yet the sacred character of the day, and the state of the times, contributed to suppress those sounds which usually distinguish populous places. The cool nights and warm days of April had generated a fog more than usually dense, which was deserting its watery bed, and stealing insidiously along the land, to unite with the vapors of the rivers and brooks, spreading a wider curtain before the placid view. As Lionel stood on the brow of the platform that crowned the eminence, the glimpses of houses and hills, of towers and ships, of places known and places forgotten, passed before his vision, through the openings in the mist, like phantoms of the imagination. The whole scene, animated and in motion, as it seemed by its changes, appeared to his excited feelings like a fanciful panorama, exhibited for his eye alone, when his enjoyment was interrupted by a voice apparently at no great dis-

tance. It was a man singing to a common English air fragments of some ballad, with a peculiarly vile nasal cadency.
Through the frequent pauses, he was enabled to comprehend
a few words which, by their recurrence, were evidently
intended for a chorus to the rest of the production. The
reader will understand the character of the whole from these
lines, which ran as follows:—

> "And they that would be free,
> Out they go;
> While the slaves, as you may see,
> Stay, to drink their p'ison tea,
> Down below!"

Lionel, after listening to this expressive ditty for a moment, followed the direction of the sounds until he encountered Job Pray, who was seated on one of the flights of
steps, which aided the ascent to the platform, cracking a
few walnuts on the boards, while he employed those intervals, when his mouth could find no better employment, in
uttering the above-mentioned strains.

"How now, Master Pray; do you come here to sing
your orisons to the goddess of liberty, on a Sunday morning?" cried Lionel; "or are you the town lark, and for
want of wings, take to this height to obtain an altitude for
your melody?"

"There's no harm in singing psalm tunes or continental
songs any day in the week," said the lad, without raising
his eyes from his occupation; "Job don't know what a lark
is, but if it belongs to the town, the soldiers are so thick,
they can't keep it on the common."

"And what objection can you have to the soldiers possessing a corner of your common?"

"They starve the cows, and then they won't give milk;
grass is sweet to beasts in the spring of the year."

"But, my life for it, the soldiers don't eat grass; your
brindles and your blacks, your reds and your whites, may
have the first offering of the spring as usual."

"But Boston cows don't love grass that British soldiers
have trampled on," said the sullen lad.

"This is, indeed, carrying notions of liberty to refinement!" exclaimed Lionel, laughing.

Job shook his head threateningly, as he looked up and said, "Don't you let Ralph hear you say anything ag'in liberty!"

"Ralph! who is he, lad? your genius? where do you keep the invisible, that there is danger of his overhearing what I say?"

"He's up there in the fog," said Job, pointing significantly towards the foot of the beacon, which a dense volume of vapor was enwrapping, probably attracted up the tall post that supported the grate.

Lionel gazed at the smoky column for a moment, when the mists began to desolve, and amid their evolutions he beheld the dim figure of his aged fellow passenger. The old man was still clad in his simple, tarnished vestments of gray, which harmonized so singularly with the mists as to impart a look almost ethereal to his wasted form. As the medium through which he was seen became less cloudy, his features grew visible, and Lionel could distinguish the uneasy, rapid glances of his eyes, which seemed to roam over the distant objects with an earnestness that appeared to mock the misty veil that was floating before so much of the view. While Lionel stood fixed to the spot, gazing at this irregular being with that secret awe which the other had succeeded in inspiring, the old man waved his hand impatiently, as if he would cast aside his shroud. At that instant a bright sunbeam darted into the vapor, illuminating his person, and melting the mist into thin air. The anxious, haggard, and severe expression of his countenance changed at the touch of the ray, and he smiled with a softness and attraction that thrilled the nerves of the other, as he called aloud to the sensitive young soldier,—

"Come hither, Lionel Lincoln, to the foot of this beacon, where you may gather warnings, which, if properly heeded, will guide you through many and great dangers unharmed."

"I am glad you have spoken," said Lionel, advancing to his side; "you appeared like a being of another world, wrapped in that mantle of fog, and I felt tempted to kneel, and ask a benediction."

"And am I not a being of another world! Most of my interests are already in the grave, and I tarry here only for a space, because there is a great work to be done, which cannot be performed without me. My view of the world of spirits, young man, is much clearer and more distinct than yours of this variable scene at your feet. There is no mist to obstruct the eye, nor any doubt as to the colors it presents."

"You are happy, sir, in the extremity of your age, to be so assured. But I fear your sudden determination last night subjected you to inconvenience in the tenement of this changeling."

"The boy is a good boy," said the old man, stroking the head of the natural complacently; "we understand each other, Major Lincoln, and that shortens introductions, and renders communion easy."

"That you feel alike on one subject, I have already discovered; but there, I should think, the resemblance and the intelligence must end."

"The propensities of the mind, in its infancy and in its maturity, are but a span apart," said the stranger; "the amount of human knowledge is but to know how much we are under the dominion of our passions; and he who has learned by experience how to smother the volcano, and he who never felt its fires, are surely fit associates."

Lionel bowed in silence to an opinion so humbling to the other, and, after a pause of a moment, adverted to their situation :—

"The sun begins to make himself felt, and when he has driven away these ragged remnants of the fog, we shall see those places each of us has frequented in his day."

"Shall we find them as we left them, think you? or will you see the stranger in possession of the haunts of your infancy?"

"Not the stranger, certainly, for we are the subjects of one king; children who own a common parent."

"I will not reply that he has proved himself an unnatural father," said the old man, calmly; "the gentleman who now fills the British throne is less to be censured than his advisers, for the oppression of his reign."

"Sir," interrupted Lionel, "if such allusions are made to the person of my sovereign, we must separate; for it ill becomes a British officer to hear his master mentioned with levity."

"Levity!" repeated the other, slowly. "It is a fault, indeed, to accompany gray locks and wasted limbs! but your jealous watchfulness betrays you into error. I have breathed in the atmosphere of kings, young man, and know how to separate the individual and his purpose from the policy of his government. 'T is the latter that will sever this great empire, and deprive the third George of what has so often and so well been termed 'the brightest jewel in his crown.'"

"I must leave you, sir," said Lionel; "the opinions you so freely expressed during our passage, were on principles which I can hardly call opposed to our own constitution, and might be heard, not only without offence, but frequently with admiration; but this language approaches to treason!"

"Go, then," returned the unmoved stranger; "descend to yon degraded common, and bid your mercenaries seize me—'t will be only the blood of an old man, but 't will help to fatten the land; or send your merciless grenadiers to torment their victim before the axe shall do its work; a man who has lived so long, can surely spare a little of his time to the tormentors!"

"I could have thought, sir, that you might spare such a reproach to me," said Lionel.

"I do spare it, and I do more; I forgot my years, and solicit forgiveness. But had you known slavery, as I have done, in its worst of forms, you would know how to prize the inestimable blessing of freedom."

"Have you ever known slavery, in your travels, more closely than in what you deem the violations of principle?"

"Have I not?" said the stranger, smiling bitterly. "I have known it as man should never know it—in act and will. I have lived days, months, and even years, to hear others coldly declare my wants; to see others dole out their meagre pittances to my necessities, and to hear others as-

sume the right to express the sufferings and to control the
enjoyments of sensibilities that God has given to me only ! ''

"To endure such thraldom, you must have fallen into
the power of the infidel barbarians.''

"Ah ! boy, I thank you for the words ; they were indeed
worthy of the epithets ; infidels, that denied the precepts of
our blessed Redeemer, and barbarians, that treated one having a soul, and possessing reason like themselves, as a beast
of the field.''

"Why did n't you come to Boston, Ralph, and tell that
to the people in Funnel Hall?'' exclaimed Job ; " ther 'd
ha' been a stir about it ! ''

"Child, I did come to Boston, again and again, in
thought; and the appeals that I made to my townsmen
would have moved the very roof of old Faneuil, could they
have been uttered within her walls. But 't was in vain !
they had the power, and like demons—or, rather, like
miserable men—they abused it.''

Lionel, sensibly touched, was about to reply in a suitable
manner, when he heard a voice calling his own name aloud,
as if the speaker were ascending the opposite acclivity of
the hill. The instant the sounds reached his ears, the old
man rose from his seat, on the foundation of the beacon,
and gliding over the brow of the platform, followed by Job,
they descended into a volume of mist, that was still clinging
to the side of the hill, with amazing swiftness.

"Why, Leo ! thou lion in name, and deer in activity ! ''
exclaimed the intruder, as he surmounted the steep ascent,
"what can have brought you up into the clouds so early !
Whew ! a man needs a Newmarket training to scale such
a precipice. But, Leo, my dear fellow, I rejoice to see you ;
we knew you were expected in the first ship, and as I was
coming from morning parade, I met a couple of grooms in
the 'Lincoln green,' you know, leading each a blooded
charger ; faith, one of them would have been quite con-
venient to climb this accursed hill on—whew and whew-w,
again ! well, I knew the liveries at a glance ; as to the
horses, I hope to be better acquainted with them hereafter.
'Pray, sir,' said I, to one of the liveried scoundrels, 'whom

do you serve?' 'Major Lincoln, of Ravenscliffe,' said he, with a look as impudent as if he could have said, like you and I, his sacred majesty the king. That's the answer of the servants of your ten-thousand-a-year men! Now, if any fool had been asked such a question, his answer would have been, craven dog as he is, 'Captain Polwarth, of the 47th'; leaving the inquirer, though it should even be some curious maiden, who had taken a fancy to the *tout ensemble* of my outline, in utter ignorance that there is such a place in the world as Polwarth Hall!"

During this voluble speech, which was interrupted by sundry efforts to regain the breath lost in the ascent, Lionel shook his friend cordially by the hand, and attempted to express his own pleasure at the meeting. The failure of wind, however, which was a sort of besetting sin with Captain Polwarth, had now compelled him to pause, and gave time to Lionel for a reply.

"This hill is the last place where I should have expected to meet you," he said. "I took it for granted you would not be stirring till nine or ten at least, when it was my intention to inquire you out, and to give you a call before I paid my respects to the commander-in-chief."

"Ah! you may thank his excellency, the 'Hon. Thomas Gage, governor and commander-in-chief in and over the Province of Massachusetts Bay, and vice-admiral of the same,' as he styles himself in his proclamations, for this especial favor; though between ourselves, Leo, he is about as much governor *over* the province, as he is owner of those hunters you have just landed."

"But why am I to thank him for this interview?"

"Why! look about you, and tell me what you behold—nothing but fog—nay, I see *there* is a steeple, and *yonder* is the smoking sea, and *here* are the chimneys of Hancock's house beneath us, smoking, too, as if their rebellious master were at home, and preparing his feed! but everything in sight is essentially smoky, and there is a natural aversion, in us epicures, to smoke. Nature dictates that a man who has as much to do in a day, in carrying himself about, as your humble servant, should not cut his rest too abruptly in the morning. But the honorable Thomas, govornor and vice-admiral, etc., has ordered us under arms with the sun —officers as well as men ! "

"Surely that is no great hardship to a soldier," returned Lionel; "and moreover, it seems to agree with you marvellously. Now I look again, Polwarth, I am amazed. Surely you are not in a light-infantry jacket ! "

"Certes—what is there in that so wonderful ? " returned the other, with great gravity. "Don't I become the dress ? or is it the dress that does not adorn me, that you look ready to die with mirth? Laugh it out, Leo. I am used to it these three days ; but what is there, after all, so remarkable in Peter Polwarth's commanding a company of light infantry? Am I not just five feet, six and one eighth of an inch ?—the precise height ! "

"You appear to have been so accurate in your longitudinal admeasurement, that you must carry one of Harrison's timepieces in your pocket; did it ever suggest itself to you to use a quadrant also ? "

"For my latitude ! I understand you, Leo ; because I am shaped a little like mother earth, does it argue that I cannot command a light-infantry company ? "

"Ay, even as Joshua commanded the sun. But the stopping of the planet itself is not a greater miracle, in my eyes, than to see you in that attire."

"Well, then, the mystery shall be explained, but first let us be seated on this beacon," said Captain Polwarth, establishing himself with great method in the place so lately occupied by the attenuated form of the stranger. "A true soldier husbands his resources for a time of need ; that word, husbands, brings me at once to the point—I am in love."

"That is surprising ! "

"But what is much more so, I would fain be married."

"It must be a woman of no mean endowments that could excite such desires in Captain Polwarth, of the 47th, and of Polwarth Hall ! "

"She is a woman of great qualifications, Major Lincoln," said the lover, with a sudden gravity that indicated his gayety of manner was not entirely natural. "In figure she may be said to be done to a turn. When she is grave, she walks with the stateliness of a show-beef; when she runs, 't is with the activity of a turkey; and when at rest, I can only compare her to a dish of venison—savory, delicate, and what one can never get enough of."

"You have, to adopt your own metaphors, given such a 'rare' sketch of her person, I am 'burning' to hear something of her mental qualifications."

"My metaphors are not poetical, perhaps, but they are the first that offer themselves to my mind, and they are natural. Her accomplishments exceed her native gifts greatly. In the first place, she is witty; in the second, she is as impertinent as the devil; and in the third, as inveterate a little traitor to King George as there is in all Boston."

"These are strange recommendations to your favor!"

"The most infallible of all recommendations. They are piquant, like savory sauces, which excite the appetite, and season the dish. Now her treason (for it amounts to that in fact) is like olives, and gives a gusto to the generous port of my loyalty. Her impertinence is oil to the cold salad of my modesty, and her acid wit mingles with the sweetness of my temperament, in that sort of pleasant combination with which sweet and sour blend in sherbet."

"It would be idle for me to gainsay the charms of such a woman," returned Lionel, a good deal amused with the droll mixture of seriousness and humor in the other's manner; "now, for her connection with the light infantry —she is not of the light corps of her own sex, Polwarth?"

"Pardon me, Major Lincoln; I cannot joke on this subject. Miss Danforth is of one of the best families in Boston."

"Danforth! not Agnes, surely!"

"The very same!" exclaimed Polwarth, in surprise; "what do you know of her?"

"Only that she is a sort of cousin of my own, and that we are inmates of the same house. We bear equal affinity to Mrs. Lechmere, and the good lady has insisted that I shall make my home in Tremont street."

"I rejoice to hear it! At all events, our intimacy may now be improved to some better purpose than eating and drinking. But to the point; there were certain damnable innuendoes getting into circulation concerning my proportions, which I considered it prudent to look down at once."

"In order to do which, you had only to look thinner."

"And do I not, in this appropriate dress? To be perfectly serious with you, Leo—for to you I can freely unburden myself—you know what a set we are in the 47th; let them once fasten an opprobrious term or a nickname on you, and you take it to the grave, be it ever so burdensome."

"There is a way, certainly, to check ungentleman-like liberties," said Lionel, gravely.

"Poh! poh! a man would n't wish to fight about a pound more or a pound less of fat! Still, the name is a great deal, and first impressions are everything. Now, who ever thinks of Grand Cairo as a village? of the Grand Turk and Great Mogul as little boys? or who would believe, by hearsay, that Captain Polwarth, of the light infantry, could weigh one hundred and eighty?"

"Add twenty to it."

"Not a pound more, as I am a sinner. I was weighed in the presence of the whole mess no later than last week, since when I have rather lost than gained an ounce, for this early rising is no friend to a thriving condition. 'T was in my night-gown, you 'll remember, Leo, for we, who tally so often, can't afford to throw in boots and buckles, and all those sorts of things, like your feather-weights."

"But I marvel how Nesbitt was induced to consent to the appointment," said Lionel; "he loves a little display."

"I am your man for that," interrupted the captain; "we are embodied, you know, and I make more display, if that be what you require, than any captain in the corps. But I will whisper a secret in your ear. There has been a nasty business here lately, in which the 47th has gained no new laurels —a matter of tarring and feathering, about an old rusty musket."

"I have heard something of the affair already," returned Lionel, "and was grieved to find the men justifying some of

4

their own brutal conduct last night by the example of their commander.''

'' Mum—'t is a delicate matter—well, that tar has brought the colonel into particularly bad odor in Boston, especially among the women, in whose good graces we are all of us lower than I have ever known scarlet coats to stand before. Why, Leo, the Mohairs are altogether the better men here! But there is not an officer in the whole army who has made more friends in the place than your humble servant. I have availed myself of my popularity, which just now is no trifling thing, and partly by promises, and partly by secret interest, I have the company; to which, you know, my rank in the regiment gives me an undoubted title.''

'' A perfectly satisfactory explanation; a most commendable ambition on your part, and a certain symptom that the peace is not to be disturbed; for Gage would never permit such an arrangement, had he any active operations in his eye.''

'' Why, there I think you are more than half right; these Yankees have been talking, and resolving, and approbating their resolves, as they call it, these ten years past; and what does it all amount to? To be sure, things grow worse and worse every day; but Jonathan is an enigma to me. Now you know, when we were in the cavalry together,—God forgive me the suicide I committed in exchanging into the foot, which I never should have done, could I have found in all England such a thing as an easy goer or safe leaper,—but then, if the Commons took offence at a new tax, or a stagnation in business, why, they got together in mobs, and burnt a house or two, frightened a magistrate, and perhaps hustled a constable; then in we come at a hand gallop, you know, flourished our swords, and scattered the ragged devils to the four winds; then the courts did the rest, leaving us a cheap victory at the expense of a little wind, which was amply compensated by an increased appetite for dinner. But here it is altogether a different sort of thing.''

'' And what are the most alarming symptoms, just now, in the colonies?'' asked Major Lincoln, with a sensible interest in the subject.

" They refuse their natural aliment to uphold what they call their principles; the women abjure tea, and the men abandon their fisheries! There has been hardly such a thing as even a wild duck brought into the market this spring, in consequence of the Port Bill, and yet they grow more stubborn every day. If it should come to blows, however, thank God! we are strong enough to open a passage for ourselves to any part of the continent where provisions may be plentier; and I hear more troops are already on the way."

" If it should come to blows, which Heaven forbid," said Major Lincoln, " we shall be besieged where we now are."

" Besieged!" exclaimed Polwarth, in evident alarm; " if I thought there was the least prospect of such a calamity, I would sell out to-morrow. It is bad enough now; our mess-table is never decently covered, but if there should come a siege, 't would be absolute starvation. No, no, Leo, their minute-men, and their long-tailed rabble, would hardly think of besieging four thousand British soldiers with a fleet to back them. Four thousand! if the regiments I hear named are actually on the way, there will be eight thousand of us— as good men as ever wore—"

" Light-infantry jackets," interrupted Lionel. " But the regiments are certainly coming; Clinton, Burgoyne, and Howe had an audience to take leave, on the same day with myself. The service is exceedingly popular with the king, and our reception, of course, was most gracious; though I thought the eye of royalty looked on me as if it remembered one or two of my juvenile votes in the House, on the subject of these unhappy dissensions."

" You voted against the Port Bill," said Polwarth, " out of regard to me?"

" No; there I joined the ministry. The conduct of the people of Boston had provoked the measure, and there were hardly two minds in Parliament on that question."

" Ah! Major Lincoln, you are a happy man," said the captain; " a seat in Parliament at five and twenty! I must think that I should prefer just such an occupation to all others; the very name is taking—a seat! You have two members for your borough; who fills the second now?"

"Say nothing on that subject, I entreat you," whispered Lionel, pressing the arm of the other as he rose; "'t is not filled by him who should occupy it, as you know. Shall we descend to the common? there are many friends that I could wish to see before the bell calls us to church."

"Yes; this is a church-going, or rather a meeting-going place; for most of the good people forswear the use of the word church, as we abjure the supremacy of the pope," returned Polwarth, following in his companion's footsteps. "I never think of attending any of their schism shops, for I would any day rather stand sentinel over a baggage wagon than stand up to hear one of their prayers. I can do very well at the King's Chapel, as they call it; for when I am once comfortably fixed on my knees, I make out as well as my lord archbishop of Canterbury; though it has always been matter of surprise to me how any man can find breath to go through their work of a morning."

They descended the hill, as Lionel replied, and their forms were soon blended with those of twenty others, who wore scarlet coats, on the common.

CHAPTER V.

" For us, and for our tragedy,
Here stooping to your clemency,
We beg your hearing patiently."

Hamlet.

WE must now carry the reader back a century, in order to clear our tale of every appearance of ambiguity. Reginald Lincoln was a cadet of an extremely ancient and wealthy family, whose possessions were suffered to continue as appendages to a baronetcy, throughout all the changes which marked the eventful periods of the commonwealth and the usurpation of Cromwell. He had himself, however, inherited little more than a morbid sensibility, which, even in that age, appeared to be a sort of heirloom to his family. While still a young man, he had married a woman to whom he was much attached, who died in giving birth to her first child. The grief of the husband took a direction towards religion ; but unhappily, instead of deriving from his researches the healing consolation with which our faith abounds, his mind became soured by the prevalent but discordant views of the attributes of the Deity ; and the result of his conversion was to leave him an ascetic puritan and an obstinate predestinarian. That such a man, finding but little to connect him with his native country, should revolt at the impure practices of the court of Charles, is not surprising ; and accordingly, though not at all implicated in the guilt of the regicides, he departed for the religious province of Massachusetts Bay, in the first years of the reign of that merry prince.

It was not difficult for a man of the rank and reputed

sanctity of Reginald Lincoln to obtain both honorable and lucrative employments in the plantations, and, after the first glow of his awakened ardor in behalf of spiritual matters had a little abated, he failed not to improve a due portion of his time by a commendable attention to temporal things. To the day of his death, however, he continued a gloomy, austere, and bigoted religionist, seemingly too regardless of the vanities of this world to permit his pure imagination to mingle with its dross, even while he submitted to discharge its visible duties. Notwithstanding this elevation of mind, his son, at the decease of his father, found himself in the possession of many goodly effects; which were, questionless, the accumulations of a neglected use during the days of his sublimated progenitor.

Young Lionel so far followed in the steps of his worthy parent as to continue gathering honors and riches into his lap; though, owing to an early disappointment, and the inheritance of the "heirloom" already mentioned, it was late in life before he found a partner to share his happiness. Contrary to all the usual calculations that are made on the choice of a man of self-denial, he was then united to a youthful and gay Episcopalian, who had little, beside her exquisite beauty and good blood to recommend her. By this lady he had four children, three sons and a daughter, when he also was laid in the vault by the side of his deceased parent. The eldest of these sons was yet a boy when he was called to the mother country to inherit the estates and honors of his family. The second, named Reginald, who was bred to arms, married, had a son, and lost his life in the wilds where he was required to serve, before he was five-and-twenty. The third was the grandfather of Agnes Danforth, and the daughter was Mrs. Lechmere.

The family of Lincoln, considering the shortness of their marriages, had been extremely prolific while in the colonies, according to that wise allotment of Providence, which ever seems to regulate the functions of our nature by our wants; but the instant it was reconveyed to the populous island of Britain, it entirely lost its reputation for fruitfulness. Sir Lionel lived to a good age, married, but died childless; notwithstanding, when his body lay in state, it was under a splendid roof, and in halls so capacious that they would have afforded comfortable shelter to the whole family of Priam.

By this fatality it became necessary to cross the Atlantic once more to find an heir to the wide domains of Ravenscliffe, and to one of the oldest baronetcies in the kingdom.

We have planted and reared this genealogical tree to but little purpose, if it be necessary to tell the reader that the individual who had now become the head of his race was the orphan son of the deceased officer. He was married, and the father of one blooming boy, when this elevation, which was not unlooked-for, occurred. Leaving his wife and child behind him, Sir Lionel immediately proceeded to England to assert his rights and secure his possessions. As he was the nephew and acknowledged heir of the late incumbent, he met with no opposition to the more important parts of his claims. Across the character and fortunes of this gentleman, however, a dark cloud had early passed, which prevented the common eye from reading the events of his life, like those of other men, in its open and intelligible movements. After his accession to fortune and rank, but little was known of him, even by his earliest and most intimate associates. It was rumored, it is true, that he had been detained in England for two years by a vexatious contention for a petty appendage to his large estates, a controversy which was, however, known to have been decided in his favor, before he was recalled to Boston by the sudden death of his wife. This calamity befell him during the period when the war of '56 was raging in its greatest violence; a time when the energies of the colonies were directed to the assistance of the mother country, who, according to the language of the day, was zealously endeavoring to defeat the ambitious views of the French, in this hemisphere; or, what amounted to the same thing in effect, in struggling to advance her own.

It was an interesting period, when the mild and peaceful colonists were seen to shake off their habits of forbearance, and to enter into the strife with an alacrity and spirit that soon emulated the utmost daring of their more practised confederates. To the amazement of all who knew his fortunes, Sir Lionel Lincoln was seen to embark in many of the most desperate adventures that distinguished the war with a hardihood that rather sought death than courted honor. He had been, like his father, trained to arms, but the regiment in which he held the commission of lieutenant-colonel, was serving his master in the most eastern of his dominions, while the uneasy soldier was thus rushing from point to point, hazarding his life, and more than once shedding his blood, in the enterprises that signalized the war in the most western.

This dangerous career, however, was at length suddenly and mysteriously checked. By the influence of some powerful agency, that was never explained, the baronet was induced to take his son, and embark once more for the land of their fathers, from which the former had never been known to return. For many years, all those inquiries which the laudable curiosity of the townsmen and townswomen of Mrs. Lechmere prompted them to make, concerning the fate of her nephew (and we leave each of our readers to determine their numbers), were answered by that lady with the most courteous reserve, and sometimes with such exhibitions of emotion, as we have already attempted to describe in her first interview with his son. But constant dropping will wear away a stone. At first there were rumors that the baronet had committed treason, and had been compelled to exchange Ravenscliffe for a less comfortable dwelling in the Tower of London. This report was succeeded by that of an unfortunate private marriage with one of the princesses of the house of Brunswick; but a reference to the calendars of the day showed that there was no lady of a suitable age disengaged; and this amour, so creditable to the provinces, was necessarily abandoned. Finally, the assertion was made, with much more of the confidence of truth, that the unhappy Sir Lionel was the tenant of a private madhouse.

The instant this rumor was circulated, a film fell from every eye, and none were so blind as not to have seen indications of insanity in the baronet long before; and not a few were enabled to trace his legitimate right to lunacy through the hereditary bias of his race. To account for its sudden exhibition was a more difficult task, and exercised the ingenuity of an exceedingly ingenious people for a long period.

The more sentimental part of the community, such as the maidens and bachelors, and those votaries of Hymen who had twice and thrice proved the solacing power of the God, did not fail to ascribe the misfortune of the baronet to the unhappy loss of his wife ; a lady to whom he was known to be most passionately attached. A few, the relics of the good old school, under whose intellectual sway the incarnate persons of so many godless dealers in necromancy had been made to expiate their abominations, pointed to the calamity as a merited punishment on the backslidings of a family that had once known the true faith ; while a third, and by no means a small class, composed of those worthies who braved the elements in King Street, in quest of filthy lucre, did not hesitate to say, that the sudden acquisition of vast wealth had driven many a better man mad. But the time was approaching, when the apparently irresistible propensity to speculate on the fortunes of a fellow-creature was made to yield to more important considerations. The hour soon arrived when the merchant forgot his momentary interests to look keenly into the distant effects that were to succeed the movements of the day ; which taught the fanatic the wholesome lesson, that Providence smiled most beneficently on those who most merited, by their own efforts, its favors ; and which even purged the breast of the sentimentalist of its sickly tenant, to be succeeded by the healthy and ennobling passion of love of country.

It was about this period that the contest for principle between the Parliament of Great Britain and the colonies of North America commenced, that in time led to those important results which have established a new era in political liberty, as well as a mighty empire. A brief glance at the nature of this controversy may assist in rendering many of the allusions in this legend more intelligible to some of its readers.

The increasing wealth of the provinces had attracted the notice of the English ministry so early as the year 1763. In that year the first effort to raise a revenue which was to meet the exigencies of the empire, was attempted by the passage of a law to impose a duty on certain stamped paper, which was made necessary to give validity to contracts. This method of raising a revenue was not new in itself, nor was the imposition heavy in amount. But the Americans, not less sagacious than wary, perceived at a glance the importance of the principles involved in the admission of a right as belonging to anybody to lay taxes, in which they were not represented. The question was not without its difficulties, but the direct and plain argument was clearly on the side of the colonists. Aware of the force of their reasons, and perhaps a little conscious of the strength of their numbers, they approached the subject with a spirit which betokened this consciousness, but with a coolness that denoted the firmness of their purpose. After a struggle of nearly two years, during which the law was rendered completely profitless by the unanimity among the people, as well as by a species of good-humored violence that rendered it exceedingly inconvenient, and perhaps a little dangerous, to the servants of the crown to exercise their obnoxious functions, the ministry abandoned the measure. But, at the same time that the law was repealed, the Parliament maintained its right to bind the colonies in all cases whatsoever, by recording a resolution to that effect in its journals.

That an empire whose several parts were separated by oceans, and whose interests were so often conflicting, should become unwieldy, and fall, in time, by its own weight, was an event that all wise men must have expected to arrive. But that the Americans did not contemplate such a division at that early day, may be fairly inferred, if there were no other testimony in the matter, by the quiet and submission that pervaded the colonies the instant the repeal of the Stamp Act was known. Had any desire for premature independence existed, the Parliament had unwisely furnished abundant fuel to feed the flame, in the very resolution already mentioned. But, satisfied with the solid advantages they had secured, peaceful in their habits, and loyal in their feelings, the colonists laughed at the empty dignity of their self-constructed rulers, while they congratulated each other on their own more substantial success. If the besotted servants of the king had learned wisdom by the past, the storm would have blown over, and another age would have witnessed the events which we are about to relate. Things were hardly suffered, however, to return to their old channels again, before the ministry attempted to revive their claims by new impositions. The design to raise a revenue had been defeated in the case of the Stamp Act, by the refusal of the colonists to use the paper ; but in the present instance, expedients were adopted, which, it was thought, would be more effective—as in the case of tea, where the duty was paid by the East India Company in the first instance, and the exaction was to be made on the Americans, through their appetites. These new innovations on their rights were met by the colonists with the same promptitude, but with much more of seriousness, than in the former instances. All the provinces south of the Great Lakes acted in concert on this occasion ; and preparations were made to render not only their remonstrances and petitions more impressive by a unity of action, but their more serious struggles also, should an appeal to force become necessary. The tea was stored or sent back to England, in most cases ; though, in the town of Boston, a concurrence of circumstances led to the violent measure, on the part of the people, of throwing a large quantity of the offensive article into the sea. To punish this act, which took place in the early part of 1774, the port of Boston was closed, and different laws were enacted in Parliament, which were intended to bring the people back to a sense of their dependence on the British power.

Although the complaints of the colonists were hushed during the short interval that had succeeded the suspension of the efforts of the ministry to tax them, the feelings of alienation which were engendered by the attempt had not time to be lost before the obnoxious subject was revived in its new shape. From 1763 to the period of our tale, all the younger part of the population of the provinces had grown into manhood, but they were no longer imbued with that profound respect for the mother country which had been transmitted from their ancestors, or with that deep loyalty to the crown that usually characterizes a people who view the pageant of royalty through the medium of distance. Still, those who guided the feelings and controlled the judgments of the Americans were averse to a dismemberment of the empire, a measure which they continued to believe both impolitic and unnatural.

In the meantime, though equally reluctant to shed blood, the adverse parties prepared for that final struggle which seemed to be unavoidably approaching. The situation of the colonies was now so peculiar, that it may be doubted whether history furnishes a precise parallel. Their fealty to the prince was everywhere acknowledged, while the laws which emanated from his counsellors were sullenly disregarded and set at naught. Each province possessed its distinct government, and in most of them the political influence of the crown was direct and great ; but the time had arrived when it was superseded by a moral feeling that defied the machinations and intrigues of the ministry. Such of the provincial legislatures as possessed a majority of the "Sons of Liberty," as they who resisted the unconstitutional attempts of the ministry were termed, elected delegates to meet in a general congress to consult on the ways and means of effecting the common objects. In one or two provinces, where the inequality of representation afforded a different result, the people supplied the deficiencies by acting in their original capacity. This body, meeting, unlike conspirators, with the fearless confidence of integrity, and acting under the excitement of a revolution in sentiment, possessed an influence which, at a later day, has been denied to their more legally constituted successors. Their recommendations possessed all the validity of laws, without incurring their odium. While, as the organ of their fellow-subjects, they still continued to petition and remonstrate, they did not forget to oppose, by such means

as were then thought expedient, the oppressive measures
of the ministry.

An association was recommended to the people, for those
purposes that are amply expressed in the three divisions
which were significantly given to the subjects, in calling
them by the several names of "non-importation," "non-
exportation," and "non-consumption resolutions." These
negative expedients were all that was constitutionally in
their power, and, throughout the whole controversy, there
had been a guarded care not to exceed the limits which the
laws had affixed to the rights of the subject. Though no
overt act of resistance was committed, they did not, however, neglect such means as were attainable, to be prepared
for the last evil, whenever it should arrive. In this manner, a feeling of resentment and disaffection was daily increasing throughout the provinces, while in Massachusetts
Bay, the more immediate scene of our story, the disorder
in the body politic seemed to be inevitably gathering to its
head.

The great principles of the controversy had been blended,
in different places, with various causes of local complaint,
and in none more than in the town of Boston. The inhabitants of this place had been distinguished for an early,
open, and fearless resistance to the ministry. An armed
force had long been thought necessary to intimidate this
spirit, to effect which the troops were drawn from different
parts of the provinces, and concentrated in this devoted
town. Early in 1774, a military man was placed in the
executive chair of the province, and an attitude of more
determination was assumed by the government. One of
the first acts of this gentleman, who held the high station
of lieutenant-general, and who commanded all the forces
of the king in America, was to dissolve the colonial assembly. About the same time a new charter was sent
from England, and a material change was contemplated in
the polity of the colonial government. From this moment
the power of the king, though it was not denied, became
suspended in the province. A provincial congress was
elected, and assembled within seven leagues of the capital,

where they continued, from time to time, to adopt such measures as the exigencies of the time were thought to render necessary. Men were enrolled, disciplined, and armed, as well as the imperfect means of the colony would allow. These troops, who were no more than the *élite* of the inhabitants, had little else to recommend them besides their spirit, and their manual dexterity with fire-arms. From the expected nature of their service, they were not unaptly termed "minute-men." The munitions of war were seized, and hoarded with a care and diligence that showed the character of the impending conflict.

On the other hand General Gage adopted a similar course of preparation and prevention, by fortifying himself in the stronghold which he possessed, and by anticipating the intentions of the colonists, in their attempts to form magazines, whenever it was in his power. He had an easy task in the former, both from the natural situation of the place he occupied, and the species of force he commanded.

Surrounded by broad and chiefly by deep waters, except at one extremely narrow point, and possessing its triple hills, which are not commanded by any adjacent eminences, the peninsula of Boston could, with a competent garrison, easily be made impregnable, especially when aided by a superior fleet. The works erected by the English general were, however, by no means of magnitude ; for it was well known that the whole park of the colonists could not exceed some dozen pieces of field artillery, with a small battering train that must be entirely composed of old and cumbrous ship-guns. Consequently, when Lionel arrived in Boston, he found a few batteries thrown up on the eminences, some of which were intended as much to control the town, as to repel an enemy from without, while lines were drawn across the neck which communicated with the main. The garrison consisted of something less than five thousand men, besides which there was a fluctuating force of seamen and marines, as the vessels of war arrived and departed.

All this time, there was no other interruption to the intercourse between the town and the country, than such as unavoidably succeeded the stagnation of trade, and the dis-

trust engendered by the aspect of affairs. Though numberless families had deserted their homes, many known whigs
continued to dwell in their habitations, where their ears
were deafened by the sounds of the British drums, and
where their spirits were but too often galled by the sneers
of the officers, on the uncouth military preparations of their
countrymen. Indeed, an impression had spread further than
among the idle and thoughtless youths of the army, that the
colonists were but little gifted with martial qualities; and
many of their best friends in Europe were in dread, lest an
appeal to force should put the contested points forever at
rest, by proving the incompetency of the Americans to
maintain them to the last extremity.

In this manner, both parties stood at bay; the people
living in perfect order and quiet, without the administration
of law, sullen, vigilant, and, through their leaders, secretly
alert; and the army, gay, haughty, and careless of the consequences, though far from being oppressive or insolent, until after the defeat of one or two abortive excursions into
the country in quest of arms. Each hour, however, was
rapidly adding to the disaffection on one side, and to the
contempt and resentment on the other, through numberless
public and private causes that belong rather to history than
to a legend like this. All extraordinary occupations were
suspended, and men awaited the course of things in anxious
expectation. It was known that the Parliament, instead of
retracting their political errors, had imposed new restraints,
and, as has been mentioned, it was also rumored that
regiments and fleets were on their way to enforce them.

How long a country could exist in such a primeval condition remained to be seen, though it was difficult to say when
or how it was to terminate. The people of the land appeared to slumber; but, like vigilant and wary soldiers,
they might be said to sleep on their arms; while the troops
assumed, each day, more of that fearful preparation which
gives, even to the trained warrior, a more martial aspect,
though both parties still continued to manifest a becoming
reluctance to shed blood.

CHAPTER VI.

" Would he were fatter! but I fear him not:
  Seldom he smiles ; and smiles in such a sort,
  As if he mocked himself, and scorned his spirit
  That could be moved to smile at anything."
                                        Julius Cæsar.

I N the course of the succeeding week, Lionel acquired a
  knowledge of many minor circumstances relating to
  the condition of the colonies, which may be easily imagined as incidental to the times, but which would
greatly excel our limits to relate. He was received by his
brethren in arms with that sort of cordiality that a rich, high-
spirited, and free, if not a jovial comrade, was certain of
meeting among men who lived chiefly for pleasure and appearance. Certain indications of more than usually important movements were discovered among the troops the first
day of the week, and his own condition in the army was in
some measure affected by the changes. Instead of joining
his particular regiment, he was ordered to hold himself in
readiness to take a command in the light corps, which had
begun its drill for the service that was peculiar to such troops.
As it was well known that Boston was Major Lincoln's place
of nativity, the commander-in-chief, with the indulgence and
kindness of his character, granted to him, however, a short
respite from duty, in order that he might indulge in the feelings natural to his situation. It was soon generally understood that Major Lincoln, though intending to serve with the
army in America, should the sad alternative of an appeal to
arms become necessary, had permission to amuse himself in
such a manner as he saw fit, for two months from the date
of his arrival. Those who affected to be more wise than com-

mon, saw, or thought they saw, in this arrangement, a deep-laid plan on the part of Gage, to use the influence and address of the young provincial among his connections and natural friends, to draw them back to those sentiments of loyalty which it was feared so many among them had forgotten to entertain. But it was the characteristic of the times to attach importance to trifling incidents, and to suspect a concealed policy in movements which emanated only in inclination.

There was nothing, however, in the deportment or manner of life adopted by Lionel to justify any of these conjectures. He continued to dwell in the house of Mrs. Lechmere in person, though, unwilling to burden the hospitality of his aunt too heavily, he had taken lodgings in a dwelling at no great distance, where his servants resided, and where it was generally understood that his visits of ceremony and friend-ship were to be received. Captain Polwarth did not fail to complain loudly of this arrangement, as paralyzing at once all the advantages he had anticipated from enjoying the *entrée* to the dwelling of his mistress, in the right of his friend. But as the establishment of Lionel was supported with much of that liberality which was becoming in a youth of his large fortune, the exuberant light-infantry officer found many sources of consolation in the change, which could not have existed had the staid Mrs. Lechmere presided over the domestic department. Lionel and Polwarth had been boys together at the same school, members of the same college at Oxford, and subsequently, for many years, com-rades in the same corps. Though, perhaps, no two men in their regiment were more essentially different in mental as well as physical constitution, yet by that unaccountable ca-price which causes us to like our opposites, it is certain that no two gentlemen in the service were known to be on better terms, or to maintain a more close and unreserved intimacy. It is unnecessary to dilate here on this singular friendship; it occurs every day, between men still more discordant, the result of accident and habit, and is often, as in the present instance, cemented by unconquerable good-nature in one of the parties. For this latter qualification Captain

5

Polwarth was eminent, if for no other. It contributed quite as much as his science in the art of living, to the thriving condition of the corporeal moiety of the man, and it rendered a communion with the less material part at all times inoffensive, if not agreeable.

On the present occasion, the captain took charge of the internal economy of Lionel's lodgings, with a zeal which he did not even pretend was disinterested. By the rules of the regiment he was compelled to live nominally with the mess, where he found his talents and his wishes fettered by divers indispensable regulations, and economical practices, that could not be easily overleaped ; but with Lionel, just such an opportunity offered for establishing rules of his own, and disregarding expenditure, as he had been long pining for in secret. Though the poor of the town were, in the absence of employment, necessarily supported by large contributions of money, clothing, and food, which were transmitted to their aid from the farthermost parts of the colonies, the markets were not yet wanting in all the necessaries of life, to those who enjoyed the means of purchasing. With this disposition of things, therefore, he became well content, and within the first fortnight after the arrival of Lionel, it became known to the mess that Captain Polwarth took his dinners regularly with his old friend, Major Lincoln ; though in truth the latter was enjoying, more than half the time, the hospitality of the respective tables of the officers of the staff.

In the meantime Lionel cultivated his acquaintance in Tremont Street, where he still slept, with an interest and assiduity that the awkwardness of his first interview would not have taught us to expect. With Mrs. Lechmere, it is true, he made but little progress in intimacy ; for, equally formal, though polite, she was at all times enshrouded in a cloud of artificial, but cold management, that gave him little opportunity, had he possessed the desire, to break through the reserve of her calculating temperament. With his more youthful kinswomen, the case was, however, in a few days, entirely reversed. Agnes Danforth, who had nothing to conceal, began insensibly to yield to the manliness and grace of his manner. and before the end of the first week, she maintained the rights of the colonists, laughed at the follies of the officers, and then acknowledged her own prejudices, with a familiarity and good-humor that soon made her, in her turn, a favorite with her English cousin, as she termed Lionel. But he found the demeanor of Cecil Dynevor much more embarrassing, if not inexplicable. For days she would be distant, silent, and haughty, and then again, as it were by sudden impulses, she became easy and natural; her whole soul beaming in her speaking eyes, or her innocent and merry humor breaking through the bounds of her restraint, and rendering not only herself, but all around her, happy and delighted. Full many an hour did Lionel ponder on this unaccountable difference in the manner of this young lady, at different moments. There was a secret excitement in the very caprices of her humors, that had a piquant interest in his eyes, and which, aided by her exquisite form and intelligent face, gradually induced him to become a more close observer of their waywardness, and consequently a more assiduous attendant on her movements. In consequence of this assiduity, the manner of Cecil grew, almost imperceptibly, less variable, and more uniformly fascinating, while Lionel, by some unaccountable oversight, soon forgot to notice its changes, or even to miss the excitement.

In a mixed society, where pleasure, company, and a multitude of objects conspired to distract the attention, such alterations would be the result of an intercourse for months, if they ever occurred; but in a town like Boston, from which most of those with whom Cecil had once mingled were already fled, and where, consequently, those who remained behind lived chiefly for themselves and by themselves, it was no more than the obvious effect of very apparent causes. In this manner something like good-will, if not a deeper interest in each other, was happily effected within that memorable fortnight, which was teeming with events vastly more important in their results than any that can appertain to the fortunes of a single family.

The winter of 1774-75 had been as remarkable for its mildness, as the spring was cold and lingering. Like every season in our changeable climate, however, the chilling days of March and April were intermingled with some, when a genial sun recalled the ideas of summer, which, in their turn, were succeeded by others, when the torrents of cold rain, that drove before the easterly gales, would seem to repel every advance towards a milder temperature. Many of those stormy days occurred in the middle of April, and during their continuance Lionel was necessarily compelled to keep himself housed.

He had retired from the parlor of Mrs. Lechmere, one evening, when the rain was beating against the windows of the house, in nearly horizontal lines, to complete some letters which, before dining, he had commenced to the agent of his family, in England. On entering his own apartment he was startled to find the room, which he had left vacant, and which he expected to find in the same state, occupied in a manner that he could not anticipate. The light of a strong wood fire was blazing on the hearth, and throwing about, in playful changes, the flickering shadows of the furniture, and magnifying each object into some strange and fantastical figure. As he stepped within the door, his eye fell upon one of these shadows, which extended along the wall, and bending against the ceiling, exhibited the gigantic but certain outlines of the human form. Recollecting that he had left his letters open, and a little distrusting the discretion of Meriton, Lionel advanced lightly, for a few feet, so far as to be able to look round the drapery of his bed, and, to his amazement, perceived that the intruder was not his valet, but the aged stranger. The old man sat holding in his hand the open letter which Lionel had been writing, and continued so deeply absorbed in its contents that the footsteps of the other were still disregarded. A large coarse overcoat, dripping with water, concealed most of his person, though the white that strayed about his face and the deep lines of his remarkable countenance could not be mistaken.

"I was ignorant of this unexpected visit," said Lionel, advancing quickly into the centre of the room, "or I should not have been so tardy in returning to my apartment, where, sir, I fear you must have found your time irksome, with nothing but that scrawl to amuse you."

The old man dropped the paper from before his features, and betrayed, by the action, the large drops that followed each other down his hollow cheeks, until they fell even to the floor. The haughty and displeased look disappeared from the countenance of Lionel at this sight, and he was on the point of speaking in a more conciliating manner, when the stranger, whose eye had not quailed before the angry frown it encountered, anticipated his intention.

"I comprehend you, Major Lincoln," he said, calmly; "but there can exist justifiable reasons for a greater breach of faith than this of which you accuse me. Accident, and not intention, has put me in possession, here, of your most secret thoughts on a subject that has deep interest for me. You have urged me often, during our voyage, to make you acquainted with all that you most desire to know ; to which request, as you may remember, I have ever been silent."

"You have said, sir, that you are master of a secret in which my feelings, I will acknowledge, are deeply interested, and I have urged you to remove my doubts by declaring the truth ; but I do not perceive—"

"How a desire to possess my secret gives me a claim to inquire into yours, you would say," interrupted the stranger ; "nor does it. But an interest in your affairs, that you cannot yet understand, and which is vouched for by these scalding tears, the first that have fallen in years from a fountain that I had thought dried, should and must satisfy you."

"It does," said Lionel, deeply affected by the melancholy tones of his voice ; "it does, it does, and I will listen to no further explanation on the unpleasant subject. You see nothing there, I am sure, of which a son can have reason to be ashamed."

"I see much here, Lionel Lincoln, of which a father would have reason to be proud," returned the old man. "It was the filial love which you have displayed in this paper which has drawn these drops from my eyes ; for he who has lived as I have done, beyond the age of man, without knowing the love that the parent feels for its off-spring, or which the child bears to the author of its being, must have outlived his natural sympathies, not to be conscious of his misfortune, when chance makes him sensible of affections like these."

"You have never been a father, then?" said Lionel, drawing a chair nigh to his aged companion, and seating himself with an air of powerful interest that he could not control.

"Have I not told you that I am alone?" returned the old man, with a solemn manner. After an impressive pause, he continued, though his tones were husky and low, "I have been both husband and parent in my day, but 't is so long since that no selfish tie remains to bind me to earth. Old age is the neighbor of death, and the chill of the grave is to be found in its warmest breathings."

"Say not so," interrupted Lionel, "for you do injustice to your own warm nature ; you forget your zeal in behalf of what you deem these oppressed colonies."

"'T is no more than the flickering of the dying lamp, which flares and dazzles most when its source of heat is nighest to extinction. But though I may not infuse into your bosom a warmth that I do not possess myself, I can point out the dangers with which life abounds, and serve as a beacon when no longer useful as a pilot. It is for such a purpose, Major Lincoln, that I have braved the tempest of to-night."

"Has anything occurred which, by rendering danger pressing, can make such an exposure necessary?"

"Look at me," said the old man earnestly : "I have seen most of this flourishing country a wilderness ; my recollection goes back into those periods when the savage and the beast of the forest contended with our fathers for much of that soil which now supports its hundreds of thousands in plenty ; and my time is to be numbered, not by years, but by ages. For such a being, think you there can yet be many months, or weeks, or even days in store?"

Lionel dropped his eyes, in embarrassment, to the floor, as he answered.—

"You cannot have very many years, surely, to hope for, but with the activity and temperance you possess, days and months confine you, I trust, in limits much too small."

"What!" exclaimed the other, stretching forth a color-less hand, in which even the prominent veins partook in the appearance of a general decay of nature; "with these wasted limbs, these gray hairs, and this sunken and sepul-chral cheek, would you talk to me of years! to me, who have not the effrontery to petition for even minutes, were they worth the prayer—so long already has been my probation!"

"It is certainly time to think of the change, when it approaches so very near."

"Well, then, Lionel Lincoln, old, feeble, and on the threshold of eternity as I stand, yet am I not nearer to my grave than that country, to which you have pledged your blood, is to a mighty convulsion, which will shake her institutions to their foundations."

"I cannot admit the signs of the times to be quite so por-tentous as your fears would make them," said Lionel, smil-ing a little proudly. "Though the worst that is apprehended should arrive, England will feel the shock but as the earth bears an eruption of one of its volcanoes! But we talk in idle figures, sir; know you anything to justify the appre-hension of immediate danger?"

The face of the stranger lighted with a sudden and startling gleam of intelligence, and a sarcastic smile passed across his wan features, as he answered slowly,—

"They only have cause to fear, who will be the losers by the change! A youth who casts off the trammels of his guardians is not apt to doubt his ability to govern himself. England has held these colonies so long in leading-strings, that she forgets her offspring is able to go alone."

"Now, sir, you exceed even the wild projects of the most daring among those who call themselves the 'Sons of Lib-erty,' as if liberty existed in any place more favored or more nurtured than under the blessed Constitution of England! The utmost required is what they term a redress of griev-ances, many of which, I must think, exist only in imagina-tion."

"Was a stone ever known to roll upward? Let there be but one drop of American blood spilt in anger, and its stain will become indelible."

"Unhappily the experiment has been already tried; and yet years have rolled by, while England keeps her footing and authority good."

"Her authority!" repeated the old man: "see you not, Major Lincoln, in the forbearance of this people, when they felt themselves in the wrong, the existence of the very principles that will render them invincible and unyielding when right? But we waste our time; I came to conduct you to a place where, with your own ears, and with your own eyes, you may hear and see a little of that spirit which pervades the land. You will follow?"

"Not, surely, in such a tempest!"

"This tempest is but a trifle to that which is about to break upon you, unless you retrace your steps; but follow, I repeat: if a man of my years disregards the night, ought an English soldier to hesitate?"

The pride of Lionel was touched; and remembering an engagement he had previously made with his aged friend to accompany him to a scene like this, he made such changes in his dress as would serve to conceal his profession, threw on a large cloak to protect his person, and was about to lead the way himself, when he was aroused by the voice of the other.

"You mistake the route," he said; "this is to be a secret, and I hope a profitable visit; none must know of your presence; and if you are a worthy son of your honorable father, I need hardly add that my faith is pledged for your discretion."

"The pledge will be respected, sir," said Lionel, haughtily; "but in order to see what you wish, we are not to remain here?"

"Follow, then, and be silent," said the old man, turning and opening the doors which led into a little apartment lighted by one of those smaller windows already mentioned in describing the exterior of the building. The passage was dark and narrow; but, observing the warnings of his companion, Lionel succeeded in descending, in safety, a flight of steps which formed a private communication between the offices of the dwelling and its upper apartments. They paused an instant at the bottom of the stairs, where the youth expressed his amazement that a stranger should be so much more familiar with the building than he who had for so many days made it his home.

"Have I not often told you," returned the old man, with a severity in his voice which was even apparent in its suppressed tones, "that I have known Boston for near a hundred years? How many edifices like this does it contain, that I should not have noted its erection! But follow in silence, and be prudent."

He now opened a door which conducted them through one end of the building, into the courtyard in which it was situated. As they emerged into the open air, Lionel perceived the figure of a man, crouching under the walls, as if seeking a shelter from the driving rain. The moment they appeared, this person arose, and followed as they moved towards the street.

"Are we not watched?" said Lionel, stopping to face the unknown. "Whom have we skulking in our footsteps?"

"'T is the boy," said the old man, for whom we must adopt the name of Ralph, which it would appear was the usual term used by Job when addressing his mother's guest, "'t is the boy, and he can do us no harm. God has granted to him a knowledge between much of what is good and that which is evil, though the mind of the child is, at times, sadly weakened by his bodily ailings. His heart, however, is with his country, at a moment when she needs all hearts to maintain her rights."

The young British officer bowed his head to meet the tempest, and smiled scornfully within the folds of his cloak, which he drew more closely around his form, as they met the gale in the open streets of the town. They had passed swiftly through many narrow and crooked ways, before another word was uttered between the adventurers. Lionel mused on the singular and indefinable interest that he took in the movements of his companion, which could draw him at a time like this from the shelter of Mrs. Lechmere's roof.

to wander he knew not whither, and on an errand which might even be dangerous to his person. Still he followed, unhesitatingly ; for with these passing thoughts were blended the recollection of the many recent and interesting communications he had held with the old man during their long and close association in the ship ; nor was he wanting in a natural interest for all that involved the safety and happiness of the place of his birth. He kept the form of his aged guide in his eye, as the other moved before him, careless of the tempest which beat on his withered frame, and he heard the heavy footsteps of Job in his rear, who had closed so near his own person as to share, in some measure, in the shelter of his ample cloak. But no other living being seemed to have ventured abroad ; and even the few sentinels they passed, instead of pacing in front of those doors which it was their duty to guard, were concealed behind the angles of walls, or sought shelter under the projections of some favoring roof. At moments the wind rushed into the narrow avenues of the streets, along which it swept, with a noise not unlike the hollow roaring of the sea, and with a violence which was nearly irresistible. At such times, Lionel was compelled to pause, and even frequently to recede a little from his path, while his guide, supported by his high purpose, and but little obstructed by his garments, seemed, to the bewildered imagination of his follower, to glide through the night with a facility that was supernatural. At length the old man, who had got some distance ahead of his followers, suddenly paused, and allowed Lionel to approach to his side. The latter observed, with surprise, that he had stopped before the root and stump of a tree, which had once grown on the borders of a street, and which appeared to have been recently felled.

" Do you see this remnant of the Elm ? " said Ralph, when the others had stopped also. " Their axes have succeeded in destroying the mother plant, but her scions are flourishing throughout a continent ! "

" I do not comprehend you," returned Lionel ; " I see here nothing but the stump of some tree ; surely the ministers of the king are not answerable that it stands no longer ! "

"The ministers of the king are answerable to their master, that it has ever become what it is ; but speak to the boy at your side ; he will tell you of its virtues."

Lionel turned towards Job, and perceived, by the obscure light of the moon, to his surprise, that the changeling stood with his head bared to the storm, regarding the root with an extraordinary degree of reverence.

"This is all a mystery to me," he said ; "what do you know about this stump to stand in awe of, boy ? "

" 'T is the root of 'Liberty-tree,' " said Job, "and 't is wicked to pass it without making your manners ! "

"And what has this tree done for liberty, that it has merited so much respect ? "

"What ! why, did you ever see a tree afore this that could write and give notices of town-meetin' da's, or that could tell the people what the king meant to do with the tea, and his stamps ! "

"And could this marvellous tree work such miracles ? "

"To be sure it could, and it did, too. You let stingy Tommy think to get above the people with any of his cunning over night, and you might come here next morning, and read a warning on the bark of this tree, that would tell all about it, and how to put down his deviltries, written out fair, in a hand as good as Master Lovell himself could put on paper, the best day of his grand scholarship."

"And who puts the paper there ? "

"Who ! " exclaimed Job, a little positively ; "why, Liberty came in the night, and pasted it up herself. When Nab could n't get a house to live in, Job used to sleep under the tree, sometimes ; and many a night has he seen Liberty with his own eyes come and put up the paper."

"And was it a woman ? "

"Do you think Liberty was such a fool as to come every time in woman's clothes, to be followed by the rake-helly soldiers about the streets ? " said Job, with great contempt in his manner. "Sometimes she did, though, and sometimes she did n't, just as it happened. And Job was in the tree when old Noll had to give up his ungodly stamps ; though he did n't do it till the 'Sons of Liberty' had chucked his stamp-shop in the dock, and hung him and Lord Boot together, on the branches of the old Elm!"

"Hung!" said Lionel, unconsciously drawing back from the spot ; "was it ever a gallows?"

"Yes, for iffigies," said Job, laughing ; "I wish you could have been here to see how the old boot, with Satan sticking out on 't, whirled about when they swung it off! They give the old boy a big shoe to put his cloven huff in!"

Lionel, who was familiar with the peculiar sound that his townsmen gave to the letter *u*, now comprehended the allusion to the Earl of Bute, and, beginning to understand more clearly the nature of the transactions and the uses to which that memorable tree had been applied, he expressed his desire to proceed.

The old man had suffered Job to make his own explanations, though not without a curious interest in the effect they would produce on Lionel ; but the instant the request was made to advance, he turned, and once more led the way. Their course was now directed more towards the wharves ; nor was it long before their conductor turned into a narrow court, and entered a house of rather mean appearance, without even observing the formality of announcing his visit by the ordinary summons of rapping at its door. A long, narrow, and dimly-lighted passage conducted them to a spacious apartment far in the court, which appeared to have been fitted as a place for the reception of large assemblages of people. In this room were collected at least a hundred men, seemingly intent on some object of more than usual interest, by the gravity and seriousness of demeanor apparent in every countenance.

As it was Sunday, the first impression of Lionel, on entering the room, was, that his old friend, who often betrayed a keen sensibility on subjects of religion, had brought him there with a design to listen to some favorite exhorter of his peculiar tenets, and as a tacit reproach for a neglect of the usual ordinances of that holy day, of which the conscience of the young man suddenly accused him, on finding himself unexpectedly mingled in such a throng. But after he had forced his person among a dense body of men, who stood at the lower end of the apartment, and became a silent observer of the scene, he was soon made to perceive his error. The weather had induced all present to appear in such garments as were best adapted to protect them from its fury; and their exteriors were rough, and perhaps a little forbidding; but there was a composure and decency in the air common to the whole assembly, which denoted that they were men who possessed, in a high degree, the commanding quality of self-respect. A very few minutes sufficed to teach Lionel that he was in the midst of a meeting collected to discuss questions connected with the political movements of the times, though he felt himself a little at a loss to discover the precise results it was intended to produce. To every question there were one or two speakers, men who expressed their ideas in a familiar manner, and with the peculiar tones and pronunciation of the province, that left no room to believe them to be orators of a higher character than the mechanics and tradesmen of the town. Most, if not all of them, wore an air of deliberation and coldness, that would have rendered their sincerity in the cause they had apparently espoused a little equivocal, but for occasional expressions of coarse, and sometimes biting invective, that they expended on the ministers of the crown, and for the perfect and firm unanimity that was manifested, as each expression of the common feeling was taken, after the manner of deliberative bodies. Certain resolutions, in which the most respectful remonstrances were singularly blended with the boldest assertions of constitutional principles, were read, and passed without a dissenting voice, though with a calmness that indicated no very strong excitement. Lionel was peculiarly struck with the language of these written opinions, which were expressed with a purity, and sometimes with an elegance of style, which plainly showed that the acquaintance of the sober artisan with the instrument through whose periods he was blundering, was quite recent, and far from being very intimate. The eyes of the young soldier wandered from face to face with a strong desire to detect the secret movers of the scene he was witnessing; nor was he long without selecting one individual as an object peculiarly deserving of his suspicions. It was a man apparently but just entering into middle age, of an appearance, both in person and in such parts of his dress as escaped from beneath his overcoat, that denoted him to be of a class altogether superior to the mass of the assembly. A deep but manly respect was evidently paid to this gentleman by those who stood nearest to his person ; and once or twice there were close and earnest communications passing between him and the more ostensible leaders of the meeting, which roused the suspicions of Lionel in the manner related. Notwithstanding the secret dislike that the English officer suddenly conceived against a man that he fancied was thus abusing his powers, by urging others to acts of insubordination, he could not conceal from himself the favorable impression made by the open, fearless, and engaging countenance of the stranger. Lionel was so situated as to be able to keep his person, which was partly concealed by the taller forms that surrounded him, in constant view ; nor was it long before his earnest and curious gaze caught the attention of the other. Glances of marked meaning were exchanged between them during the remainder of the evening, until the chairman announced that the objects of the convocation were accomplished, and dissolved the meeting.

Lionel raised himself from his reclining attitude against the wall, and submitted to be carried by the current of human bodies into the dark passage, through which he had entered the room. Here he lingered a moment, with a view to recover his lost companion, and with a secret wish to scan more narrowly the proceedings of the man whose air and manner had so long chained his attention. The crowd had sensibly diminished before he was aware that few remained besides himself, nor would he then have discovered that he was likely to become an object of suspicion to those few, had not a voice at his elbow recalled his recollection.

"Does Major Lincoln meet his countrymen to-night as one who sympathizes in their wrongs, or as the favored and prosperous officer of the crown?" asked the very man for whose person he had so long been looking in vain.

"Is sympathy with the oppressed incompatible with loyalty to my prince?" demanded Lionel.

"That it is not," said the stranger, in a friendly accent, "is apparent from the conduct of many gallant Englishmen among us, who espouse our cause; but we claim Major Lincoln as a countryman."

"Perhaps, sir, it would be indiscreet just now to disavow that title, let my dispositions be as they may," returned Lionel, smiling a little haughtily; "this may not be as secure a spot in which to avow one's sentiment, as the town common, or the palace of St. James."

"Had the king been present to-night, Major Lincoln, would he have heard a single sentence opposed to that constitution which has declared him a member too sacred to be offended?"

"Whatever may have been the legality of your sentiments, sir, they surely have not been expressed in language altogether fit for a royal ear."

"It may not have been adulation, or even flattery, but it is truth, a quality no less sacred than the rights of kings."

"This is neither a place nor an occasion, sir," said the young soldier, quickly, "to discuss the rights of our common master; but if, as from your manner and your language I think not improbable, we should meet hereafter in a higher sphere, you will not find me at a loss to vindicate his claims."

The stranger smiled with meaning, and as he bowed before he fell back and was lost in the darkness of the passage, he replied,—

"Our fathers have often met in such society, I believe; God forbid that their sons should ever encounter in a less friendly manner."

Lionel, now finding himself alone, groped his way into the street, where he perceived Ralph and the changeling in waiting for his appearance. Without demanding the cause of the other's delay, the old man proceeded by the side of his companions, with the same indifference to the tempest as before, towards the residence of Mrs. Lechmere.

"You have now had some evidence of the spirit that per-

vades this people," said Ralph, after a few moments of
silence; "think you still there is no danger that the volcano will explode?"

"Surely everything I have heard and seen to-night confirms such an opinion," returned Lionel. "Men on the
threshold of rebellion seldom reason so closely, and with
such moderation. Why, the very fuel for the combustion,
the rabble themselves, discuss their constitutional principles,
and keep under the mantle of law, as though they were a
club of learned Templars."

"Think you that the fire will burn less steadily, because
what you call the fuel has been prepared by the seasoning
of time?" returned Ralph. "But this comes from sending
a youth into a foreign land for his education! The boy
rates his sober and earnest countrymen on a level with the
peasants of Europe."

So much Lionel was able to comprehend; but notwithstanding the old man muttered vehemently to himself for
some time longer, it was in a tone too indistinct for his ear
to understand his meaning. When they arrived in a part
of the town with which Lionel was familiar, his aged guide
pointed out his way, and took his leave, saying,—

"I see that nothing but the last, and dreadful argument
of force, will convince you of the purpose of the Americans
to resist their oppressors. God avert the evil hour! but
when it shall come, as come it must, you will learn your
error, young man, and, I trust, will not disregard the natural ties of country and kindred."

Lionel would have spoken in reply, but the rapid steps
of Ralph rendered his wishes vain; for, before he had
time for utterance, his emaciated form was seen gliding,
like an immaterial being, through the sheets of driving
rain, and was soon lost to the eye, as it vanished in the dim
shades of night, followed by the more substantial frame of
the idiot.

CHAPTER VII.

"Sergeant, you shall. Thus are poor servitors,
When others sleep upon their quiet beds,
Constrained to watch in darkness, rain, and cold."
King Henry VI.

TWO or three days of fine, balmy spring weather succeeded the storm, during which Lionel saw no more of his aged fellow-voyager. Job, however, attached himself to the British soldier with a confiding helplessness that touched the heart of his young protector, who gathered from the circumstance a just opinion of the nature of the abuses that the unfortunate changeling was frequently compelled to endure from the brutal soldiery. Meriton performed the functions of master of the wardrobe to the lad, by Lionel's express commands, with evident disgust, but with manifest advantage to the external appearance, if with no very sensible evidence of having added to the comfort of his charge. During this short period, the slight impression made on Lionel by the scene related in the preceding chapter, faded before the cheerful changes of the season, and the increasing interest which he felt in the society of his youthful kinswomen. Polwarth relieved him from all cares of a domestic nature, and the peculiar shade of sadness, which at times had been so very perceptible in his countenance, was changed to a look of a' more brightening and cheerful character. Polwarth and Lionel had found an officer, who had formerly served in the same regiment with them in the British Islands, in command of a company of grenadiers, which formed part of the garrison of Boston. This gentle-

6

man, an Irishman, of the name of M'Fuse, was qualified to do great honor to the culinary skill of the officer of light infantry, by virtue of a keen natural gusto for whatever possessed the inherent properties of a savory taste, though utterly destitute of any of that remarkable scientific knowledge which might be said to distinguish the other in the art. He was, in consequence of this double claim on the notice of Lionel, a frequent guest at the nightly banquets prepared by Polwarth. Accordingly, we find him, on the evening of the third day in the week, seated with his two friends around a board plentifully garnished by the care of that gentleman, on the preparations for which more than usual skill had been exerted, if the repeated declarations of the disciple of Heliogabalus, to that effect, were entitled to ordinary credit.

" In short, Major Lincoln," said Polwarth, in continuance of his favorite theme, while seated before the table, " a man may live anywhere, provided he possesses food—in England, or out of England, it matters not. Raiment may be necessary to appearance, but food is the only indispensable that nature has imposed on the animal world ; and, in my opinion, here is a sort of obligation on every man to be satisfied, who has wherewithal to appease the cravings of his appetite. Captain M'Fuse, I will thank you to cut that sirloin with the grain."

"What matters it, Polly," said the captain of grenadiers, with a slight Irish accent, and with the humor of his countrymen strongly depicted in his fine, open, manly features, "which way a bit of meat is divided, so there be enough to allay the cravings of the appetite ? "

"It is a collateral assistance to nature that should never be neglected," returned Polwarth, whose gravity and seriousness at his banquets were not easily disturbed ; " it facilitates mastication and aids digestion, two considerations of great importance to military men, sir, who have frequently such little time for the former, and no rest after their meals to complete the latter."

"He reasons like an army contractor, who wishes to make one ration do the work of two, when transportation is high," said M'Fuse, winking to Lionel. "According to your principles, then, Polly, a potato is your true campaigner, for that is a cr'ature you may cut any way without disturbing the grain, provided the article be a little m'aly."

"Pardon me, Captain M'Fuse," said Polwarth; "a potato should be broken, and not cut at all; there is no vegetable more used, and less understood, than the potato."

"And is it you, Pater Polwarth, of Nesbitt's light infantry," interrupted the grenadier, laying down his knife and fork with an air of infinite humor, "that will tell Dennis M'Fuse how to carve a potato! I will yield to the right of an Englishman over the chivalry of an ox, your sirloins, and your lady-rumps, if you please; but in my own country, one end of every farm is a bog, and the other a potato field—'t is an Irishman's patrimony that you are making so free with, sir!"

"The possession of a thing, and the knowledge how to use it, are two very different properties—"

"Give me the property of possession, then," again interrupted the ardent grenadier, "especially when a morsel of the green island is in dispute; and trust an old soldier of the Royal Irish to carve his own enjoyments. Now, I'll wager a month's pay—and that to me is as much as if the major should say, 'Done for a thousand,' that you can't tell how many dishes can be made, and are made every day in Ireland, out of so simple a thing as a potato."

"You roast and boil; and use them in stuffing tame birds, sometimes, and—"

"All old woman's cookery!" interrupted M'Fuse, with an affectation of great contempt in his manner. "Now, sir, we have them with butter, and without butter—that counts two; then we have the fruit p'aled; and—"

"Impaled," said Lionel, laughing. "I believe this nice controversy must be referred to Job, who is amusing himself in the corner there, I see, with the very subject of the dispute transfixed on his fork in the latter condition."

"Or suppose, rather," said M'Fuse, "as it is a matter to exercise the judgment of Solomon, we make a potato umpire of Master Seth Sage, yonder, who should have some of the wisdom of the royal Jew, by the sagacity of his countenance as well as of his name."

"Don't you call Seth r'yal," said Job, suspending his occupation on the vegetable. "The king is r'yal and fla'nty, but neighbor Sage lets Job come in and eat like a Christian."

"That lad there is not altogether without reason, Major Lincoln," said Polwarth; "on the contrary, he discovers an instinctive knowledge of good from evil, by favoring us with his company at the hour of meals."

"The poor fellow finds but little at home to tempt him to remain there, I fear," said Lionel; "and as he was one of the first acquaintances I made on returning to my native land, I have desired Mr. Sage to admit him at all proper hours; and especially, Polwarth, at those times when he can have an opportunity of doing homage to your skill."

"I am glad to see him," said Polwarth; "for I love an uninstructed palate, as much as I admire *naïveté* in a woman. Be so good as to favor me with a cut from the breast of that wild goose, M'Fuse,—not quite so far forward, if you please; your migratory birds are apt to be tough about the wing,—but simplicity in eating is, after all, the great secret of life; that and a sufficiency of food."

"You may be right this time," replied the grenadier, laughing; "for this fellow made one of the flankers of the flock, and did double duty in wheeling, I believe, or I have got him against the grain too! But, Polly, you have not told us how you improve in your light-infantry exercises of late."

By this time, Polwarth had made such progress in the essential part of his meal, as to have recovered in some measure his usual tone of good-nature, and he answered with less gravity,—

"If Gage does not work a reformation in our habits, he will fag us all to death. I suppose you know, Leo, that all the flank companies are relieved from the guards to learn a new species of exercise. They call it relieving us, but the only relief I find in the matter is when we lie down to fire, —there is a luxurious moment or two then. I must confess."

"I have known the fact, any time these ten days, by your moanings," returned Lionel. "But what do you argue from this particular exercise, Captain M'Fuse? Does Gage contemplate more than the customary drills?"

"You question me now, sir, on a matter in which I am uninstructed," said the grenadier. "I am a soldier, and obey my orders, without pretending to inquire into their objects or merits; all I know is, that both grenadiers and light infantry are taken from the guards; and that we travel over a good deal of solid earth each day, in the way of marching and countermarching, to the manifest discomfiture and reduction of Polly, there, who loses flesh as fast as he gains ground."

"Do you think so, Mac?" cried the delighted captain of light infantry. "Then I have not all the detestable motion in vain. They have given us little Harry Skip as a drill-officer, who, I believe, has the most restless foot of any man in his majesty's service. Do you join with me in opinion, Master Sage? You seem to meditate on the subject as if it had some secret charm."

The individual to whom Polwarth addressed this question, and who has been already named, was standing with a plate in his hand, in an attitude that bespoke close attention, with a sudden and deep interest in the discourse, though his eyes were bent on the floor, and his face was averted as if, while listening earnestly, he had a particular desire to be unnoticed. He was the owner of the house in which Lionel had taken his quarters. His family had been some time before removed into the country, under the pretence of his inability to maintain them in a place destitute of business and resources, like Boston; but he remained himself, for the double purpose of protecting his property and serving his guests. This man partook, in no small degree, of the qualities, both of person and mind, which distinguish a large class among his countrymen. In the former, he was rather over than under the middle stature; was thin, angular, and awkward, but possessing an unusual proportion of sinew and bone. His eyes were small, black, scintillating, and it was not easy to fancy that the intelli-

gence they manifested was unmingled with a large proportion of shrewd cunning. The rest of his countenance was
meagre, sallow, and rigidly demure. Thus called upon, on
a sudden, by Polwarth for an opinion, Seth answered, with
the cautious reserve with which he invariably delivered
himself,—

"The adjutant is an uneasy man ; but that, I suppose, is
so much the better for a light-infantry officer. Captain
Polwarth must find it considerably jading to keep the step,
now the general has ordered these new doings with the
soldiers."

"And what may be your opinion of these doings, as you
call them, Mr. Sage?" asked M'Fuse. "You, who are a
man of observation, should understand your countrymen ;
will they fight?"

"A rat will fight if the cats pen him," said Seth, without
raising his eyes from his occupation.

"But do the Americans conceive themselves to be
penned?"

"Why, that is pretty much as people think, captain.
The country was in a great touse about the stamps and the
tea, but I always said such folks as did n't give their notes-
of-hand, and had no great relish for anything more than
country food, would n't find themselves cramped by the laws,
after all."

"Then you see no great oppression in being asked to pay
your bit of a tax, Master Sage," cried the grenadier, "to
maintain such a worthy fellow as myself in a decent equipage to fight your battles?"

"Why, as to that, captain, I suppose we can do pretty
much the whole of our own fighting, when occasion calls ;
though I don't think there is much stomach for such doings
among the people, without need."

"But what do you think the 'Committee of Safety,'
and your 'Sons of Liberty,' as they call themselves, really
mean, by their parades of 'minute-men,' their gathering of
provisions, carrying off the cannon, and such other formidable and appalling preparations,—ha ! honest Seth ? Do
they think to frighten British soldiers with the roll of a

drum, or are they amusing themselves, like boys in the holidays, with playing war?"

"I should conclude," said Seth, with undisturbed gravity and caution, "that the people are pretty much engaged, and in earnest."

"To do what?" demanded the Irishman. "To forge their own chains, that we may fetter them in truth?"

"Why, seeing that they have burnt the stamps, and thrown the tea into the harbor," returned Seth, "and, since that, have taken the management into their own hands, I should rather conclude that they have pretty much determined to do what they think best."

Lionel and Polwarth laughed aloud, and the former observed,—

"You appear not to come to conclusions with our host, Captain M'Fuse, notwithstanding so much is determined. Is it well understood, Mr. Sage, that large reinforcements are coming to the colonies, and to Boston in particular?"

"Why, yes," returned Seth; "it seems to be pretty generally contemplated on."

"And what is the result of these contemplations?"

Seth paused a moment, as if uncertain whether he was master of the other's meaning, before he replied,—

"Why, as the country is considerably engaged in the business, there are some who think, if the ministers don't open the port, that it will be done without much further words by the people."

"Do you know," said Lionel, gravely, "that such an attempt would lead directly to a civil war?"

"I suppose it is safe to calculate that such doings would bring on disturbances," returned his phlegmatic host.

"And you speak of it, sir, as a thing not to be deprecated or averted by every possible means in the power of the nation!"

"If the port is opened, and the right to tax given up," said Seth, calmly, "I can find a man in Boston who'll engage to let them draw all the blood that will be spilt, from his own veins, for nothing."

"And who may that redoubtable individual be, Master

Sage?" cried M'Fuse. "Your own plethoric person? How now, Doyle—to what am I indebted for the honor of this visit?"

This sudden question was put by the captain of grenadiers to the orderly of his own company, who at that instant filled the door of the apartment with his huge frame, in the attitude of military respect, as if about to address his officer.

"Orders have come down, sir, to parade the men at half an hour after tattoo, and to be in readiness for active service."

The three gentlemen rose together from their chairs at this intelligence, while M'Fuse exclaimed. "A night-march! Pooh! We are to be sent back to garrison duty, I suppose; the companies in the line grow sleepy, and wish a relief. Gage might have taken a more suitable time, than to put gentlemen on their march so soon after such a feast as this of yours, Polly."

"There is some deeper meaning to so extraordinary an order," interrupted Lionel; "there goes the tap of the tattoo, this instant! Are no other troops but your company ordered to parade?"

"The whole battalion is under the same orders, your honor, and so is the battalion of light infantry; I was commanded to report it so to Captain Polwarth, if I saw him."

"This bears some meaning, gentlemen," said Lionel, "and it is necessary to be looked to. If either corps leaves the town to-night, I will march with it as a volunteer; for it is my business, just now, to examine into the state of the country."

"That we shall march to-night, is sure, your honor," added the sergeant, with the confidence of an old soldier; "but how far, or on what road, is known only to the officers of the staff; though the men think we are to go out by the colleges."

"And what has put so learned an opinion in their silly heads?"demanded his captain.

"One of the men who has been on leave, has just got in, and reports that a squad of gentlemen from the army dined near them, your honor, and that as night set in they mounted, and began to patrol the roads in that direction. He was met and questioned by four of them as he crossed the flats."

"All this confirms my conjectures," cried Lionel ; "there is a man who might now prove of important service—Job —where is the simpleton, Meriton ?"

"He was called out, sir, a minute since, and has left the house."

"Then send in Mr. Sage," continued the young man, musing as he spoke. A moment after it was reported to him that Seth had strangely disappeared also.

"Curiosity has led him to the barracks," said Lionel, "where duty calls you, gentlemen. I will despatch a little business, and join you there in an hour ; you cannot march short of that time."

The bustle of a general departure succeeded. Lionel threw his cloak into the arms of Meriton, to whom he delivered his orders, took his arms, and making his apologies to his guests, he left the house with the manner of one who saw a pressing necessity to be prompt. M'Fuse proceeded to equip himself with the deliberation of a soldier who was too much practised to be easily disconcerted. Notwithstanding his great deliberation, the delay of Polwarth, however, eventually vanquished the patience of the grenadier, who exclaimed, on hearing the other repeat, for the fourth time, an order concerning the preservation of certain viands, to which he appeared to cling in spirit, after a carnal separation was directed by fortune.

"Poh ! poh ! man," exclaimed the Irishman ; "why will you bother yourself on the eve of a march with such epicurean propensities ! It 's the soldier who should show your hermits and anchorites an example of mortification : besides, Polly, this affectation of care and provision is the less excusable in yourself—you, who have been well aware that we were to march on a secret expedition this very night on which you seem so much troubled."

"I !" exclaimed Polwarth ; "as I hope to eat another meal, I am as ignorant as the meanest corporal in the army of the whole transaction. Why do you suspect otherwise?"

"Trifles tell the old campaigner when and where the blow is to be struck," returned M'Fuse, coolly drawing his military overcoat tighter to his large frame; " have I not, with my own eyes, seen you, within the hour, provision a certain captain of light infantry after a very heavy fashion? Damn it, man! do you think I have served these five-and-twenty years, and do not know that when a garrison begins to fill its granaries, it expects a siege?"

"I have paid no more than a suitable compliment to the entertainment of Major Lincoln," returned Polwarth; "but so far from having had any very extraordinary appetite, I have not found myself in a condition to do all the justice I could wish to several of the dishes. Mr. Meriton, I will thank you to have the remainder of that bird sent down to the barracks, where my man will receive it; and, as it may be a long march and a hungry one, add the tongue, and a fowl, and some of the ragout; we can warm it up at any farm-house. We'll take the piece of beef, Mac; Leo has a particular taste for a cold cut; and you might put up the ham, also; it will keep better than anything else, if we should be out long—and—and—I believe that will do, Meriton."

"I am as much rejoiced to hear it as I should be to hear a proclamation of war read at Charing Cross," cried M'Fuse; "you should have been a commissary, Polly; nature meant you for an army sutler!"

"Laugh as you will, Mac," returned the good-humored Polwarth; "I shall hear your thanks when we halt for breakfast; but I attend you now."

As they left the house, he continued, "I hope Gage means no more than to push us a little in advance with a view to protect the foragers and the supplies of the army. Such a situation would have very pretty advantages; for a system might be established that would give the mess of the light corps the choice of the whole market."

"'T is a mighty preparation about some old iron gun, which would cost a man his life to put a match to," returned

M'Fuse, cavalierly ; "for my part, Captain Polwarth, if we are to fight these colonists at all, I would do the thing like a man, and allow the lads to gather together a suitable arsenal, that when we come to blows, it may be a military affair. As it now stands, I should be ashamed, as I am a soldier and an Irishman, to bid my fellows pull a trigger or make a charge on a set of peasants, whose fire-arms look more like rusty water-pipes than muskets, and who have half a dozen cannon with touch-holes that a man may put his head in, with muzzles just large enough to throw marbles."

"I don't know, Mac," said Polwarth, while they diligently pursued their way towards the quarters of their men ; "even a marble may destroy a man's appetite for his dinner ; and the countrymen possess a great advantage over us in commanding the supplies ; the difference in equipments would not more than balance the odds."

"I wish to disturb no gentleman's opinion on matters of military discretion, Captain Polwarth," said the grenadier, with an air of high martial pride ; "but I take it there exists a material difference between a soldier and a butcher, though killing be a business common to both. I repeat, sir, I hope that this secret expedition is for a more worthy object than to deprive those poor devils, with whom we are about to fight, of the means of making a good battle ; and I add, sir, that such is sound military doctrine, without regarding who may choose to controvert it."

"Your sentiments are generous and manly, Mac ; but, after all, there is both a physical and moral obligation on every man to eat ; and if starvation be the consequence of permitting your enemies to bear arms, it becomes a solemn duty to deprive them of their weapons. No, no ; I will support Gage in such a measure, at present, as highly military."

"And he is much obliged to you, sir, for your support," returned the other. "I apprehend, Captain Polwarth, whenever the Lieutenant-general Gage finds it necessary to lean on anyone for extraordinary assistance, he will remember that there is a regiment called the Royal Irish in the

country, and that he is not entirely ignorant of the qualities
of the people of his own nation. You have done well, Captain Polwarth, to choose the light-infantry service ; they are
a set of foragers, and can help themselves ; but the grenadiers, thank God, love to encounter men, and not cattle, in
the field.''

How long the good-nature of Polwarth would have endured the increasing taunts of the Irishman, who was exasperating himself gradually by his own arguments, there is no
possibility of determining ; for their arrival at the barracks
put an end to the controversy and to the feelings it was
beginning to engender.

CHAPTER VIII.

"Preserve thy sighs, unthrifty girl!
To purify the air;
Thy tears to thread, instead of pearl,
On bracelets of thy hair."

DAVENANT.

LIONEL might have blushed to acknowledge the secret and inexplicable influence which his unknown and mysterious friend Ralph had obtained over his feelings, but which induced him, on leaving his own quarters thus hastily, to take his way into the lower parts of the town, in quest of the residence of Abigail Pray. He had not visited the sombre tenement of this woman since the night of his arrival, but its proximity to the well-known town-hall, as well as the quaint architecture of the building itself, had frequently brought its exterior under his observation in the course of his rambles through the place of his nativity. A guide being consequently unnecessary, he took the most direct and frequented route to the Dock Square. When Lionel issued into the street, he found a deep darkness already enveloping the peninsula of Boston, as if nature had lent herself to the secret designs of the British commandant. The fine strain of a shrill fife was playing among the naked hills of the place, accompanied by the occasional and measured taps of the sullen drum; and, at moments, the full, rich notes of the horns would rise from the common, and, borne on the night air, sweep along the narrow streets, causing the nerves of the excited young soldier to thrill with a stern pleasure, as he stepped proudly along. The practised ear, however, detected no other sounds in the music than the usual nightly signal of rest ; and when the last melting strains of the horns seemed to be lost in the clouds, a stillness fell upon the town like the deep and slumbering quiet of midnight. He paused a moment before the gates of Province House, and after examining, with an attentive eye, the windows of the building, he spoke to the grenadier, who had stopped in his short walk to note the curious stranger.

"You should have company within, sentinel," he said, "by the brilliant light from those windows."

The rattling of Lionel's side-arms, as he pointed with his hand in the direction of the illuminated apartment, taught the soldier that he was addressed by his superior, and he answered respectfully,—

"It does not become one such as I, to pretend to know much of what his betters do, your honor ; but I stood before the quarters of General Wolfe the very night we went up to the Plains of Abram ; and I think an old soldier can tell when a movement is at hand without asking his superiors any impertinent questions."

"I suppose, from your remark, the general holds a council to-night ?" said Lionel.

"No one has gone in, sir, since I have been posted," returned the sentinel, "but the lieutenant-colonel of the 10th, that great Northumbrian lord, and the old major of marines. A great war-dog is that old man, your honor, and it is not often he comes to Province House for nothing."

"A good night to you, my old comrade," said Lionel, walking away ; "'t is probably some consultation concerning the new exercises that you practise."

The grenadier shook his head, as if unconcerned, and resumed his march with his customary steadiness. A very few minutes now brought Lionel before the low door of Abigail Pray, where he again stopped, struck with the contrast between the gloomy, dark, and unguarded threshold over which he was about to pass, and the gay portal he had just left. Urged, however, by his feelings, the young man paused but a moment before he tapped lightly for admission. After repeating his summons, and hearing no reply, he lifted the latch and entered the building without further ceremony. The large and vacant apartment in which he found himself was silent and dreary as the still streets he had quitted. Groping his way towards the little room in the tower, where he met the mother of Job, as before related, Lionel found that apartment also tenantless and dark. He was turning in disappointment to quit the place, when a feeble ray fell from the loft of the building, and settled on the foot of a rude ladder which formed the means of communication with its upper apartments. Hesitating a single moment how to decide, he then yielded to his anxiety, and ascended to the floor above, with steps as light as extreme caution could render them. Like the basement, the building was subdivided here into a large open wareroom, and a small rudely finished apartment in each of its towers. Following the rays from a candle, he stood on the threshold of one of these little rooms, in which he found the individual of whom he was in quest. The old man was seated on the only broken chair which the loft contained, and before him, on the simple bundle of straw which would seem, by the garments thrown loosely over the pile, to be intended as his place of rest, lay a large map, spread for inspection, which his glazed and sunken eyes appeared to be intently engaged in marking. Lionel hesitated again, while he regarded the white hairs which fell across the temples of the stranger, as he bowed his head in his employment, imparting a wild and melancholy expression to his remarkable countenance, and seeming to hallow their possessor by the air of great age and attendant care that they imparted.

"I have come to seek you," the young man at length said, "since you no longer deem me worthy of your care."

"You come too late," returned Ralph, without betraying the least emotion at the suddenness of the interruption, or even raising his eyes from the map he studied so intently ; "too late at least to avert calamity, if not to learn wisdom from its lessons."

"You know, then, of the secret movements of the night !"

"Old age, like mine, seldom sleeps," returned Ralph, looking for the first time at his visitor; "for the eternal night of death promises a speedy repose. I, too, served an apprenticeship in my youth to your trade of blood."

"Your watchfulness and experience have then detected the signs of preparation in the garrison? Have they also discovered the objects and probable consequences of the enterprise?"

"Both. Gage weakly thinks to crush the germ of liberty which has already quickened in the land, by lopping its feeble branches, when it is rooted in the hearts of the people. He thinks that bold thoughts can be humbled by the destruction of magazines."

"It is then only a measure of precaution that he is about to take?"

The old man shook his head mournfully as he answered,—

"It will prove a measure of blood."

"I intend to accompany the detachment into the country," said Lionel; "it will probably take post at some little distance in the interior, and it will afford me a fitting opportunity to make those inquiries which you know are so near my heart, and in which you have promised to assist; it is to consult on the means, that I have now sought you."

The countenance of the stranger seemed to lose its character of melancholy reflection, as Lionel spoke, and his eyes moved, vacant and unmeaning, over the naked rafters above him, passing in their wanderings across the surface of the unheeded map again, until they fell upon the face of the astonished youth, where they remained settled for more than a minute, fixed in the glazed, riveted look of death. The lips of Lionel had already opened in anxious inquiry, when the expression of life shot again into the features of Ralph, with the suddenness, and with an appearance of the physical reality with which light flashes from the sun when emerging from a cloud.

"You are ill!" Lionel exclaimed.

"Leave me," said the old man, "leave me."

"Surely not at such a moment, and alone."

"I bid you leave me; we shall meet as you desire, in the country."

"You would then have me accompany the troops, and expect your coming?"

"Both."

"Pardon me," said Lionel, dropping his eyes in embarrassment, and speaking with hesitation ; "but your present abode, and the appearance of your attire, is an evidence that old age has come upon you when you are not altogether prepared to meet its sufferings."

"You would offer me money?"

"By accepting it, I shall become the obliged party."

"When my wants exceed my means, young man, your offer shall be remembered. Go, now ; there is no time for delay."

"But I would not leave you alone ; the woman, the termagant, is better than none."

"She is absent."

"And the boy—the changeling has the feelings of humanity, and would aid you in extremity."

"He is better employed than in propping the steps of a useless old man. Go then, I entreat—I command, sir, that you leave me."

The firm if not haughty manner in which the other repeated his desire, taught Lionel that he had nothing more to expect at present, and he obeyed reluctantly, by slowly leaving the apartment ; and as soon as he had descended the ladder, he began to retrace his steps towards his own quarters. In crossing the light drawbridge thrown over the narrow dock already mentioned, his contemplations were first disturbed by the sounds of voices at no great distance, apparently conversing in tones that were not intended to be heard by every ear. It was a moment when each unusual incident was likely to induce inquiry, and Lionel stopped to examine two men, who, at a little distance, held their secret and suppressed communications. He had, however, paused but an instant, when the whisperers separated : one walking leisurely up the centre of the square, entering under one of the arches of the market-place, and the other coming directly across the bridge on which he himself was standing.

7

"What, Job, do I find you here, whispering and plotting in the Dock Square!" exclaimed Lionel; "what secrets can you have, that require the cover of night?"

"Job lives there, in the old ware'us'," said the lad sullenly; "Nab has plenty of house-room, now the king won't let the people bring in their goods."

"But whither are you going? into the water? surely the road to your bed cannot be through the town dock."

"Nab wants fish to eat, as well as a ruff to keep off the rain," said Job, dropping lightly from the bridge into a small canoe, which was fastened to one of its posts, "and now the king has closed the harbor, the fish have to come up in the dark; for come they will; Boston fish ain't to be shut out by acts of Parliament!"

"Poor lad!" exclaimed Lionel, "return to your home and your bed; here is money to buy food for your mother, if she suffers; you will draw a shot from some of the sentinels by going about the harbor thus at night."

"Job can see a ship farther than a ship can see Job," returned the other; "and if they should kill Job, they need n't think to shoot a Boston boy without some stir."

Further dialogue was precluded; the canoe gliding along the outer dock into the harbor, with a stillness and swiftness that showed the idiot was not ignorant of the business which he had undertaken. Lionel resumed his walk, and was passing the head of the square, when he encountered, face to face, under the light of a lamp, the man whose figure he had seen but a minute before to issue from beneath the town-hall. A mutual desire to ascertain the identity of each other drew them together.

"We meet again, Major Lincoln!" said the interesting stranger Lionel remembered to have seen at the political meeting. "Our interviews appear to be ordained in secret places."

"And Job Pray would seem to be the presiding spirit," returned the young soldier. "You parted from him but now?"

"I trust, sir," said the stranger, gravely, "that this is not a land, nor have we fallen on times, when and where an honest man dare not say that he has spoken to whom he pleases.''

"Certainly, sir, it is not for me to prohibit the inter-course,'' returned Lionel. "You spoke of our fathers; mine is well known to you, it would seem, though to me you are a stranger.''

"And may be so yet a little longer," said the other, "though I think the time is at hand when men will be known in their true characters; until then, Major Lincoln, I bid you adieu.''

Without waiting for any reply, the stranger took a different direction from that which Lionel was pursuing, and walked away with the swiftness of one who was pressed with urgent business. Lionel soon ascended into the upper part of the town, with the intention of going into Tremont Street, to communicate his design to accompany the expedition. It was now apparent to the young man that a rumor of a contemplated movement of the troops was spreading secretly, but swiftly, among the people. He passed several groups of earnest and excited townsmen, conferring together at the corners of the streets, from some of whom he overheard the startling intelligence that the neck, the only approach to the place by land, was closed by a line of sentinels; and that guard-boats from the vessels of war were encircling the peninsula in a manner to intercept the communication with the adjacent country. Still no indications of a military alarm could be discovered, though, at times a stifled hum, like the notes of busy preparation, was borne along by the damp breezes of the night, and mingled with those sounds of a spring evening which increased as he approached the skirts of the dwellings. In Tremont Street, Lionel found no appearance of that excitement, which was spreading so rapidly in the old and lower parts of the town. He passed into his own room without meeting any of the family, and having completed his brief arrangements, he was descending to inquire for his kinswomen, when the voice of Mrs. Lechmere, proceeding from a small apartment appropriated to her own use, arrested his steps. Anxious to take leave

in person, he approached the half open door, and would
have asked permission to enter had not his eye rested on
the person of Abigail Pray, who was in earnest conference
with the mistress of the mansion.

"A man aged, and poor, say you?" observed Mrs. Lechmere, at that instant.

"And one that seems to know all," interrupted Abigail,
glancing her eyes about with an expression of superstitious
terror.

"All!" echoed Mrs. Lechmere, her lip trembling more
with apprehension than age; "and he arrived with Major
Lincoln, say you?"

"In the same ship; and it seems that Heaven has ordained
that he shall dwell with me in my poverty, as a punishment
for my great sin!"

"But why do you tolerate his presence, if it be irksome?"
said Mrs. Lechmere; "you are at least the mistress of your
own dwelling."

"It has pleased God that my home shall be the home of
any who are so miserable as to need one. He has the same
right to live in the warehouse that I have."

"You have the rights of a woman, and of first possession,"
said Mrs. Lechmere, with that unyielding severity of manner
that Lionel had often observed before; "I would turn him
into the street, like a dog."

"Into the street!" repeated Abigail, again looking about
her in secret terror; "speak lower, Madam Lechmere, for
the love of Heaven. I dare not even look at him: he reminds
me of all I have ever known, and of all the evil I have ever
done, by his scorching eye—and yet I cannot tell why; and
then Job worships him as a god, and if I should offend him,
he could easily worm from the child all that you and I wish
so much—"

"How!" exclaimed Mrs. Lechmere, in a voice husky
with horror, "have you been so base as to make a confidant
of that fool?"

"That fool is the child of my bosom," said Abigail, raising
her hands, as if imploring pardon for the indiscretion. "Ah!
Madam Lechmere, you, who are rich, and great, and happy,

and have such a sweet and sensible grandchild, cannot
know how to love one like Job ; but when the heart is loaded
and heavy, it throws its burden on any that will bear it ;
and Job is my child, though he is but little better than an
idiot ! ''

It was by no trifling exertion of his breeding that Lionel
was enabled to profit by the inability of Mrs. Lechmere to
reply, and to turn away from the spot, and cease to listen
to a conversation that was not intended for his ear. He
reached the parlor, and threw himself on one of its settees,
before he was conscious that he was no longer alone or
unobserved.

"What ! Major Lincoln returned from his revels thus early,
and armed like a bandit, to his teeth ! '' exclaimed the playful voice of Cecil Dynevor, who, unheeded, was in possession
of the opposite seat, when he entered the room.

Lionel started, and rubbed his forehead, like a man awak-
ing from a dream, as he answered,—

"Yes, a bandit, or any other opprobrious name you please ;
I deserve them all.''

"Surely,'' said Cecil, turning pale, "none other dare use
such language of Major Lincoln, and he does it unjustly ! ''

"What foolish nonsense have I uttered, Miss Dynevor?''
cried Lionel, recovering his recollection. "I was lost in
thought, and heard your language without comprehending
its meaning.''

"Still, you are armed ; a sword is not a usual instrument
at your side, and now you bear even pistols ! ''

"Yes,'' returned the young soldier, laying aside his dangerous implements ; "yes, I am about to march as a volunteer, with a party that go into the country to-night, and I
take these because I would affect something very warlike,
though you well know how peaceably I am disposed.''

"March into the country—and in the dead of night ! ''
said Cecil, catching her breath, and turning pale. "And
does Lionel Lincoln volunteer on such a duty ? ''

"I volunteer to perform no other duty than to be a witness
of whatever may occur ; you are not more ignorant yourself
of the nature of the expedition than I am at this moment.''

"Then remain where you are," said Cecil, firmly, "and enlist not in an enterprise that may be unholy in its purposes and disgraceful in its results."

"Of the former I am innocent, whatever they may be, nor will they be affected by my presence or absence. There is little danger of disgrace in accompanying the grenadiers and light infantry of this army, Miss Dynevor, though it should be against treble their numbers of chosen troops."

"Then it would seem," said Agnes Danforth, speaking as she entered the room, "that our friend Mercury, that feather of a man, Captain Polwarth, is to be one of these night depredators! Heaven shield the hen-roosts!"

"You have, then, heard the intelligence, Agnes?"

"I have heard that men are arming, and that boats are rowing round the town in all directions, and that it is forbidden to enter or quit Boston, as we were wont to do, Cecil, at such hours and in such fashion as suited us plain Americans," said Agnes, endeavoring to conceal her deep vexation in affected irony. "God only can tell in what all these oppressive measures will end."

"If you go only as a curious spectator of the depredations of the troops," continued Cecil, "are you not wrong to lend them even the sanction of your name?"

"I have yet to learn that there will be depredations."

"You forget, Cecil," interrupted Agnes Danforth, scornfully, "that Major Lincoln did not arrive until after the renowned march from Roxbury to Dorchester! Then the troops gathered their laurels under the face of the sun; but it is easy to conceive how much more glorious their achievements will become when darkness shall conceal their blushes!"

The blood rushed across the fine features of Lionel, but he laughed as he arose to depart, saying,—

"You compel me to beat the retreat, my spirited coz. If I have my usual fortune in this forage, your larder, however, shall be the better for it. I kiss my hand to you, for it would be necessary to lay aside the scarlet, to dare to approach with a more peaceable offering. But here I may make an approach to something like amity."

He took the hand of Cecil, who frankly met his offer, and insensibly suffered herself to be led to the door of the building while he continued speaking.

"I would, Lincoln, that you were not to go," she said, when they stopped on the threshold ; "it is not required of you as a soldier ; and as a man, your own feelings should teach you to be tender of your countrymen."

"It is as a man that I go, Cecil," he answered. "I have motives that you cannot suspect."

"And is your absence to be long?"

"If not for days, my object will be unaccomplished ; but," he added, pressing her hand gently, "you cannot doubt my willingness to return when occasion may offer."

"Go, then," said Cecil, hastily, and perhaps unconsciously extricating herself, "go, if you have secret reasons for your conduct ; but remember that the acts of every officer of your rank are keenly noted."

"Do you then distrust me, Cecil?"

"No—no—I distrust no one, Major Lincoln ; go—go—and—and—we shall see you, Lionel, the instant you return."

He had not time to reply, for she glided into the building so rapidly as to give the young man an opportunity only to observe, that, instead of rejoining her cousin, her light form passed up the great stairs with the swiftness and grace of a fairy.

CHAPTER IX.

"Hang out our banners on the outward walls :
The cry is still, *They come.*"

Macbeth.

LIONEL had walked from the dwelling of Mrs. Lechmere to the foot of Beacon Hill, and had even toiled up some part of the steep ascent, before he recollected why he was thus wandering by himself at that unusual hour. Hearing, however, no sounds that denoted an immediate movement of the troops, he then yielded, unconsciously, to the nature of his sensations, which just at that moment rendered his feelings jealous of communication with others, and continued to ascend until he gained the summit of the eminence. From this elevated stand he paused to contemplate the scene which lay in the obscurity of night at his feet, while his thoughts returned from the flattering anticipations in which he had been indulging, to consider the more pressing business of the hour. There arose from the town itself a distant buzzing, like the hum of suppressed agitation, and lights were seen to glide along the streets, or flit across the windows, in a manner which denoted that a knowledge of the expedition had become general within its dwellings. Lionel turned his head towards the common, and listened long and anxiously, but in vain, to detect a single sound that could betray any unusual stir among the soldiery. Towards the interior, the darkness of night had fallen heavily, dimming the amphitheatre of hills that encircled the place, and enshrouding the vales and lowlands between them and the water with an impenetrable veil of gloom. There were moments, indeed, when he imagined he overheard some indications among the people of the opposite shore, that they were apprised of the impending descent; but on listening more attentively, the utmost of which his ear could assure him was the faint lowing of cattle from the meadows, or the plash of oars from a line of boats, which, by stretching far along the shores, told both the nature and the extent of the watchfulness that was deemed necessary for the occasion.

While Lionel stood thus, on the margin of the little platform of earth that had been formed by levelling the apex of the natural cone, musing on the probable results of the measure his superiors had been resolving to undertake, a dim light shed itself along the grass, and glancing upward, danced upon the beacon with strong and playful rays.

"Scoundrel!" exclaimed a man, springing from his place of concealment, at the foot of the post, and encountering him face to face, "do you dare to fire the beacon?"

"I would answer by asking how you dare to apply so rude an epithet to me, did I not see the cause of your error," said Lionel. "The light is from yonder moon, which is just emerging from the ocean."

"Ah! I see my error," returned his rough assailant. "By heavens, I would have sworn, at first, 'twas the beacon!"

"You must, then, believe in the traditional witchcraft of this country; for nothing short of necromancy could have enabled me to light those combustibles at this distance."

"I don't know; 'tis a strange people we have got among —they stole the cannon from the gun-house, here, a short time since, when I would have said the thing was impossible. It was before your arrival, sir; for I now believe I address myself to Major Lincoln, of the 47th."

"You are nearer the truth this time than in your first conjecture as to my character," said Lionel; "but have I met one of the gentlemen of our mess?"

The stranger now explained that he was a subaltern in a different regiment, but that he well knew the person of the other. He added that he had been ordered to watch on the hill to prevent any of the inhabitants lighting the beacon,

or making any other signal which might convey into the
country a knowledge of the contemplated inroad.

"This matter wears a more serious aspect than I had
supposed," returned Lionel, when the young man had
ended his apologies and explanation; "the commander-
in-chief must intend more than we are aware of, by employ
ing officers in this manner to do the duties of privates."

"We poor subs know but little, and care less what he
means," cried the ensign; "though I will acknowledge that
I can see no sufficient reason why British troops should put
on coats of darkness to march against a parcel of guessing,
canting countrymen, who would run at the sight of their
uniforms under a bright sun. Had I my will, the tar above
us, there, should blaze a mile high, to bring down the heroes
from Connecticut River. The dogs would cow before two
full companies of grenadiers. Ha! listen, sir; there they
go, now; the pride of our army! I know them by their
heavy tread."

Lionel did listen attentively, and plainly distinguished
the measured step of a body of disciplined men, moving
rapidly across the common, as if marching towards the
water-side. Hastily bidding his companion good-night,
he threw himself over the brow of the hill, and taking the
direction of the sounds, he arrived at the shore at the same
instant with the troops. Two dark masses of human bodies
were halted in order, and as Lionel skirted the columns, his
experienced eye judged that the force collected before him
could be but little short of a thousand men. A group of
officers was clustered on the beach, and he approached it,
rightly supposing that it was gathered about the leader of
the party. This officer proved to be the lieutenant-colonel
of the 10th, who was in close conversation with the old
major of marines alluded to by the sentinel who stood before
the gates of Province House. To the former of these the
young soldier addressed himself, demanding leave to accompany the detachment as a volunteer. After a few words of
explanation his request was granted, though each forbore to
touch in the slightest manner on the secret objects of the
expedition.

Lionel now found his groom, who had followed the troops with his master's horses, and, after giving his orders to the man, he proceeded in quest of his friend Polwarth, whom he soon discovered, posted in all the stiffness of military exactness, at the head of the leading platoon of the column of light infantry. As it was apparent, both from the position they occupied, as well as by the boats that had been collected at the point, that the detachment was not to leave the peninsula by its ordinary channel of communication with the country, there remained no alternative but to await patiently the order to embark. The delay was but short, and, as the most perfect order was observed, the troops were soon seated, and the boats pulled heavily from the land just as the rays of the moon, which had been some time playing among the hills and gilding the spires of the town, diffused themselves softly over the bay, and lighted the busy scene, with an effect not unlike the sudden rising of the curtain at the opening of some interesting drama. Polwarth had established himself by the side of Lionel, much to the ease of his limbs, and as they moved slowly into the light, all those misgivings which had so naturally accompanied his musings on the difficulties of a partisan irruption, vanished before the loveliness of the time, and possibly before the quietude of the action.

"There are moments when I could fancy the life of a sailor," he said, leaning indolently back, and playing with one hand in the water. "This pulling about in boats is easy work, and must be capital assistance for a heavy digestion, inasmuch as it furnishes air with as little violent exercise as may be. Your marine should lead a merry life of it!"

"They are said to murmur at the clashing of their duties with those of the sea-officers," said Lionel; "and I have often heard them complain of a want of room to make use of their legs."

"Humph!" ejaculated Polwarth; "the leg is a part of a man for which I see less actual necessity than for any other portion of his frame. I often think there has been a sad mistake in the formation of the animal : as, for instance, one can be a very good waterman, as you see, without legs—a good fiddler, a firstrate tailor, a lawyer, a doctor, a parson, a very tolerable cook, and, in short, anything but a dancing-master. I see no use in a leg, unless it be to have the gout; at any rate, a leg of twelve inches is as good as one a mile long, and the saving might be appropriated to the nobler parts of the animal, such as the brain and the stomach."

"You forget the officer of light infantry," said Lionel, laughing.

"You might give him a couple of inches more; though as everything in this wicked world is excellent only by comparison, it would amount to the same thing, and on my system a man would be just as fit for the light infantry without as with legs; and he would get rid of a good deal of troublesome manœuvring, especially of this new exercise. It would then become a delightful service, Leo; for it may be said to monopolize all the poetry of military life, as you may see. Neither the imagination nor the body can require more than we enjoy at this moment, and of what use, I would ask, are our legs?—if anything, they are incumbrances in this boat. Here we have a soft moon, and softer seats—smooth water and a stimulating air; on one side a fine country, which, though but faintly seen, is known to be fertile and rich to abundance; and on the other a pictur-esque town, stored with the condiments of every climate : even those rascally privates look mellowed by the moon-beams, with their scarlet coats and glittering arms ! Did you meet Miss Danforth in your visit to Tremont Street, Major Lincoln ? "

"That pleasure was not denied me."

"Knew she of these martial proceedings ? "

"There was something exceedingly belligerent in her humor."

"Spoke she of the light infantry, or of any who serve in the light corps ? "

"Your name was certainly mentioned," returned Lionel, a little dryly ; "she intimated that the hen-roosts were in danger."

"Ah ! she is a girl of a million ! her very acids are

sweet ! the spices were not forgotten when the dough of
her composition was mixed ; would that she were here !
five minutes of moonshine to a man in love is worth a whole
summer of a broiling sun ; 't would be a master-stroke to
entice her into one of our picturesque marches ; your partisan is the man to take everything by surprise—women and
fortifications ! Where now are your companies of the line ;
your artillery and dragoons ; your engineers and staff ? night-
capped and snoring to a man, while we enjoy here the very
dessert of existence ; I wish I could hear a nightingale.''

"You have a solitary whippoorwill whistling his notes, as
if in lamentation at our approach.''

"Too dolorous, and by far too monotonous ; 't is like eating pig for a month. But why are our fifes asleep ?''

"The precautions of a whole day should hardly be defeated by the tell-tale notes of our music," said Lionel ;
"your spirits get the better of your discretion. I should
think the prospect of a fatiguing march would have lowered
your vein.''

"A fico for fatigue !'' exclaimed Polwarth ; "we only go
out to take a position at the colleges to cover our supplies
—we are for school, Leo : only fancy the knapsacks of the
men to be satchels,—humor my folly,—and you may believe yourself once more a boy.''

The spirits of Polwarth had indeed undergone a sudden
change, when he found the sad anticipations which crossed
his mind on first hearing of a night inroad, so agreeably disappointed by the comfortable situation he occupied ; and he
continued conversing in the manner described, until the
boats reached an unfrequented point that projected a little
way into that part of the bay which washed the western
side of the peninsula of Boston. Here the troops landed,
and were again formed with all possible despatch. The
company of Polwarth was posted, as before, at the head of
the column of light infantry ; and an officer of the staff riding a short distance in front, it was directed to follow his
movements. Lionel ordered his groom to take the route of
the troops with the horses, and placing himself once more by
the side of the captain, they proceeded at the appointed signal.

"Now for the shades of old Harvard!" said Polwarth, pointing towards the humble buildings of the university, "you shall feast this night on reason, while I will make a more sub—Ha! what can that blind quartermaster mean by taking this direction? Does he not see that the meadows are half covered with water?"

"Move on, move on with the light infantry," cried the stern voice of the old major of marines, who rode but a short distance in their rear. "Do you falter at the sight of water?"

"We are not wharf-rats," said Polwarth.

Lionel seized him by the arm, and before the disconcerted captain had time to recollect himself, he was borne through a wide pool of stagnant water, mid-leg deep.

"Do not let your romance cost your commission," said the major, as Polwarth floundered out of his difficulties; "here is an incident at once for your private narrative of the campaign."

"Ah! Leo," said the captain, with a sort of comical sorrow, "I fear we are not to court the muses by this hallowed moon to-night."

"You can assure yourself of that, by observing that we leave the academical roofs on our left—our leaders take the highway."

They had by this time extricated themselves from the meadows, and were moving on a road which led into the interior.

"You had better order up your groom, and mount, Major Lincoln," said Polwarth, sullenly: "a man need husband his strength, I see."

"'T would be folly now; I am wet, and must walk for safety."

With the departure of Polwarth's spirits the conversation began to flag, and the gentlemen continued their march with only such occasional communications as arose from the passing incidents of their situation. It very soon became apparent, both by the direction given to the columns, as well as by the hurried steps of their guide, that the march was to be forced, as well as of some length. But as the

air was getting cool, even Polwarth was not reluctant to
warm his chilled blood by more than ordinary exertion.
The columns opened for the sake of ease, and each man
was permitted to consult his own convenience, provided he
preserved his appointed situation, and kept even pace with
his comrades. In this manner the detachment advanced
swiftly, a general silence pervading the whole, as the spirits
of the men settled into that deep sobriety which denotes
much earnestness of purpose. At first, the whole country
appeared buried in a general sleep ; but as they proceeded,
the barking of the dogs, and the tread of the soldiery, drew
the inhabitants of the farm-houses to their windows, who
gazed in mute wonder at the passing spectacle, across which
the mellow light of the moon cast a glow of brilliancy.
Lionel had turned his head from studying the surprise depicted in the faces of the members of one of these disturbed
families, when the tones of a distant church-bell came
sweeping down the valley in which they marched, ringing
peal on peal, in the quick, spirit-stirring sounds of an alarm.
The men raised their heads in wondering attention, as they
advanced ; but it was not long before the reports of fire-
arms were heard echoing among the hills, and bell began to
answer bell in every direction, until the sounds blended
with the murmurs of the night air, or were lost in distance.
The whole country was now filled with every organ of
sound that the means of the people furnished, or their ingenuity could devise, to call the population to arms. Fires
blazed along the heights, the bellowing of the conchs and
horns mingled with the rattling of the muskets and the
varied tones of the bells, while the swift clattering of horses'
hoofs began to be heard, as if their riders were dashing
furiously along the flanks of the party.

"Push on, gentlemen, push on!" shouted the old veteran of marines, amid the din. "The Yankees have awoke,
and are stirring,—we have yet a long road to journey.
Push on, light infantry, the grenadiers are on your heels!"

The advance quickened their steps, and the whole body
pushed for their unknown object with as much rapidity as
the steadiness of military array would admit. In this man-

ner the detachment continued to proceed for some hours, without halting, and Lionel imagined that they had advanced several leagues into the country. The sounds of the alarm had now passed away, having swept far inland, until the faintest evidence of its existence was lost to the ear, though the noise of horsemen, riding furiously along the by-ways, yet denoted that men were still hurrying past them, to the scene of the expected strife. As the deceitful light of the moon was blending with the truer colors of the day, the welcome sound of "Halt!" was passed from the rear up to the head of the column of light infantry.

"Halt!" repeated Polwarth, with instinctive readiness, and with a voice that sent the order through the whole length of their extended line; "halt, and let the rear close; if my judgment in walking be worth so much as an anchovy, they are some miles behind us, by this time. A man needs to have crossed his race with the blood of Flying Childers for this sort of work! The next command should be to break our fasts. Tom, you brought the trifles I sent you from Major Lincoln's quarters?"

"Yes, sir," returned his man; "they are on the major's horses, in the rear, as—"

"The major's horses in the rear, you ass, when food is in such request in the front! I wonder, Leo, if a mouthful couldn't be picked up in yon farm-house?"

"Pick yourself off that stone, and make the men dress; here is Pitcairn closing to the front with the whole battalion."

Lionel had hardly spoken before an order was passed to the light infantry to look to their arms, and for the grenadiers to prime and load. The presence of the veteran who rode in front of the column, and the hurry of the moment, suppressed the complaints of Polwarth, who was in truth an excellent officer, as it respected what he himself termed the "quiescent details of service." Three or four companies of the light corps were detached from the main body, and formed in the open marching order of their exercise, when the old marine, placing himself at their head, gave forth the order to advance again at a quick step. The road now led into a vale, and at some distance a small hamlet of houses

was dimly seen through the morning haze, clustered around
one of the humble, but decent temples, so common in Massachusetts. The halt, and the brief preparations that succeeded, had excited a powerful interest in the whole of the
detachment, who pushed earnestly forward, keeping on the
heels of the charger of their veteran leader, as he passed
over the ground at a small trot. The air partook of the
scent of morning, and the eye was enabled to dwell distinctly on surrounding objects, quickening, aided by the
excitement of the action, the blood of the men who had
been toiling throughout the night in uncertain obscurity
along an unknown, and, apparently, interminable road.
Their object now seemed before them and attainable, and
they pressed forward to achieve it in animated but silent
earnestness. The plain architecture of the church and of
its humble companions had just become distinct, when three
or four armed horsemen were seen attempting to anticipate
their arrival, by crossing the head of the column from a
by-path.

"Come in," cried an officer of the staff in front, "come
in, or quit the place!"

The men turned, and rode briskly off, one of their party
flashing his piece in a vain attempt to give the alarm. A
low mandate was now passed through the ranks to push on,
and in a few moments they entered on a full view of the
hamlet, the church, and the little green on which it stood.
The forms of men were seen moving swiftly across the latter, as a roll of a drum broke from the spot; and there
were glimpses of a small body of countrymen, drawn up in
the affectation of military parade.

"Push on, light infantry!" cried their leader, spurring
his horse, and advancing with the staff at so brisk a trot as
to disappear round an angle of the church.

Lionel pressed forward with a beating heart, for a crowd
of horrors rushed across his imagination at the moment,
when the stern voice of the major of marines was again
heard, shouting,—

"Disperse, ye rebels, disperse! Throw down your arms,
and disperse!"

8

These memorable words were instantly followed by the reports of pistols, and the fatal mandate of "Fire!" when a loud shout arose from the whole body of the soldiery, who rushed upon the open green, and threw in a close discharge on all before them.

"Great God!" exclaimed Lionel, "what is it ye do? Ye fire at unoffending men! Is there no law but force? Beat up their pieces, Polwarth; stop their fire."

"Halt!" cried Polwarth, brandishing his sword fiercely among his men. "Come to an order, or I'll fell ye to the earth!"

But the excitement which had been gathering to a head for so many hours, and the animosity which had so long been growing between the troops and the people, were not to be repressed at a word. It was only when Pitcairn himself rode in among the soldiers, and, aided by his officers, beat down their arms, that the uproar was gradually quelled, and something like order was again restored. Before this was effected, however, a few scattering shot were thrown back from their flying adversaries, though without material injury to the British.

When the firing had ceased, officers and men stood gazing at each other for a few moments, as if even they could foresee some of the mighty events which were to follow the deeds of that hour. The smoke slowly arose, like a lifted veil, from the green, and, mingling with the fogs of morning, drove heavily across the country, as if to communicate the fatal intelligence that the final appeal to arms had been made. Every eye was bent inquiringly on the fatal green, and Lionel beheld, with a feeling allied to anguish, a few men at a distance, writhing and struggling in their wounds, while some five or six bodies lay stretched upon the grass in the appalling quiet of death. Sickening at the sight, he turned, and walked away by himself, while the remainder of the troops, alarmed by the reports of the arms, were eagerly pressing up from the rear to join their comrades. Unwittingly he approached the church, nor did he awake from the deep abstraction into which he had fallen, until he was aroused by the extraordinary spectacle of Job Pray, issuing from the edifice with an air in which menace was singularly blended with resentment and fear. The changeling pointed earnestly to the body of a man, who, having been wounded, had crept for refuge near to the door of the temple, in which he had so often worshipped that Being to whom he had been thus hurriedly sent to render his last and great account, and said solemnly,—

"You have killed one of God's creatures; and he'll remember it!"

"I would it were one only," said Lionel; "but they are many, and none can tell where the carnage is to cease."

"Do you think," said Job, looking furtively around to assure himself that no other overheard him, "that the king can kill men in the Bay Colony as he can in London? They'll take this up in old Funnel, and 't will ring again, from the North End to the Neck."

"What can they do, boy, after all?" said Lionel, forgetting at the moment that he whom he addressed had been denied the reason of his kind; "the power of Britain is too mighty for these scattered and unprepared colonies to cope with, and prudence would tell the people to desist from resistance while yet they may."

"Does the king believe there is more prudence in London than there is in Boston?" returned the simpleton; "he need n't think, because the people were quiet at the massacre, there'll be no stir about this. You have killed one of God's creatures," added the lad, "and he'll remember it!"

"How came you here, sirrah?" demanded Lionel, suddenly recollecting himself; "did you not tell me that you were going out to fish for your mother?"

"And if I did," returned the other sullenly, "ain't there fish in the ponds as well as in the bay, and can't Nab have a fresh taste? Job don't know there is any act of Parliament ag'in taking brook trout."

"Fellow, you are attempting to deceive me! Some one is practising on your ignorance, and knowing you to be a fool, is employing you on errands that may one day cost your life."

"The king can't send Job on arr'nds," said the lad, proudly; "for there is no law for it, and Job won't go."

"Your knowledge will undo you, simpleton. Who should teach you these niceties of the law?"

"Why, do you think the Boston people so dumb as not to know the law?" asked Job, with unfeigned astonishment, "and Ralph, too—he knows as much law as the king; he told me it was ag'in all law to shoot at the minute-men, unless they fired first, because the colony has a right to train whenever it pleases."

"Ralph!" said Lionel, eagerly; "can Ralph be with you, then? 't is impossible; I left him ill, and at home—neither would he mingle in such a business as this, at his years."

"I expect Ralph has seen bigger armies than the light infantry, and grannies, and all the soldiers left in town put together," said Job, evasively.

Lionel was far too generous to practise on the simplicity of his companion, with a view to extract any secret which might endanger his liberty, but he felt a deep concern in the welfare of a young man who had been thrown in his way in the manner already related. He therefore pursued the subject, with the double design to advise Job against any dangerous connections, and to relieve his own anxiety on the subject of the aged stranger. But to all his interrogatories the lad answered guardedly, and with a discretion which denoted that he possessed no small share of cunning, though a higher order of intellect had been denied him.

"I repeat to you," said Lionel, losing his patience, "that it is important for me to meet the man whom you call Ralph in the country, and I wish to know if he is to be seen near here."

"Ralph scorns a lie," returned Job; "go where he promised to meet you, and see if he don't come."

"But no place was named; and this unhappy event may embarrass him, or frighten him—"

"Frighten him!" repeated Job, shaking his head with solemn earnestness; "you can't frighten Ralph!"

" His daring may prove his misfortune. Boy, I ask you for the last time whether the old man—"

Perceiving Job to shrink back timidly, and lower in his looks, Lionel paused, and casting a glance behind him, beheld the captain of grenadiers standing with folded arms, silently contemplating the body of the American.

" Will you have the goodness to explain to me, Major Lincoln," said the captain, when he perceived himself observed, " why this man lies here dead?"

" You see the wound in his breast?"

" It is a palpable and baistly truth, that he has been shot—but why, or with what design?"

" I must leave that question to be answered by our superiors, Captain M'Fuse," returned Lionel. " It is, however, rumored that the expedition is out to seize certain magazines of provisions and arms which the colonists have been collecting, it is feared, with hostile intentions."

" I had my own sagacious thoughts that we were bent on some such glorious errand," said M'Fuse, with strong contempt expressed in his hard features. " Tell me, Major Lincoln—you are certainly but a young soldier, though being of the staff, you should know—does Gage think we can have a war with the arms and ammunition all on one side? We have had a long p'ace, Major Lincoln, and now, when there is a small prospect of some of the peculiarities of our profession arising, we are commanded to do the very thing which is most likely to def'ate the object of war."

" I do not know that I rightly understand you, sir," said Lionel ; " there can be but little glory gained by such troops as we possess, in a contest with the unarmed and undisciplined inhabitants of any country."

" Exactly my maining, sir ; it is quite obvious that we understand each other thoroughly, wlthout a word of circumlocution. The lads are doing very well at present, and if left to themselves a few months longer, it may become a creditable affair. You know as well as I do, Major Lincoln, that time is necessary to make a soldier, and if they are hurried into the business, you might as well be chasing a mob up Ludgate Hill, for the honor you will gain. A discrate officer would nurse this little matter, instead of resorting to such precipitation. To my id'aas, sir, the man before us has been butchered, and not slain in honorable battle ! "

"There is much reason to fear that others may use the same term in speaking of the affair," returned Lionel ; "God knows how much cause we may have to lament the death of the poor man."

"On that topic, the man may be said to have gone through a business that was to be done, and is not to be done over again," said the captain, very coolly, " and therefore his death can be no very great calamity to himself, whatever it may be to us. If these minute-men—and, as they stand but a minute, they 'arn their name like worthy fellows—if these minute-men, sir, stood in your way, you should have whipped them from the green with your ramrods."

"Here is one who may tell you that they are not to be treated like children either," said Lionel, turning to the place which had been so recently occupied by Job Pray, but which, to his surprise, he now found vacant. While he was yet looking around him, wondering whither the lad could so suddenly have withdrawn, the drums beat the signal to form, and a general bustle among the soldiery showed them to be on the eve of further movements. The two gentlemen instantly rejoined their companions, walking thoughtfully towards the troops, though influenced by such totally different views of the recent transactions.

During the short halt of the advance, the whole detachment was again united, and a hasty meal had been taken. The astonishment which succeeded the rencontre had given place, among the officers, to a military pride, capable of sustaining them in much more arduous circumstances. Even the ardent looks of professional excitement were to be seen in most of their countenances, as with glittering arms, waving banners, and timing their march to the enlivening music of their band, they wheeled from the fatal spot, and advanced again, with proud and measured steps, along the highway. If such was the result of the first encounter on the lofty and tempered spirits of the gentlemen of the detachment, its effect on the common hirelings in the ranks was still more palpable and revolting. Their coarse jests, and taunting looks, as they moved by the despised victims of their disciplined skill, together with the fierce and boastful expression of brutal triumph, which so many among them betrayed, exhibited the infallible evidence, that, having tasted of blood, they were now ready, like tigers, to feed on it till they glutted.

CHAPTER X.

"There was mounting 'mong Græmes of the Netherby clan;
Fosters, Fenwicks, and Musgraves, they rode and they ran;
There was racing, and chasing, on Cannobie Lea."

Marmion.

THE pomp of military parade, with which the troops marched from the village of Lexington, as the little hamlet was called, where the foregoing events occurred, soon settled again into the sober and business-like air of men earnestly bent on the achievement of their object. It was no longer a secret that they were to proceed two leagues farther into the interior, to destroy the stores already mentioned, and which were now known to be collected at Concord, the town where the Congress of Provincial Delegates, who were substituted by the colonists for the ancient legislatures of the province, held their meetings. As the march could not now be concealed, it became necessary to resort to expedition, in order to insure its successful termination. The veteran officer of marines, so often mentioned, resumed his post in front, and at the head of the same companies of the light corps, which he had before led, pushed in advance of the heavier column of the grenadiers. Polwarth, by this arrangement, perceived himself again included among those on whose swiftness of foot so much depended. When Lionel rejoined his friend, he found him at the head of his men, marching with so grave an air, as at once induced the major to give him credit for regrets much more commendable than such as were connected with his physical distress. The files were once more opened for room, as well as for air, which was becoming necessary, as a hot sun began to dissipate the mists of the morning, and shed that enervating influence on the men so peculiar to the first warmth of an American spring.

"This has been a hasty business altogether, Major Lincoln," said Polwarth, as Lincoln took his wonted station at the side of the other, and dropped mechanically into the regular step of the party; "I know not that it is quite as lawful to knock a man in the head as a bullock."

"You then agree with me in thinking our attack hasty, if not cruel?"

"Hasty! most unequivocally. Haste may be called the distinctive property of the expedition; and whatever destroys the appetite of an honest man, may be set down as cruel. I have not been able to swallow a mouthful of breakfast, Leo. A man must have the cravings of a hyena, and the stomach of an ostrich, to eat and digest with such work as this of ours before his eyes."

"And yet the men regard their acts with triumph!"

"The dogs are drilled into it. But you saw how sober the provincials looked in the matter: we must endeavor to soothe their feelings in the best manner we can."

"Will they not despise our consolation and apologies, and look rather to themselves for redress and vengeance?"

Polwarth smiled contemptuously, and there was an air of pride about him that gave an appearance of elasticity even to his heavy tread, as he answered,—

"The thing is a bad thing, Major Lincoln, and, if you will, a wicked thing; but take the assurance of a man who knows the country well, there will be no attempts at vengeance; and as for redress, in a military way, the thing is impossible."

"You speak with a confidence, sir, that should find its warranty in an intimate acquaintance with the weakness of the people."

"I have dwelt two years, Major Lincoln, in the very heart of the country," said Polwarth, without turning his eyes from the steady gaze he maintained on the long road which lay before him, "even three hundred miles beyond the uninhabited districts; and I should know the character of the nation, as well as its resources. In respect to the latter, there is no esculent thing within its borders, from a humming-bird to a buffalo, or from an artichoke to a watermelon, that I have not, on some occasion or other, had tossed up, in a certain way—therefore, I can speak with confidence, and do not hesitate to say, that the colonists will never fight; nor, if they had the disposition, do they possess the means to maintain a war."

"Perhaps, sir," returned Lionel, sharply, "you have consulted the animals of the country too closely to be acquainted with its spirits?"

"The relation between them is intimate; tell me what food a man diets on, and I will furnish you with his character. 'T is morally impossible that a people who eat their pudding before the meats, after the fashion of these colonists, can ever make good soldiers, because the appetite is appeased before the introduction of the succulent nutriment of the flesh, into—"

"Enough! spare me the remainder," interrupted Lionel; "too much has been said already to prove the inferiority of the American to the European animal, and your reasoning is conclusive."

"Parliament must do something for the families of the sufferers."

"Parliament!" echoed Lionel, with bitter emphasis; "yes, we shall be called on to pass resolutions to commend the decision of the general, and the courage of the troops; and then, after we have added every possible insult to the injury, under the conviction of our imaginary supremacy, we may hear of some paltry sum to the widows and orphans cited as an evidence of the unbounded generosity of the nation!"

"The feeding of six or seven broods of young Yankees is no such trifle, Major Lincoln," returned Polwarth; "and there I trust the unhappy affair will end. We are now marching on Concord, a place with a most auspicious name, where we shall find repose under its shadows, as well as the food of his home-made parliament, which they have gotten together. These considerations alone support me under the fatigue of this direful trot with which old Pitcairn goes over

the ground—does the man think he is hunting with a pack
of beagles at his heels?''

The opinion expressed by his companion, concerning the
martial propensities of the Americans, was one too common
among the troops to excite any surprise in Lionel ; but disgusted with the illiberality of the sentiment, and secretly
offended at the supercilious manner with which the other
expressed these injurious opinions of his countrymen, he
continued his route in silence, while Polwarth speedily lost
his loquacious propensity in a sense of the fatigue that as-
sailed every muscle and joint in his body.

That severe training of the corps, concerning which the
captain vented such frequent complaints, now stood the advance in good service.   It was apparent that the whole
country was in a state of high alarm, and small bodies of
armed men were occasionally seen on the heights that flanked
their route, though no attempts were made to revenge the
deaths of those who fell at Lexington.   The march of the
troops was accelerated rather with a belief that the colonists
might remove, or otherwise secrete the stores, than from any
apprehension that they would dare to oppose the progress of
the chosen troops of the army.   The slight resistance of the
Americans in the rencontre of that morning, was already a
jest among the soldiers, who sneeringly remarked, that the
term of '' minute-men '' was deservedly applied to warriors
who had proved themselves so dexterous at flight.   In short,
every opprobrious and disrespectful epithet that contempt
and ignorance could invent, was freely lavished on the for-
bearing mildness of the suffering colonists.   In this temper
the troops reached a point whence the modest spire and roofs
of Concord became visible.   A small body of colonists retired through the place as the English advanced, and the
detachment entered the town without the least resistance,
and with the appearance of conquerors.   Lionel was not long
in discovering, from such of the inhabitants as remained,
that, notwithstanding their approach had been known for
some time, the events of that morning were yet a secret from
the people of the village.   Detachments from the light corps
were immediately sent in various directions ; some to search

for the ammunition and provisions, and some to guard the approaches to the place. One, in particular, followed the retreating footsteps of the Americans, and took post at a bridge, at some little distance, which cut off the communication with the country to the northward.

In the meantime the work of destruction was commenced in the town, chiefly under the superintendence of the veteran officer of the marines. The few male inhabitants who remained in their dwellings were of necessity peaceable, though Lionel could read, in their flushed cheeks and gleaming eyes, the secret indignation of men who, accustomed to the protection of the law, now found themselves subjected to the insults and wanton abuses of a military inroad. Every door was flung open, and no place was held sacred from the rude scrutiny of the licentious soldiery. Taunts and execrations soon mingled with the seeming moderation with which the search had commenced, and loud exultation was betrayed, even among the officers, as the scanty provisions of the colonists were gradually brought to light. It was not a moment to respect private rights, and the freedom and ribaldry of the men were on the point of becoming something more serious, when the report of fire-arms was heard suddenly to issue from the post held by the light infantry, at the bridge. A few scattering shot were succeeded by a volley, which was answered by another with the quickness of lightning, and then the air became filled with the incessant rattling of a sharp conflict. Every arm was suspended, and each tongue became mute with astonishment, and the men abandoned their occupations, as these unexpected sounds of war broke on their ears. The chiefs of the party were seen in consultation, and horsemen rode furiously into the place, to communicate the nature of this new conflict. The rank of Major Lincoln soon obtained for him a knowledge that it was thought impolitic to communicate to the whole detachment. Notwithstanding it was apparent that they who brought the intelligence were anxious to give it the most favorable aspect, he soon discovered that the same body of Americans, which had retired at their approach, having attempted to return to their homes in the

town, had been fired on at the bridge, and in the skirmish
which succeeded, the troops had been compelled to give way
with loss. The effect of this prompt and spirited conduct
on the part of the provincials produced a sudden alteration,
not only in the aspect, but also in the proceedings of the
troops. The detachments were recalled, and the drums
beat to arms ; and, for the first time, both officers and men
seemed to recollect that they had six leagues to march
through a country that hardly contained a friend. Still, few
or no enemies were visible, with the exception of those men
of Concord, who had already drawn blood freely from the
invaders of their domestic sanctuaries. The dead, and all
the common wounded, were left where they had fallen ; and
it was thought an unfavorable omen among the observant
of the detachment, that a wounded young subaltern, of rank
and fortune, was also abandoned to the mercy of the exasperated Americans. The privates caught the infection from
their officers, and Lionel saw, that in place of the high and
insulting confidence with which the troops had wheeled into
the streets of Concord, that they left them, when the order
was given to march, with faces bent anxiously on the surrounding heights, and with looks that bespoke a consciousness of the dangers that were likely to beset the long road
which lay before them.

Their apprehensions were not groundless. The troops
had hardly commenced their march before a volley was
fired upon them from the protection of a barn, and as they
advanced, volley succeeded volley, and musket answered
musket from behind every cover that offered to their assailants. At first these desultory and feeble attacks were but
little regarded ; a brisk charge, and a smart fire of a few
moments never failed to disperse their enemies, when the
troops again proceeded for a short distance unmolested.
But the alarm of the preceding night had gathered the
people over an immense extent of country ; and, having
waited for information, those nearest to the scene of action
were already pressing forward to the assistance of their
friends. There was but little order, and no concert among
the Americans ; but each party, as it arrived, pushed into

the fray, hanging on the skirts of their enemies, or making spirited, though ineffectual efforts to stop their progress. While the men from the towns behind them pressed upon their rear, the population in their front accumulated in bodies, like a rolling ball of snow, and before half the distance between Concord and Lexington was accomplished, Lionel perceived that the safety of their boasted power was in extreme jeopardy. During the first hour of these attacks, while they were yet distant, desultory, and feeble, the young soldier had marched by the side of M'Fuse, who shook his head disdainfully whenever a shot whistled near him, and did not fail to comment freely on the folly of commencing a war thus prematurely, which, if properly nursed, might, to use his own words, " be in time brought to something pretty and interesting."

"You perceive, Major Lincoln," he added, " that these provincials have got the first elements of the art, for the rascals fire with exceeding accuracy, when the distance is considered ; and six months or a year of close drilling would make them good for something in a regular charge. They have got a smart crack to their p'aces, and a pretty whiz to their lead already ; if they could but learn to deliver their fire in platoons, the lads might make some impression on the light infantry even now ; and in a year or two, sir, they would not be unworthy of the favors of the grenadiers."

Lionel listened to this, and much other similar discourse, with a vacant ear ; but as the combat thickened, the blood of the young man began to course more swiftly through his veins ; and at length, excited by the noise and the danger which was pressing more closely around them, he mounted, and, riding to the commander of the detachment, tendered his assistance as a volunteer aid, having lost every other sensation in youthful blood, and the pride of arms. He was immediately charged with orders for the advance, and driving his spurs into his steed, he dashed through the scattered line of fighting and jaded troops, and galloped to its head. Here he found several companies, diligently employed in clearing the way for their comrades, as new foes appeared at every few rods that they advanced. Even as Lionel

approached, a heavy sheet of fire flashed from a close barn-
yard, full in the faces of the leading files, sending the swift
engines of death into the very centre of the party.

"Wheel a company of the light infantry, Captain Polwarth," cried the old major of marines, who battled stoutly
in the van, "and drive the skulking scoundrels from their
ambush."

"O! by the sweets of ease, and the hopes of a halt! but
here is another tribe of these white savages!" responded
the unfortunate captain. "Look out, my brave men!
blaze away over the walls on your left—give no quarter
to the annoying rascals—get the first shot—give them a
foot of your steel."

While venting such terrible denunciations and commands,
which were drawn from the peaceable captain by the force
of circumstances, Lionel beheld his friend disappear amid
the buildings of the farmyard in a cloud of smoke, followed
by his troops. In a few minutes afterwards, as the line
toiled its way up the hill on which this scene occurred, Polwarth reappeared, issuing from the fray with his face
blackened and grimed with powder, while a sheet of flame
arose from the spot, which soon laid the devoted buildings
of the unfortunate husbandman in ruins.

"Ha! Major Lincoln," he cried, as he approached the
other, "do you call these light infantry movements! to me
they are the torments of the damned! Go, you who have
influence, and, what is better, a horse, go to Smith, and tell
him if he will call a halt, I will engage, with my single company, to seat ourselves in any field he may select, and keep
these blood-suckers at bay for an hour, while the detachment can rest and satisfy their hunger—trusting that he
will then allow time for his defenders to perform the same
necessary operations. A night-march—no breakfast—a
burning sun—mile after mile—no halt, and nothing but
fire, fire—'t is opposed to every principle in physics, and
even to the anatomy of man, to think he can endure it!"

Lionel endeavored to encourage his friend to new exertions, and, turning away from their leader, spoke cheeringly,
and with a martial tone, to his troops. The men cheered

as they passed, and dashed forward to new encounters ; the Americans yielding sullenly, but necessarily, to the constant charges of the bayonet, to which the regulars resorted to dislodge them. As the advance moved on again, Lionel turned to contemplate the scene in the rear. They had now been marching and fighting for two hours with little or no cessation ; and it was but too evident that the force of the assailants was increasing, both in numbers and in daring at each step they took. On either side of the highway, along the skirts of every wood or orchard, in the open fields, and from every house, barn, or cover in sight, the flash of fire-arms was to be seen, while the shouts of the English grew, at each instant, feebler and less inspiriting. Heavy clouds of smoke rose above the valley into which he looked, and mingled with the dust of the march, drawing an impenetrable veil before the view; but as the wind, at moments, shoved it aside, he caught glimpses of the worried and faltering platoons of the party, sometimes breasting and repulsing an attack with spirit, and at others shrinking from the contest, with an ill-concealed desire to urge their retreat to the verge of an absolute flight. Young as he was, Major Lincoln knew enough of his profession to understand that nothing but the want of concert, and of a unity of command among the Americans, saved the detachment from total destruction. The attacks were growing extremely spirited, and not unfrequently close and bloody, though the discipline of the troops enabled them still to bear up against this desultory and divided warfare, when Lionel heard, with a pleasure he could not conceal, the loud shouts that arose from the van, as the cheering intelligence was proclaimed through the ranks, that the cloud of dust in their front was raised by a chosen brigade of their comrades which had come most timely to their succor, with the heir of Northumberland at its head. The Americans gave way as the two detachments joined, and the artillery of the succors opened upon their flying parties, giving a few minutes of stolen rest to those who needed it so much. Polwarth threw himself flat on the earth, as Lionel dismounted at his side, and his example was followed by the whole party, who lay panting,

under the heat and fatigue, like worried deer, that had
succeeded in throwing the hounds from their scent.

"As I am a gentleman of simple habits, and a man innocent of all this bloodshed, Major Lincoln," said the captain,
"I pronounce this march to be a most unjust draft on the
resources of human nature. I have journeyed at least five
leagues between this spot and that place of discord that they
falsely call Concord, within two hours, amidst dust, smoke,
groans, and other infernal cries, that would cause the best-
trained racer in England to bolt; and breathing an air, all
the time, that would boil an egg in two minutes and a quarter, if fairly exposed to it."

"You overrate the distance—'t is but two leagues by the
stones—"

"Stones!" interrupted Polwarth. "I scorn their lies:
I have a leg here that is a better index for miles, feet, or
even inches, than was ever chiselled in stone."

"We must not contest this idle point," returned Lionel,
"for I see the troops are about to dine; and we have need
of every moment to reach Boston before the night closes
around us."

"Eat!—Boston!—night!" slowly repeated Polwarth,
raising himself on one arm, and staring wildly about him.
"Surely no man among us is so mad as to talk of moving
from this spot short of a week: it would take half that
time to receive the internal refreshment necessary to our
systems, and the remainder to restore us healthy appetites."

"Such, however, are the orders of the Earl Percy, from
whom I learn that the whole country is rising in our front."

"Ay, but they are fellows who slept peacefully in their
beds the past night; and I dare say that every dog among
them ate his half pound of pork, together with additions
suitable for a breakfast, before he crossed his threshold this
morning. But with us the case is different. It is incumbent on two thousand British troops to move with deliberation, if it should be only for the credit of his majesty's arms.
No, no; the gallant Percy too highly respects his princely
lineage and name, to assume the appearance of flight before
a mob of base-born hinds!"

9

The intelligence of Lionel was nevertheless true; for, after a short halt, allowing barely time enough to the troops to eat a hasty meal, the drums again beat the signal to march, and Polwarth, as well as many hundred others, was reluctantly compelled to resume his feet, under the penalty of being abandoned to the fury of the exasperated Americans. While the troops were in a state of rest, the field-pieces of the reinforcement kept their foes at a distance; but the instant guns were limbered, and the files had once more opened for room, the attacks were renewed from every quarter, with redoubled fury. The excesses of the troops, who had begun to vent their anger by plundering and firing the dwellings that they passed, added to the bitterness of the attacks; and the march had not been renewed many minutes, before a fiercer conflict raged along its skirts than had been before witnessed on that day.

"Would to God that the Northumbrian would form us in order of battle, and make a fair field with the Yankees!" groaned Polwarth, as he toiled his way once more with the advance. "Half an hour would settle the matter, and a man would then possess the gratification of seeing himself a victor, or at least of knowing that he was comfortably and quietly dead."

"Few of us would ever arrive in the morning, if we left the Americans a night to gather in; and a halt of an hour would lose us the advantages of the whole march," returned Lionel. "Cheer up, my old comrade, and you will establish your reputation for activity forever. Here comes a party of the provincials over the crest of the hill to keep you in employment."

Polwarth cast a look of despair at Lionel, as he muttered in reply,—

"Employment! God knows that there has not been a single muscle, sinew, or joint in my body in a state of wholesome rest for four-and-twenty hours!" Then turning to his men, he cried, with tones so cheerful and animated, that they seemed to proceed from a final and closing exertion, as he led them gallantly into the approaching fray—"Scatter the dogs, my brave friends! Away with them like gnats, like mosquitoes, like leeches, as they are! Give it them—lead and steel by handfuls—"

"On—push on with the advance!" shouted the old major of marines, who observed the leading platoons to stagger.

The voice of Polwarth was once more heard in the din, and their irregular assailants sullenly yielded before the charge.

"On—on with the advance!" cried fifty voices out of a cloud of smoke and dust that was moving up the hill, on whose side this encounter occurred.

In this manner the war continued to roll slowly onward, following the weary and heavy footsteps of the soldiery, who had now toiled for many miles, surrounded by the din of battle, and leaving in their path the bloody impressions of their footsteps. Lionel was enabled to trace their route, far towards the north, by the bright red spots which lay scattered in alarming numbers along the highway, and in the fields, through which the troops occasionally moved. He even found time, in the intervals of rest, to note the difference in the characters of the combatants. Whenever the ground or the circumstances admitted of a regular attack, the dying confidence of the troops would seem restored; and they moved up to the charge with the bold carriage which high discipline inspires, rending the air with shouts, while their enemies melted before their power in sullen silence, never ceasing to use their weapons, however, with an expertness that rendered them doubly dangerous. The direction of the columns frequently brought the troops over ground that had been sharply contested in front, and the victims of these short struggles came under the eyes of the detachment. It was necessary to turn a deaf ear to the cries and prayers of many wounded soldiers, who, with horror and abject fear written on every feature of their countenances, were the helpless witnesses of the retreating files of their comrades. On the other hand, the American lay in his blood, regarding the passing detachment with a stern and indignant eye, that appeared to look far beyond his individual suffering. Over one body, Lionel pulled the reins of his horse, and he paused a moment to consider the spectacle. It was the lifeless form of a man, whose white locks, hollow cheeks, and emaciated frame, denoted that the bullet which had stricken him to the earth had anticipated the irresistible decrees of time but a very few days. He had fallen on his back, and his glazed eye expressed, even in death, the honest resentment he had felt while living; and his palsied hand continued to grasp the firelock, old and time-worn, like its owner, with which he had taken the field in behalf of his country.

"Where can a contest end which calls such champions to its aid!" exclaimed Lionel, observing that the shadow of another spectator fell across the wan features of the dead; "who can tell where this torrent of blood can be stayed, or how many are to be its victims!"

Receiving no answer, he raised his eyes, and discovered that he had unwittingly put this searching question to the very man whose rashness had precipitated the war. It was the major of marines, who sat looking at the sight, for a minute, with an eye as vacant as the one that seemed to throw back his wild gaze, and then, rousing from his trance he buried his rowels in the flanks of his horse, and disappeared in the smoke that enveloped a body of the grenadiers, waving his sword on high, and shouting,—

"On—push on with the advance!"

Major Lincoln slowly followed, musing on the scene he had witnessed, when, to his surprise, he encountered Polwarth, seated on a rock by the roadside, looking with a listless and dull eye at the retreating columns. Checking his charger, he inquired of his friend if he was hurt.

"Only melted," returned the captain; "I have outdone the speed of man this day, Major Lincoln, and can do no more. If you see any of my friends in dear England, tell them that I met my fate as a soldier should, stationary; though I am actually melting away in rivulets, like the snows of April."

"Good God! you will not remain here to be slain by the provincials, by whom you see we are completely enveloped?"

"I am preparing a speech for the first Yankee who may approach. If he be a true man, he will melt into tears at my sufferings this day—if a savage, my heirs will be spared the charges of my funeral!"

Lionel would have continued his remonstrances, but a fierce encounter between a flanking party of the troops and a body of Americans, drove the former close upon him; and, leaping the wall, he rallied his comrades, and turned the tide of battle in their favor. He was drawn far from the spot by the vicissitudes of the combat, and there was a moment, while passing from one body of the troops to another, that he found himself unexpectedly alone, in a most dangerous vicinity to a small wood. The hurried call of "Pick off that officer!" first aroused him to his extreme danger, and he had mechanically bowed himself on the neck of his charger, in expectation of the fatal messengers, when a voice was heard among the Americans, crying, in tones that caused every nerve in his body to thrill,—

"Spare him! for the love of that God you worship, spare him!"

The overwhelming sensations of the moment prevented flight, and the young man beheld Ralph, running with frantic gestures, along the skirts of the cover, beating up the fire-arms of twenty Americans, and repeating his cries in a voice that did not seem to belong to a human being; then, in the confusion which whirled through his brain, Lionel thought himself a prisoner, as a man, armed with a long rifle, glided from the wood, and laid his hand on the rein of his bridle, saying earnestly,—

"'T is a bloody day, and God will remember it; but if Major Lincoln will ride straight down the hill, the people won't fire for fear of hitting Job; and when Job fires, he'll shoot that granny who's getting over the wall, and there'll never be a stir about it in Funnel Hall."

Lionel wheeled away quicker than thought, and as his charger took long and desperate leaps down the slight declivity, he heard the shouts of the Americans behind him, the crack of Job's rifle, and the whizzing of the bullet which the changeling sent, as he had promised, in a direction to do him no harm. On gaining a place of comparative safety, he found Pitcairn in the act of abandoning his bleeding horse, the close and bitter attacks of the provincials rendering it no longer safe for an officer to be seen riding on the flanks of the detachment. Lionel, though he valued his steed highly, had also received so many intimations of the dangerous notice he had attracted, that he was soon obliged to follow this example ; and he saw, with deep regret, the noble animal scouring across the fields with a loose rein, snorting and snuffing the tainted air. He now joined a party of the combatants on foot, and continued to animate them to new exertions during the remainder of the tedious way.

From the moment the spires of Boston met the view of the troops, the struggle became intensely interesting. New vigor was imparted to their weary frames by the cheering sight, and, assuming once more the air of high martial training, they bore up against the assaults of their enemies with renewed spirit. On the other hand, the Americans seemed aware that the moments of vengeance were passing swiftly away, and boys, and gray-headed men, the wounded and the active, crowded around their invaders, as if eager to obtain a parting blow. Even the peaceful ministers of God were known to take the field on that memorable occasion, and, mingling with their parishioners, to brave every danger in a cause which they believed in consonance with their holy calling. The sun was sinking over the land, and the situation of the detachment had become nearly desperate, when Percy abandoned the idea of reaching the Neck, across which he had proudly marched that morning from Boston, and strained every nerve to get the remainder of his command within the peninsula of Charlestown. The crests and the sides of the heights were alive with men, and as the shades of evening closed about the combatants, the bosoms of the Americans beat high with hope, while they witnessed the faltering steps and slackened fire of the troops. But high discipline finally so far prevailed as to snatch the English from the very grasp of destruction, and enabled them to gain the narrow entrance to the desired shelter just as night had come apparently to seal their doom.

Lionel stood leaning against a fence, as this fine body of men, which a few hours before had thought themselves equal to a march through the colonies, defiled slowly and heavily by him, dragging their weary and exhausted limbs up the toilsome ascent of Bunker Hill. The haughty eyes of most of the officers were bent to the earth in shame, and the common herd, even in that place of security, cast many an anxious glance behind them, to assure themselves that the despised inhabitants of the province were no longer pressing on their footsteps. Platoon after platoon passed, each man compelled to depend on his own wearied limbs for support, until Lionel at last saw a solitary horseman slowly ascending among the crowd. To his utter amazement and great joy, as this officer approached, he beheld Polwarth, mounted on his own steed, riding towards him, with a face of the utmost complacency and composure. The dress of the captain was torn in many places, and the housings of the saddle were cut into ribbons, while here and there a spot of clotted blood, on the sides of the beast, served to announce the particular notice the rider had received from the Americans. The truth was soon extorted from the honest soldier. The love of life had returned with the sight of the abandoned charger. He acknowledged it had cost him his watch to have the beast caught; but, once established in the saddle, no danger, nor any remonstrances, could induce him to relinquish a seat which he found so consoling after all the fatigue and motion of that evil day, in which he had been compelled to share in the calamities of those who fought on the side of the crown in the memorable battle of Lexington.

CHAPTER XI.

"Fluel.   Is it not lawful, an' please your majesty,
To tell how many is killed?"

King Henry V.

WHILE a strong party of the royal troops took post on the height which commanded the approach to their position, the remainder penetrated deeper into the peninsula, or were transported by the boats of the fleet to the town of Boston. Lionel and Polwarth passed the strait with the first division of the wounded, the former having no duty to detain him any longer with the detachment, and the latter stoutly maintaining that his corporeal sufferings gave him an undoubted claim to include his case among the casualties of the day.   Perhaps no officer in the army of the king felt less chagrin at the result of this inroad than Major Lincoln ; for, notwithstanding his attachment to his prince and adopted country, he was keenly sensitive on the subject of the reputation of his real countrymen, a sentiment that is honorable to our nature, and which never deserts any that do not become disloyal to its purest and noblest impulses.   Even while he regretted the price at which his comrades had been taught to appreciate the characters of those whose long and mild forbearance had been misconstrued into pusillanimity, he rejoiced that the eyes of the more aged would now be opened to the truth, and that the mouths of the young and thoughtless were to be forever closed in shame.   Although the actual losses of the two detachments were probably concealed from motives of policy, it was early acknowledged to amount to about one sixth of the whole number employed.

On the wharf, Lionel and Polwarth separated ; the latter agreeing to repair speedily to the private quarters of his friend, where he promised himself a solace for the compulsory abstinence and privations of his long march, and the former taking his way toward Tremont Street, with a view to allay the uneasiness which the secret and flattering whisperings of hope taught him to believe his fair young kinswomen would feel in his behalf. At every corner he encountered groups of earnest townsmen, listening with greedy ears to the particulars of the contest, a few walking away dejected at the spirit exhibited by that country they had vilified to its oppressors ; but most of them regarding the passing form of one whose disordered dress announced his participation in the affair, with glances of stern satisfaction. As Lionel tapped at the door of Mrs. Lechmere, he forgot his fatigue ; and when it opened, and he beheld Cecil standing in the hall, with every lineament of her fine countenance expressing the power of her emotions, he no longer remembered those trying dangers he had so lately escaped.

"Lionel ! " exclaimed the young lady, clasping her hands with joy,—"himself, and unhurt ! " The blood rushed from her heart across her face to her forehead, and burying her shame in her hands, she burst into a flood of tears, and fled his presence.

Agnes Danforth received him with undisguised pleasure, nor would she indulge in a single question to appease her burning curiosity, until thoroughly assured of his perfect safety. Then, indeed, she remarked, with a smile of triumph seated on her arch features,—

"Your march has been well attended, Major Lincoln ; from the upper windows I have seen some of the honors which the good people of Massachusetts have paid to their visitors."

"On my soul, if it were not for the dreadful consequences which must follow, I rejoice, as well as yourself, in the events of the day," said Lincoln ; "for a people are never certain of their rights until they are respected."

"Tell me, then, all, cousin Lincoln, that I may know how to boast of my parentage."

The young man gave her a short, but distinct and impartial account of all that had occurred, to which his fair listener attended with undisguised interest.

"Now, then," she exclaimed, as he ended, "there is an end forever of those biting taunts that have so long insulted our ears! But you know," she added, with a slight blush, and a smile most comically arch, "I had a double stake in the fortunes of the day,—my country, and my true love!"

"O! be at ease; your worshipper has returned, whole in body, and suffering in mind only through your cruelty; he performed the route with wonderful address, and really showed himself a soldier in danger."

"Nay, Major Lincoln," returned Agnes, still blushing, though she laughed; "you do not mean to insinuate that Peter Polwarth has walked forty miles between the rising and setting of the sun?"

"Between two sunsets he has done the deed, if you except a trifling *promenade à cheval*, on my own steed, whom Jonathan compelled me to abandon, and of whom he took, and maintained the possession, too, in spite of dangers of every kind."

"Really," exclaimed the wilful girl, clasping her hands in affected astonishment, though Lionel thought he could read inward satisfaction at his intelligence, "the prodigies of the man exceed belief! One wants the faith of father Abraham to credit such marvels! Though, after the repulse of two thousand British soldiers by a body of husbandmen, I am prepared for an exceeding use of my credulity."

"The moment is, then, auspicious for my friend," whispered Lionel, rising to follow the flitting form of Cecil Dynevor, which he saw gliding into the opposite room, as Polwarth himself entered the apartment. "Credulity is said to be the great weakness of your sex, and I must leave you a moment exposed to the failing, and that, too, in the dangerous company of the subject of our discourse."

"Now would you give half your hopes of promotion, and all your hopes of a war, Captain Polwarth, to know in what manner your character has been treated in your absence!" cried Agnes, blushing slightly. "I shall not, however, satisfy the cravings of your curiosity, but let it serve as a stimulant to better deeds than have employed you since we met last."

"I trust Lincoln has done justice to my service," returned the good-humored captain, "and that he has not neglected to mention the manner in which I rescued his steed from the rebels?"

"The what, sir?" interrupted Agnes, with a frown. "How did you style the good people of Massachusetts Bay?"

"I should have said the excited dwellers in the land, I believe. Ah! Miss Agnes, I have suffered this day as man never suffered before; and all on your behalf—"

"On my behalf! Your words require explanation, Captain Polwarth."

"'T is impossible," returned the captain; "there are feelings and actions connected with the heart that will admit of no explanation. All I know is, that I have suffered unutterably on your account, to-day; and what is unutterable is in a great degree inexplicable."

"I shall set this down for what I understand occurs regularly in a certain description of *tête-à-têtes*,—the expression of an unutterable thing! Surely, Major Lincoln had some reason to believe he left me at the mercy of my credulity!"

"You slander your own character, fair Agnes," said Polwarth, endeavoring to look piteously; "you are neither merciful nor credulous, or you would long since have believed my tale, and taken pity on my misery."

"Is not sympathy a sort—a kind—in short, is not sympathy a dreadful symptom in a certain disease?" asked Agnes, resting her eyes on the floor, and affecting a girlish embarrassment.

"Who can gainsay it?" cried the captain; "'t is the infallible way for a young lady to discover the bent of her inclinations. Thousands have lived in ignorance of their own affections until their sympathies have been awakened. But what means the question, my fair tormentor? May I dare to flatter myself that you at length feel for my pains?"

"I am sadly afraid 't is but too true, Polwarth," returned Agnes, shaking her head, and continuing to look exceedingly grave.

Polwarth moved, with something like animation again, nigher to the amused girl, and attempted to take her hand, as he said,—

"You restore me to life with your sweet acknowledgments; I have lived for six months like a dog under your frowns, but one kind word acts like a healing balm, and restores me to myself again!"

"Then my sympathy is evaporated!" returned Agnes. "Throughout this long and anxious day have I fancied myself older than my good, staid, great-aunt; and whenever certain thoughts have crossed my mind, I have even imagined a thousand of the ailings of age had encircled me,—rheumatism, gouts, asthmas, and numberless other aches and pains, exceeding unbecoming to a young lady of nineteen. But you have enlightened me, and given vast relief to my apprehensions, by explaining it to be no more than sympathy. You see, Polwarth, what a wife you will obtain, should I ever, in a weak moment, accept you; for I have already sustained one half your burdens!"

"A man is not made to be in constant motion, like the pendulum of that clock, Miss Danforth, and yet feel no fatigue," said Polwarth, more vexed than he would permit himself to betray; "yet I flatter myself there is no officer in the light infantry—you understand me to say the light infantry—who has passed over more ground, within four-and-twenty hours, than the man who hastens, notwithstanding his exploits, to throw himself at your feet, even before he thinks of his ordinary rest."

"Captain Polwarth," said Agnes, rising, "for the compliment, if compliment it be, I thank you; but," she added, losing her affected gravity in a strong natural feeling that shone in her dark eyes, and illuminated the whole of her fine countenance, as she laid her hand impressively on her heart, "the man who will supplant the feelings which nature has impressed here, must not come to my feet, as you call it, from a field of battle, where he has been contending

with my kinsmen, and helping to enslave my country. You
will excuse me, sir, but as Major Lincoln is at home here,
permit me, for a few minutes, to leave you to his hospitality."

She withdrew as Lionel re-entered, passing him on the
threshold.

"I would rather be a leader in a stage-coach, or a running footman, than in love!" cried Polwarth; "'t is a dog's
life, Leo, and this girl treats me like a cart-horse! But what
an eye she has! I could have lighted my cigar by it,—my
heart is a heap of cinders. Why, Leo, what aileth thee?
throughout the whole of this damnable day, I have not before
seen thee bear such a troubled look!"

"Let us withdraw to my private quarters," muttered the
young man, whose aspect and air expressed the marks of
extreme disturbance; "'t is time to repair the disasters of
our march."

"All that has been already looked to," said Polwarth,
rising and limping, with sundry grimaces, in the best manner he was able, in a vain effort to equal the rapid strides
of his companion. "My first business on leaving you was
to borrow a conveyance of a friend, in which I rode to your
place; and my next was to write to little Jimmy Craig, to
offer an exchange of my company for his,—for from this
hour henceforth I denounce all light infantry movements,
and shall take the first opportunity to get back again into
the dragoons; as soon as I have effected which, Major Lincoln, I propose to treat with you for the purchase of that
horse. After that duty was performed,—for, if self-preservation be commendable, it became a duty,—I made out a bill
of fare for Meriton, in order that nothing might be forgotten; after which, like yourself, Lionel, I hastened to the
feet of my mistress. Ah! Major Lincoln, you are a happy
man; for you there is no reception, but smiles,—and charms
so—"

"Talk not to me, sir, of smiles," interrupted Lionel, impatiently, "nor of the charms of women. They are all alike,
capricious and unaccountable."

"Bless me!" exclaimed Polwarth, staring about him in
wonder; "there is then favor for none, in this place, who

battle for the king ! There is a strange connection between Cupid and Mars, love and war ; for here did I, after fighting all day like a Saracen, a Turk, Jenghis Khan, or, in short, anything but a good Christian, come with full intent to make a serious offer of my hand, commission, and of Polwarth Hall, to that treasonable vixen, when she repulses me with a frown and a sarcasm as biting as the salutation of a hungry man. But what an eye the girl has, and what a bloom, when she is a little more seasoned than common ! Then you, too, Lionel, have been treated like a dog ! ''

"Like a fool, as I am," said Lionel, pacing haughtily over the ground at a rate that soon threw his companion too far in the rear to admit of further discourse until they reached the place of their destination. Here, to the no small surprise of both gentlemen, they found a company collected that neither was prepared to meet. At a side-table sat M'Fuse, discussing, with singular relish, some of the cold viands of the previous night's repast, and washing down his morsels with deep potations of the best wine of his host. In one corner of the room Seth Sage was posted, with the appearance of a man in duress, his hands being tied before him, from which depended a long cord, that might, on emergency, be made to serve the purpose of a halter. Opposite to the prisoner, for such in truth he was, stood Job, imitating the example of the captain of grena-diers, who now and then tossed some fragment of his meal into the hat of the simpleton. Meriton and several of the menials of the establishment were in waiting.

"What have we here ! " cried Lionel, regarding the scene with a curious eye. " Of what offence has Mr. Sage been guilty, that he bears those bonds? ''

" Of the small crimes of tr'ason and homicide," returned M'Fuse, " if shooting at a man, with a hearty mind to kill him, can make murder."

"It can't," said Seth, raising his eyes from the floor, where he had hitherto kept them in demure silence ; " a man must kill with wicked intent to commit murder—"

" Hear to the blackguard, detailing the law as if he were my lord chief-justice of the King's Bench ! " interrupted the grenadier; "and what was your own wicked intention, ye skulking vagabond, but to kill me! I'll have you tried and hung for the same act."

"It's ag'in reason to believe that any jury will convict one man for the murder of another that ain't dead," said Seth; "there's no jury to be found in the Bay colony to do it."

"Bay colony, ye murdering thief and rebel!" cried the captain; "I'll have ye transported to England; ye shall be both transported and hung. By the Lord, I'll carry ye back to Ireland with me, and I'll hang ye up in the green island itself, and bury ye, in the heart of winter, in a bog—"

"But what is the offence," demanded Lionel, "that calls forth these severe threats?"

"The scoundrel has been out—"

"Out!"

"Ay, out! Damn it, sir, has not the whole country been like so many bees in search of a hive? Is your memory so short that ye forget, already, Major Lincoln, the tramp the blackguards have given you over hill and dale, through thick and thin?"

"And was Mr. Sage, then, found among our enemies to-day?"

"Did n't I see him pull trigger on my own stature three times within as many minutes?" returned the angry captain; "and did n't he break the handle of my sword? And have not I a bit of lead he calls a buckshot in my shoulder as a present from the thief?"

"It's ag'in all law to call a man a thief," said Job, "unless you can prove it upon him; but it ain't ag'in law to go in and out of Boston as often as you choose."

"Do you hear the rascals! They know every angle of the law as well, or better than I do myself, who am the son of a Cork counsellor. I dare to say, you were among them too, and that ye deserve the gallows as well as your commendable companion there."

"How is this?" said Lionel, turning quickly away from Job, with a view to prevent a reply that might endanger the safety of the changeling. "Did you not only mingle in this rebellion, Mr. Sage, but also attempt the life of a gentleman who may be said, almost, to be an inmate of your own house?"

"I conclude," returned Seth, "it's best not to talk too much, seeing that no one can foretell what may happen."

"Hear to the cunning reprobate! he has not the grace to acknowledge his own sins, like an honest man," interrupted M'Fuse; "but I can save him that small trouble. I got tired, you must know, Major Lincoln, of being shot at like noxious vermin, from morning till night, without making some return to the compliments of those gentlemen who are out on the hills; and I took advantage of a turn, ye see, to double on a party of the uncivilized demons. This lad, here, got three good pulls at me, before we closed and made an end of them with the steel, all but the fellow, who, having a becoming look for a gallows, I brought him in, as you see, for an exchange, intending to hang him the first favorable opportunity."

"If this be true, we must give him into the hands of the proper authorities," said Lionel, smiling at the confused account of the angry captain; "for it remains to be seen yet what course will be adopted with the prisoners in this singular contest."

"I should think nothing of the matter," returned M'Fuse, "if the reprobate had not tr'ated me like a beast of the field, with his buckshot, and taking his aim each time, as though I had been a mad dog. Ye villain, do you call yourself a man, and aim at a fellow-creature as you would at a brute?"

"Why," said Seth, sullenly, "when a man has pretty much made up his mind to fight, I conclude it's best to take aim, in order to save ammunition and time."

"You acknowledge the charge, then?" demanded Lionel.

"As the major is a moderate man, and will hear to reason, I will talk the matter over with him rationally," said Seth, disposing himself to speak more to the purpose. "You see I had a small call to Concord early this morning—"

"Concord!" exclaimed Lionel.

"Yes, Concord," returned Seth, laying great stress on the first syllable, and speaking with an air of extreme innocence: "it lies hereaway, say twenty or one-and-twenty miles—"

"Damn your Concords, and your miles, too!" cried Polwarth. "Is there a man in the army who can forget the deceitful place? Go on with your defence, without talking to us of the distance, who have measured the road by inches."

"The captain is hasty and rash!" said the deliberate prisoner. "But being there, I went out of the town with some company that I happened in with; and after a time, we concluded to return; and so, as we came to a bridge about a mile beyond the place, we received considerable rough treatment from some of the king's troops, who were standing there—"

"What did they?"

"They fired at us, and killed two of our company, besides other threatening doings. There were some among us that took the matter up in considerable earnest, and there was a sharp toss about it for a few minutes; though finally the law prevailed."

"The law!"

"Certain. 'T is ag'in all law, I believe the major will own, to shoot peaceable men on the public highway!"

"Proceed with your tale in your own way."

"That is pretty much the whole of it," said Seth, warily. "The people rather took that, and some other things that happened at Lexington, to heart, and I suppose the major knows the rest."

"But what has all this to do with your attempt to murder me, you hypocrite!" demanded M'Fuse. "Confess the whole, ye thief, that I may hang you with an aisy conscience."

"Enough," said Lionel; "the man has acknowledged sufficient already to justify us in transferring him to the custody of others. Let him be taken to the main guard, and delivered as a prisoner of this day."

"I hope the major will look to the things," said Seth,

10

who instantly prepared to depart, but stopped on the threshold to speak. "I shall hold him accountable for all."

"Your property shall be protected, and I hope your life
may not be in jeopardy," returned Lionel, waving his hand
for those who guarded him to proceed. Seth turned, and
left his own dwelling with the same quiet air which had
distinguished him throughout the day; though there were
occasional flashes from his quick, dark eyes, that looked like
the glimmerings of a fading fire. Notwithstanding the
threatening denunciation he had encountered, he left the
house with a perfect conviction, that if his case were to be
tried by those principles of justice which every man in the
colony so well understood, it would be found that both he and
his fellows had kept thoroughly on the windy side of the law.

During this singular and characteristic discourse, Polwarth, with the solitary exception we have recorded, had
employed his time in forwarding the preparations for the
banquet.

As Seth and his train disappeared, Lionel cast a furtive
look at Job, who was a quiet and apparently an undisturbed
spectator of the scene, and then turned his attention suddenly
to his guests, as if fearful the folly of the changeling might
betray his agency also in the deeds of the day. The simplicity of the lad, however, defeated the kind intentions of
the major, for he immediately observed, without the least
indication of fear,—

"The king can't hang Seth Sage for firing back, when
the rake-helly soldiers began first."

"Perhaps you were out too, Master Solomon," cried
M'Fuse, "amusing yourself at Concord, with a small party
of select friends?"

"Job did n't go any farther than Lexington," returned
the lad; "and he has n't got any friend, except old Nab."

"The devil has possessed the minds of the people!" continued the grenadier. "Lawyers and doctors, praists and
sinners, old and young, big and little, beset us in our march,
and here is a fool to be added to the number! I dare say
that fellow, now, has attempted murder in his day, too."

"Job scorns such wickedness," returned the unmoved

simpleton; "he only shot one granny, and bit an officer in the arm."

"D' ye hear that, Major Lincoln?" cried M'Fuse, jumping from the seat, which, notwithstanding the bitterness of his language, he had hitherto perseveringly maintained; "d' ye hear that shell of a man, that effigy, boasting of having killed a grenadier?"

"Hold!" interrupted Lionel, arresting his excited companion by the arm; "remember we are soldiers, and that the boy is not a responsible being. No tribunal would ever sentence such an unfortunate creature to a gibbet; and in general, he is as harmless as a babe—"

"The devil burn such babes! A pretty fellow is he to kill a man of six feet! and with a ducking gun, I'll engage. I'll not hang the rascal, Major Lincoln, since it is your particular wish—I'll only have him buried alive."

Job continued perfectly unmoved in his chair; and the captain, ashamed of his resentment against such unconscious imbecility, was soon persuaded to abandon his intentions of revenge, though he continued muttering his threats against the provincials, and his denunciations against such "an unmanly spacies of warfare," until the much-needed repast was ended.

Polwarth, having restored the equilibrium of his system by a hearty meal, hobbled to his bed, and M'Fuse, without any ceremony, took possession of another of the apartments in the tenement of Mr. Sage. The servants withdrew to their own entertainment; and Lionel, who had been sitting for the last half hour in melancholy silence, now unexpectedly found himself alone with the changeling. Job had waited for this moment with exceeding patience; but when the door closed on Meriton, who was the last to retire, he made a movement that indicated some communication of more than usual importance, and succeeded in attracting the attention of his companion.

"Foolish boy!" exclaimed Lionel, as he met the unmeaning eye of the other, "did I not warn you that wicked men might endanger your life? How was it that I saw you in arms to-day against the troops?"

"How came the troops in arms ag'in Job?" returned the changeling. "They need n't think to wheel about the Bay province, clashing their godless drums and trumpets, burning housen, and shooting people, and find no stir about it!"

"Do you know that your life has been twice forfeited within twelve hours, by your own confession : once for murder, and again for treason against your king? You have acknowledged killing a man!"

"Yes," said the lad, with undisturbed simplicity, "Job shot the granny; but he did n't let the people kill Major Lincoln."

"True, true," said Lionel, hastily : "I owe my life to you, and that debt shall be cancelled at every hazard. But why have you put yourself into the hands of your enemies so thoughtlessly? What brings you here to-night?"

"Ralph told me to come; and if Ralph told Job to go into the king's parlor, he would go."

"Ralph!" exclaimed Lionel, stopping in his hurried walk across the room; "and where is he?"

"In the old ware'us'; and he has sent me to tell you to come to him; and what Ralph says, must be done."

"He here too! Is the man crazed? Would not his fears teach him—"

"Fears!" interrupted Job, with singular disdain; "you can't frighten Ralph. The grannies could n't frighten him, nor the light infantry could n't hit him, though he eat nothing but their smoke the whole day. Ralph's a proper warrior!"

"And he waits me, you say, in the tenement of your mother?"

"Job don't know what tenement means, but he 's in the old ware'us'."

"Come, then," said Lionel, taking his hat, "let us go to him : I must save him from the effects of his own rashness, though it cost my commission!"

He left the room while speaking, and the simpleton followed close at his heels, well content with having executed his mission without encountering any greater difficulties.

CHAPTER XII.

"This play is the image of a murder done in Vienna!
Gonzago is the duke's name; his wife, Baptista:
You shall see, anon; 't is a knavish piece of work."

Hamlet.

THE agitation and deep excitement produced by the events of the day had not yet subsided in the town, when Lionel found himself again in its narrow streets. Men passed swiftly by him, as if bent on some unusual and earnest business; and more than once the young soldier detected the triumphant smiles of the women, as they looked curiously out on the scene, from their half-open windows, and their eyes detected the professional trappings of his dress. Strong bodies of the troops were marching in different directions, and in a manner which denoted that the guards were strengthening, while the few solitary officers he met watched his approaching figure with cautious jealousy, as if they apprehended a dangerous enemy in every form they encountered.

The gates of Province House were open, and, as usual, guarded by armed men. As Lionel passed leisurely along, he perceived that the grenadier to whom he had spoken on the preceding evening, again held his watch before the portal of the governor.

"Your experience did not deceive you, my old comrade," said Lionel, lingering a moment to address him; "we have had a warm day."

"So it is reported in the barracks, your honor," returned the soldier; "our company was not ordered out, and we are to stand double duty. I hope to God the next time there is anything to do, the grenadiers of the ——th may not be left behind—it would have been for the credit of the army had they been in the field to-day."

"Why do you think so, my veteran? The men who were out are thought to have behaved well; but it was impossible to make head against a multitude in arms."

"It is not my place, your honor, to say, this man did well, and that man behaved amiss," returned the proud old soldier; "but when I hear of two thousand British troops turning their backs, or quickening their march, before all the rabble this country can muster, I want the flank companies of the ——th to be at hand, if it should be only that I may say I have witnessed the disgraceful sight with my own eyes."

"There is no disgrace where there is no misconduct," said Lionel.

"There must have been misconduct somewhere, your honor, or such a thing could not have happened; consider, your honor, the very flower of the army! Something must have been wrong; and although I could see the latter part of the business from the hills, I can hardly believe it to be true." As he concluded, he shook his head, and continued his steady pace along his allotted ground, as if unwilling to pursue the humiliating subject any further. Lionel passed slowly on, musing on that deep-rooted prejudice, which had even taught this humble menial of the crown to regard with contempt a whole nation, because they were believed to be dependants.

The Dock Square was stiller than usual, and the sounds of revelry which it was usual to hear at that hour from the adjacent drinking-houses, were no longer audible. The moon had not yet risen, and Lionel passed under the dark arches of the market with a quick step, as he now remembered that one in whom he felt so deep an interest awaited his appearance. Job, who had followed in silence, glided by him on the drawbridge, and stood holding the door of the old building in his hand, when he reached its threshold. Lionel found the large space in the centre of the warehouse, as usual, dark and empty, though the dim light of a candle

glimmered through the fissures in a partition which separated an apartment in one of the little towers that was occupied by Abigail Pray, from the ruder parts of the edifice.
Low voices were also heard issuing from this room, and
Major Lincoln, supposing he should find the old man and
the mother of Job in conference together, turned to request
the lad would precede him, and announce his name. But
the changeling had also detected the whispering sounds,
and it would seem with a more cunning ear, for he turned
and darted through the door of the building with a velocity
that did not abate until Lionel, who watched his movements
with amazement, saw his shuffling figure disappear among
the shambles of the market-place. Thus deserted by his
guide, Lionel groped his way towards the place where he
believed he should find the door which led into the tower.
The light deceived him; for, as he approached it, his eye
glanced through one of the crevices of the wall, and he
again became an unintentional witness of another of those
interviews, which evinced the singular and mysterious
affinity between the fortunes of the affluent and respected
Mrs. Lechmere and the miserable tenant of the warehouse.
Until that moment, the hurry of events and the crowd of
reflections which had rushed over the mind of the young
man, throughout the busy time of the last twenty-four
hours, had prevented his recalling the hidden meaning of
the singular discourse of which he had already been an
auditor. But now, when he found his aunt led into these
haunts of beggary, by a feeling he was not weak enough
to attribute to her charity, he stood rooted to the spot by a
curiosity which, at the same time that he found it irresistible, he was willing to excuse, under a strong impression
that these private communications were in some way connected with himself.

Mrs. Lechmere had evidently muffled her person in a
manner that was intended to conceal this mysterious visit
from any casual observer of her movements; but the hoops
of her large calash were now so far raised as to admit a
distinct view of her withered features, and of the hard eye
which shot forth its selfish, worldly glances, from amid the

surrounding decay of nature. She was seated, both in indulgence to her infirmities, and from that assumption of superiority she never neglected in the presence of her inferiors, while her companion stood before her, in an attitude that partook more of restraint than of respect.

"Your weakness, foolish woman," said Mrs. Lechmere, in those stern, repulsive tones she so well knew how to use, when she wished to intimidate, "will yet prove your ruin. You owe it to respect for yourself, to your character, and even to your safety, that you should exhibit more firmness, and show yourself above this weak and idle superstition."

"My ruin! and my character!" returned Abigail, looking about her with a haggard eye and a trembling lip; "what is ruin, Madam Lechmere, if this poverty be not called so? or what loss of character can bring upon me more biting scorn than I am now ordained to suffer for my sins?"

"Perhaps," said Mrs. Lechmere, endeavoring to affect a kinder tone, though dislike was still too evident in her manner, "in the hurry of my grand-nephew's reception, I have forgotten my usual liberality."

The woman took the piece of silver which Mrs. Lechmere slowly placed in her hand, and held it in her open palm for several moments, regarding it with a vacant look, which the other mistook for dissatisfaction.

"The troubles, and the decreasing value of property, have sensibly affected my income," continued the richly clad and luxurious Mrs. Lechmere; "but if that should be too little for your immediate wants, I will add to it another crown."

"'T will do—'t will do," said Abigail, clenching her hand over the money, with a grasp that was convulsive; "yes, yes, 't will do. O, Madam Lechmere, humbling and sinful as that wicked passion is, would to God that no motive worse than avarice had proved my ruin!"

Lionel thought his aunt cast an uneasy and embarrassed glance at her companion, which he construed into an expression that betrayed there were secrets even between these strange confidants ; but the momentary surprise exhibited in her features soon gave place to her habitual look of guarded and severe formality ; and she replied, with an air of coldness, as if she would repulse any approach to an acknowledgment of their common transgression,—

"The woman talks like one who is beside herself! Of what crime has she been guilty, but such as those to which our nature is liable ! "

"True, true," said Abigail Pray, with a half-stifled, hysterical laugh, "'t is our guilty, guilty nature, as you say. But I grow nervous, I believe, as I grow old and feeble, Madam Lechmere ; and I often forget myself. The sight of the grave, so very near, is apt to bring thoughts of repentance to such as are more hardened even than I."

"Foolish girl! " said Mrs. Lechmere, endeavoring to screen her pallid features, by drawing down her calash, with a hand that trembled more with terror than with age ; "why should you speak thus freely of death, who are but a child?"

Lionel heard the faltering, husky tones of his aunt, as they appeared to die in her throat, but nothing more was distinctly audible, until, after a long pause, she raised her face, and looked about her again with her severe, unbending eye, and continued,—

"Enough of this folly, Abigail Pray—I have come to learn more of your strange inmate."

"O! 'tis not enough, Madam Lechmere," interrupted the conscience-stricken woman ; "we have so little time left us for penitence and prayer, that there never can be enough, I fear, to answer our mighty transgressions. Let us speak of the grave, Madam Lechmere, while we can yet do it on this side of eternity."

"Ay! speak of the grave, while out of its damp cloisters ; 't is the home of the aged," said a third voice, whose hollow tones might well have issued from some tomb, "and I am here to join in the wholesome theme."

"Who—who—in the name of God, who art thou?" exclaimed Mrs. Lechmere, forgetting her infirmities, and her secret compunctions in new emotions, and rising involuntarily from her seat; "tell me, I conjure thee, who thou art?"

"One, aged like thyself, Priscilla Lechmere, and standing on the threshold of that final home of which you would discourse. Speak on, then, ye widowed women; for if ever ye have done aught that calls for forgiveness, 't is in the grave ye shall find the heavenly gift of mercy offered to your unworthiness."

By changing the position of his body a little, Lionel was now enabled to command a view of the whole apartment. In the doorway stood Ralph, immovable in his attitude, with one hand raised high towards heaven, and the other pointing impressively downward, as if about to lay bare the secrets of that tomb, of which his wasted limbs, and faded lineaments, marked him as a fit tenant, while his searching eyeballs glared about him, from the face of one to the other, with that look of quickness and penetration, that Abigail Pray had so well described as "scorching." Within a few feet of the old man, Mrs. Lechmere remained standing, rigid and motionless as marble, her calash fallen back, and her death-like features exposed, with horror and astonishment rooted in every muscle, as, with open mouth, and eyes riveted on the intruder, she gazed as steadily as if placed in that posture by the chisel of the statuary. Abigail shaded her eyes with her hand, and buried her face in the folds of her garments, while strong convulsive shudderings ran through her frame, and betrayed the extent of the emotions she endeavored to conceal. Amazed at what he had witnessed, and concerned for the apparent insensibility of his aunt, whose great age rendered such scenes dangerous, Lionel was about to rush into the apartment, when Mrs. Lechmere so far recovered her faculties as to speak, and the young man lost every consideration in a burning curiosity, which was powerfully justified by his situation.

"Who is it that calls me by the name of Priscilla?" said Mrs. Lechmere; "none now live who can claim to be so familiar."

"Priscilla—Priscilla," repeated the old man, looking about him, as if he would require the presence of another; "it is a soft and pleasant sound to my ears, and there is one that owns it besides thee, as thou knowest."

"She is dead; years have gone by since I saw her in her coffin; and I would forget her, and all like her, who have proved unworthy of my blood."

"She is *not* dead!" shouted the old man, in a voice that rung through the naked rafters of the edifice like the unearthly tones of some spirit of the air; "she lives—she lives! ay, she yet lives!"

"Lives!" repeated Mrs. Lechmere, recoiling a step before the forward movement of the other; "why am I so weak as to listen! 'tis impossible."

"Lives!" exclaimed Abigail Pray, clasping her hands with agony. "O! would to God she did live! but did I not see her a bloated, disfigured corpse? did I not with these very hands place the grave-clothes about her once lovely frame? O! no—she is dead—dead—and I am a—"

"'Tis some madman that asserts these idle tales," exclaimed Mrs. Lechmere, with a quickness that interrupted the criminal epithet the other was about to apply to herself. "The unfortunate girl is long since dead, as we know; why should we reason with a maniac?"

"Maniac!" repeated Ralph, with an expression of the most taunting irony; "no—no—no—such an one there is, as you and I well know, but 'tis not I who am mad— thou art rather crazed thyself, woman; thou hast made one maniac already, wouldst thou make another?"

"I!" said Mrs. Lechmere, without quailing before the ardent look she encountered; "that God who bestows reason, recalls his gift at will; 'tis not I who exercise such power."

"How sayest thou, Priscilla Lechmere?" cried Ralph, stepping with an inaudible tread so nigh as to grasp, unperceived, her motionless arm with his own wasted fingers; "yes—I will call thee Priscilla, little as thou deservest such a holy name; dost thou deny the power to craze? where, then, is the head of thy boasted race? the proud baronet of Devonshire, the wealthy, and respected, and once happy companion of princes—thy nephew, Lionel Lincoln? Is he

in the halls of his fathers?—leading the armies of his king?
—ruling and protecting his household? or is he the tenant of
a gloomy cell? thou knowest he is—thou knowest he is—
and, woman, thy vile machinations have placed him there!"

"Who is it that dare thus speak to me?" demanded
Mrs. Lechmere, rallying her faculties with a mighty effort,
to look down this charge; "if my unhappy nephew is
indeed known to thee, thy own knowledge will refute this
base accusation—"

"Known to me! I would ask what is hid from me? I
have looked at thee, and observed thy conduct, woman, for
the life of man; and nothing that thou hast done is hid
from me. I tell thee, I know all. Of this sinful woman
here, also, I know all. Have I not told thee, Abigail Pray,
of thy most secret transgressions?"

"O! yes—yes; he is indeed acquainted with what I
had thought was now concealed from every eye but that of
God!" cried Abigail, with superstitious terror.

"Nor of thee am I ignorant, thou miserable widow of
John Lechmere; and of Priscilla, too, do I not know all?"

"All!" again exclaimed Abigail.

"All!" repeated Mrs. Lechmere, in a voice barely
audible; when she sunk back in her chair, in a state of
total insensibility. The breathless interest he felt in all
that had passed, could detain Lionel no longer from rushing to the assistance of his aunt. Abigail Pray, who, it
would seem, had been in some measure accustomed to such
scenes with her lodger, retained, however, sufficient self-
command to anticipate his motions; and, when he had
gained the door, he found her already supporting, and
making the usual applications to Mrs. Lechmere. It became necessary to divest the sufferer of part of her attire,
and Abigail, assuring Lionel of her perfect competency to
act by herself, requested him to withdraw, not only on that
account, but because she felt assured that nothing could
prove more dangerous to her reviving patient, than his
unexpected presence. After lingering a moment, until he
witnessed the signs of returning life, Lionel complied with
the earnest entreaties of the woman; and, leaving the

room, he groped his way to the foot of the ladder, with a determination to ascend to the apartment of Ralph, in order to demand at once explanation of what he had just seen and heard. He found the old man seated in his little tower, his hand shading his eyes from the feeble light of the miserable candle, and his head drooping upon his bosom, like one in pensive musing. Lionel approached him, without appearing to attract his attention, and was compelled to speak, in order to announce his presence.

"I have received your summons, by Job," he said, "and have obeyed it."

"'T is well," returned Ralph.

"Perhaps I should add, that I have been an astonished witness of your interview with Mrs. Lechmere, and have heard the bold and unaccountable language you have seen proper to use to that lady."

The old man now raised his head, and Lionel saw the bright rays from his eyes quicken, as he answered,—

"You then heard the truth, and witnessed its effects on a guilty conscience."

"I also heard what you call the truth, in connection, as you know, with the names most dear to me."

"Art certain of it, boy?" returned Ralph, looking the other steadily in the face; "has no other become dearer to you, of late, than the authors of your being? Speak, and remember that you answer one of no common knowledge."

"What mean you, sir? is it nature to love any as we do a parent?"

"Away with this childish simplicity," continued the other sternly; "the grandchild of that wretched woman below—do you not love her, and can I put trust in thee?"

"What trust is there incompatible with affection for a being so pure as Cecil Dynevor?"

"Ay," murmured the old man in an undertone, "her mother was pure, and why may not the child be worthy of its parentage?" He paused, and a long, and, on the part of Lionel, a painful and embarrassing silence succeeded, which was at length broken by Ralph, who said, abruptly,—
"You were in the field to-day, Major Lincoln."

" Of that you must be certain, as I owe my life to your kind interposition. But why have you braved the danger of an arrest, by trusting your person in the power of the troops? Your presence and activity among the Americans must be known to many in the army besides myself."

"And would they think of searching for their enemies within the streets of Boston, when the hills without are filling with armed men? My residence in this building is known only to the woman below, who dare not betray me, her worthy son, and to you. My movements are secret and sudden, when men least expect them. Danger cannot touch such as I."

" But," said Lionel, hesitating with embarrassment, " ought I to conceal the presence of one whom I know to be inimical to my king?"

" Lionel Lincoln, you overrate your courage," interrupted Ralph, smiling in scorn. " You dare not shed the blood of him who has spared your own. But enough of this: we understand each other, and one old as I should be a stranger to fear."

" No, no," said a low solemn voice, from a dark corner of the apartment, where Job had stolen unseen, and was now nestled in security: " you can't frighten Ralph."

" The boy is a worthy boy, and he knows good from evil; what more is necessary to man in this wicked world?" muttered Ralph, in those quick and indistinct tones that characterized his manner.

"Whence came you, fellow, and why did you abandon me so abruptly?" demanded Lionel.

"Job has just been into market, to see if he could n't find something that might be good for Nab," returned the lad.

"Think not to impose on me with this nonsense! Is food to be purchased at any hour of the night, though you had the means?"

" Now that is convincing the king's officers don't know everything," said the simpleton, laughing within himself. " Here 's as good a pound-bill, old tenor, as was ever granted by the Bay colony; and meat 's no such rarity, that a man, who has a pound-bill, old tenor, in his pocket, can't go under old Funnel when he pleases, for all their acts of Parliament."

"You have plundered the dead!" cried Lionel, observing that Job exhibited in his hand several pieces of silver, besides the note he had mentioned.

"Don't call Job a thief!" said the lad, with a threatening air: "there's law in the Bay yet, though people don't use it; and right will be done to all, when the time comes. Job shot a granny, but he's no thief."

"You were then paid for your secret errand, last night, foolish boy, and have been tempted to run into danger by money. Let it be the last time. In future, when you want, come to me for assistance."

"Job won't go of arr'nds for the king, if he'd give him his golden crown, with all its di'monds and flauntiness, unless Job pleases, for there's no law for it."

Lionel, with a view to appease the irritated lad, now made a few kind and conciliating remarks, but the change-ling did not deign to reply, falling back in his corner in a sullen manner, as if he would repair the fatigue of the day by a few moments of sleep. In the meantime, Ralph had sunk into a profound revery, when the young soldier remembered that the hour was late, and he had yet obtained no explanation of the mysterious charges. He therefore alluded to the subject in a manner which he thought best adapted to obtain the desired intelligence. The instant Lionel mentioned the agitation of his aunt, his companion raised his head again, and a smile like that of fierce exulta-tion lighted the wan face of the old man, who answered, pointing with an emphatic gesture to his own bosom,—

"'Twas here, boy—'t was here. Nothing short of the power of conscience, and a knowledge like that of mine, could strike that woman speechless in the presence of any-thing human."

"But what is this extraordinary knowledge? I am in some degree the natural protector of Mrs. Lechmere; and, independent of my individual interest in your secret, have a right, in her behalf, to require an explanation of such seri-ous allegations."

"In her behalf!" repeated Ralph.   "Wait, impetuous young man, until she bids you push the inquiry: it shall then be answered, in a voice of thunder."

"If not in justice to my aged aunt, at least remember your repeated promises to unfold that sad tale of my own domestic sorrows, of which you claim to be the master."

"Ay, of that, and much more, am I in possession," returned the old man, smiling, as if conscious of his knowledge and power.   "If you doubt it, descend and ask the miserable tenant of this warehouse, or the guilty widow of John Lechmere."

"Nay, I doubt nothing but my own patience; the moments fly swiftly, and I have yet to learn all I wish to know."

"This is neither the time, nor is it the place where you are to hear the tale," returned Ralph.   "I have already said that we shall meet beyond the colleges for that purpose."

"But after the events of this day, who can tell when it will be in the power of an officer of the crown to visit the colleges in safety?"

"What!" cried the old man, laughing aloud, in the bitterness of his scorn, "has the boy found the strength and the will of the despised colonists so soon!   But I pledge to thee my word, that thou shalt yet see the place, and in safety.   Yes, yes, Priscilla Lechmere, thy hour is at hand, and thy doom is sealed forever!"

Lionel again mentioned his aunt, and alluded to the necessity of his soon rejoining her, as he already heard footsteps below, which indicated that preparations were making for her departure.   But his petitions and remonstrances were now totally unheeded: his aged companion was pacing swiftly up and down his small apartment, muttering incoherent sentences, in which the name of Priscilla was alone audible, and his countenance betraying the inward workings of absorbing and fierce passions.   In a few moments more, the shrill voice of Abigail was heard calling upon her son, in a manner which plainly denoted her knowledge that the changeling was concealed somewhere about the building. Job heard her calls repeated, until the tones of her voice became angry and threatening, when he stole slowly from his corner, and moved towards the ladder, with a sunken brow and lingering steps. Lionel now knew not how to act. His aunt was still ignorant of his presence, and he thought if Abigail Pray had wished him to appear, he would in some manner be soon included in the summons. He had also his own secret reasons for wishing his visits to Ralph unknown. Accordingly he determined to watch the movements below, under the favor of the darkness, and to be governed entirely by circumstances. He took no leave of his companion on departing, for long use had so far accustomed him to the eccentric manner of the old man, that he well knew any attempt to divert his attention from his burning thoughts would be futile at a moment of such intense excitement.

From the head of the ladder, where Lionel took his stand, he saw Mrs. Lechmere, preceded by Job with a lantern, walking, with a firmer step than he could have hoped for, towards the door, and he overheard Abigail cautioning her wilful son to light her visitor to a neighboring corner, where it appeared a conveyance was in waiting. On the threshold, his aunt turned, and, the light from the candle of Abigail falling on her features, Lional caught a full view of her cold, hard eye, which had regained all its worldly expression, though softened a little by a deeper shade of thought than usual.

"Let the scene of to-night be forgotten, my good Abigail," she said. "Your lodger is a nameless being, who has gleaned some idle tale, and wishes to practise on our credulity to enrich himself. I will consider more of it ; but on no account do you hold any further communion with him. I must remove you, my trusty woman ; this habitation is unworthy of you, and of your dutiful son, too. I must see you better lodged, my good Abigail—indeed I must."

Lionel could distinguish the slight shudder that passed through the frame of her companion, as she alluded to the doubtful character of Ralph ; but, without answering, Abigail held the door open for the departure of her guest. The instant Mrs. Lechmere disappeared, Lionel glided down the ladder, and stood before the astonished woman.

"When I tell you I have heard all that passed to-night," he abruptly said, "you will see the folly of any further attempt at concealment. I now demand so much of your secret as affects the happiness of me or mine."

"No—no—not of me, Major Lincoln," said the terrified female ; "not of me, for the love of God, not of me : I have sworn to keep it, and one oath"— Her emotions choked her, and her voice became indistinct.

Lionel regretted his vehemence, and, ashamed to extort a confession from a woman, he attempted to pacify her feelings, promising to require no further communication at that time.

"Go—go," she said, motioning him to depart, "and I shall be well again. Leave me, and then I shall be alone with that terrible old man, and my God !"

Perceiving her earnestness, he reluctantly complied, and, meeting Job on the threshold, he ceased to feel any further uneasiness for her safety.

During his rapid walk to Tremont Street, Major Lincoln thought intently on all he had heard and witnessed. He remembered the communications by which Ralph had attained such a powerful interest in his feelings, and he fancied he could discover a pledge of the truth of the old man's knowledge in the guilt betrayed by the manner of his aunt. From Mrs. Lechmere his thoughts recurred to her lovely grandchild, and for a moment he was perplexed, by endeavoring to explain her contradictory deportment towards himself : at one time she was warm, frank, and even affectionate ; and at another, as in the short and private interview of that very evening, cold, constrained, and repulsive. Then, again, he recollected the object which had chiefly induced him to follow his regiment to his native country ; and the recollection was attended by that shade of dejection which such reflections never failed to cast across his intelligent features. On reaching the house, he ascertained the safe return of Mrs. Lechmere, who had already retired to her room, attended by her lovely relatives. Lionel immediately followed their example ; and as the excitement of that memorable and busy day subsided, it was succeeded by a deep sleep, that fell on his senses like the forgetfulness of the dead.

CHAPTER XIII.

"Now let it work : Mischief, thou art afoot :
Take then what course thou wilt !"

SHAKESPEARE.

THE alarm of the inroad passed swiftly by the low shores of the Atlantic, and was heard echoing among the rugged mountains west of the rivers, as if borne along on a whirlwind. The male population, between the rolling waters of Massachusetts Bay and the limpid stream of the Connecticut, rose as one man ; and as the cry of blood was sounded far inland, the hills and valleys, the highways and footpaths, were seen covered with bands of armed husbandmen, pressing eagerly towards the scene of the war. Within eight-and-forty hours after the fatal meeting at Lexington, it was calculated that more than a hundred thousand men were in arms ; and near one fourth of that number was gathered before the peninsulas of Boston and Charlestown. They who were precluded by distance and a want of military provisions, to support such a concourse, from participating in the more immediate contest, lay by in expectation of the arrival of that moment when their zeal might also be put to severer trials. In short, the sullen quietude in which the colonies had been slumbering for a year, was suddenly and rudely broken by the events of that day ; and the patriotic among the people rose with such a cry of indignation on their lips, that the disaffected, who were no insignificant class in the more southern provinces, were compelled to silence, until the first burst of revolutionary excitement had an opportunity to subside, under the never failing influence of time and suffering.

Gage, secure in his position, and supported by a constantly increasing power, as well as the presence of a formidable fleet, looked on the gathering storm with a steady eye, and with that calmness which distinguished the mild benevolence of his private character. Though the attitude and the intentions of the Americans could no longer be mistaken, he listened with reluctant ears to the revengeful advice of his counsellors, and rather strove to appease the tumult than to attempt crushing it by a force which, though a month before it had been thought equal to the united power of the peaceful colonists, he now prudently deemed no more than competent to protect itself within its watery boundaries. Proclamations were, however, fulminated against the rebels ; and such other measures as were thought indispensable to assert the dignity and authority of the crown, were promptly adopted. Of course, these harmless denunciations were disregarded, and all his exhortations to return to an allegiance, which the people still denied had ever been impaired, were lost amid the din of arms, and the popular cries of the time. These appeals of the British general, as well as sundry others made by the royal governors, who yet held their rule throughout all the provinces, except the one in which the scene of our tale is laid, were answered by the people in humble but manly petitions to the throne for justice ; and in loud remonstrances to the Parliament, requiring to be restored to the possession of those rights and immunities which should be secured to all who enjoyed the protection of their common constitution. Still the power and prerogatives of the prince were deeply respected, and were alluded to in all public documents, with the veneration which was thought due to the sacredness of his character and station. But that biting, though grave sarcasm, which the colonists knew so well how to use, was freely expended on his ministers, who were accused of devising the measures so destructive to the peace of the empire. In this manner passed some weeks after the series of skirmishes which were called the battle of Lexington, from the circumstance of commencing at the hamlet of that name, both parties continuing to prepare for a mightier exhibition of their power and daring.

Lionel had by no means been an unconcerned spectator of these preparations. The morning after the return of the detachment, he applied for a command, equal to his just expectations. But while he was complimented on the spirit and loyalty he had manifested on the late occasion, it was intimated to the young man that he might be of more service to the cause of his prince, by devoting his time to the cultivation of his interest among those powerful colonists with whom his family was allied by blood, or connected by long and close intimacies. It was even submitted to his own judgment whether it would not be well, at some auspicious moment, to trust his person without the defences of the army, in the prosecution of this commendable design. There was so much that was flattering to the self-love, and soothing to the pride of the young soldier, artfully mingled with these ambiguous proposals, that he became content to await the course of events, having, however, secured a promise of obtaining a suitable military command in the case of further hostilities. That such an event was at hand, could not well be concealed from one much less observing than Major Lincoln.

Gage had already abandoned his temporary position in Charlestown, for the sake of procuring additional security by concentrating his force. From the hills of the peninsula of Boston, it was apparent that the colonists were fast assuming the front of men who were resolved to beleaguer the army of the king. Many of the opposite heights were already crowned with hastily-formed works of earth, and a formidable body of these unpractised warriors had set themselves boldly down before the entrance to the isthmus, cutting off all communication with the adjacent country, and occupying the little village of Roxbury, directly before the muzzles of the British guns, with a hardiness that would not have disgraced men much longer tried in the field, and more inured to its dangers.

The surprise created in the army by these appearances of skill and spirit among the hitherto despised Americans, in some measure ceased when the rumor spread itself in their camp, that many gentlemen of the provinces, who had served with credit in the forces of the crown, at former periods, were mingled with the people in stations of responsibility and command. Among others Lionel heard the names of Ward and Thomas; men of liberal attainments, and of some experience in arms. Both were regularly commissioned by the congress of the colony as leaders of their forces; and under their orders were numerous regiments duly organized, possessing all the necessary qualifications of soldiers, excepting the two indispensable requisites of discipline and arms. Lionel heard the name of Warren mentioned oftener than any other in the circles of Province House, and with that sort of bitterness, which, even while it bespoke their animosity, betrayed the respect of his enemies. This gentleman, who until the last moment had braved the presence of the royal troops, and fearlessly advocated his principles, while encircled with their bayonets, was now known to have suddenly disappeared from among them, abandoning home, property, and a lucrative profession; and by sharing in the closing scenes of the day of Lexington, to have fairly cast his fortunes on the struggle. But the name which in secret possessed the greatest charm for the ear of the young British soldier, was that of Putnam, a yeoman of the neighboring colony of Connecticut, who, as the uproar of the alarm whirled by him, literally deserted his plough, and mounting a beast from its team, made an early halt, after a forced march of a hundred miles, in the foremost ranks of his countrymen. While the name of this sturdy American was passing in whispers among the veterans who crowded the levees of Gage, a flood of melancholy and tender recollections flashed through the brain of the young man. He remembered the frequent and interesting communications which, in his boyhood, he had held with his own father, before the dark shade had passed across the reason of Sir Lionel, and, in every tale of murderous combats with the savage tenants of the wilds, in each scene of danger and of daring that had distinguished the romantic warfare of the wilderness, and even in strange and fearful encounters with the beasts of the forest, the name of this man was blended with a species of chivalrous fame that is seldom obtained in an enlightened age, and never undeservedly. The great wealth of the family of Lincoln, and the high expectations of its heir, had obtained for the latter a military rank which at that period was rarely enjoyed by any but such as had bought the distinction by long and arduous services. Consequently, many of his equals had shared in those trials of his father, in which the "Lion heart" of America had been so conspicuous for his deeds. By these grave veterans, who should know him best, the name of Putnam was always mentioned with strong and romantic affection ; and when the notable scheme of detaching him, by the promise of office and wealth, from the cause of the colonists, was proposed by the cringing counsellors who surrounded the commander-in-chief, it was listened to with a contemptuous incredulity by the former associates of the old partisan, that the result of the plan fully justified. Similar inducements were offered to others among the Americans, whose talents were thought worthy of purchase ; but so deep root had the principles of the day taken, that not a man of any note was found to listen to the proposition.

While these subtle experiments were adopted in the room of more energetic measures, troops continued to arrive from England, and, before the end of May, many leaders of renown appeared in the councils of Gage, who now possessed a disposable force of not less than eight thousand bayonets. With the appearance of these reinforcements, the fallen pride of the army began to revive ; and the spirits of the haughty young men, who had so recently left the gay parades of their boasted island, were chafed by the reflection that such an army should be cooped within the narrow limits of the peninsula by a band of half-armed husbandmen, destitute alike of the knowledge of war, and of most of its munitions. This feeling was increased by the taunts of the Americans themselves, who now turned the tables on their adversaries, applying, among other sneers, the term of "elbow-room" freely to Burgoyne, one of those chieftains of the royal army, who had boasted unwittingly of the intention of himself and his compeers to widen the limits of the army immediately on their arrival at the scene of the contest. The aspect of things within the British camp began to indicate, however, that their leaders were serious in the intention to extend their possessions, and all eyes were again turned to the heights of Charlestown, the spot most likely to be first occupied.

No military positions could be more happily situated, as respects locality, to support each other, and to extend and weaken the lines of their enemies, than the two opposite peninsulas so often mentioned. The distance between them was but six hundred yards, and the deep and navigable waters, by which they were nearly surrounded, rendered it easy for the royal general to command, at any time, the assistance of the heaviest vessels of the fleet, in defending either place. With these advantages before them, the army gladly heard those orders issued, which, it was well understood, indicated an approaching movement to the opposite shores.

It was now eight weeks since the commencement of hostilities, and the war had been confined to the preparations detailed, with the exception of one or two sharp skirmishes on the islands of the harbor, between the foragers of the army and small parties of the Americans, in which the latter well maintained their newly acquired reputation for spirit.

With the arrival of the regiments from England, gayety had once more visited the town, though such of the inhabitants as were compelled to remain against their inclinations, continued to maintain that cold reserve, in their deportment, which effectually repelled all the efforts of the officers to include them in the wanton festivities of the time. There were a few, however, among the colonists, who had been bribed, by offices and emoluments, to desert the good cause of the land; and as some of these had already been rewarded by offices which gave them access to the ear of the royal governor, he was thought to be unduly and unhappily influenced by the pernicious counsels with which they poisoned his mind, and prepared him for acts of injustice and harshness, that both his unbiassed feelings and ordinary opinions would have condemned. A few days succeeding

the affair of Lexington, a meeting of the inhabitants had
been convened, and a solemn compact was made between
them and the governor, that such as chose to deliver up
their arms might leave the place, while the remainder were
promised a suitable protection in their own dwellings. The
arms were delivered, but that part of the conditions which
related to the removal of the inhabitants was violated under
slight and insufficient pretexts. This, and various other
causes incidental to military rule, embittered the feelings of
the people, and furnished new causes of complaint; while,
on the other hand, hatred was rapidly usurping the place of
contempt, in the breasts of those who had been compelled
to change their sentiments with respect to a people that they
could never love. In this manner, resentment and distrust
existed, with all the violence of personality, within the
place itself, affording an additional reason to the troops for
wishing to extend their limits. Notwithstanding these inau-
spicious omens of the character of the contest, the native
kindness of Gage, and perhaps a desire to rescue a few of
his own men from the hands of the colonists, induced him
to consent to an exchange of the prisoners made in the
inroad; thus establishing, in the outset, a precedent to distinguish the controversy from an ordinary rebellion against
the loyal authority of the sovereign. A meeting was held,
for this purpose, in the village of Charlestown, at that time
unoccupied by either army. At the head of the American
deputation appeared Warren, and the old partisan of the
wilderness already mentioned, who, by a happy, though not
uncommon constitution of temperament, was as forward in
deeds of charity as in those of daring. At this interview,
several of the veterans of the royal army were present, having passed the strait to hold a last, friendly converse with
their ancient comrade, who received them with the frankness
of a soldier, while he rejected their subtle endeavors to
entice him from the banners under which he had enlisted,
with a sturdiness as unpretending as it was inflexible.

While these events were occurring at the great scene of
the contest, the hum of preparation was to be heard throughout the whole of the wide extent of the colonies. In various

places slight acts of hostility were committed, the Americans no longer waiting for the British to be the aggressors, and everywhere such military stores as could be reached, were seized, peaceably or by violence, as the case required. The concentration of most of the troops in Boston had, however, left the other colonies comparatively but little to achieve, though, while they still rested, nominally, under the dominion of the crown, they neglected no means within their power to assert their rights in the last extremity.

At Philadelphia, "the Congress of the Delegates from the United Colonies," the body that controlled the great movements of a people who now first began to act as a distinct nation, issued their manifestoes, supporting in a masterly manner their principles, and proceeded to organize an army that should be as competent to maintain them as circumstances would allow. Gentlemen who had been trained to arms in the service of the king, were invited to resort to their banners, and the remainder of the vacancies were filled by the names of the youthful, the bold, and adventurous, who were willing to risk their lives in a cause where even success promised so little personal advantage. At the head of this list of untrained warriors, the congress placed one of their own body, a man already distinguished for his services in the field, and who has since bequeathed to his country the glory of an untarnished name.

CHAPTER XIV.

"Thou shalt see me at Philippi."
Julius Cæsar.

DURING this period of feverish excitement, while the appearance and privations of war existed with so little of its danger or its action, Lionel had not altogether forgotten his personal feelings, in the powerful interest created by the state of public affairs. Early on the morning succeeding the night of the scene between Mrs. Lechmere and the inmates of the warehouse, he had repaired again to the spot, to relieve the intense anxiety of his mind, by seeking a complete explanation of all those mysteries which had been the principal ligament that bound him to a man, little known, except for his singularities.

The effects of the preceding day's battle were already visible in the market-place, where, as Lionel passed, he saw few or none of the countrymen who usually crowded the square at that hour. In fact, the windows of the shops were opened with caution, and men looked out upon the face of the sun as if doubting of its appearance and warmth, as in seasons of ordinary quiet; jealousy and distrust having completely usurped the place of security within the streets of the town. Notwithstanding the hour, few were in their beds, and those who appeared, betrayed by their looks that they had passed the night in watchfulness. Among the number was Abigail Pray, who received her guest in the little tower, surrounded by everything as he had seen it the past evening, nothing altered, except her own dark eye, which at times looked like a gem of price set in her squalid features, but which now appeared haggard and sunken, participating, more markedly than common, in the general air of misery that pervaded the woman.

"I have intruded at a somewhat unusual hour, Mrs. Pray," said Lionel, as he entered; "but business of the last moment requires that I should see your lodger. I suppose he is above : it will be well to announce my visit."

Abigail shook her head with an air of solemn meaning, as she answered, in a subdued voice, "He is gone!"

"Gone!" exclaimed Lionel. "Whither, and when?"

"The people seem visited by the wrath of God, sir," returned the woman. "Old and young, the sick and well, are crazy about the shedding of blood; and it's beyond the might of man to say where the torrent will be stayed."

"But what has this to do with Ralph? Where is he? Woman, you are not playing me false?"

"I! Heaven forbid that I should ever be false again! and to you least of all God's creatures! No, no, Major Lincoln; the wonderful man, who seems to have lived so long that he can even read our secret thoughts, as I had supposed man could never read them, has left me, and I know not whether he will ever return."

"Ever! You have not driven him by violence from under your miserable roof?"

"My roof is like that of the fowls of the air—'tis the roof of any who are so unfortunate as to need it. There is no spot on earth, Major Lincoln, that I can call mine : but one day there will be one—yes, yes, there will be a narrow house provided for us all; and God grant that mine may be as quiet as the coffin is said to be! I lie not, Major Lincoln —no, this time I am innocent of deceit—Ralph and Job have gone together, but whither I know not, unless it be to join the people without the town. They left me as the moon rose, and he gave me a parting and a warning voice, that will ring in my ears until they are deafened by the damps of the grave!"

"Gone to join the Americans, and with Job!" returned Lionel, musing, and without attending to the closing words of Abigail. "Your boy will purchase peril with this madness, Mrs. Pray, and should be looked to."

"Job is not one of God's accountables, nor is he to be treated like other children," returned the woman. "Ah Major Lincoln, a healthier, and a stouter, and a finer boy was not to be seen in the Bay province, till the child had reached his fifth year ; then, then it was that the judgment of Heaven fell on mother and son—sickness made him what you see, a being with the form, but without the reason of man, and I have grown the wretch I am. But it has all been foretold, and warnings enough have I had of it all ; for is it not said, that *He* 'will visit the sins of the fathers upon the children until the third and fourth generation'? Thank God, my sorrows and sins will end with Job, for there never can be a third to suffer !''

"If," said Lionel, "there be any sin which lies heavy at your heart, every consideration, whether of justice or repentance, should induce you to confess your errors to those whose happiness may be affected by the knowledge, if any such there be."

The anxious eye of the woman raised itself to meet the look of the young man ; but quailing before the piercing gaze it encountered, she quickly turned it upon the litter and confusion of her disordered apartment. Lionel waited some time for a reply ; but finding that she remained obstinately silent, he continued,—

"From what has already passed, you must be conscious that I have good reasons to believe that my feelings are deeply concerned in your secret; make, then, your confession of the guilt which seems to bear you down so heavily ; and in return for the confidence, I promise you my forgiveness and protection."

As Lionel pressed thus directly the point so near his heart, the woman shrunk away from her situation near him, and her countenance lost, as he proceeded, its remarkable expression of compunction, in a forced look of deep surprise, that showed she was no novice in dissimulation, whatever might be the occasional warnings of her conscience.

"Guilt !" she repeated, in a slow and tremulous voice : "we are all guilty, and would be lost creatures, but for the blood of the Mediator."

" Most true. But you have spoken of crimes that infringe
the laws of man, as well as those of God."

" I ! Major Lincoln—I a disorderly law-breaker !" exclaimed Abigail, affecting to busy herself in arranging her
apartment. " It is not such as I that have leisure or courage to break the laws ! Major Lincoln is trying a poor
lone woman, to make his jokes with the gentlemen of his
mess this evening : 't is certain we all of us have our burdens of guilt to answer for. Surely Major Lincoln could n't
have heard Minister Hunt preach his sermon, the last Sabbath, on the sins of the town ! "

Lionel colored highly at the artful imputation of the
woman, that he was practising on her sex and unprotected
situation ; and, greatly provoked in secret, at her duplicity,
he became more guarded in his language, endeavoring to
lead her on, by kindness and soothing, to the desired communications. But all his ingenuity was met by more than
equal abilities on the part of Abigail, from whom he only
obtained expressions of surprise, that he could have mistaken her language for more than the usual acknowledgment of errors, that are admitted to be common to our lost
nature. In this particular, the woman was in no respect
singular ; the greater number of those who are loudest in
their confessions and denunciations on the abandoned nature
of our hearts, commonly resenting, in the deepest manner,
the imputation of individual offences. The more earnest
and pressing his inquiries became, the more wary she grew,
until, disgusted with her pertinacity, and secretly suspecting
her of foul play with her lodger, he left the house in anger,
determining to keep a close eye on her movements, and, at
a suitable moment, to strike such a blow as should bring
her not only to confession, but to shame.

Under the influence of this momentary resentment, and
unable to avoid harboring the most unpleasant suspicions
of his aunt, the young man determined, that very morning,
to withdraw himself entirely, as a guest, from her dwelling.
Mrs. Lechmere, who, if she knew at all that Lionel had
been a witness of her intercourse with Ralph, must have
received the intelligence from Abigail, received him, at

breakfast, with a manner that betrayed no such consciousness. She listened to his excuses for removing with evident concern ; and more than once, as Lionel spoke of the probable nature of his future life, now that hostilities had commenced—the additional trouble his presence would occasion to one of her habits and years—of his great concern in her behalf—and, in short, of all that he could devise in the way of apology for the step, he saw her eyes turned anxiously on Cecil, with an expression which, at another time, might have led him to distrust the motives of her hospitality. The young lady herself, however, evidently heard the proposal with great satisfaction, and, when her grandmother appealed to her opinion, whether he had urged a single good reason for the measure, she answered, with a vivacity that had been a stranger to her manner of late,—

"Certainly, my dear grandmamma, the best of all reasons—his inclinations. Major Lincoln tires of us, and of our humdrum habits, and—and in my eyes, true politeness requires that we should suffer him to leave us for his barracks, without a word of remonstrance."

"My motive must be greatly mistaken, if a desire to leave you—"

"O, sir, the explanation is not required. You have urged so many reasons, cousin Lionel, that the true and moving motive is yet kept behind the curtain. It must and can be no other than *ennui*."

"Then I will remain," said Lionel ; "for anything is better than to be suspected of insensibility."

Cecil looked both gratified and disappointed ; she played with her spoon a moment in embarrassment, bit her beautiful lip with vexation, and then said, in a more friendly tone,—

"I must then exonerate you from the imputation. Go to your own quarters, if it be agreeable, and we will believe your incomprehensible reasons for the change ; besides, as a kinsman, we shall see you every day, you know."

Lionel had now no longer any excuse for not abiding by his avowed determination ; and, notwithstanding Mrs. Lechmere parted from her interesting nephew with an exhibition of reluctance that was in singular contrast with her usually cold and formal manner, the desired removal was made in the course of that very morning.

When this change was accomplished, week after week slipped by in the manner related in the preceding chapter, during which the reinforcements continued to arrive, and general after general appeared in the place to support the unenterprising Gage in the conduct of the war. The timid amongst the colonists were appalled as they heard the long list of proud and boasted names recounted. There was Howe, a man sprung from a noble race, long known for their deeds in arms, and whose chief had already shed his blood on the soil of America ; Clinton, another cadet of an illustrious house, better known for his personal intrepidity and domestic kindness, than for the rough qualities of the warrior ; and the elegant and accomplished Burgoyne, who had already purchased a name in the fields of Portugal and Germany, which he was destined soon to lose in the wilds of America. In addition to these might be mentioned Pigot, Grant, Robertson, and the heir of Northumberland, each of whom led a brigade in the cause of his prince ; besides a host of men of lesser note, who had passed their youth in arms, and were now about to bring their experience to the field, in opposition to the untrained husbandmen of the plains of New England. As if this were not sufficient to overwhelm their inexperienced adversaries, the pride of arms had gathered many of the young among the noble and chivalric in the British empire, to the point on which all eyes were turned ; amongst whom, the one who afterwards added the fairest wreath to the laurels of his ancestors, was the joint heir of Hastings and Moria, the gallant, but, as yet, untried boy of Rawdon. Amongst such companions, many of whom had been his associates in England, the hours of Lionel passed swiftly by, leaving him but little leisure to meditate on those causes which had brought him also to the scene of contention.

One warm evening, towards the middle of June, Lionel became a witness of the following scene, through the open doors which communicated between his private apartment and the room which Polwarth had dedicated to what he called "the knowing mess." M'Fuse was seated at a table, with a ludicrous air of magisterial authority, while Polwarth held a station at his side, which appeared to partake of the double duties of a judge and a scribe. Before this formidable tribunal Seth Sage was arraigned, as it would seem, to answer for certain offences alleged to have been committed in the field of battle. Ignorant that his landlord had not received the benefit of the late exchange, and curious to know what all the suppressed roguery he could detect in the demure countenances of his friends might signify, Lionel dropped his pen, and listened to the succeeding dialogue.

"Now answer to your offences, you silly fellow, with a wise name," M'Fuse commenced, in a voice that did not fail, by its harsh cadences, to create some of that awe which, by the expression of the speaker's eye, it would seem he labored to produce; "speak out with the freedom of a man, and the compunctions of a Christian, if you have them. Why should I not send you at once to Ireland, that ye may get your deserts on three pieces of timber, the one being laid crosswise for the sake of convenience? If you have a contrary reason, bestow it without delay, for the love you bear your own angular deformities."

The wags did not altogether fail in their object, Seth betraying a good deal more uneasiness than it was usual for the man to exhibit even in situations of uncommon peril. After clearing his throat, and looking about him, to gather from the eyes of the spectators which way their sympathies inclined, he answered with a very commendable fortitude,—

"Because it 's ag'in all law."

"Have done with your interminable perplexities of the law," cried M'Fuse, "and do not bother honest gentlemen with its knavery, as if they were no more than so many proctors in big wigs! 'T is the Gospel you should be thinking of, you godless reprobate, on account of that final end you will yet make, one day, in most indecent hurry."

"To your purpose, Mac," interrupted Polwarth, who perceived that the erratic feelings of his friend were beginning already to lead him from the desired point; "or I will pro-

12

pound the matter myself, in a style that would do credit to a mandamus counsellor."

"The mandamuses are all agin the charter, and the law too," continued Seth, whose courage increased as the dialogue bore more directly upon his political principles; "and to my mind it 's quite convincing, that if ministers calculate largely on upholding them, there will be great disturbances, if not a proper fight in the land; for the whole country is in a blaze!"

"Disturbances, thou immovable iniquity! thou quiet assassin!" roared M'Fuse; "do ye not call a light of a day a disturbance? or do ye tarm skulking behind fences, and laying the muzzle of a musket on the head of Job Pray, and the breech of a mullein-stalk, while ye draw upon a fellow-creature, a commendable method of fighting? Now answer me to the truth, and disdain all lying, as ye would 'ating anything but cod on a Saturday, who were the two men that fired into my very countenance, from the unfortunate situation among the mulleins that I have detailed to you?"

"Pardon me, Captain M'Fuse," said Polwarth, "if I say that your zeal and indignation run ahead of your discretion. If we alarm the prisoner in this manner, we may defeat the ends of justice. Besides, sir, there is a reflection contained in your language, to which I must dissent. A real *dumb* is not to be despised, especially when served up in wrapper, and between two coarser fish, to preserve the steam. I have had my private meditations on the subject of getting up a Saturday's club, in order to enjoy the bounty of the Bay, and for improving the cookery of the cod."[1]

"And let me tell you, Captain Polwarth," returned the grenadier, cocking his eye fiercely at the other, "that your

[1] It may be a fit matter of inquiry for the antiquarian, to learn whether the captain ever put his project in execution; and if so, whether he has not the merit of founding that famous association, which, to this hour, maintains the catholic custom of the east, by feasting on the last day of the week and on the staple of New England; and which is said to assemble regularly, with much good-fellowship, around more good wine than is ever encountered at any other board in the known world.

epicurean propensities lead you to the verge of cannibalism ; for sure it may be called *that*, when you speak of 'ating, while the life of a fellow-cr'ature is under discussion for its termination—"

"I conclude," interrupted Seth, who was greatly averse to all quarrelling, and who thought he saw the symptoms of a breach between his judges, "the captain wishes to know who the two men were that fired on him a short time before he got the hit in the shoulder ?"

"A short time, ye marvellous hypocrite !—'t was as quick as pop and slap could make it."

"Perhaps there might be some mistake, for a great many of the troops were much disguised—"

"Do ye insinuate that I got drunk before the enemies of my king ?" roared the grenadier. "Harkye, Mister Sage ; I ask you in a genteel way, who the two men were that fired on me, in the manner detailed ; and remember that a man may tire of putting questions which are never answered."

"Why," returned Seth, who, however expert at prevarication, eschewed, with religious horror, a direct lie, "I pretty much conclude that they—the captain is sure the place he means was just beyond Menotomy ?"

"As sure as men can be," said Polwarth, "who possess the use of their eyes."

"Then Captain Polwarth can give testimony to the fact ?"

"I believe Major Lincoln's horse carries a small bit of your lead to this moment, Master Sage."

Seth yielded to this accumulation of evidence against him ; and knowing, moreover, that the grenadier had literally made him a prisoner in the act of renewing his fire, he sagaciously determined to make a merit of necessity, and candidly to acknowledge his agency in inflicting the wounds. The utmost, however, that his cautious habits would permit him to say, was,—

"Seeing there can't well be any mistake, I seem to think the two men were chiefly Job and I."

"Chiefly, you lath of uncertainty !" exclaimed M'Fuse ;

"if there was any chief in that cowardly assassination of wounding a Christian, and of also hurting a horse—which, though nothing but a dumb baste, has better blood than runs in your beggarly veins—'t was your own ugly proportions. But I rejoice that you come to the confessional! I can now see you hung with felicity. If you have anything to say, urge it at once, why I should not embark you for Ireland by the first vessel, in a letter to my lord-lieutenant, with a request that he 'll give you an early procession, and a dacent funeral."

Seth belonged to a class of his countrymen, amongst whom, while there was a superabundance of ingenuity, there was literally no joke. Deceived by the appearance of anger, which had in reality blended with the assumed manner of the grenadier, as he dwelt upon the irritating subject of his own injuries, the belief of the prisoner in the sacred protection of the laws became much shaken, and he began to reflect very seriously on the insecurity of the times, as well as on the despotic nature of the military power. The little humor he had inherited from his Puritan ancestors was, though exceedingly quaint, altogether after a different fashion from the off-hand, blundering wit of the Irishman; and that manner which he did not possess, he could not entirely comprehend; so that, as far as a very visible alarm furthered the views of the two conspirators, they were quite successful. Polwarth now took pity on his evident embarrassment, and observed, with a careless manner,—

"Perhaps I can make a proposal, by which Mr. Sage may redeem his neck from the halter, and at the same time essentially serve an old friend."

"Hear ye that, thou confounder of men and bastes!" cried M'Fuse. "Down on your knees, and thank Mr. Pater Polwarth for the charity of his insinuation."

Seth was not displeased to hear such amicable intentions announced; but, habitually cautious in all bargaining, he suppressed the exhibition of his satisfaction, and said, with an air of deliberation that would have done credit to the keenest trader in King Street, that "he should like to hear the terms of agreement, before he gave his conclusion."

" They are simply these," returned Polwarth : " you shall receive your passports and freedom to-night, on condition that you sign this bond, whereby you will become obliged to supply our mess, as usual, during the time the place is invested, with certain articles of food and nourishment, as herein set forth, and according to the prices mentioned, which the veriest Jew in Duke's Place would pronounce to be liberal. Here, take the instrument, and ' read and mark,' in order that we may ' inwardly digest.' "

Seth took the paper, and gave it that manner of investigation that he was wont to bestow on everything which affected his pecuniary interests. He objected to the price of every article, all of which were altered in compliance with his obstinate resistance ; and he moreover insisted that a clause should be inserted to exonerate him from the penalty, provided the intercourse should be prohibited by the authorities of the colony ; after which he continued,—

" If the captain will agree to take charge of the things, and become liable, I will conclude to make the trade."

" Here is a fellow who wants boot in a bargain for his life ! " cried the grenadier. " But we will humor his covetous inclination, Polly, and take charge of the chattels. Captain Polwarth and myself pledge our words to their safe-keeping. Let me run my eyes over the articles," continued the grenadier, looking very gravely at the several covenants of the bond. " Faith, Pater, you have bargained for a goodly larder ! Baif, mutton, pigs, turnips, potatoes, melons, and other fruits—there 's a blunder, now, that would keep an English mess on a grin for a month, if an Irishman had made it ! as if a melon was a fruit, and a potato was not ! The devil a word do I see that you have said about a mouthful, except aitables, either ! Here, fellow, clap your learning to it, and I 'll warrant you we yet get a meal out of it, in some manner or other."

" Would n't it be as well to put the last agreement in the writings, too," said Seth, " in case of accidents ? "

" Hear how a knave halters himself ! " cried M'Fuse : " he has the individual honor of two captains of foot, and is willing to exchange it for their joint bond ! The request is too

raisonable to be denied, Polly, and we should be guilty of
pecuniary suicide to reject it ; so place a small article at the
bottom, explanatory of the mistake the gentleman has fallen
into.''

Polwarth did not hesitate to comply, and in a very few
minutes everything was arranged to the perfect satisfaction
of the parties ; the two soldiers felicitating themselves on
the success of a scheme which seemed to avert the principal
evils of the leaguer from their own mess ; and Seth finding
no difficulty in complying with an agreement which was
likely to prove so profitable, however much he doubted its
validity in a court of justice. The prisoner was now declared
at liberty, and was advised to make his way out of the place,
with as little noise as possible, and under favor of the pass
he held. Seth gave the bond a last and most attentive perusal, and then departed, well contented to abide by its conditions, and not a little pleased to escape from the grenadier,
the expression of whose half-comic, half-serious eye, occasioned him more perplexity than any other subject which had
ever before occupied his astuteness. After the disappearance of the prisoner, the two worthies repaired to their
nightly banquet, laughing heartily at the success of their
notable invention.

Lionel suffered Seth to pass from the room, without speaking ; but, as the man left his own abode with a lingering and
doubtful step, the young soldier followed him into the street,
without communicating to any one that he had witnessed
what had passed, with the laudable intention of adding his
own personal pledge for the security of the household goods
in question. He, however, found it no easy achievement to
equal the speed of a man who had just escaped from a long
confinement, and who now appeared inclined to indulge his
limbs freely in the pleasure of an unlimited exercise. The
velocity of Seth continued unabated, until he had conducted
Lionel far into the lower parts of the town, where the latter
perceived him to encounter a man, with whom he turned
suddenly under an arch which led into a dark and narrow
court. Lionel instantly increased his speed, and as he entered beneath the passage, he caught a glimpse of the lank

figure of the object of his pursuit, gliding through the opposite entrance to the court; and, at the same moment, he encountered the man who had apparently induced the deviation in his route. As Lionel stepped a little on one side, the light of the lamp fell full on the form of the other, and he recognized the person of the active leader of the caucus (as the political meeting he had attended was called), though so disguised and muffled that, but for the accidental opening of the folds of his cloak, the unknown might have passed his nearest friend without discovery.

"We meet again!" exclaimed Lionel, in the quickness of surprise; "though it would seem that the sun is never to shine on our interviews."

The stranger started, and betrayed an evident wish to continue his walk, as though the other had mistaken his person; then, as if suddenly recollecting himself, he turned and approached Lionel, with easy dignity, and answered,—

"The third time is said to contain the charm! I am happy to find that I meet Major Lincoln unharmed, after the dangers he so lately encountered."

"The dangers have probably been exaggerated by those who wish ill to the cause of our master," returned Lionel, coldly.

There was a calm, but proud smile on the face of the stranger, as he replied,—

"I shall not dispute the information of one who bore so conspicuous a part in the deeds of that day. Still you will remember, though the march to Lexington was, like our own accidental rencontres, in the dark, that a bright sun shone upon the retreat, and nothing has been hid."

"Nothing need be concealed," replied Lionel, nettled by the proud composure of the other, "unless, indeed, the man I address is afraid to walk the streets of Boston in open day."

"The man you address, Major Lincoln," said the stranger, advancing in his warmth a step nearer to Lionel, "has dared to walk the streets of Boston both by day and by night, when the bullies of him you call your master have strutted their hour in the security of peace; and, now a

nation is up to humble their pretensions, shall he shrink
from treading his native soil when he will ? "

" This is bold language from an enemy within a British
camp ! Ask yourself what course my duty requires of
me."

" That is a question which lies between Major Lincoln
and his conscience," returned the stranger ; " though," he
added, after a momentary pause, and in a milder tone, as if
he recollected the danger of his situation, " the gentlemen
of his name and lineage were not apt to be informers, when
they dwelt in the land of their birth."

" Neither is their descendant. But let this be the last
of our interviews, until we can meet as friends, or, as enemies should, where we may discuss these topics at the points
of our weapons."

" Amen ! " said the stranger, seizing the hand of the young
man, and pressing it with the warmth of a generous emula-
tion ; " that hour may not be far distant, and may God
smile only on the just cause ! "

Without uttering more, he drew the folds of his dress
more closely around his form, and walked so swiftly away
that Lionel, had he possessed the inclination, could not have
found an opportunity to arrest his progress. As all expectation of overtaking Seth was now lost, the young soldier
returned slowly and thoughtfully towards his quarters.

The two or three succeeding days were distinguished by
an appearance of more than usual preparation among the
troops, and it became known that officers of rank had closely
reconnoitred the grounds of the opposite peninsula. Lionel
patiently awaited the progress of events ; but as the proba-
bility of active service increased, his wishes to make another
effort to probe the secret of the tenant of the warehouse
revived, and he took his way towards the Dock Square,
with that object, on the night of the fourth day from the
preceding interview with the stranger. It was long after
the tattoo had laid the town in that deep quiet which follows
the bustle of a garrison ; and, as he passed along, he saw
none but the sentinels pacing their short limits, or an occasional officer, returning at that late hour from his revels or

his duty. The windows of the warehouse were dark, and its inhabitants, if any it had, were wrapped in deep sleep. Restless and excited, Lionel pursued his walk through the narrow and gloomy streets of the North End, until he unexpectedly found himself issuing upon the open space that is tenanted by the dead, on Copp's Hill. On this eminence the English general had caused a battery of heavy cannon to be raised, and Lionel, unwilling to encounter the challenge of the sentinels, inclining a little to one side, proceeded to the brow of the hill, and, seating himself on a stone, began to muse deeply on his own fortunes, and the situation of the country.

The night was obscure, but the thin vapors which appeared to overhang the place opened at times, when a faint starlight fell from the heavens, and rendered the black hulls of the vessels of war, that lay moored before the town, and the faint outlines of the opposite shores, dimly visible. The stillness of midnight rested on the scene, and when the loud calls of " All 's well ! " ascended from the ships and batteries, the momentary cry was succeeded by a quiet as deep as if the universe slumbered under this assurance of safety. At such an instant, when even the light breathings of the night air were audible, the sound of rippling waters, like that occasioned by raising a paddle with extreme caution, was borne to the ear of the young soldier. He listened intently, and then, bending his eyes in the direction of the faint sounds, he saw a small canoe gliding along the surface of the water, and soon shoot upon the gravelly shore, at the foot of the hill, with a motion so easy and uniform as scarcely to curl a wave on the land. Curious to know who could be moving about the harbor at this hour, in such a secret manner, Lionel was in the act of rising to descend, when he saw the dim figure of a man land from the boat, and climb the hill, directly in a line with his own position. Suppressing even the sounds of his breath, and drawing his body back within the deep shadow cast from a point of the hill, a little above him, Lionel waited until the figure had approached within ten feet of him, when it stopped, and appeared, like himself, to be endeavoring to suppress all

other sounds and feelings in the absorbing act of deep attention. The young soldier loosened his sword in its sheath,
before he said,—

"We have chosen a private spot, and a secret hour, sir,
for our meditations!"

Had the figure possessed the impalpable nature of an
immaterial being, it could not have received this remark, so
startling from its suddenness, with greater apathy than did
the man to whom it was addressed. He turned slowly towards the speaker, and seemed to look at him earnestly,
before he answered, in a low, menacing voice,—

"There's a granny on the hill, with a gun and baggonet,
walking among the cannon, and if he hears people talking
down here, he'll make them prisoners, though one of them
should be Major Lincoln."

"Ha! Job," said Lionel; "and is it you I meet prowling
about like a thief at night? On what errand of mischief
have you been sent this time?"

"If Job's a thief for coming to see the graves on Copp's,"
returned the lad, sullenly," there's two of them."

"Well answered, boy!" said Lionel, with a smile. "But
I repeat, on what errand have you returned to the town at
this unseasonable and suspicious hour?"

"Job loves to come up among the graves before the cocks
crow; they say the dead walk when living men sleep."

"And would you hold communion with the dead, then?"

"'T is sinful to ask them many questions, and such as you
do put should be made in the Holy Name," returned the
lad, in a tone so solemn, that, connected with the place and
the scene, it caused the blood of Lionel to thrill. "But Job
loves to be near them, to use him to the damps, agin the time
he shall be called to walk himself in a sheet at midnight."

"Hush!" said Lionel. "What noise is that?"

Job stood a moment, listening as intently as his companion, before he answered,—

"There's no noise but the moaning of the wind in the
bay, or the sea tumbling on the beaches of the islands."

"'T is neither," said Lionel; "I heard the low hum of a
hundred voices, or my ears have played me falsely,"

"Maybe the spirits speak to each other," said the lad; "they say their voices are like the rushing winds."

Lionel passed his hand across his brow, and endeavored to recover the tone of his mind, which had been strangely disordered by the solemn manner of his companion, and walked slowly from the spot, closely attended by the silent changeling. He did not stop until he had reached the inner angle of the wall that inclosed the field of the dead, when he paused, and, leaning on the fence, again listened intently.

"Boy, I know not how your silly conversation may have warped my brain," he said, "but there are surely strange and unearthly sounds lingering about this place, to-night! By heavens! there is another rush of voices, as if the air above the water were filled with living beings; and then, again, I think I hear a noise as if heavy weights were falling to the earth."

"Ay," said Job, "'t is the clods on the coffins; the dead are going into their graves ag'in, and 't is time that we should leave them their own grounds."

Lionel hesitated no longer, but he rather ran than walked from the spot, with a secret horror that, at another moment, he would have blushed to acknowledge; nor did he perceive that he was still attended by Job, until he had descended some distance down Lynn Street. Here he was addressed by his companion, in his usually quiet and unmeaning tones,—

"There's the house that the governor built, who went down into the sea for money!" he said. "He was a poor boy once, like Job, and now they say his grandson is a great lord, and the king knighted the grand'ther too. It's pretty much the same thing whether a man gets his money out of the sea or out of the earth; the king will make him a lord for it."

"You hold the favors of royalty cheap, fellow," returned Lionel, glancing his eye carelessly at the "Phipps' House," as he passed; "you forget that I am to be some day one of your despised knights!"

"I know it," said Job; "and you come from America,

too. It seems to me that all the poor boys go from America to the king to be great lords, and all the sons of the great lords come to America to be made poor boys. Nab says Job is the son of a great lord, too!"

"Then Nab is as great a fool as her child," said Lionel; "but, boy, I would see your mother in the morning, and I expect you to let me know at what hour I may visit her."

Job did not answer, and Lionel, on turning his head, perceived that he was suddenly deserted by the changeling, who was already gliding back towards his favorite haunt among the graves. Vexed at the wild humors of the lad, Lionel hastened to his quarters, and threw himself in his bed, though he heard the loud cries of "All's well!" again and again, before the strange phantasies, which continued to cross his mind, would permit him to obtain the rest he sought.

CHAPTER XV.

"We are finer gentlemen, no doubt, than the plain farmers we are about to encounter. Our hats carry a smarter cock, our swords hang more gracefully by our sides, and we make an easier figure in a ball-room ; but let it be remembered, that the most finished maccaroni amongst us, would pass for an arrant clown at Pekin."

Letter from a Veteran Officer, etc.

WHEN the heavy sleep of morning fell upon his senses, visions of the past and future mingled with wild confusion in the dreams of the youthful soldier. The form of his father stood before him, as he had known it in his childhood, fair in the proportions and vigor of manhood, regarding him with those eyes of benignant, but melancholy affection, which characterized their expression after he had become the sole joy of his widowed parent. While his heart was warming at the sight, the figure melted away, and was succeeded by fantastic phantoms, which appeared to dance among the graves on Copp's, led along in those gambols, which partook of the ghastly horrors of the dead, by Job Pray, who glided among the tombs like a being of another world. Sudden and loud thunder then burst upon them, and the shadows fled into their secret places, from whence he could see, ever and anon, some glassy eyes and spectral faces, peering out upon him, as if conscious of the power they possessed to chill the blood of the living. His visions now became painfully distinct, and his sleep was oppressed with their vividness, when his senses burst their unnatural bonds, and he awoke. The air of morning was breathing through his open curtains, and the light of day had already shed itself upon the dusky roofs of the town. Lionel arose from his bed, and had paced his chamber several times, in a vain effort to shake off the images that had haunted his slumbers, when the sounds which broke upon the stillness of the air became too plain to be longer mistaken by a practised ear.

"Ha!" he muttered to himself, "I have been dreaming but by halves; these are the sounds of no fancied tempest, but cannon, speaking most plainly to the soldier!"

He opened his window and looked out upon the surrounding scene. The roar of artillery was now quick and heavy, and Lionel bent his eyes about him to discover the cause of this unusual occurrence. It had been the policy of Gage to await the arrival of his reinforcements before he struck a blow which was intended to be decisive; and the Americans were well known to be too scantily supplied with the munitions of war, to waste a single charge of powder in any of the vain attacks of modern sieges. A knowledge of these facts gave an additional interest to the curiosity, with which Major Lincoln endeavored to penetrate the mystery of so singular a disturbance. Window after window in the adjacent buildings soon exhibited, like his own, its wondering and alarmed spectator. Here and there a half-dressed soldier, or a busy townsman, was seen hurrying along the silent streets, with steps that denoted the eagerness of his curiosity. Women began to rush wildly from their dwellings, and then, as the sounds broke on their ears with tenfold heaviness in the open air, they shrunk back into their habitations in pallid dismay. Lionel called to three or four of the men, as they hurried by; but, turning their eyes wildly towards his window, they passed on without answering, as if the emergency were too pressing to admit of speech. Finding his repeated inquiries fruitless, he hastily dressed himself, and descended to the street. As he left his own door, a half-clad artillerist hurried past him, adjusting his garments with one hand, and bearing in the other some of the lesser implements of the particular corps in which he served.

"What means the firing, sergeant," demanded Lionel, "and whither do you hasten with those fusees?"

"The rebels, your honor, the rebels!" returned the soldier looking back to speak, without ceasing his speed; "and I go to my guns!"

"The rebels!" repeated Lionel; "what can we have to fear from a mob of countrymen, in such a position? That fellow has slept from his post, and apprehensions for himself mingle with this zeal for his king!"

The townspeople now began to pour from their dwellings in scores; and Lionel imitated their example, and took his course towards the adjacent height of Beacon Hill. He toiled his way up the steep ascent, in company with twenty more, without exchanging a syllable with men who appeared as much astonished as himself at this early interruption of their slumbers, and in a few minutes he stood on a little grassy platform, surrounded by a hundred interested gazers. The sun had just lifted the thin veil of mist from the bosom of the waters, and the eye was permitted to range over a wide field beneath the light vapor. Several vessels were moored in the channels of the Charles and Mystic, to cover the northern approaches to the place; and as he beheld the column of white smoke that was wreathing about the masts of a frigate among them, Lionel was no longer at a loss to comprehend whence the firing proceeded. While he was yet gazing, uncertain of the reasons which demanded this show of war, immense fields of smoke burst from the side of a ship of the line, who also opened her deep-mouthed cannon, and presently her example was followed by several floating batteries, and lighter vessels, until the wide amphitheatre of hills that encircled Boston was filled with the echoes of a hundred pieces of artillery.

"What can it mean, sir?" exclaimed a young officer of his own regiment, addressing Major Lincoln; "the sailors are in downright earnest, and they scale their guns with shot, I know, by the rattling of the reports."

"I can boast of a vision no better than your own," returned Lionel; "for no enemy can I see. As the guns seem pointed at the opposite peninsula, it is probable a party of the Americans are attempting to destroy the grass which lies newly mown in the meadows."

The young officer was in the act of assenting to this conjecture, when a voice was heard above their heads, shouting,—

"There goes a gun from Copp's! They need n't think to frighten the people with their rake-helly noises; let them blaze away till the dead get out of their graves; the Bay-men will keep the hill!"

Every eye was immediately turned upward, and the wondering and amused spectators discovered Job Pray, seated in the grate of the beacon, his countenance, usually so vacant, gleaming with exultation, while he continued waving his hat high in the air, as gun after gun was added to the uproar of the cannonade.

"How now, fellow!" exclaimed Lionel; "what see you, and where are the Bay-men of whom you speak?"

"Where?" returned the simpleton, clapping his hands with childish delight. "Why, where they came at dark midnight, and where they 'll stand at open noonday! The Bay-men can look into the windows of old Funnel at last; and now let the reg'lars come on, and they 'll teach the godless murderers the law."

Lionel, a little irritated with the bold language of Job, called to him, in an angry voice,—

"Come down from that perch, fellow, and explain yourself, or this grenadier shall lift you from your seat, and transfer you to the post for a little of that wholesome correction which you need."

"You promised that the grannies should never flog Job ag'in," said the changeling, crouching down in the grate, whence he looked out at his threatened chastiser with a lowering and sullen eye; "and Job agreed to run your arr'nds, and not take any of the king's crowns in pay."

"Come down, then, this instant, and I will remember the compact."

Comforted by this assurance, which was made in a more friendly tone, Job threw himself carelessly from his iron seat, and clinging to the post, he slid swiftly to the earth, where Major Lincoln immediately arrested him by the arm, and demanded,—

" Where are those Bay-men, I once more ask ? "

" There ! " repeated Job, pointing over the low roofs of the town, in the direction of the opposite peninsula. " They dug their cellar on Breed's, and now they are fixing the underpinnin', and next you 'll see what a raising they 'll invite the people to ! "

The instant the spot was named, all those eyes which had hitherto gazed at the vessels themselves, instead of searching for the object of their hostility, were turned on the green eminence which rose a little to the right of the village of Charlestown, and every doubt was at once removed by the discovery. The high, conical summit of Bunker Hill lay naked and unoccupied, as on the preceding day ; but on the extremity of a more humble ridge, which extended within a short distance of the water, a low bank of earth had been thrown up, for purposes which no military eye could mistake. This redoubt, small and inartificial as it was, commanded by its position the whole of the inner harbor of Boston, and even endangered, in some measure, the occupants of the town itself. It was the sudden appearance of this magical mound, as the mists of the morning had dispersed, which roused the slumbering seamen ; and it had already become the target of all the guns of the shipping in the bay. Amazement at the temerity of their countrymen held the townsmen silent, while Major Lincoln, and the few officers who stood nigh him, saw, at a glance, that this step on the part of their adversaries would bring the affairs of the leaguer to an instant crisis. In vain they turned their wondering looks on the neighboring eminence, and around the different points of the peninsula, in quest of those places of support with which soldiers generally intrench their defences. The husbandmen opposed to them had seized upon the point best calculated to annoy their foes, without regard to the consequences ; and in a few short hours, favored by the mantle of night, had thrown up their work with a dexterity that was only exceeded by their boldness. The truth flashed across the brain of Major Lincoln with his first glance, and he felt his cheeks glow as he remembered the low and indistinct murmurs which the night air had wafted to his ears,

13

and those unexplicable fancies which had even continued to
haunt him till dispersed by truth and the light of day. Motioning to Job to follow he left the hill with a hurried step ;
and when they gained the common, he turned and said
sternly, to his companion,—

"Fellow, you have been privy to this midnight work !"

"Job has enough to do in the day, without laboring in
the night, when none but the dead are out of their places
of rest," returned the lad, with a look of mental imbecility which immediately disarmed the resentment of the
other.

Lionel smiled as he again remembered his own weakness,
and repeated to himself,—

"The dead ! ay, these are the works of the living ; and
bold men are they who have dared to do the deed. But tell
me, Job,—for 't is in vain to attempt deceiving me any
longer,—what number of Americans did you leave on the
hill, when you crossed the Charles to visit the graves on
Copp's, the past night?"

"Both hills were crowded," returned the other ; "Breed's
with the people, and Copp's with the ghosts ; Job believes
the dead rose to see their children digging so nigh them !"

"'T is probable," said Lionel, who believed it wisest to
humor the wild conceits of the lad, in order to disarm his
cunning ; "but, though the dead are invisible, the living
may be counted."

"Job did count five hundred men, marching over the nose
of Bunker, by starlight, with their picks and spades ; and
then he stopped, for he forgot whether seven or eight hundred
came next."

"And after you ceased to count, did many others pass?"

"The Bay colony is n't so poorly off for men, that it can't
muster a thousand at a raising."

"But you had a master workman on the occasion ; was it
the wolf hunter of Connecticut?"

"There is no occasion to go from the province to find a
workman to lay out a cellar! Dickey Gridley is a Boston
boy !"

"Ah ! he is the chief ! We can have nothing to fear,

then, since the Connecticut woodsman is not at their head!"

"Do you think old Prescott, of Pepperel, will quit the hill while he has a kernel of powder to burn? No, no, Major Lincoln, Ralph himself ain't a stouter warrior; and you can't frighten Ralph!"

"But if they fire their cannon often, their small stock of ammunition will soon be consumed, and then they must unavoidably run."

Job laughed tauntingly, and with an appearance of high scorn, before he answered,—

"Yes, if the Bay-men were as dumb as the king's troops, and used such big guns! But the cannon of the colony want but little brimstone, and there's but a few of them. Let the rake-hellies go up to Breed's,—the people will teach them the law!"

Lionel had now obtained all he expected to learn from the simpleton concerning the force and condition of the Americans; and as the moments were too precious to be wasted in vain discourse, he bid the lad repair to his quarters that night, and left him. On entering his own lodgings, Major Lincoln shut himself up in his private apartment, and passed several hours in writing, and examining important papers. One letter, in particular, was written, read, torn, and re-written, five or six times, until at length, he placed his seal, and directed the important paper with a sort of carelessness that denoted his patience was exhausted by repeated trials. These documents were intrusted to Meriton, with orders to deliver them to their several addresses, unless countermanded before the following day; and the young man hastily swallowed a late and light breakfast. While shut up in his closet, Lionel had several times thrown aside his pen to listen, as the hum of the place penetrated to his retirement, and announced the excitement and bustle which pervaded the streets of the town. Having at length completed the task he had assigned himself, he caught up his hat, and took his way, with hasty steps, into the centre of the place.

Cannon were rattling over the rough pavements, followed

by ammunition-wagons, and officers and men of the artillery were seen in swift pursuit of their pieces. Aide-de-camps were riding furiously through the streets, charged with important messages; and here and there an officer might be seen issuing from his quarters, with a countenance in which manly pride struggled powerfully with inward dejection, as he caught the last glance of anguish, which followed his retiring form, from eyes that had been used to meet his own with looks of confidence and love. There was, however, but little time to dwell on these flitting glimpses of domestic woe, amid the general bustle and glitter of the scene. Now and then the strains of martial music broke up through the windings of the crooked avenues, and detachments of the troops wheeled by, on their way to the appointed place of embarkation. While Lionel stood a moment at the corner of a street, admiring the firm movement of a body of grenadiers, his eye fell on the powerful frame and rigid features of M'Fuse, marching at the head of his company with that gravity which regarded the accuracy of the step amongst the most important incidents of life. At a short distance from him was Job Pray, timing his paces to the tread of the soldier, and regarding the gallant show with stupid admiration, while his ear unconsciously drank the inspiriting music of their band. As this fine body of men passed on, it was immediately succeeded by a battalion in which Lionel instantly recognized the facings of his own regiment. The warm-hearted Polwarth led his forward files, and, waving his hand, he cried,—

"God bless you, Leo! God bless you! we shall make a fair stand-up fight of this; there is an end of all stag-hunting."

The notes of the horns rose above his voice, and Lionel could do no more than return his cordial salute; when, recalled to his purpose by the sight of his comrades, he turned, and pursued his way to the quarters of the commander-in-chief.

The gate of Province House was thronged with military men; some waiting for admittance, and others entering and departing with the air of those who were charged with the execution of matters of the deepest moment. The name of Major Lincoln was hardly announced before an aid appeared to conduct him into the presence of the governor, with a politeness and haste that several gentlemen, who had been in waiting for hours, deemed in a trifling degree unjust.

Lionel, however, having little to do with murmurs which he did not hear, followed his conductor, and was immediately ushered into the apartment, where a council of war had just closed its deliberations. On the threshold of its door he was compelled to give way to an officer, who was departing in haste, and whose powerful frame seemed bent a little in the intensity of thought, as his dark, military countenance lighted for an instant with the salutation he returned to the low bow of the young soldier. Around this chief a group of younger men immediately clustered, and as they departed in company, Lionel was enabled to gather, from their conversation, that they took their way for the field of battle. The room was filled with officers of high rank; though here and there was to be seen a man in civil attire, whose disappointed and bitter looks announced him to be one of those mandamus counsellors whose evil advice had hastened the mischief their wisdom could never repair. From out a small circle of these mortified civilians, the unpretending person of Gage advanced to meet Lionel, forming a marked contrast, by the simplicity of its dress, to the military splendor that was glittering around him.

" In what can I oblige Major Lincoln?'' he said, taking the young man by the hand cordially, as if glad to get rid of the troublesome counsellors he had so unceremoniously quitted.

" 'Wolfe's own' has just passed me, on its way to the boats, and I have ventured to intrude on your excellency to inquire if it were not time its major resumed his duty.''

A shade of thought was seated for a moment on the placid features of the general, and he then answered, with a friendly smile,—

" 'T will be no more than an affair of outposts, and must be quickly ended. But should I grant the request of every brave young man whose spirit is up to-day, it might cost his majesty's service the life of some officer that would make the purchase of the pile of earth too dear."

"But may I not be permitted to say, that the family of Lincoln is of the province, and its example should not be lost on such an occasion?"

"The loyalty of the colonies is too well represented here to need the sacrifice," said Gage, glancing his eyes carelessly at the expecting group behind him. "My council have decided on the officers to be employed, and I regret that Major Lincoln's name was omitted, since I know it will give him pain; but valuable lives are not to be lightly and unnecessarily exposed."

Lionel bowed in submission; and, after communicating the little he had gathered from Job Pray, he turned away, and found himself near another officer of high rank, who smiled as he observed his disappointed countenance, and, taking him by the arm, led him from the room, with a freedom suited to his fine figure and easy air.

"Then, like myself, Lincoln, you are not to battle for the king to-day," he said, on gaining the antechamber. "Howe has the luck of the occasion, if there can be luck in so vulgar an affair. But *allons;* accompany me to Copp's, as a spectator, since they deny us parts in the drama; and perhaps we may pick up materials for a pasquinade, though not for an epic."

"Pardon me, General Burgoyne," said Lionel, "if I view the matter with more serious eyes than yourself."

"Ah! I had forgot that you were a follower of Percy in the hunt of Lexington!" interrupted the other; "we will call it a tragedy, then, if it better suits your humor. For myself, Lincoln, I weary of these crooked streets and gloomy houses, and, having some taste for the poetry of nature, would have long since looked out upon the deserted fields of these husbandmen, had the authority, as well as the inclination, rested with me. But Clinton is joining us; he, too, is for Copp's, where we can all take a lesson in arms, by studying the manner in which Howe wields his battalions."

A soldier of middle age now joined them, whose stout frame, while it wanted the grace and ease of the gentleman who still held Lionel by the arm, bore a martial character to which the look of the quiet and domestic Gage was a stranger ; and, followed by their several attendants, the whole party immediately left the government-house to take their destined position on the eminence so often mentioned.

As they entered the street, Burgoyne relinquished the arm of his companion, and moved with becoming dignity by the side of his brother general. Lionel gladly availed himself of this alteration, to withdraw a little from the group, whose steps he followed at such a distance as permitted him to observe those exhibitions of feeling, on the part of the inhabitants, which the pride of the others induced them to overlook. Pallid and anxious female faces were gleaming out upon them from every window, while the roofs of the houses, and the steeples of the churches, were beginning to throng with more daring, and equally interested spectators. The drums no longer rolled along the narrow streets, though, occasionally, the shrill strain of a fife was heard from the water, announcing the movements of the troops to the opposite peninsula. Over all was heard the incessant roaring of the artillery, which, untired, had not ceased to rumble in the air since the appearance of light, until the ear, accustomed to its presence, had learnt to distinguish the lesser sounds we have recorded.

As the party descended into the lower passages of the town, it appeared deserted by everything having life ; the open windows and neglected doors betraying the urgency of the feelings which had called the population to situations more favorable for observing the approaching contest. This appearance of intense curiosity excited the sympathies of even the old and practised soldiers ; and, quickening their paces, the whole soon rose from among the gloomy edifices to the open and unobstructed view from the hill.

The whole scene now lay before them. Nearly in their front was the village of Charlestown, with its deserted streets, and silent roofs, looking like a place of the dead ; or, if the signs of life were visible within its open avenues, 't was merely some figure moving swiftly in the solitude, like one who hastened to quit the devoted spot. On the opposite point of the southeastern face of the peninsula, and at the distance of a thousand yards, the ground was already covered by masses of human beings in scarlet, with their arms glittering in a noonday sun. Between the two, though in the more immediate vicinity of the silent town, the rounded ridge already described rose abruptly from a flat that was bounded by the water, until, having attained an elevation of some fifty or sixty feet, it swelled gradually to the little crest, where was planted the humble object that had occasioned all this commotion. The meadows on the right were still peaceful and smiling, as in the most quiet days of the province, though the excited fancy of Lionel imagined that a sullen stillness lingered about the neglected kilns in their front, and over the whole landscape, that was in gloomy consonance with the approaching scene. Far on the left, across the waters of the Charles, the American camp had poured forth its thousands to the hills; and the whole population of the country, for many miles inland, had gathered to a point, to witness a struggle charged with the fate of their nation. Beacon Hill rose from out the appalling silence of the town of Boston, like a pyramid of living faces, with every eye fixed on the fatal point; and men hung along the yards of the shipping, or were suspended on cornices, cupolas, and steeples, in thoughtless security, while every other sense was lost in the absorbing interest of the sight. The vessels of war had hauled deep into the rivers, or, more properly, those narrow arms of the sea which formed the peninsula, and sent their iron missiles with unwearied industry across the low passage which alone opened the means of communication between the self-devoted yeoman on the hill, and their distant countrymen. While battalion landed after battalion on the point, cannon-balls from the battery of Copp's and the vessels of war were glancing up the natural glacis that surrounded the redoubt, burying themselves in its earthen parapet, or plunging with violence into the deserted sides of the loftier height which lay a few hundred yards in its rear; and the black and smoking bombs appeared to hover above the spot, as if pausing to select the places in which to plant their deadly combustibles.

Notwithstanding these appalling preparations and ceaseless annoyances, throughout that long and anxious morning, the stout husbandmen on the hill had never ceased their steady efforts to maintain, to the uttermost extremity, the post they had so daringly assumed. In vain the English exhausted every means to disturb their stubborn foes; the pick, the shovel, and the spade continued to perform their offices; and mound rose after mound, amidst the din and danger of the cannonade, steadily, and as well as if the fanciful conceits of Job Pray embraced their real objects, and the laborers were employed in the peaceful pursuits of their ordinary lives. This firmness, however, was not like the proud front which high training can impart to the most common mind; for, ignorant of the glare of military show; in the simple and rude vestments of their calling; armed with such weapons as they had seized from the hooks above their own mantels; and without even a banner to wave its cheering folds above their heads, they stood, sustained only by the righteousness of their cause, and those deep moral principles which they had received from their fathers, and which they intended this day should show were to be transmitted untarnished to their children. It was afterwards known that they endured their labors and their dangers even in want of that sustenance which is so essential to support animal spirits in moments of calmness and ease; while their enemies, on the point, awaiting the arrival of their latest bands, were securely devouring a meal, which to hundreds amongst them proved to be their last. The fatal instant now seemed approaching. A general movement was seen among the battalions of the British, who began to spread along the shore, under cover of the brow of the hill—the lingering boats having arrived with the rear of their detachments—and officers hurried from regiment to regiment with the final mandates of their chief. At this moment a body of Americans appeared on the crown of Bunker Hill, and descending swiftly by the road, disappeared in the meadows to the left of their own redoubt. This band was followed by others, who, like themselves, had broken through the dangers of the narrow pass, by braving the fire of the shipping, and who also hurried to join their comrades on the lowland. The British general determined at once to anticipate the arrival of further reinforcements, and gave forth the long-expected order to prepare for the attack.

CHAPTER XVI.

" Th' imperious Briton, on the well-fought ground,
  No cause for joy, or wanton triumph, found ;
  But saw, with grief, their dreams of conquest vain,
  Felt the deep wounds, and mourned their vet'rans slain."

HUMPHREYS.

T HE Americans had made a show, in the course of that fearful morning, of returning the fire of their enemies, by throwing a few shot from their light field-pieces, as if in mockery of the tremendous cannonade which they sustained. But as the moment of severest trial approached, the same awful stillness which had settled upon the deserted streets of Charlestown hovered around the redoubt. On the meadows, to its left, the recently arrived bands hastily threw the rails of two fences into one, and, covering the whole with the mown grass that surrounded them, they posted themselves along the frail defence, which answered no better purpose than to conceal their weakness from their adversaries. Behind this characteristic rampart, several bodies of husbandmen, from the neighboring provinces of New Hampshire and Connecticut, lay on their arms, in sullen expectation. Their line extended from the shore to the base of the ridge, where it terminated several hundred feet behind the works ; leaving a wide opening, in a diagonal direction, between the fence and an earthen breastwork, which ran a short distance down the declivity of the hill, from the northeastern angle of the redoubt. A few hundred yards in the rear of this rude disposition, the naked crest of Bunker Hill rose, unoccupied and undefended ; and the streams of the Charles and Mystic, sweeping around its base, approached so near each other as to blend the sounds of their rippling. It was across this low and narrow isthmus that the royal frigates poured a stream of fire that never ceased, while around it hovered the numerous parties of the undisciplined Americans, hesitating to attempt the dangerous passage.

In this manner Gage had, in a great degree, surrounded the devoted peninsula with his power; and the bold men, who had so daringly planted themselves under the muzzles of his cannon, were left, as already stated, unsupported, without nourishment, and with weapons from their own gun-hooks, singly to maintain the honor of their nation. Including men of all ages and conditions, there might have been two thousand of them; but, as the day advanced, small bodies of their countrymen, taking counsel of their feelings, and animated by the example of the old partisan of the woods, who crossed and recrossed the neck, loudly scoffing at the danger, broke through the fire of the shipping in time to join in the closing and bloody business of the hour.

On the other hand, Howe led more than an equal number of the chosen troops of his prince; and as boats continued to ply between the two peninsulas throughout the afternoon, the relative disparity continued undiminished to the end of the struggle. It was at this point in our narrative that, deeming himself sufficiently strong to force the defences of his despised foes, the arrangements immediately preparatory to such an undertaking were made in full view of the excited spectators. Notwithstanding the security with which the English general marshalled his warriors, he felt that the approaching contest would be a battle of no common incidents. The eyes of tens of thousands were fastened on his movements, and the occasion demanded the richest display of the pageantry of war.

The troops formed with beautiful accuracy, and the columns moved steadily along the shore, and took their assigned stations under cover of the brow of the eminence. Their force was in some measure divided; one moiety attempting the toilsome ascent of the hill, and the other moving along the beach, or in the orchards of the more level ground, towards the husbandmen on the meadows. The latter soon disappeared behind some fruit-trees and the brick-kilns just mentioned. The advance of the royal columns up the ascent was slow and measured, giving time to their field-guns to add their efforts to the uproar of the cannonade, which broke out with new fury as the battalions prepared to march. When each column arrived at the allotted point, it spread the gallant array of its glittering warriors under a bright sun.

"It is a glorious spectacle!" murmured the graceful chieftain by the side of Lionel, keenly alive to all the poetry of his alluring profession. "How exceeding soldier-like! and with what accuracy his 'first-arm ascends the hill,' towards his enemy!"

The intensity of his feelings prevented Major Lincoln from replying, and the other soon forgot that he had spoken, in the overwhelming anxiety of the moment. The advance of the British line, so beautiful and slow, resembled rather the ordered steadiness of a drill, than an approach to a deadly struggle. Their standards fluttered proudly above them; and there were moments when the wild music of their bands was heard rising on the air, and tempering the ruder sounds of the artillery. The young and thoughtless in their ranks turned their faces backward, and smiled exultingly, as they beheld steeples, roofs, masts, and heights, teeming with their thousands of eyes, bent on the show of their bright array. As the British lines moved in open view of the little redoubt, and began slowly to gather around its different faces, gun after gun became silent, and the curious artillerist, or tired seaman, lay extended on his heated piece, gazing in mute wonder at the spectacle. There was just then a minute when the roar of the cannonade seemed passing away like the rumbling of distant thunder.

"They will not fight, Lincoln," said the animated leader at the side of Lionel; "the military front of Howe has chilled the hearts of the knaves, and our victory will be bloodless!"

"We shall see, sir—we shall see!"

These words were barely uttered. when platoon after platoon, among the British, delivered its me, the blaze of musketry flashing swiftly around the brow of the hill, and was immediately followed by heavy volleys that ascended from the orchard. Still no answering sound was heard from the Americans, and the royal troops were soon lost to the eye, as they slowly marched into the white cloud which their own fire had alone created.

"They are cowed, by heavens—the dogs are cowed!" once more cried the gay companion of Lionel, "and Howe is within two hundred feet of them, unharmed!"

At that instant a sheet of flame glanced through the smoke, like lightning playing in a cloud, while at one report a thousand muskets were added to the uproar. It was not altogether fancy which led Lionel to imagine that he saw the smoky canopy of the hill to wave, as if the trained warriors it enveloped faltered before this close and appalling discharge; but, in another instant, the stimulating war-cry, and the loud shouts of the combatants, were borne across the strait to his ears, even amid the horrid din of the combat. Ten breathless minutes flew by like a moment of time, and the bewildered spectators on Copp's were still gazing intently on the scene, when a voice was raised among them, shouting,—

"Hurrah! let the rake-hellies go up to Breed's—the people will teach 'em the law!"

"Throw the rebel scoundrel from the hill! Blow him from the muzzle of a gun!" cried twenty soldiers in a breath.

"Hold!" exclaimed Lionel; "'t is a simpleton, an idiot, a fool!"

But the angry and savage murmurs as quickly subsided, and were lost in other feelings, as the bright-red lines of the royal troops were seen issuing from the smoke, waving and recoiling before the still vivid fire of their enemies.

"Ha!" said Burgoyne; "'t is some feint to draw the rebels from their hold!"

"'T is a palpable and disgraceful retreat!" muttered the stern warrior nigh him, whose truer eye detected at a glance

the discomfiture of the assailants. "'T is another base retreat before the rebels !"

"Hurrah !" shouted the reckless changeling again;
"there come the reg'lars out of the orchard, too ! See the
grannies skulking behind the kilns ! Let them go on to
Breed's—the people will teach 'em the law !"

No cry of vengeance preceded the act this time, but fifty
of the soldiery rushed, as by a common impulse, on their
prey. Lionel had not time to utter a word of remonstrance,
before Job appeared in the air, borne on the uplifted arms
of a dozen men, and at the next instant he was seen rolling
down the steep declivity, with a velocity that carried him to
the water's edge. Springing to his feet, the undaunted
changeling once more waved his hat in triumph, and shouted
forth again his offensive challenge. Then, turning, he
launched his canoe from its hiding-place among the adjacent
lumber, amid a shower of stones, and glided across the
strait; his little bark escaping unnoticed in the crowd of
boats that were rowing in all directions. But his progress
was watched by the uneasy eye of Lionel, who saw him
land and disappear, with hasty steps, in the silent streets of
the town.

While this trifling by-play was enacting, the great drama
of the day was not at a stand. The smoky veil, which
clung around the brow of the eminence, was lifted by the
air, and sailed heavily away to the southwest, leaving the
scene of the bloody struggle again open to the view. Lionel
witnessed the grave and meaning glances which the two
lieutenants of the king exchanged as they simultaneously
turned their glasses from the fatal spot, and, taking the one
proffered by Burgoyne, he read their explanation in the
numbers of the dead that lay profusely scattered in front of
the redoubt. At this instant, an officer from the field held
an earnest communication with the two leaders; when,
having delivered his orders, he hastened back to his boat,
like one who felt himself employed in matters of life and
death.

"It shall be done, sir," repeated Clinton, as the other
departed, his own honest brow sternly knit under high mar-

tial excitement. "The artillery have their orders, and the work will be accomplished without delay."

"This, Major Lincoln," cried his more sophisticated companion, "this is one of the trying duties of the soldier! To fight, to bleed, or even to die, for his prince, is his happy privilege; but it is sometimes his unfortunate lot to become the instrument of vengeance."

Lionel waited but a moment for an explanation; the flaming balls were soon seen taking their wide circuit in the air, and carrying their desolation among the close and inflammable roofs of the opposite town. In a very few minutes, a dense, black smoke arose from the deserted buildings, and forked flames played actively along the heated shingles, as though rioting in their unmolested possession of the place. He regarded the gathering destruction in painful silence; and, on bending his looks towards his companions, he fancied, notwithstanding the language of the other, that he read the deepest regret in the averted eye of him who had so unhesitatingly uttered the fatal mandate to destroy.

In scenes like these we are attempting to describe, hours appear to be minutes, and time flies as imperceptibly as life slides from beneath the feet of age. The disordered ranks of the British had been arrested at the base of the hill, and were again forming under the eyes of their leaders, with admirable discipline and extraordinary care. Fresh battalions, from Boston, marched with high military pride into the line, and everything betokened that a second assault was at hand. When the moment of stupid amazement which succeeded the retreat of the royal troops had passed, the troops and batteries poured out their wrath with tenfold fury on their enemies. Shot were incessantly glancing up the gentle acclivity, madly ploughing across its grassy surface, while black and threatening shells appeared to hover above the work, like the monsters of the air, about to swoop upon their prey.

Still all lay quiet and immovable within the low mounds of earth, as if none there had a stake in the issue of the bloody day. For a few moments only, the tall figure of an aged man was seen slowly moving along the summit of the rampart, calmly regarding the dispositions of the English general in the more distant part of his line, and after exchanging a few words with a gentleman, who joined him in his dangerous lookout, they disappeared together behind the grassy banks. Lionel soon detected the name of Prescott of Pepperel, passing through the crowd in low murmurs, and his glass did not deceive him when he thought, in the smaller of the two, he had himself descried the graceful person of the unknown leader of the "caucus."

All eyes were now watching the advance of the battalions, which once more drew nigh the point of contest. The heads of the columns were already in view of their enemies, when a man was seen swiftly ascending the hill from the burning town; he paused amid the peril, on the natural glacis, and swung his hat triumphantly, and Lionel even fancied he heard the exulting cry, as he recognized the ungainly form of the simpleton, before it plunged into the work.

The right of the British once more disappeared in the orchard, and the columns in front of the redoubt again opened with all the imposing exactness of their high discipline. Their arms were already glittering in a line with the green faces of the mound, and Lionel heard the experienced warrior at his side murmuring to himself,—

"Let him hold his fire, and he will go in at the point of the bayonet!"

But the trial was too great for even the practised courage of the royal troops. Volley succeeded volley, and in a few moments they had again curtained their ranks behind the misty screen produced by their own fire. Then came the terrible flash from the redoubt, and the eddying volumes from the adverse hosts rolled into one cloud, enveloping the combatants in its folds, as if to conceal their bloody work from the spectators. Twenty times, in the short space of as many minutes, Major Lincoln fancied he heard the incessant roll of the American musketry die away before the heavy and regular volleys of the troops; and then he thought the sounds of the latter grew more faint, and were given at longer intervals.

The result, however, was soon known. The heavy bank of smoke, which now even clung along the ground, was broken in fifty places ; and the disordered masses of the British were seen driven before their deliberate foes in wild confusion. The flashing swords of the officers in vain attempted to arrest the torrent, nor did the flight cease, with many of the regiments, until they had even reached their boats. At this moment a hum was heard in Boston, like the sudden rush of wind, and men gazed in each other's faces with undisguised amazement. Here and there a low sound of exultation escaped some unguarded lip, and many an eye gleamed with a triumph that could no longer be suppressed. Until this moment the feelings of Lionel had vacillated between the pride of country and his military spirit ; but, losing all other feelings in the latter sensation, he now looked fiercely about him, as if he would seek the man who dare exult in the repulse of his comrades. The poetic chieftain was still at his side, biting his nether lip in vexation ; but his more tried companion had suddenly disappeared. Another quick glace fell upon his missing form in the act of entering a boat at the foot of the hill. Quicker than thought Lionel was on the shore, crying, as he flew to the water's edge,—

"Hold ! for God's sake, hold ! Remember the 47th is in the field, and that I am its major ! "

"Receive him," said Clinton, with that grim satisfaction with which men acknowledge a valued friend in moments of great trial ; " and then row for your lives, or, what is of more value, for the honor of the British name."

The brain of Lionel whirled as the boat shot along its watery bed, but before it had gained the middle of the stream he had time to consider the whole of the appalling scene. The fire had spread from house to house, and the whole village of Charlestown, with its four hundred buildings, was just bursting into flames. The air seemed filled with whistling balls, as they hurtled above his head, and the black sides of the vessels of war were vomiting their sheets of flame with unwearied industry. Amid this tumult, the English general and his companions sprung to land. The former rushed into the disordered ranks, and by his presence and voice recalled the men of one regiment to their duty. But long and loud appeals to their spirit and their ancient fame were necessary to restore a moiety of their former confidence to men who had been thus rudely repulsed, and who now looked along their thinned and exhausted ranks, missing, in many instances, more than half the well-known countenances of their fellows. In the midst of the faltering troops stood their stern and unbending chief; but of all those gay and gallant youths, who followed in his train as he had departed from Province House that morning, not one remained, but in his blood. He alone seemed undisturbed in that disordered crowd; and his mandates went forth as usual, calm and determined. At length the panic, in some degree, subsided, and order was once more restored as the high-spirited and mortified gentlemen of the detachment regained their lost authority.

The leaders consulted together, apart, and the dispositions were immediately renewed for the assault. Military show was no longer affected, but the soldiers laid down all the useless implements of their trade, and many even cast aside their outer garments, under the warmth of a broiling sun, added to the heat of the conflagration, which began to diffuse itself along the extremity of the peninsula. Fresh companies were placed in the columns, and most of the troops were withdrawn from the meadows, leaving merely a few skirmishers to amuse the Americans who lay behind the fence. When each disposition was completed, the final signal was given to advance.

Lionel had taken post in his regiment, but marching on the skirt of the column, he commanded a view of most of the scene of battle. In his front moved a battalion, reduced to a handful of men in the previous assaults. Behind these came a party of the marine guards, from the shipping, led by their own veteran major; and next followed the dejected Nesbitt and his corps, amongst whom Lionel looked in vain for the features of the good-natured Polwarth. Similar columns marched on their right and left, encircling three sides of the redoubt by their battalions.

A few minutes brought him in full view of that humble and unfinished mound of earth, for the possession of which so much blood had that day been spilt in vain. It lay, as before, still as if none breathed within its bosom, though a terrific row of dark tubes were arrayed along its top, following the movements of the approaching columns, as the eyes of the imaginary charmers of our own wilderness are said to watch their victims. As the uproar of the artillery again grew fainter, the crash of falling streets, and the appalling sounds of the conflagration on their left, became more audible. Immense volumes of black smoke issued from the smouldering ruins, and, bellying outward, fold beyond fold, it overhung the work in a hideous cloud, casting its gloomy shadow across the place of blood.

A strong column was now seen ascending, as if from out the burning town, and the advance of the whole became quick and spirited. A low call ran through the platoons, to note the naked weapons of their adversaries, and it was followed by the cry of "To the bayonet! to the bayonet!"

"Hurrah! for the Royal Irish!" shouted M'Fuse, at the head of the dark column from the conflagration.

"Hurrah!" echoed a well-known voice from the silent mound; "let them come on to Breed's; the people will teach 'em the law!"

Men think at such moments with the rapidity of lightning, and Lionel had even fancied his comrades in possession of the work, when the terrible stream of fire flashed in the faces of the men in front.

"Push on with the ——th," cried the veteran major of marines,—"push on, or the 18th will get the honor of the day!"

"We cannot," murmured the soldiers of the ——th; "their fire is too heavy!"

"Then break, and let the marines pass through you!"

The feeble battalion melted away, and the warriors of the deep, trained to conflicts of hand to hand, sprang forward, with a loud shout, in their places. The Americans, ex-

hausted of their ammunition, now sunk sullenly back, a few
hurling stones at their foes in desperate indignation. The
cannon of the British had been brought to enfilade their short
breastwork, which was no longer tenable ; and as the columns approached closer to the low rampart, it became a
mutual protection to the adverse parties.

"Hurrah ! for the Royal Irish ! " again shouted M'Fuse,
rushing up the trifling ascent, which was but of little more
than his own height.

"Hurrah ! " repeated Pitcairn, waving his sword on another angle of the work, "the day 's our own ! "

One more sheet of flame issued out of the bosom of the
work, and all those brave men, who had emulated the ex-
amples of their officers, were swept away, as though a whirlwind had passed along. The grenadier gave his war-cry
once more, before he pitched headlong among his enemies ;
while Pitcairn fell back into the arms of his own child. The
cry of "Forward, 47th ! " rung through their ranks, and in
their turn this veteran battalion gallantly mounted the ram-
parts. In the shallow ditch Lionel passed the expiring
marine, and caught the dying and despairing look from his
eyes, and in another instant he found himself in the presence
of his foes. As company followed company into the defence-
less redoubt, the Americans sullenly retired by its rear, keeping the bayonets of the soldiers at bay with clubbed muskets
and sinewy arms. When the whole issued upon the open
ground, the husbandmen received a close and fatal fire from
the battalions, which were now gathering around them on
three sides. A scene of wild and savage confusion then succeeded to the order of the fight, and many fatal blows were
given and taken, the *mêlée* rendering the use of fire-arms
nearly impossible for several minutes.

Lionel continued in advance, pressing on the footsteps of
the retiring foe, stepping over many a lifeless body in his
difficult progress. Notwithstanding the hurry, and vast
disorder of the fray, his eye fell on the form of the graceful
stranger, stretched lifeless on the parched grass, which had
greedily drank his blood. Amid the ferocious cries and
fiercer passions of the moment, the young man paused, and

glanced his eyes around him with an expression that said he thought the work of death should cease. At this instant the trappings of his attire caught the glaring eyeballs of a dying yeoman, who exerted his wasting strength to sacrifice one more worthy victim to the *manes* of his countrymen. The whole of the tumultuous scene vanished from the senses of Lionel at the flash of the musket of this man, and he sunk beneath the feet of the combatants, insensible of further triumph, and of every danger.

The fall of a single officer, in such a contest, was a circumstance not to be regarded ; and regiments passed over him, without a single man stooping to inquire into his fate. When the Americans had disengaged themselves from the troops, they descended into the little hollow between the two hills, swiftly, and like a disordered crowd, bearing off most of their wounded, and leaving but few prisoners in the hands of their foes. The formation of the ground favored their retreat, as hundreds of bullets whistled harmlessly above their heads ; and by the time they gained the acclivity of Bunker, distance was added to their security. Finding the field lost, the men at the fence broke away in a body from their position, and abandoned the meadows ; the whole moving in confused masses behind the crest of the adjacent height. The shouting soldiery followed in their footsteps, pouring in fruitless and distant volleys ; but on the summit of Bunker their tired platoons were halted, and they beheld the throng move fearlessly through the tremendous fire that enfiladed the low pass, as little injured as though most of them bore charmed lives.

The day was now drawing to a close. With the disappearance of their enemies, the ships and batteries ceased their cannonade ; and presently not a musket was heard in that place where so fierce a contest had so long raged. The troops commenced fortifying the outward eminence, on which they rested, in order to maintain their barren conquest ; and nothing further remained for the achievement of the royal lieutenants but to go and mourn over their victory.

CHAPTER XVII.

"She speaks, yet she says nothing : what of that ?
Her eye discourses,—I will answer it."

Romeo and Juliet.

ALTHOUGH the battle of Bunker Hill was fought while the grass yet lay on the meadows, the heats of summer had been followed by the nipping frosts of November; the leaf had fallen in its hour, and the tempests and biting colds of February had succeeded, before Major Lincoln left that couch where he had been laid, when carried, in total helplessness, from the fatal heights of the peninsula. Throughout the whole of that long period, the hidden bullet had defied the utmost skill of the British surgeons; nor could all their science and experience embolden them to risk cutting certain arteries and tendons in the body of the heir of Lincoln, which were thought to obstruct the passage to that obstinate lead, which, all agreed, alone impeded the recovery of the unfortunate sufferer. This indecision was one of the penalties that poor Lionel paid for his greatness; for had it been Meriton who lingered, instead of his master, it is quite probable the case would have been determined at a much earlier hour. At length, a young and enterprising leech, with the world before him, arrived from Europe, who, possessing greater skill or more effrontery (the effects are sometimes the same) than his fellows, did not hesitate to decide at once on the expediency of an operation. The medical staff of the army sneered at this bold innovator, and at first were content with such silent testimonials of their contempt. But when the friends of the patient, listening, as usual, to the whisperings of hope, consented that the confident man of probes should use his instruments, the voices of his contemporaries became not only loud, but clamorous. There was a day or two when even the watch-worn and jaded subalterns of the army forgot the dangers and hardships of the siege, to attend with demure and instructed countenances to the unintelligible jargon of the "Medici" of their camp; and men grew pale, as they listened, who had never been known to exhibit any symptoms of the disgraceful passion before their more acknowledged enemies. But when it became known that the ball was safely extracted, and the patient was pronounced convalescent, a calm succeeded, that was much more portentous to the human race than the preceding tempest; and in a short time the daring practitioner was universally acknowledged to be the founder of a new theory. The degrees of M.D. were showered upon his honored head from half the learned bodies in Christendom, while many of his enthusiastic admirers and imitators became justly entitled to the use of the same magical symbols, as annexments to their patronymics, with the addition of the first letter of the alphabet. The ancient reasoning was altered to suit the modern facts, and before the war was ended, some thousands of the servants of the crown, and not a few of the patriotic colonists, were thought to have died, scientifically, under the favor of this important discovery.

We might devote a chapter to the minute promulgation of such an event, had not more recent philosophers long since upset the practice (in which case the theory seems to fall, as a matter of course), by the renewal of those bold adventures, which teach us, occasionally, something new in the anatomy of man; as in the science of geography, the sealers of New England have been able to discover Terra Australia, where Cook saw nothing but water; or Parry finds veins and arteries in that part of the American continent which had so long been thought to consist of worthless cartilage.

Whatever may have been the effects of the operation on the surgical science, it was healthful, in the first degree, to its subject. For seven weary months Lionel lay in a state in which he might be said to exist, instead of live, but little conscious of surrounding occurrences ; and, happily for him-self, nearly insensible to pain and anxiety. At moments the flame of life would apparently glimmer like the dying lamp, and then both the fears and hopes of his attendants were disappointed, as the patient dropped again into that state of apathy in which so much of his time was wasted. From an erroneous opinion of his master's sufferings, Meri-ton had been induced to make a free use of soporifics, and no small part of Lionel's insensibility was produced by an excessive use of that laudanum, for which he was indebted to the mistaken humanity of his valet. At the moment of the operation, the adventurous surgeon had availed himself of the same stupefying drug, and many days of dull, heavy, and alarming apathy succeeded, before his system, finding itself relieved from its unnatural inmate, resumed its health-ful functions, and began to renew its powers. By a singular good fortune, his leech was too much occupied by his own novel honors, to follow up his success, *secundum artem*, as a great general pushes a victory to the utmost ; and that matchless doctor, Nature, was permitted to complete the cure.

When the effects of the anodynes had subsided, the pa-tient found himself entirely free from uneasiness, and dropped into a sweet and refreshing sleep that lasted for many hours without interruption. He awoke a new man ; with his body renovated, his head clear, and his recollec-tions, though a little confused and wandering, certainly better than they had been since the moment when he fell in the *mêlée* on Breed's. This restoration to all the nobler properties of life occurred about the tenth hour of the day ; and as Lionel opened his eyes, with understanding in their expression, they fell upon a cheerfulness which a bright sun, assisted by the dazzling light of the masses of snow without, had lent to every object in his apartment. The curtains of the windows had been opened, and every article of the fur-niture was arranged with a neatness that manifested the studied care which presided over his illness. In one corner, it is true, Meriton had established himself in an easy chair, with an arrangement of attitude which spoke more in favor of his consideration for the valet than the master, while he was comforting his faculties for a night of watchfulness, by the sweet, because stolen, slumbers of the morning.

A flood of recollections broke into the mind of Lionel together, and it was some little time before he could so far separate the true from the imaginary, as to attain a tolerably clear comprehension of what had occurred in the little age he had been dozing. Raising himself on one elbow, without difficulty, he passed his hand once or twice slowly over his face, and then trusted his voice in a summons to his man. Meriton started at the well-known sounds, and after diligently rubbing his eyes, like one who awakes by surprise, he arose and gave the customary reply.

"How now, Meriton!" exclaimed Major Lincoln; "you sleep as sound as a recruit on post, and I suppose you have been stationed like one, with twice-told orders to be vigilant."

The valet stood with open mouth, as if ready to devour his master's words with more senses than one ; and then, as Lionel concluded, passed his hands in quick succession over his eyes, as before, though with a very different object, ere he answered,—

"Thank God, sir, thank God! you look like yourself once more, and we shall live again as we used to. Yes, yes, sir ; you'll do now,—you'll do this time. That's a miracle of a man, is the great Lon'non surgeon! and now we shall go back to Soho, and live like civilizers. Thank God, sir, thank God! you smile again ; and I hope if anything should go wrong, you'll soon be able to give me one of those awful looks that I am so used to, and which makes my heart jump into my mouth, when I know I've been forgetful!"

The poor fellow, in whom long service had created a deep attachment to his master, which had been greatly increased by the solicitude of a nurse, was compelled to cease his unconnected expressions of joy, while he actually wept. Lionel was too much affected by this evidence of feeling, to continue the dialogue, for several minutes; during which time he employed himself in putting on part of his attire, assisted by the gulping valet, when, drawing his *robe-de-chambre* around his person, he leaned on the shoulder of his man, and took the seat which the other had so recently quitted.

"Well, well, Meriton, that will do," said Lionel, giving a deep hem, as though his breathing was obstructed; "that will do, silly fellow; I trust I shall live to give you many a frown, and some few guineas, yet. I have been shot, I know——"

"Shot, sir!" interrupted the valet, "you have been downright and unlawfully murdered! you were first shot, and then baggoneted, and after that a troop of horse rode over you. I had it from one of the Royal Irish, who lay by your side the whole time, and who now lives to tell of it; a good honest fellow is Terence; and if such a thing was possible that your honor was poor enough to need a pension, he would cheerfully swear to your hurts at the King's Bench, or War Office; Bridewell, or St. James'; it's all one to the like of him."

"I dare say, I dare say," said Lionel, smiling, though he mechanically passed his hand over his body, as his valet spoke of the bayonet; "but the poor fellow must have transferred some of his own wounds to my person; I own the bullet, but object to the cavalry and the steel."

"No, sir, *I* own the bullet, and it shall be buried with me in my dressing-box, at the head of my grave," said Meriton, exhibiting the flattened bit of lead, exultingly, in the palm of his hand; "it has been in my pocket these thirteen days, after tormenting your honor for six long months, hid in the what-d' ye-call-'em muscles, away behind the thingumy artery. But snug as it was, we got it out! He is a miracle, is the great Lon'non surgeon!"

Lionel reached over to his purse, which Meriton had placed regularly on the table, each morning, in order to remove it again at night, and, dropping several guineas in the hand of his valet, said,——

"So much lead must need some gold to sweeten it. Put up the unseemly thing, and never let me see it again!"

Meriton coolly took the opposing metals, and after glancing his eyes at the guineas, with a readiness that embraced their amount in a single look, he dropped them carelessly into one pocket, while he restored the lead to the other with an exceeding attention to its preservation. He then turned his hand to the customary duties of his station.

"I remember well to have been in a fight on the heights of Charlestown, even to the instant when I got my hurt," continued his master; "and I even recollect many things that have occurred since; a period which appears like a whole life to me. But after all, Meriton, I believe my ideas have not been remarkable for their clearness."

"Lord, sir, you have talked to me, and scolded me, and praised me, a hundred and a hundred times over again ; but you have never scolded as sharp like as you can, nor have you ever spoken and looked as bright as you do this morning !"

"I am in the house of Mrs. Lechmere," again continued Lionel, examining the room ; "I know this apartment and those private doors too well to be mistaken."

"To be sure you are, sir ; Madam Lechmere had you brought here from the field to her own house, and one of the best it is in Boston, too; and I expect that madam would somehow lose her title to it, if anything serious should happen to us !"

"Such as a bayonet, or a troop of horse ! but why do you fancy any such thing?"

"Because, sir, when madam comes here of an afternoon, which she did daily, before she sickened, I heard her very often say to herself, if you should be so unfortunate as to die, there would be an end to all her hopes of her house."

"Then it is Mrs. Lechmere who visits me daily," said Lionel, thoughtfully ; "I have recollections of a female form hovering around my bed, though I had supposed it more youthful and active than that of my aunt."

"And you are quite right, sir ; you have had such a nurse the whole time as is seldom to be met with. For making a posset or a gruel, I 'll match her with the oldest woman in the wards of Guy's ; and, to my taste, the best barkeeper at the Lon'non is a fool to her at a negus."

"These are high accomplishments, indeed! and who may be their mistress?"

"Miss Agnus, sir; a rare good nurse is Miss Agnus Danforth! though in point of regard to the troops, I should n't presume to call her at all distinguishable."

"Miss Danforth," repeated Lionel, dropping his expecting eyes, in disappointment, from the face of Meriton to the floor; "I hope she has not sustained all this trouble on my account alone? There are women enough in the establishment; one would think such offices might be borne by the domestics; in short, Meriton, was she without an assistant in all these little kindnesses?"

"*I* helped her, you know, sir, all I could; though my neguses never touch the right spot, like Miss Agnus'."

"One would think, by your account, that I have done little else than guzzle port wine for six months," said Lionel, pettishly.

"Lord, sir, you would n't drink a thimbleful from a glass, often; which I always took for a bad symptom; for I'm certain 't was no fault of the liquor, if it was n't drunk."

"Well, enough of your favorite beverage! I sicken at the name already. But, Meriton, have not others of my friends called to inquire after my fate?"

"Certainly, sir; the commander-in-chief sends an aid or a servant every day; and Lord Percy left his card more than—"

"Poh! these are calls of courtesy. But I have relatives in Boston—Miss Dynevor, has she left the town?"

"No, sir," said the valet, very coolly resuming the duty of arranging the vials on the night-table; "she is not much of a moving body, is that Miss Cecil."

"She is not ill, I trust?" demanded Lionel.

"Lord, it goes through me, part joy and part fear, to hear you speak again so quick and brisk, sir! No, she is n't downright ailing, but she has n't the life and knowledge of things, as her cousin, Miss Agnus."

"Why do you think so, fellow?"

"Because, sir, she is mopy, and don't turn her hand to any of the light lady's work in the family. I have seen her sit in that very chair, where you are now, sir, for hours together, without moving; unless it was some nervous start when you groaned, or breathed a little upward through your honor's nose. I have taken it into my consideration, sir, that she poetizes; at all events, she likes what I calls quietude."

"Indeed!" said Lionel, pursuing the conversation with an interest that would have struck a more observant man as remarkable. "What reason have you for suspecting Miss Dynevor of manufacturing rhymes?"

"Because, sir, she has often a bit of paper in her hand; and I have seen her read the same thing over and over again, till I'm sure she must know it by heart; which your poetizers always do with what they writes."

"Perhaps it was a letter?" cried Lionel, with a quickness that caused Meriton to drop a vial he was dusting, at the expense of its contents.

"Bless me, Master Lionel, how strong, and like old times you speak!"

"I believe I am amazed to find you know so much of the divine art, Meriton."

"Practice makes perfect, you know, sir," said the simpering valet. "I can't say I ever did much in that way, though I wrote some verses on a pet pig, as died down at Ravenscliffe, the last time we was there; and I got considerable eclaw for a few lines on a vase which Lady Bab's woman broke one day, in a scuffle, when the foolish creature said as I wanted to kiss her; though all that knows me, knows that I needn't break vases to get kisses from the like of her!"

"Very well," said Lionel; "some day, when I am stronger, I may like to be indulged with a perusal. Go now, Meriton, to the larder, and look about you; I feel the symptoms of returning health grow strong upon me."

The gratified valet instantly departed, leaving his master to the musings of his own busy fancy.

Several minutes passed away before the young man raised his head from the hand that supported it, and then it was only done when he thought he heard a light footstep near him. His ear had not deceived him, for Cecil Dynevor herself stood within a few feet of the chair, which concealed, in a great measure, his person from her view. It was apparent, by her attitude and her tread, that she expected to find the sick where she had seen him last, and where, for so many dreary months, his listless form had been stretched in apathy. Lionel followed her graceful movements with his eyes, and as the airy band of her morning-cap waved aside at her own breathing, he discovered the unnatural paleness that was seated on her speaking features. But when she drew the folds of the bed-curtains, and missed the invalid, thought is not quicker than the motion with which she turned her light person towards the chair. Here she encountered the eyes of the young man, beaming on her with delight, and expressing all that animation and intelligence to which they had so long been strangers. Yielding to the surprise and the gush of her feelings Cecil flew to his feet, and clasping one of his extended hands in both her own, she cried,—

"Lionel, dear Lionel, you are better! God be praised! you look well again!"

Lionel gently extricated his hand from the warm and unguarded pressure of her soft fingers, and drew forth a paper which she had unconsciously committed to his keeping.

"This, dearest Cecil," he whispered to the blushing maiden, "this is my own letter, written when I knew my life to be at imminent hazard, and speaking the purest thoughts of my heart. Tell me, then, it has not been thus kept for nothing?"

Cecil dropped her face between her hands for a moment, in burning shame, and then, as all the emotions of the moment crowded around her heart, she yielded to them as a woman, and burst into a paroxysm of tears. It is needless to dwell on those consoling and seducing speeches of the young man, which soon succeeded in luring his companion not only from her sobs, but even from her confusion, and permitted her to raise her beautiful countenance to his ardent gaze, bright and confiding as his fondest wishes could have made it.

The letter of Lionel was too direct, not to save her pride, and it had been too often perused for a single sentence to be soon forgotten. Besides, Cecil had watched over his couch too fondly and too long, to indulge in any of those little coquetries which are sometimes met with in similar scenes. She said all that an affectionate, generous, and modest female would say on such an occasion; and it is certain that, well as Lionel looked on waking, the little she uttered had the effect to improve his appearance tenfold.

"And you received my letter on the morning after the battle?" said Lionel, leaning fondly over her, as she still, unconsciously, kneeled by his side.

"Yes—yes; it was your order that it should be sent to me only in case of your death; but for more than a month you were numbered as among the dead by us all. O! what a month was that!"

"'T is past, my sweet friend, and, God be praised! I may now look forward to health and happiness."

"God be praised, indeed!" murmured Cecil, the tears again rushing to her eyes. "I would not live that month over again, Lionel, for all that this world can offer!"

"Dearest Cecil," he replied, "I can only repay this kindness and suffering on my account, by shielding you from the rude contact of the world, even as your father would protect you, were he again in being."

She looked up in his face with all the soul of a woman's confidence beaming in her eyes, as she answered,—

"You will, Lincoln, I know you will; you have sworn it, and I should be a wretch to doubt you."

He drew her unresisting form into his arms, and folded her to his bosom. In another moment, a noise, like one ascending the stairs, was heard through the open door of the room, when all the feelings of her sex rushed to the breast of Cecil. She sprung on her feet, and, hardly allowing time to the delighted Lionel to note the burning tints that suffused her whole face, she darted from the room with the rapidity and lightness of an antelope.

CHAPTER XVIII.

"Dead, for a ducat, dead."

Hamlet.

WHILE Lionel was in the confusion of feeling produced by the foregoing scene, the intruder, after a prelude of singularly heavy and loud steps, on the floor, as if some one approached on crutches, entered by a door opposite to the one through which Cecil had so suddenly vanished. At the next moment the convalescent was saluted by the full cheerful voice of his visitor,—

"God bless you, Leo, and bless the whole of us, for we need it!" cried Polwarth, eagerly advancing to grasp the extended hands of his friend. "Meriton has told me that you have got the true mark of health—a good appetite—at last. I should have broken my neck in hurrying up to wish you joy on the moment, but I just stepped into the kitchen, without Mrs. Lechmere's leave, to show her cook how to broil the steak they are warming through for you—a capital thing after a long nap, and full of nutriment—God bless you, my dear Leo; the look of your bright eye is as stimulating to my spirits as a West India pepper is to the stomach."

Polwarth ceased shaking the hands of his reanimated friend, as with a husky voice he concluded, and turning aside under the pretence of reaching a chair, he dashed his hand before his eyes, gave a loud hem, and took his seat in silence. During the performance of this evolution, Lionel had leisure to observe the altered person of the captain. His form, though still rotund and even corpulent, was much reduced in dimensions, while, in the place of one of those lower members, with which nature furnishes the human race, he had been compelled to substitute a leg of wood, somewhat inartificially made, and roughly shod with iron. This last sad alteration, in particular, attracted the look of Major Lincoln, who continued to gaze at it with glistening eyes, for some time after the other had established himself, to his entire satisfaction, in one of the cushioned seats of the apartment.

"I see my frame-work has caught your eye, Leo," said Polwarth, raising the wooden substitute with an air of affected indifference, and tapping it lightly with his cane. "'T is not as gracefully cut, perhaps, as if it had been turned from the hands of Master Phidias ; but in a place like Boston, it is an invaluable member, inasmuch as it knows neither hunger nor cold."

"The Americans, then, press the town," said Lionel, glad to turn the subject, "and maintain the siege with vigor?"

"They have kept us in horrible bodily terror, ever since the shallow waters towards the main-land have been frozen, and opened a path directly into the heart of the place. Their Virginian generalissimo, Washington, appeared a short time after the affair over on the other peninsula—a cursed business that, Leo!—and with him came all the trimmings of a large army. Since that time they have worn a more military front, though little else has been done, excepting an occasional skirmish, but cooping us up, like so many uneasy pigeons, in our cage."

"And Gage chafes not at the confinement?"

"Gage!—we sent him off like the soups, months ago. No, no—the moment the ministry discovered that we had come to our forks, in good earnest, they chose Black Billy to preside ; and now we stand at bay with the rebels, who have already learnt that our leader is not a child at the grand entertainment of war."

"Yes, seconded by such men as Clinton and Burgoyne, and supported by the flower of our troops, the position can be easily maintained."

" No position can be easily maintained, Major Lincoln,"
said Polwarth, promptly, " in the face of starvation, both
internal and external."

" And is the case so desperate ? "

" Of that you shall judge yourself, my friend. When
Parliament shut the port of Boston, the colonies were filled
with grumblers ; and now we have opened it, and would be
glad to see their supplies, the devil a craft enters the harbor
willingly ! Ah ! Meriton, you have the steak, I see ; put
it here, where your master can have it at his elbow, and
bring another plate ; I breakfasted but indifferently well
this morning. So we are thrown completely on our own
resources. But the rebels do not let us enjoy even them in
peace. This thing is done to a turn—how charmingly the
blood follows the knife ! They have gone so far as to equip
privateers, who cut off our necessaries ; and he is a lucky
man who can get a meal like the one before us."

" I had not thought the power of the Americans could
have forced matters to such a pass."

" What I have mentioned, though of vital importance, is
not half. If a man is happy enough to obtain the materials
for a good dish—you should have rubbed an onion over
these plates, Mr. Meriton—he don't know where he is to
find fuel to cook it withal."

" Looking at the comforts with which I am surrounded,
my good friend, I cannot but fancy your imagination
heightens the distress."

" Fancy no such silly thing ; for when you get abroad,
you will find it but too exact. In the article of food, if we
are not reduced, like the men of Jerusalem, to eating one
another, we are, half the time, rather worse off, being
entirely destitute of wholesome nutriment. Let but an
unlucky log float by the town among the ice, and go forth
and witness the struggling and skirmishing between the
Yankees and our frozen fingers for its possession, and you
will become a believer ! 'T will be lucky if the water-soaked
relic of some wharf should escape without a cannonade ! I
don't tell you these things as a grumbler, Leo ; for, thank
God, I have only half as many toes as other men, to keep

warmth in ; and as for eating, a little will suffice for me, now my corporeal establishment is so sadly reduced."

Lionel paused in melancholy, as his friend attempted to jest at his misfortune, and then, by a very natural transition, for a young man in his situation, he proudly exclaimed,—

"But we gained the day, Polwarth! and drove the rebels from their intrenchments, like chaff before a whirlwind!"

"Humph!" ejaculated the captain, laying his wooden leg carefully over its more valuable fellow, and regarding it ruefully, while he spoke ; "had we made a suitable use of the bounties of nature, and turned their position, instead of running into the jaws of the beast, many might have left the field better supplied with appurtenances than are some among us at present. But dark William loves a brush, they say, and he enjoyed it, on that occasion, to his heart's content!"

"He must be grateful to Clinton for his timely presence!"

"Does the devil delight in martyrdom? The presence of a thousand rebels would have been more welcome, even at that moment ; nor has he smiled once on his good-natured assistant, since he thrust himself, in that unwelcome manner, between him and his enemy. We had enough to think of, with our dead and wounded, and in maintaining our conquest, or something more than black looks and unkind eyes would have followed the deed."

"I fear to inquire into the fortunes of the field, so many names of worth must be numbered in the loss."

"Twelve or fifteen hundred men are not to be knocked on the head out of such an army, and all the clever fellows escape. Gage, I know, calls the loss something like eleven hundred ; but, after vaporing so much about the Yankees, their prowess is not to be acknowledged in its bloom at once. A man seldom goes on one leg, but he halts a little at first, as I can say from experience—put down thirteen, Leo, as a medium, and you 'll not miscalculate largely ; yes, indeed, there were some brave young men amongst them! Those rascally light-footed gentry, that I gave up so oppor-

tunely, were finely peppered; and there were the Fusileers
had hardly men enough left to saddle their goat!"[1]

"And the marines! they must have suffered heavily; I
saw Pitcairn fall before me," said Lionel, speaking with
hesitation. "I greatly fear our old comrade, the grenadier,
did not escape with better fortune."

"Mac!" exclaimed Polwarth, casting a furtive glance at
his companion. "Ay, Mac was not as lucky in that business as he was in Germany—he-em—Mac—had an obstinate
way with him, Leo; a damned obstinate fellow in all military matters; but as generous a heart, and as free in sharing
a mess-bill as any man in his majesty's service! I crossed
the river in the same boat with him, and he entertained us
with his queer thoughts on the art of war. According to
Mac's notions of things, the grenadiers were to do all the
fighting—a damned odd way with him had Mac!"

"There are few of us without peculiarities, and I could
wish that none of them were more offensive than the trifling
prejudices of poor Dennis M'Fuse."

"Yes, yes," added Polwarth, hemming violently, as if
determined to clear his throat at every hazard; "he was a
little opinionated in trifles, such as a knowledge of war, and
matters of discipline; but in all important things as tract-
able as a child. He loved to joke, but it was impossible to
have a less difficult or more unpretending palate in one's
mess! The greatest evil I can wish him is breath in his
body, to live and enjoy, in these hard times, when things
become excellent by comparison, the sagacious provision
which his own ingenuity contrived to secure out of the
cupidity of our ancient landlord, Mister Seth Sage."

"Then that notable scheme did not entirely fall to the
ground," said Lionel, with a feverish desire to change the
subject once more. "I had thought the Americans were
too vigilant to admit the intercourse."

[1] This regiment in consequence of some tradition, kept a goat, with
gilded horns, as a memorial. Once a year it celebrated a festival, in
which the bearded quadruped acted a conspicuous part. In the battle
of Bunker Hill, the corps was distinguished alike for its courage and
its losses.

"Seth has been too sagacious to permit them to obstruct it. The prices acted like a soporific on his conscience, and by using your name, I believe, he has formed some friend of sufficient importance amongst the rebels to protect him in his trade. His supplies made their appearance twice a week as regularly as the meats follow the soups in a well-ordered banquet."

"You then can communicate with the country, and the country with the town ! Although Washington may wink at the proceeding, I should fear the scowl of Howe."

"Why, in order to prevent suspicions of unfair practices, and at the same time to serve the cause of humanity, so the explanation reads, you know, our sapient host has seen fit to employ a fool as his agent in the intercourse ; a fellow, as you may remember, of some notoriety ; a certain simpleton, who calls himself Job Pray."

Lionel continued silent for many moments, during which time his recollections began to revive, and his thoughts glanced over the scenes that occurred in the first months of his residence in Boston. It is quite possible that a painful, though still general and indefinite feeling mingled with his musings ; for he evidently strove to expel some such unwelcome intruder, as he resumed the discourse with a strong appearance of forced gayety.

"Ay, ay, I well remember poor Job,—a fellow, once seen and known, not easily to be forgotten. He used, of old, to attach himself greatly to my person, but I suppose, like the rest of the world, I am neglected when in retirement."

"You do the lad injustice ; he not only makes frequent inquiries, after his slovenly manner, I acknowledge, concerning your condition, but sometimes he seems better informed in the matter than myself, and can requite my frequent answers to his questions, by imparting, instead of receiving, intelligence of your improvement ; more especially since the ball has been extracted.

"That should be very singular, too," said Lionel, with a still more thoughtful brow.

"Not so very remarkable, Leo, as one would at first imagine," interrupted his companion ; "the lad is not wanting in sagacity, as he manifested by his choice of dishes at our old mess-table. Ah! Leo, Leo, we may see many a discriminating palate, but where shall we go to find another such a friend! one who could eat and joke, drink and quarrel with a man, in a breath, like poor Dennis, who is gone from among us forever! There was a piquancy about poor Mac, that acted on the dulness of life like condiments on the natural appetite!"

Meriton, who was diligently brushing his master's coat, an office that he performed daily, though the garment had not been worn in so long a period, stole a glance at the averted eye of the major, and understanding its expression to indicate a determined silence, he ventured to maintain the discourse in his own unworthy person.

"Yes, sir, a nice gentleman was Captain M'Fuse, and one as fought as stoutly for the king as any gentleman in the army, all agrees. It was a thousand pities such a fine figure of a man had n't a better idea of dress; it is n't all, sir, as is gifted in that way. But everybody says he's a detrimental loss, though there's some officers in town who consider so little how to wear their ornaments, that if they were to be shot, I am sure no one would miss them."

"Ah! Meriton," cried the full-hearted Polwarth, "I see you are a youth of more observation than I had suspected. Mac had all the seeds of a man in him, though some of them might not have come to maturity. There was a flavor in his humor, that served as a relish to every conversation in which he mingled. Did you serve the poor fellow up in handsome style, Meriton, for his last worldly exhibition?"

"Yes, indeed, sir; we gave him as ornamental a funeral as can be seen out of Lon'non. Besides the Royal Irish, all the grenadiers was out; that is, all as was n't hurt, which was near half of them. As I knowed the regard Master Lionel had for the captain, I dressed him with my own hands; I trimmed his whiskers, sir, and altered his hair more in front; and seeing that his honor was getting a little gray, I threw on a sprinkling of powder, and as handsome a corpse was Captain M'Fuse as any gentleman in the army, let the other be who he may!"

The eyes of Polwarth twinkled, and he blew his nose with a noise not unlike the sound of a clarion, ere he rejoined,—

"Yes, yes, time and hardships had given a touch of frost to the head of the poor fellow; but it is a consolation to know that he died like a soldier, and not by the hands of that vulgar butcher, Nature; and that, being dead, he was removed according to his deserts!"

"Indeed, sir," said Meriton, with a solemnity worthy of the occasion, "we gave him a great procession; a great deal can be made out of his majesty's uniform, on such festivities, and it had a wonderful look about it! Did you speak, sir?"

"Yes," added Lionel, impatiently; "remove the cloth; and go, inquire if there be letters for me."

The valet submissively obeyed, and after a short pause the dialogue was resumed by the gentlemen on subjects of a less painful nature.

As Polwarth was exceedingly communicative, Lionel soon obtained a very general, and, to do the captain suitable justice, an extremely impartial account of the situation of the hostile forces, as well as of all the leading events that had transpired since the day of Breed's. Once or twice the invalid ventured an allusion to the spirit of the rebels, and to the unexpected energy they had discovered; but Polwarth heard them all in silence, answering only by a melancholy smile, and, in the last instance, by a significant gesture towards his unnatural supporter. Of course, after this touching acknowledgment of his former error, his friend waived the subject for others less personal.

He learned that the royal general maintained his hardly-earned conquest on the opposite peninsula, where he was as effectually beleaguered, however, as in the town of Boston itself. In the meantime, while the war was conducted in earnest at the point where it commenced, hostilities had broken out in every one of those colonies, south of the St. Lawrence and the Great Lakes, where the presence of the royal troops invited an appeal to force. At first, while the colonists acted under the impulses of the high enthusiasm of a sudden rising, they had been everywhere successful. A general army had been organized, as already related, and divisions were employed at different points to effect those conquests which, in that early state of the struggle, were thought to be important to the main result. But the effects of their imperfect means and divided power were already becoming visible. After a series of minor victories, Montgomery had fallen in a most desperate and unsuccessful attempt to carry the impregnable fortress of Quebec; and, ceasing to be the assailants, the Americans were gradually compelled to collect their resources to meet that mighty effort of the crown which was known to be not far distant. As thousands of their fellow-subjects in the mother country manifested a strong repugnance to the war, the ministry so far submitted to the influence of that free spirit, which first took deep root in Britain, as to turn their eyes to those States of Europe, who made a trade in human life, in quest of mercenaries to quell the temper of the colonists. In consequence, the fears of the timid amongst the Americans were excited by rumors of the vast hordes of Russians and Germans, who were to be poured into their country, with the fell intent to make them slaves. Perhaps no step of their enemies had a greater tendency to render them odious in the eyes of the Americans, than this measure of introducing foreigners to decide a quarrel purely domestic. So long as none but men who had been educated in those acknowledged principles of justice and law, known to both people, were admitted to the contest, there were visible points, common to each, which might render the struggle less fierce, and in time lead to a permanent reconciliation. But they reasoned not inaptly, when they asserted, that in a contest rendered triumphant by slaves, nothing but abject submission could ensue to the conquered. It was like throwing away the scabbard, and, by abandoning reason, submitting the result to the sword alone. In addition to the estrangement these measures were gradually increasing between the people of the mother country and the colonies, must be added the change it produced amongst the latter in their habits of regarding the person of their prince.

During the whole of the angry discussion, and the recriminations, which preceded the drawing of blood, the colonists had admitted, to the fullest extent, not only in their language, but in their feelings, that fiction of the British law, which says "The king can do no wrong." Throughout the wide extent of an empire, on which the sun was never known to set, the English monarch could boast of no subjects more devoted to his family and person, than the men who now stood in arms against what they honestly believed to be the unconstitutional encroachments of his power. Hitherto the whole weight of their resentment had justly fallen on the advisers of the prince, who himself was thought to be ignorant, as he was probably innocent, of the abuses so generally practised in his name. But as the contest thickened, the natural feelings of the man were thought to savor of the political acts he was required to sanction with his name. It was soon whispered, amongst those who had the best means of intelligence, that the feelings of the sovereign were deeply interested in the maintenance of what he deemed his prerogative, and the ascendency of that body of the representatives of his empire, which he met in person and influenced by his presence. Ere long this opinion was rumored abroad, and as the minds of men began to loosen from their ancient attachments and prejudices, they confounded, by a very natural feeling, the head with the members; forgetting that "Liberty and Equality" formed no part of the trade of princes. The name of the monarch was daily falling into disrepute; and as the colonial writers ventured to allude more freely to his person and power, the glimmerings of that light were seen, which was a precursor of the rise of "the stars of the West" amongst the national symbols of the earth. Until then, few had thought, and none had ventured to speak openly, of independence, though events had been silently preparing the colonists for such a final measure.

Allegiance to the prince was the last and only tie to be severed; for the colonies already governed themselves in all matters, whether of internal or foreign policy, as effectually as any people could, whose right to do so was not generally acknowledged. But as the honest nature of George III. admitted of no disguise, mutual disgust and alienation were the natural consequences of the reaction of sentiment between the prince and his western people.[1]

All this, and much more of minute detail, was hastily commented on by Polwarth, who possessed, in the midst of his epicurean propensities, sterling good sense, and great integrity of intention. Lionel was chiefly a listener, nor did he cease the greedy and interesting employment until warned by his weakness, and the stroke of a neighboring clock, that he was trespassing too far on prudence. His friend then assisted the exhausted invalid to his bed ; and after giving him a world of good advice, together with a warm pressure of the hand, he stumped his way out of the room, with a noise that brought, at every tread, an echo from the heart of Major Lincoln.

[1] The prejudices of the king of England were unavoidable in his insulated situation, but his virtues and integrity were exclusively the property of the man. His speech to our first minister after the peace cannot be too often recorded : " I was the last man in my kingdom to acknowledge your independence, and I shall be the last to violate it."

CHAPTER XIX.

"God never meant that man should scale the heavens
    By strides of human wisdom."

COWPER.

A VERY few days of gentle exercise in the bracing air of the season, were sufficient to restore the strength of the invalid, whose wounds had healed while he lay slumbering under the influence of the anodynes prescribed by his leech. Polwarth, in consideration of the dilapidated state of his own limbs, together with the debility of Lionel, had so far braved the ridicule of the army, as to set up one of those comfortable and easy conveyances, which, in the good old times of colonial humility, were known by the quaint and unpretending title of tompungs. To equip this establishment, he had been compelled to impress one of the fine hunters of his friend. The animal had been taught, by virtue of much training from his groom, aided a little, perhaps, by the low state of the garners of the place, to amble through the snow as quietly as if he were conscious of the altered condition of his master's health. In this safe vehicle the two gentlemen might be seen daily, gliding along the upper streets of the town, and moving through the winding paths of the common, receiving the congratulations of their friends; or, in their turn, visiting others, who, like themselves, had been wounded in the murderous battle of the preceding summer, but who, less fortunate than they, were still compelled to submit to the lingering confinement of their quarters.

It was not difficult to persuade Cecil and Agnes to join in many of their short excursions, though no temptation could induce the latter to still the frown that habitually settled on her beautiful brow, whenever chance or intention brought them in contact with any of the gentlemen of the army. Miss Dynevor was, however, much more conciliating in her deportment, and even, at times, so gracious as to incur the private reproaches of her friend.

"Surely, Cecil, you forget how much our poor country-men are suffering in their miserable lodgings without the town, or you would be less prodigal of your condescension to these butterflies of the army," cried Agnes, pettishly, while they were uncloaking after one of these rides, during which the latter thought her cousin had lost sight of that tacit compact, by which most of the women of the colonies deemed themselves bound to exhibit their feminine resentments to their invaders. "Were a chief from our own army presented to you, he could not have been received in a sweeter manner than you bestowed your smile to-day on that Sir Digby Dent!"

"I can say nothing in favor of its sweetness, my acid cousin, but *that* Sir Digby Dent is a gentleman—"

"A gentleman!—yes—so is every Englishman who wears a scarlet coat, and knows how to play off his airs in the colonies!"

"And as I hope I have some claims to be called a lady," continued Cecil, quietly, "I do not know why, in the little intercourse we have, I should be rude to him."

"Cecil Dynevor!" exclaimed Agnes, with a sparkling eye, and with a woman's intuitive perception of the other's motives, "all Englishmen are not Lionel Lincolns."

"Nor is Major Lincoln an Englishman," returned Cecil, laughing, while she blushed; "though I have reason to think that Captain Polwarth may be."

"Silly, child, silly; the poor man has paid the penalty of his offence, and is to be regarded with pity."

"Have a care, my coz. Pity is one of a large connection of gentle feelings; when you once admit the first-born, you may leave open your doors to the whole family."

"Now that is exactly the point in question, Cecil—because you esteem Major Lincoln, you are willing to admire

Howe and all his myrmidons; but I can pity, and still be firm."

"*Le bon temps viendra !*"

"Never !" interrupted Agnes, with a warmth that prevented her perceiving how much she admitted; "never, at least under the guise of a scarlet coat."

Cecil smiled, but having completed her toilet, she withdrew without making any reply.

Such little discussions, enlivened more or less by the peculiar spirit of Agnes, were of frequent occurrence, though the eye of her cousin became daily more thoughtful, and the indifference with which she listened was more apparent in each succeeding dialogue.

In the meantime, the affairs of the siege, though conducted with extreme caution, amounted only to a vigilant blockade.

The Americans lay by thousands in the surrounding villages, or were hutted in strong bands nigh the batteries which commanded the approaches to the place. Notwithstanding their means had been greatly increased by the capture of several vessels loaded with warlike stores, as well as by the reduction of two important fortresses towards the Canadian frontiers, they were still too scanty to admit of that wasteful expenditure which is the usual accompaniment of war. In addition to their necessities, as a reason for forbearance, might also be mentioned the feelings of the colonists, who were anxious, in mercy to themselves, to regain their town with as little injury as possible. On the other hand, the impression made by the battle of Bunker Hill was still so vivid as to curb the enterprise of the royal commanders, and Washington had been permitted to hold their powerful forces in check, by an untrained and half-armed multitude, that was, at times, absolutely destitute of the means of maintaining even a momentary conquest.

As, however, a show of hostilities was maintained, the reports of cannon were frequently heard, and there were days when skirmishes between the advanced parties of the two hosts brought on more heavy firings, which continued for longer periods. The ears of the ladies had been long accustomed to these rude sounds, and as the trifling loss which followed was altogether confined to the outworks, they were listened to with but little or no terror.

In this manner a fortnight flew swiftly away without an incident to be related. One fine morning at the end of that period, Polwarth drove into the little courtyard of Mrs. Lechmere's residence, with all those knowing flourishes he could command, and which, in the year 1775, were thought to indicate the greatest familiarity with the properties of a tom-pung. In another minute his wooden member was heard in the passage, timing his steps, as he approached the room where the rest of the party were waiting his appearance. The two cousins stood wrapped in furs, with their smiling faces blooming beneath double rows of lace to soften the picture, while Major Lincoln was in the act of taking his cloak from Meriton, as the door opened for the admission of the captain.

"What, already dished!" exclaimed the good-natured Polwarth, glancing his eyes from one to the other; "so much the better; punctuality is the true leaven of life—a good watch is as necessary to the guest as the host, and to the host as his cook. Miss Agnes, you are amazingly murderous to-day! If Howe expects his subalterns to do their duty, he should not suffer you to go at large in his camp."

The fine eye of Miss Danforth sparkled as he proceeded, but happening to fall on his mutilated person, its expression softened, and she was content with answering with a smile,—

"Let your general look to himself; I seldom go abroad but to espy his weakness!"

The captain gave an expressive shrug of his shoulder and turning aside to his friend, said in an undertone,—

"You see how it is, Major Lincoln; ever since I have been compelled to serve myself up, like a turkey from yesterday's dinner, with a single leg, I have not been able to get a sharp reply from the young woman—she has grown an even-tempered, tasteless morsel; and I am like a two-pronged fork—only fit for carving; well, I care not how soon they cut me up entirely, since she has lost her piquancy; but shall we to the church?"

Lionel looked a little embarrassed, and fingered a paper he held in his hand, for a moment, before he handed it to the other for his perusal.

"What have we here?" continued Polwarth: "'Two officers, wounded in the late battle, desire to return thanks for their recovery'—hum—hum—hum—two?—yourself, and who is the other?"

"I had hoped it would be my old companion and school-fellow."

"Ha! what, me!" exclaimed the captain, unconsciously elevating his wooden leg, and examining it with a rueful eye; "umph! Leo, do you think a man has a particular reason to be grateful for the loss of a leg?"

"It might have been worse."

"I don't know," interrupted Polwarth, a little obstinately; "there would have been more symmetry in it, if it had been both."

"You forget your mother," continued Lionel, as though the other had not spoken; "I am very sure it will give her heartfelt pleasure."

Polwarth gave a loud hem, rubbed his hand over his face once or twice, gave another furtive glance at his solitary limb, and then answered with a little tremor in his voice,—

"Yes, yes—I believe you are quite right—a mother can love her child, though he should be chopped into mince-meat! The sex get that generous feeling after they are turned of forty—it's your young woman that is particular about proportions and correspondents."

"You consent, then, that Meriton shall hand in the request, as it reads?"

Polwarth hesitated a single instant longer, and then, as he remembered his distant mother (for Lionel had touched the right chord), his heart melted within him.

"Certainly, certainly—it might have been worse, as it was with poor Dennis—ay, let it pass for two; it shall go hard, but I find a knee to bend on the occasion. Perhaps, Leo, when a certain young lady sees I can have a *Te Deum* for my adventure, she may cease to think me such an object of pity as at present."

Lionel bowed in silence, and the captain, turning to Agnes, conducted her to the sleigh with a particularly lofty air, that he intended should indicate his perfect superiority to the casualties of war. Cecil took the arm of Major Lincoln, and the whole party were soon seated in the vehicle that was in waiting.

Until this day, which was the second Sunday since his reappearance, and the first on which the weather permitted him to go abroad, Lionel had no opportunity to observe the altered population of the town. The inhabitants had gradually left the place, some clandestinely, and others under favor of passes from the royal general, until those who remained were actually outnumbered by the army and its dependents. As the party approached the "King's Chapel," the street was crowded by military men, collected in groups, who indulged in thoughtless merriment, reckless of the wounds their light conversation inflicted on the few townsmen, who might be seen moving towards the church, with deportments suited to the solemnity of their purpose, and countenances severely chastened by a remembrance of the day, and its serious duties. Indeed, so completely had Boston lost that distinctive appearance of sobriety, which had ever been the care and pride of its people, in the levity of a garrison, that even the immediate precincts of the temple were not protected from the passing jest or rude mirth of the gay and unreflecting, at an hour when quiet was wont to settle on the whole province, as deep as if Nature had ceased her ordinary functions to unite in the worship of man. Lionel observed the change with mortification ; nor did it escape his uneasy glances, that his two female companions concealed their faces in their muffs, as if to exclude a view that brought still more painful recollections to minds early trained in the reflecting habits of the country.

When the sleigh drew up before the edifice, a dozen hands were extended to assist the ladies in their short but difficult passage into the heavy portico. Agnes coldly bowed her acknowledgments, observing, with an extremely equivocal smile, to one of the most assiduous of the young men,—

"We, who are accustomed to the climate, find no diffi-

16

culty in walking on ice, though to you foreigners it may seem so hazardous." She then bowed, and walked gravely into the bosom of the church, without deigning to bestow another glance to her right hand or her left.

The manner of Cecil, though more chastened and feminine, and consequently more impressive, was equally reserved. Like her cousin, she proceeded directly to her pew, repulsing the attempts of those who wished to detain her a moment in idle discourse, by a lady-like propriety that checked the advance of all who approached her. In consequence of the rapid movement of their companions, Lionel and Polwarth were left among the crowd of officers who thronged the entrance of the church. The former moved up within the colonnade, and passed from group to group, answering and making the customary inquiries of men engaged in the business of war. Here, three or four veterans were clustered about one of those heavy columns, that were arranged in formidable show on three faces of the building, discussing, with becoming gravity, the political signs of the times, or the military condition of their respective corps. There, three or four unfledged boys, tricked in all the vain emblems of their profession, impeded the entrance of the few women who appeared, under the pretence of admiration for the sex, while they secretly dwelt on the glitter of their own ornaments. Scattered along the whole extent of the entrance were other little knots ; some listening to the idle tale of a professed jester, some abusing the land in which it was their fate to serve, and others recounting the marvels they had witnessed in distant climes, and in scenes of peril which beggared their utmost powers of description.

Among such a collection it was not difficult, however, to find a few whose views were more elevated, and whose deportment might be termed less offensive, either to breeding or principles. With one of the gentlemen of the latter class Lionel was held for some time in discourse, in a distant part of the portico. At length the sounds of the organ were heard issuing from the church, and the gay parties began to separate, like men suddenly reminded why they were collected in that unusual place. The companion of Major Lincoln had left him, and he was himself following along the colonnade, which was now but thinly peopled, when his ear was saluted by a low voice, singing in a sort of nasal chant at his very elbow,—

"Woe unto you, Pharisees! for ye love the uppermost seats in the synagogues, and greetings in the market!"

Though Lionel had not heard the voice since the echoing cry had issued out of the fatal redoubt, he knew its first tones on the instant. Turning at this singular denunciation, he beheld Job Pray, erect and immovable as a statue, in one of the niches in front of the building, whence he gave forth his warning voice, like some oracle speaking to its devotees.

"Fellow, will no peril teach you wisdom?" demanded Lionel; "how dare you brave our resentment so wantonly?"

But his questions were unheeded. The young man, whose features looked pale and emaciated, as if he had endured recent bodily disease, whose eye was glazed and vacant, and whose whole appearance was more squalid and miserable than usual, appeared perfectly indifferent to all around him. Without even altering the riveted gaze of his unmeaning eye, he continued,—

"Woe unto you! for ye neither go in yourselves, neither suffer ye them that are entering to go in!"

"Art deaf, fool?" demanded Lionel.

In an instant the eye of the other was turned on his interrogator, and Major Lincoln felt a thrill pass through him, when he met the wild gleam of intelligence that lighted the countenance of the changeling, as he continued, in the same ominous tones,—

"Whosoever shall say to his brother, Raca, shall be in danger of the council; but whosoever shall say, Thou fool, is in danger of hell fire."

For a moment Lionel stood as if spell-bound by the manner of Job, while he uttered this dreadful anathema. But the instant the secret influence ceased, he tapped the lad lightly with his cane, and bid him descend from the niche.

"Job's a prophet," returned the other, dishonoring his declaration at the same time, by losing the singular air of momentary intelligence, in his usual appearance of mental imbecility, "it's wicked to strike a prophet. The Jews stoned the prophets, and beat them too."

"Do then as I bid you; would you stay here to be beaten by the soldiers? Go now, away; after service come to me, and I will furnish you with a better coat than the garment you wear."

"Did you never read the good book," said Job, "where it tells how you must n't take heed for food nor raiment? Nab says when Job dies he 'll go to heaven, for he gets nothing to wear and but little to eat. Kings wear their di'mond crowns and golden flauntiness; and kings always go to the dark place."

The lad suddenly ceased, and crouching into the very bottom of his niche, he began to play with his fingers, like an infant amused with the power of exercising its own members. At the same moment Lionel turned from him, attracted by the rattling of side-arms, and the tread of many feet behind him. A large party of officers, belonging to the staff of the army, had paused to listen to what was passing. Amongst them Lionel recognized, at the first glance, two of the chieftains, who, in a little advance of their attendants, were keenly eying the singular being that was squatted in the niche. Notwithstanding his surprise, Major Lincoln detected the scowl that impended over the dark brow of the commander-in-chief, while he bowed low, in deference to his rank.

"Who is this fellow, that dare condemn the mighty of the earth to such sweeping perdition?" demanded Howe; "his own sovereign amongst the number?"

"'T is an unfortunate being, wanting in intellect, with whom accident has made me acquainted," returned Major Lincoln; "who hardly knows what he utters, and least of all in whose presence he has been speaking."

"It is to such idle opinions, which are conceived by the designing, and circulated by the ignorant, that we may ascribe the wavering allegiance of the colonies," said the

British general. "I hope you can answer for the loyalty of your singular acquaintance, Major Lincoln?"

Lionel was about to reply, with some little spirit, when the companion of the frowning chief suddenly exclaimed,—

"By the feats of the feathered Hermes, but this is the identical Merry-Andrew who took the flying leap from Copp's, of which I have already spoken to you. Am I in error, Lincoln? Is not this the shouting philosopher, whose feelings were so elevated on the day of Breed's, that he could not refrain from flying, but who, less fortunate than Icarus, made his descent on *terra firma?*"

"I believe your memory is faithful, sir," said Lionel, answering the smile of the other; "the lad is often brought to trouble by his simplicity."

Burgoyne gave a gentle impulse to the arm he held, as if he thought the wretched being before them unworthy of further consideration; though secretly with a view to prevent an impolitic exhibition of the well-known propensity of his senior to push his notions of military ascendency to the extreme. Perceiving by the still darkening look of the other that he hesitated, his ready lieutenant observed,—

"Poor fellow! his treason was doubly punished, by a flight of some fifty feet down the declivity of Copp's, and the mortification of witnessing the glorious triumph of his majesty's troops. To such a wretch we may well afford forgiveness."

Howe insensibly yielded to the continued pressure of the other, and his hard features even relaxed into a scowling smile, as he said, while turning away,—

"Look to your acquaintance, Major Lincoln, or, bad as his present condition seems, he may make it worse. Such language cannot be tolerated in a place besieged. That is the word, I believe; the rebels call their mob a besieging army, do they not?"

"They do gather round our winter quarters, and claim some such distinction—"

"It must be acknowledged they did well on Breed's too! The shabby rascals fought like true men."

"Desperately, and with some discretion," answered Burgoyne; "but it was their fortune to meet those who fought better, and with greater skill. Shall we enter?"

The frown was now entirely chased from the brow of the chief, who said complacently,—

"Come, gentlemen, we are tardy; unless more industrious, we shall not be in season to pray for the king, much less ourselves."

The whole party advanced a step, when a bustle in the rear announced the approach of another officer of high rank, and the second in command entered into the colonnade, followed also by the gentlemen of his family. The instant he appeared, the self-contented look vanished from the features of Howe, who returned his salute with cold civility, and immediately entered the church. The quick-witted Burgoyne again interposed, and as he made way in his turn, he found means to whisper into the ear of Clinton some well-imagined allusion to the events of that very field, which had given birth to the heart-burnings between his brother generals, and had caused the feelings of Howe to be estranged from the man to whose assistance he owed so much. Clinton yielded to the subtle influence of the flattery, and followed his commander into the house of God, with a bland contentment that he probably mistook for a feeling much better suited to the place and the occasion. As the whole group of spectators, consisting of aids, secretaries, and idlers, without, immediately imitated the example of the general, Lionel found himself alone with the changeling.

From the moment that Job discovered the vicinity of the English leader, to that of his disappearance, the lad remained literally immovable. His eye was fastened on vacancy, his jaw had fallen in a manner to give a look of utter mental alienation to his countenance; and, in short, he exhibited the degraded lineaments and figure of a man, without his animation or intelligence. But as the last footsteps of the retiring party became inaudible, the fear, which had put to flight the feeble intellects of the simpleton, slowly left him, and raising his face, he said, in a low, growling voice,—

"Let him go out to Prospect ; the people will teach him the law ! "

" Perverse and obstinate simpleton ! " cried Lionel, dragging him, without further ceremony, from the niche ; " will you persevere in that foolish cry until you are whipped from regiment to regiment for your pains ! "

"You promised Job the grannies should n't beat him any more, and Job promised to run your arr'nds."

"Ay ! but unless you learn to keep silence, boy, I shall forget my promise, and give you up to the anger of all the grannies in town."

"Well," said Job, brightening in his look, like a fool in his exultation, "they are half of them dead, at any rate ; Job heard the biggest man among 'em roar like a ravenous lion, ' Hurrah for the Royal Irish,' but he never spoke ag'in ; though there was n't any better rest for Job's gun than a dead man's shoulder ! "

"Wretch ! " cried Lionel, recoiling from him in horror, " are your hands then stained with the blood of M'Fuse ? "

"Job did n't touch him with his hands," returned the undisturbed simpleton ; " for he died like a dog, where he fell ? "

Lionel stood a moment in utter confusion of thought ; but hearing the infallible evidence of the near approach of Polwarth in his tread, he said, in a hurried manner, and in a voice half choked by his emotions,—

"Go, fellow, go to Mrs. Lechmere's, as I bid you ; tell— tell Meriton to look to my fire."

The lad made a motion towards obeying, but checking himself, he looked up into the face of the other with a piteous and suffering look, and said,—

"See, Job's numb with cold ! Nab and Job can't get wood now ; the king keeps men to fight for it. Let Job warm his flesh a little ; his body is cold as the dead ! "

Touched to the heart by the request, and the helpless aspect of the lad, Lionel made a silent signal of assent, and turned quickly to meet his friend. It was not necessary for Polwarth to speak, in order to apprise Major Lincoln that he had overheard part of the dialogue between him and Job. His countenance and attitude sufficiently betrayed his knowledge, as well as the effect it had produced on his feelings. He kept his eyes on the form of the simpleton, as the lad shuffled his way along the icy street, with an expression that could not easily be mistaken.

"Did I not hear the name of poor Dennis?" at length he asked.

"'T was some of the idle boasting of the fool. But why are you not in the pew?"

"The fellow is a *protégé* of yours, Major Lincoln; but you may carry forbearance too far," returned Polwarth, gravely. "I come for you, at the request of a pair of beautiful blue eyes, that have inquired of each one that has entered the church, this half hour, where and why Major Lincoln has tarried."

Lionel bowed his thanks, and affected to laugh at the humor of his friend, while they proceeded together to the pew of Mrs. Lechmere without further delay.

The painful reflections excited by this interview with Job, gradually vanished from the mind of Lionel, as he yielded to the influence of the solemn service of the church. He heard the difficult and suppressed breathing of the fair being who kneeled by his side, while the minister read those thanksgivings which personally concerned himself, and no little of earthly gratitude mingled with the loftier aspirations of the youth, as he listened. He caught the timid glance of the soft eye from behind the folds of Cecil's veil, as they rose, and he took his seat as happy as an ardent young man might well be fancied, under the consciousness of possessing the best affections of a female so youthful, so lovely, and so pure.

Perhaps the service was not altogether so consoling to the feelings of Polwarth. As he recovered his solitary foot again, with some little difficulty, he cast a very equivocal glance at his dismembered person, hemmed aloud, and finished with a rattling of his wooden leg about the pew, that attracted the eyes of the whole congregation, as if he intended the ears of all present should bear testimony in whose behalf their owners had uttered their extraordinary thanksgivings.

The officiating minister was far too discreet to vex the attention of his superiors with any prolix and unwelcome exhibitions of the Christian's duty. The impressive delivery of his text required one minute. Four were consumed in the exordium. The argument was ingeniously condensed into ten more ; and the peroration of his essay was happily concluded in four minutes and a half; leaving him the satisfaction of knowing, as he was assured by fifty watches, and twice that number of contented faces, that he had accomplished his task by half a minute within the orthodox period.

For this exactitude he doubtless had his reward. Among other testimonials in his favor, when Polwarth shook his hand to thank him for his kind offices in his own behalf, he found room for a high compliment to the discourse, concluding by assuring the flattered divine, " that, in addition to its other great merits, it was done in beautiful time ! "

CHAPTER XX.

"Away; let naught to love displeasing,
My Winifreda, move your care:
Let naught delay the heavenly blessing,
Nor squeamish pride, nor gloomy fear."

Anonymous.

IT was perhaps fortunate for the tranquillity of all concerned, that, during this period of their opening confidence, the person of Mrs. Lechmere came not between
the bright image of purity and happiness that Cecil
presented in each lineament and action, and the eyes of her
lover. The singular and somewhat contradictory interests
that lady had so often betrayed in the movements of her
young kinsman, were no longer visible to awaken his slumbering suspicions. Even those inexplicable scenes, in which
his aunt had so strangely been an actor, were forgotten in
the engrossing feelings of the hour; or, if remembered at all,
were only suffered to dim the pleasing pictures of his imagination, as an airy cloud throws its passing shadows across
some cheerful and lovely landscape. In addition to those
very natural auxiliaries, love and hope, the cause of Mrs.
Lechmere had found a very powerful assistant, in the
bosom of Lionel, through an accident which had confined
her, for a long period, not only to her apartment, but to her
bed.

On that day, when the critical operation was performed
on the person of Major Lincoln, his aunt was known to
have awaited the result with intense anxiety. As soon as
the favorable termination was reported to her, she hastened
towards his room with an unguarded eagerness, which, added
to the general infirmities of her years, had nearly cost the

price of her life. Her foot became entangled in her train, in ascending the stairs, but disregarding the warning cry of Agnes Danforth, with that sort of reckless vehemence that sometimes broke through the formal decorum of her manners, she sustained, in consequence, a fall that might well have proved fatal to a much younger woman. The injury she received was severe and internal ; and the inflammation, though not high, was sufficiently protracted to arouse the apprehension of her attendants. The symptoms were, however, now abating, and her recovery no longer a matter of question.

As Lionel heard this from the lips of Cecil, the reader will not imagine the effect produced by the interest his aunt took in his welfare was at all lessened by the source whence he derived his knowledge. Notwithstanding Cecil dwelt on such a particular evidence of Mrs. Lechmere's attachment to her nephew with much earnestness, it had not escaped Major Lincoln that her name was but seldom introduced in their frequent conversations, and never, on the part of his companion, without a guarded delicacy that appeared sensitive in the extreme. As their confidence, however, increased with their hourly communications, he began gently to lift the veil which female reserve had drawn before her inmost feelings, and to read a heart whose purity and truth would have repaid a more difficult investigation.

When the party returned from the church, Cecil and Agnes immediately hastened to the apartment of the invalid, leaving Lionel in possession of the little wainscoted parlor by himself ; Polwarth having proceeded to his own quarters, with the assistance of the hunter. The young man passed a few minutes in pacing the room, musing deeply on the scene he had witnessed before the church ; now and then casting a vacant look on the fanciful ornaments of the walls, among which the armorial bearings of his own name were so frequent, and in such honorable situations. At length he heard that light footstep approach, whose sound had now become too well known to be mistaken, and in another instant he was joined by Miss Dynevor.

" Mrs. Lechmere," he said, leading her to a settee, and

placing himself by her side,—"you found her better, I trust?"

"So well, that she intends adventuring, this morning, an interview with your own formidable self. Indeed, Lionel, you have every reason to be grateful for the deep interest my grandmother takes in your welfare. Ill as she has been, her inquiries in your behalf were ceaseless; and I have known her refuse to answer any questions about her own critical condition, until her physician had relieved her anxiety concerning yours."

As Cecil spoke, the tears rushed into her eyes, and her bloom deepened with the strength of her feelings.

"It is to you, then, that much of my gratitude is due," returned Lionel; "for, by permitting me to blend my lot with yours, I find new value in her eyes. Have you acquainted Mrs. Lechmere with the full extent of my presumption? She knows of our engagement?"

"Could I do otherwise? While your life was in peril, I confined the knowledge of my interest in your situation to my own breast; but when we were flattered with the hopes of a recovery, I placed your letter in the hands of my natural adviser, and have the consolation of knowing that she approves of my—what shall I call it, Lionel?— would not folly be the better word?"

"Call it what you will, so you do not disavow it. I have hitherto forborne inquiring into the views of Mrs. Lechmere, in tenderness to her situation; but I may flatter myself, Cecil, that she will not reject me?"

For a single instant the blood rushed tumultuously over the fine countenance of Miss Dynevor, suffusing even her temples and forehead with its healthful bloom; but, as she cast a reproachful glance at her lover, it deserted even her cheeks, while she answered calmly, though with a slight exhibition of displeasure in her air,—

"It may have been the misfortune of my grandmother to view the head of her own family with too partial eyes; but, if it be so, her reward should not be distrust. The weakness is, I dare say, very natural, though not less a weakness."

For the first time Lionel fully comprehended the cause of that variable manner, with which Cecil had received his attentions, until interest in his person had stilled her sensitive feelings. Without, however, betraying the least consciousness of his intelligence, he answered,—

"Gratitude does not deserve so forbidding a name as distrust; nor will vanity permit me to call partiality in my favor a weakness."

"The word is a good and a safe term, as applied to poor human nature," said Cecil, smiling once more with all her native sweetness, "and you may possibly overlook it, when you recollect that our foibles are sometimes hereditary."

"I pardon your unkind suspicion for that gentle acknowledgment. But I may now, without hesitation, apply to your grandmother for her consent to our immediate union?"

"You would not have your epithalamium sung, when, at the next moment, you may be required to listen to the dirge of some friend!"

"The very reason you urge against our marriage, induces me to press it, Cecil. As the season advances, this play of war must end. Howe will either break out of his bounds, and drive the Americans from the hills, or seek some other point for more active warfare. In either case you would be left in a distracted and divided country, at an age too tender for your own safety, rather the guardian than the ward of your helpless parent. Surely, Cecil, you would not hesitate to accept of my protection at such a crisis, I had almost dared to say, in tenderness to yourself, as well as to my feelings."

"Say on," she answered; "I admire your ingenuity, if not your argument. In the first place, however, I do not believe your general can drive the Americans from their post so easily; for, by a very simple process in figures, that even I understand, you may find, that if one hill costs so many hundred men, that the purchase of the whole would be too dear. Nay, Lionel, do not look so grave, I implore you! Surely, surely, you do not think I would speak idly of a battle that had nearly cost your life, and—and—my happiness."

"Say on," said Lionel, instantly dismissing the momentary cloud from his brow, and smiling fondly in her anxious face ; "I admire your casuistry, and worship your feeling ; but can also deny your argument."

Reassured by his voice and manner, after a moment of extreme agitation, she continued, in the same playful tones as before,—

"But we will suppose all the hills won, and the American chief, Washington, who, though nothing but a rebel, is a very respectable one, driven into the country with his army at his heels ; I trust it is to be done without the assistance of the women ! Or, should Howe remove his forces, as you intimate, will he not leave the town behind him ? In either case, I should remain quietly where I am ; safe in a British garrison, or safer among my countrymen."

"Cecil, you are alike ignorant of the dangers and of the rude lawlessness of war. Though Howe should abandon the place, 't would be only for a time ; believe me, the ministry will never yield the possession of a town like this, which has so long dared their power, to men in arms against their lawful prince."

"You have strangely forgotten the last six months, Lionel, or you would not accuse me of ignorance of the misery that war can inflict."

"A thousand thanks for the kind admission, dearest Cecil, as well as for the hint," said the young man, shifting the ground of his argument with the consistency, as well as the readiness of a lover ; "you have owned your sentiments to me, and would not refuse to avow them again ?"

"Not to one whose self-esteem will induce him to forget the weakness ; but, perhaps, I might hesitate to do such a silly thing before the world."

"I will then put it to your heart," he continued, without regarding the smiling coquetry she had affected. "Believing the best, you will admit that another battle would be no strange occurrence ?"

She raised her anxious looks to his face, but remained silent.

"We both know, at least I know, from sad experience, that I am far from being invulnerable. Now answer me,

Cecil ; not as a female, struggling to support the false pride of her sex, but as a woman, generous and full of heart, like yourself; were the events of the last six months to recur, whether would you live them over affianced in secret, or as an acknowledged wife, who might not blush to show her tenderness to the world ?"

It was not until the large drops, that glistened at his words upon the dark lashes of Miss Dynevor, were shaken from the tremulous fringes that concealed her eyes, that she looked up, blushing, into his face, and said,—

"Do you not then think that I endured enough, as one who felt herself betrothed ; but that closer ties were necessary to fill the measure of my suffering ?"

"I cannot even thank you as I would for those flattering tears, until my question is plainly answered."

"Is this altogether generous, Lincoln ?"

"Perhaps not in appearance, but sincerely so in truth. By heaven, Cecil, I would shelter and protect you from a rude contact with the world, even as I seek my own happiness !"

Miss Dynevor was not only confused, but distressed ; she however said, in a low voice,—

"You forget, Major Lincoln, that I have one to consult, without whose approbation I can promise nothing."

"Will you, then, refer the question to her wisdom? Should Mrs. Lechmere approve of our immediate union, may I say to her that you authorize me to ask it ?"

Cecil said nothing ; but smiling through her tears, she permitted Lionel to take her hand in a manner that a much less sanguine man would have found no difficulty in construing into an assent.

"Come, then," he cried, "let us hasten to the apartment of Mrs. Lechmere ; did you not say she expected me ?" She suffered him to draw her arm through his own, and lead her from the room. Notwithstanding the buoyant hopes with which Lionel conducted his companion through the passages of the house, he did not approach the chamber of Mrs. Lechmere without some inward repugnance. It was not possible to forget entirely all that had so recently passed, or to still, effectually, those dark suspicions which had been once awakened within his bosom. His purpose, however, bore him onward, and a glance at the trembling being who now absolutely leaned on him for support, drove every consideration, in which she did not form a most prominent part, from his mind.

The enfeebled appearance of the invalid, with a sudden recollection that she had sustained so much, in consequence of her anxiety in his own behalf, so far aided the cause of his aunt, that the young man not only met her with cordiality, but with a feeling akin to gratitude.

The indisposition of Mrs. Lechmere had now continued for several weeks, and her features, aged and sunken as they were, by the general decay of nature, afforded strong additional testimony of the severity of her recent illness. Her face, besides being paler and more emaciated than usual, had caught that anxious expression, which great and protracted bodily ailing is apt to leave on the human countenance. Her brow was, however, smooth and satisfied, unless at moments, when a slight and involuntary play of the muscles betrayed that fleeting pains continued, at short intervals, to remind her of her illness. She received her visitors with a smile that was softer and more conciliating than usual, and which the pallid and careworn appearance of her features rendered deeply impressive.

"It is kind, cousin Lionel," she said, extending her withered hand to her young kinsman, "in the sick to come thus to visit the well. For after so long apprehending the worst on your account, I cannot consent that my trifling injury should be mentioned before your more serious wounds."

"Would, madam, that you had as happily recovered from their effects as myself," returned Lionel, taking her hand, and pressing it with great sincerity. "I shall never forget that you owe your illness to anxiety for me."

"Let it pass, sir; it is natural that we should feel strongly in behalf of those we love. I have lived to see you well again, and, God willing, I shall live to see this wicked rebellion crushed." She paused; and smiling for a moment on the young pair who had approached her couch, she continued, "Cecil has told me all, Major Lincoln."

"No, not all, dear madam," interrupted Lionel; "I have something yet to add; and in the commencement, I will own that I depend altogether on your pity and judgment to support my pretensions."

"Pretensions is an injudicious word, cousin Lionel; where there is a perfect equality of birth, education, and virtues, and, I may say, considering the difference in the sexes, of fortune too, it may amount to claims; but pretensions is an expression too ambiguous. Cecil, my child, go to my library; in the small, secret drawer of my escritoire, you will find a paper bearing your name; read it, my love, and then bring it hither."

She motioned to Lionel to be seated, and when the door had closed on the retiring form of Cecil she resumed the conversation.

"As we are about to speak of business, the confused girl may as well be relieved, Major Lincoln. What is this particular favor that I shall be required to yield?"

"Like any other sturdy mendicant, who may have already partaken largely of your bounty, I come to beg the immediate gift of the last and greatest boon you can bestow."

"My grandchild. There is no necessity for useless reserves between us, cousin Lionel, for you will remember that I too am a Lincoln. Let us then speak freely, like two friends, who have met to determine on a matter equally near to the heart of each."

"Such is my earnest wish, madam. I have been urging on Miss Dynevor the peril of the times, and the critical situation of the country, in both of which I have found the strongest reasons for our immediate union."

"And Cecil?—"

"Has been like herself—kind, but dutiful. She refers me entirely to your decision, by which alone she consents to be guided."

Mrs. Lechmere made no immediate reply, but her features powerfully betrayed the inward workings of her mind. It certainly was not displeasure that caused her to hesitate, her hollow eye lighting with a gleam of satisfaction that could not be mistaken ; neither was it uncertainty, for her whole countenance seemed to express rather the uncontrollable agitation which might accompany the sudden accomplishment of long-desired ends, than any doubt as to their prudence. Gradually her agitation subsided ; and as her feelings became more natural, her hard eyes filled with tears, and when she spoke, there was a softness mingled with the tremor of her voice, that Lionel had never before witnessed.

"She is a good and dutiful child, my own, my obedient Cecil ! She will bring you no wealth, Major Lincoln, that will be esteemed among your hoards, nor any proud title to add to the lustre of your honorable name ; but she will bring you what is as good, if not better—nay, I am sure it must be better—a pure and virtuous heart, that knows no guile."

" A thousand and a thousand times more estimable in my eyes, my worthy aunt ! " cried Lionel, melting before the touch of nature, which had so effectually softened the harsh feelings of Mrs. Lechmere ; " let her come to my arms penniless, and without a name ; she will be no less my wife—no less her own invaluable self."

" I spoke only by comparison, Major Lincoln ; the child of Colonel Dynevor, and the granddaughter of the Lord Viscount Cardonnell, can have no cause to blush for her lineage ; neither will the descendant of John Lechmere be a dowerless bride. When Cecil shall become Lady Lincoln, she need never wish to conceal the escutcheon of her own ancestors under the bloody hand of her husband's."

" May Heaven long avert the hour when either of us may be required to use the symbol ! " exclaimed Lionel.

" Did I not understand aright? was not your request for an instant marriage?"

" Never less in error, my dear madam ; but you surely do not forget that one lives so mutually dear to us, who has every reason to hope for many years of life ; and I trust, too, of happiness and reason."

Mrs. Lechmere looked wildly at her nephew, and then passed her hand slowly before her eyes, from whence she did not withdraw them until a universal shudder had shaken the whole of her enfeebled frame.

"You are right, my young cousin," she said, smiling faintly; "I believe my bodily weakness has impaired my memory. I was indeed dreaming of days long since past. You stood before me in the image of your desolate father, while Cecil bore that of her mother—my own long-lost but wilful Agnes! O! she was my child! my child! and God has forgotten her faults in mercy to a mother's prayers."

Lionel recoiled a step before the wild energy of the invalid's manner, in speechless amazement. A flush had passed into her pallid cheeks, and as she concluded, she clasped her hands before her, and sunk on the pillows which supported her back. Large insulated tears fell from her eyes, and, slowly moving over her wasted cheeks, dropped singly upon the counterpane. Lionel laid his hand upon the night-bell, but an expressive gesture from his aunt prevented his ringing.

"I am well again," she said; "hand me the restorative by your side."

Mrs. Lechmere drank freely from the glass, and in another minute her agitation subsided, her features settling into their rigid composure, and her eye resuming its hard expression, as though nothing had occurred to disturb her usual cold and worldly look.

"You see how much better youth can endure the ravages of disease than age, by my present weakness, Major Lincoln," she continued; "but let us return to other and more agreeable subjects—you have not only my consent, but my wish, that you should wed my grandchild. It is a happiness that I have rather hoped for than dared to expect, and I will freely add, 't is a consummation of my wishes that will render the evening of my days not only happy, but blessed."

"Then, dearest madam, why should it be delayed?—no one can say what a day may bring forth, at such a time as this, and the moment of bustle and action is not the hour to register the marriage vows."

After musing a moment, Mrs. Lechmere replied,—

"We have a good and holy custom in this religious

province, of choosing the day which the Lord has set apart for his own exclusive worship as that on which to enter into the honorable state of matrimony. Choose, then, between this or the next Sabbath for your nuptials."

Whatever might be the ardor of the young man, he was a little surprised at the shortness of the former period; but the pride of his sex would not admit of any hesitation.

"Let it be this day, if Miss Dynevor can be brought freely to consent."

"Here then she comes, to tell you that, at my request, she does. Cecil, my own sweet child, I have promised Major Lincoln that you will become his wife this day."

Miss Dynevor, who had advanced into the centre of the room before she heard the purport of this speech, stopped short, and stood like a beautiful statue, expressing astonishment and dismay. Her color went and came with alarming quickness, and the paper fell from her trembling hand to her feet, which appeared riveted to the floor.

"To-day!" she repeated, in a voice barely audible; "did you say to-day, my grandmother?"

"Even to-day, my child."

"Why this reluctance, this alarm, Cecil?" said Lionel, approaching, and leading her gently to a seat. "You know the peril of the times—you have condescended to own your sentiments—consider; the winter is breaking, and the first thaw can lead to events which may entirely alter our situation."

"All these may have weight in your eyes, Major Lincoln," interrupted Mrs. Lechmere, in a voice whose marked solemnity drew the attention of her hearers; "but I have other and deeper motives. Have I not already proved the dangers and the evils of delay? Ye are young, and ye are virtuous; why should ye not be happy? Cecil, if you love and revere me, as I think you do, you will become his wife this day."

"Let me have time to think, dearest grandmother. The tie is so new and so solemn! Major Lincoln,—dear Lionel, —you are not wont to be ungenerous; I throw myself on your kindness!"

Lionel did not speak, and Mrs. Lechmere calmly answered,—

" 'T is not at his, but my request, that you will comply."

Miss Dynevor rose from her seat by the side of Lionel, with an air of offended delicacy, and said, with a mournful smile, to her lover,—

"Illness has rendered my good mother timid and weak; will you excuse my desire to be alone with her?"

"I leave you, Cecil," he said, "but if you ascribe my silence to any other motive than tenderness to your feelings, you are unjust both to yourself and me."

She expressed her gratitude only in her looks, and he immediately withdrew, to await the result of their conversation in his own apartment. The half hour that Lionel passed in his chamber seemed half a year; but at the expiration of that short period of time, Meriton came to announce that Mrs. Lechmere desired his presence again in her room.

The first glance of her eye assured Major Lincoln that his cause had triumphed. His aunt had sunk back on her pillows, with her countenance set in a calculating and rigid expression, which indicated a satisfaction so selfish that it almost induced the young man to regret she had not failed. But when his eyes met the tearful and timid glances of the blushing Cecil, he felt that, provided she could be his without violence to her feelings, he cared but little at whose instigation she had consented.

"If I am to read my fate by your goodness, I know I may hope," he said, advancing to her side; "if in my own deserts, I am left to despair."

"Perhaps 't was foolish, Lincoln," she said, smiling through her tears, and frankly placing her hand in his, "to hesitate about a few days, when I feel ready to devote my life to your happiness. It is the wish of my grandmother that I place myself under your protection."

"Then this evening unites us forever?"

"There is no obligation on your gallantry, that it should positively take place this very evening, if any or the least difficulties present."

"But none do, nor can," interrupted Lionel. "Happily the marriage forms of the colony are simple, and we enjoy the consent of all who have any right to interfere."

"Go, then, my children, and complete your brief arrangements," said Mrs. Lechmere; "'t is a solemn knot that ye tie! it must, it will be happy!"

Lionel pressed the hand of his intended bride, and withdrew; and Cecil, throwing herself into the arms of her grandmother, gave vent to her feelings in a burst of tears. Mrs. Lechmere did not repulse her child; on the contrary, she pressed her once or twice to her heart; but still an observant spectator might have seen that her looks betrayed more of worldly pride, than of those natural emotions which such a scene ought to have excited.

CHAPTER XXI.

" Come, friar Francis, be brief; only to the plain form of marriage."
Much Ado About Nothing.

MAJOR LINCOLN had justly said, the laws regulating marriages in the Massachusetts, which were adapted to the infant state of the country, threw but few impediments in the way of the indissoluble connection. Cecil had, however, been educated in the bosom of the English Church, and she clung to its forms and ceremonies with an affection that may easily be accounted for in their solemnity and beauty. Notwithstanding the colonists often chose the weekly festival for their bridals, the rage of reform had excluded the altar from most of their temples, and it was not usual with them to celebrate their nuptials in the places of public worship. But there appeared so much of unreasonable haste, and so little of due preparation, in her own case, that Miss Dynevor, anxious to give all solemnity to an act, to whose importance she was sensibly alive, expressed her desire to pronounce her vows at that altar where she had so long been used to worship, and under that roof where she had already, since the rising of the sun, poured out the thanksgivings of her pure spirit in behalf of the man who was so soon to become her husband.

As Mrs. Lechmere had declared that the agitation of the day and her feeble condition must unavoidably prevent her witnessing the ceremony, there existed no sufficient reason for not indulging the request of her grandchild, notwithstanding it was not in strict accordance with the customs of the place. But being married at the altar, and being married in public, were not similar duties ; and in order to effect the one and avoid the other, it was necessary to postpone the ceremony until a late hour, and to clothe the whole in a cloak of mystery, that the otherwise unembarrassed state of the parties would not have required.

Miss Dynevor made no other confidant than her cousin. Her feelings being altogether elevated above the ordinarily idle considerations which are induced by time and preparations on such an occasion, her brief arrangements were soon ended, and she awaited the appointed moment without alarm, if not without emotion.

Lionel had much more to perform. He knew that the least intimation of such a scene would collect a curious and a disagreeable crowd around and in the church, and he therefore determined that his plans should be arranged in silence, and managed secretly. In order to prevent a surprise, Meriton was sent to the clergyman, requesting him to appoint an hour in the evening when he could give an interview to Major Lincoln. He was answered that at any moment after nine o'clock Dr. Liturgy would be released from the duties of the day, and in readiness to receive him. There was no alternative ; and ten was the time mentioned to Cecil when she was requested to meet him before the altar. Major Lincoln distrusted a little the discretion of Polwarth, and he contented himself with merely telling his friend that he was to be married that evening, and that he must be careful to repair to Tremont Street in order to give away the bride, appointing an hour sufficiently early for all the subsequent movements. His groom and his valet had their respective and separate orders, and long before the important moment, he had everything arranged, as he believed, beyond the possibility of a disappointment.

Perhaps there was something a little romantic, if not diseased, in the mind of Lionel that caused him to derive a secret pleasure from the hidden movements he contemplated. He was certainly not entirely free from a touch of that melancholy and morbid humor which has been mentioned as the characteristic of his race, nor did he always feel the less happy because he was a little miserable. However, either by his activity of intellect or that excellent training in life he had undergone, by being required to act early for himself, he had so far succeeded in quelling the evil spirit within him, as to render its influence quite imperceptible to others, and nearly so to himself. It had, in fine, left him what we have endeavored to represent him in these pages—not a man without faults, but certainly one of many high and generous virtues.

As the day drew to a close, the small family party in Tremont Street collected, in their usual manner, to partake of the evening repast, which was common throughout the colonies at that period. Cecil was pale, and at times a slight tremor was perceptible in the little hand which did the offices of the table; but there was a forced calmness seated in her humid eyes that betokened the resolution she had summoned to her assistance in order to comply with the wishes of her grandmother. Agnes Danforth was silent and observant, though an occasional look, of more than usual meaning, betrayed what she thought of the mystery and suddenness of the approaching nuptials. It would seem, however, that the importance of the step she was about to take had served to raise the bride above the little affectations of her sex; for she spoke of the preparations like one who owned her interest in their completion, and who even dreaded that something might yet occur to mar them.

"If I were superstitious, and had faith in omens, Lincoln," she said, "the hour and the weather might well intimidate me from taking this step. See, the wind already blows across the endless wastes of the ocean, and the snow is driving through the streets in whirlwinds!"

"It is not yet too late to countermand my orders, Cecil," he said, regarding her anxiously; "I have made all my movements so like a great commander, that it is as easy to retrograde as to advance."

"Would you then retreat before one so little formidable as I?" she returned, smiling.

"You surely understand me as wishing only to change the place of our marriage. I dread exposing you and our kind cousin to the tempest, which, as you say, after sweeping over the ocean so long, appears rejoiced to find land on which to expend its fury."

"I have not misconstrued your meaning, Lionel, nor must you be mistaken in mine. I will become your wife to-night, and cheerfully, too ; for what reason can I have to doubt you now more than formerly ? But my vows must be offered at the altar."

Agnes, perceiving that her cousin spoke with a suppressed emotion that made utterance difficult, gayly interrupted her,—

"And as for the snow, you know little of Boston girls, if you think an icicle has any terrors for them. I vow, Cecil, I do think you and I have been guilty, when children, of coasting in a hand-sled down the side of Beacon, in a worse flurry than this."

"We were guilty of many mad and silly things at ten that might not grace twenty, Agnes."

"Lord, how like a matron she speaks already ! " interrupted the other, throwing up her eyes and clasping her hands in affected admiration ; " nothing short of the church will satisfy so discreet a dame, Major Lincoln ! so dismiss your cares on her account, and begin to enumerate the cloaks and overcoats necessary to your own preservation."

Lionel made a lively reply, when a dialogue of some spirit ensued between him and Agnes, to which even Cecil listened with a beguiled ear. When the evening had advanced, Polwarth made his appearance, suitably attired, and with a face that was sufficiently knowing and important for the occasion. The presence of the captain reminded Lionel of the lateness of the hour, and without delay he hastened to communicate his plans to his friend.

At a few minutes before ten, Polwarth was to accompany the ladies in a covered sleigh to the chapel, which was not a stone's throw from their residence, where the bridegroom was to be in readiness to receive them, with the divine. Referring the captain to Meriton for further instructions, and without waiting to hear the other express his amazement at the singularity of the plan, Major Lincoln said a

few words of tender encouragement to Cecil, looked at his
watch, and throwing his cloak around him, took his hat,
and departed.

We shall leave Polwarth endeavoring to extract the
meaning of all these mysterious movements from the wilful
and amused Agnes (Cecil having retired also), and accompany the bridegroom in his progress towards the residence
of the divine.

Major Lincoln found the streets entirely deserted. The
night was not dark, for a full moon was wading among the
volumes of clouds, which drove before the tempest in dark
and threatening masses, that contrasted singularly and wildly
to the light covering of the hills and buildings of the town.
Occasionally the gusts of the wind would lift eddying
wreaths of fine snow from some roof, and whole squares
were wrapt in mist as the frozen vapor whistled by. At
times, the gale howled among the chimneys and turrets, in
a steady, sullen roaring ; and there were again moments
when the element appeared hushed, as if its fury were expended, and winter, having worked its might, was yielding
to the steady, but insensible advances of spring. There was
something in the season and the hour peculiarly in consonance with the excited temperament of the young bridegroom. Even the solitude of the streets, and the hollow
rushing of the winds, the fleeting and dim light of the moon,
which afforded passing glimpses of surrounding objects, and
then was hid behind a dark veil of shifting vapor, contributed to his pleasure. He made his way through the snow
with that species of stern joy, to which all are indebted, at
times, for moments of wild and pleasing self-abandonment.
His thoughts vacillated between the purpose of the hour,
and the unlooked-for coincidence of circumstances that had
clothed it in a dress of such romantic mystery. Once or
twice a painful and dark thought, connected with the secret
of Mrs. Lechmere's life, found its way among his more
pleasing visions, but it was quickly chased from his mind by
the image of her who awaited his movements in such confiding faith, and with such secure and dependent affection.

As the residence of Dr. Liturgy was on the North End,

which was then one of the fashionable quarters of the town, the distance required that Lionel should be diligent, in order to be punctual to his appointment. Young, active, and full of hope, he passed along the unequal pavements with great rapidity, and had the satisfaction of perceiving by his watch, when admitted to the presence of the clergyman, that his speed had even outstripped the proverbial fleetness of time itself.

The reverend gentleman was in his study, consoling himself for the arduous duties of the day, with the comforts of a large easy chair, a warm fire, and a pitcher filled with a mixture of cider and ginger, together with other articles that would have done credit to the knowledge of Polwarth in spices. His full and decorous wig was replaced by a velvet cap, his shoes were unbuckled, and his heels released from confinement. In short, all his arrangements were those of a man who, having endured a day of labor, was resolved to prove the enjoyments of an evening of rest. His pipe, though filled, and on the little table by his side, was not lighted, in compliment to the guest he expected at that hour. As he was slightly acquainted with Major Lincoln, no introduction was necessary, and the two gentlemen were soon seated; the one endeavoring to overcome the embarrassment he felt on revealing his singular errand, and the other waiting, in no little curiosity, to learn the reason why a member of Parliament, and the heir of ten thousand a year, should come abroad on such an unpropitious night.

At length Lionel succeeded in making the astonished priest understand his wishes, and paused to hear the expected approbation of his proposal.

Dr. Liturgy had listened with the most profound attention, as if to catch some clue to explain the mystery of the extraordinary proceeding, and when the young man concluded, he unconsciously lighted his pipe, and began to throw out large clouds of smoke, like a man who felt there was a design to abridge his pleasures, and who was consequently determined to make the most of his time.

"Married! To be married in church! and after the night lecture?" he muttered in a low voice between his long-drawn puffs. " 'T is my duty, certainly, Major Lincoln, to marry parishioners—"

"In the present instance, as I know my request to be irregular, sir," interrupted the impatient Lionel, "I will make it your interest also." While speaking, he took a well-filled purse from his pocket, and, with an air of much delicacy, laid a small pile of gold by the side of the silver spectacle-case of the divine, as if to show him the difference in the value of the two metals.

Dr. Liturgy bowed his acknowledgments, and insensibly changed the stream of smoke to the opposite corner of his mouth, so as to leave the view of the glittering boon unobstructed. At the same time he raised the heel of one shoe, and threw an anxious glance at the curtained window, to inquire into the state of the weather.

"Could not the ceremony be performed at the house of Mrs. Lechmere?" he asked; "Miss Dynevor is a tender child, and I fear the cold air of the chapel might do her no service."

"It is her wish to go to the altar, and you are sensible it is not my part to question her decision in such a matter."

" 'T is a pious inclination; though I trust she knows the distinction between the spiritual and the temporal church. The laws of the colonies are too loose on the subject of marriages, Major Lincoln; culpably and dangerously loose!"

"But as it is not in our power to alter, my good sir, you will permit me to profit by them, imperfect as they are?"

"Undeniably; it is part of my office to christen, to marry, and to bury; a duty which, I often say, covers the beginning, the middle, and the end of existence. But permit me to help you to a little of my beverage, Major Lincoln; we call it 'Samson,' in Boston; you will find the 'Danite' a warm companion for a February night in this climate."

"The mixture is not inaptly named, sir," said Lionel, after wetting his lips, "if strength be the quality most considered."

"Ah! you have him from the lap of a Delilah; but it is unbecoming in one of my cloth to meddle with aught of the harlot."

He laughed at his own wit, and made a more spirituous than spiritual addition to his glass, while he continued,—

"We divide it into 'Samson with his hair off,' and 'Samson with his hair on'; and I believe myself the most orthodox in preferring the man of strength in his native comeliness. I pledge you, Major Lincoln; may the middle of your days be as happy as the charming young lady you are about to espouse may well render them; and your end, sir, that of a good churchman, and a faithful subject."

Lionel, who considered this compliment as an indication of his success, now rose, and said a few words on the subject of their meeting in the chapel. The divine, who manifestly possessed no great relish for the duty, made sundry slight objections to the whole proceeding, which were, however, soon overcome by the arguments of the bridegroom. At length, every difficulty was happily adjusted, save one, and that the epicurean doctor stoutly declared to be a serious objection to acting in the matter. The church fires were suffered to go down, and his sexton had been taken from the chapel, that very evening, with every symptom on him of the terrible pestilence which then raged in the place, adding, by its danger, to the horrors and the privations of the siege.

"A clear case of the small-pox, I do assure you, Major Lincoln," he continued, "and contracted, without doubt, from some emissaries sent into the town for that purpose, by the wicked devices of the rebels."

"I have heard that each party accuses the other of resorting to these unjustifiable means of annoyance," returned Lionel; "but, as I know our own leader to be above such baseness, I will not suspect any other man of it without proof."

"Too charitable by half, sir, much too charitable! But let the disease come whence it will, I fear my sexton will prove its victim."

"I will take the charge on myself of having the fires renewed," said Lionel; "the embers must yet be in the stoves, and we have still an hour of time before us."

As the clergyman was much too conscientious to retain

possession of the gold without fully entitling himself to the ownership, he had long before determined to comply, notwithstanding the secret yearnings of his flesh. Their plans were now soon arranged, and Lionel, after receiving the key of the chapel, took his leave for a time.

When Major Lincoln found himself in the street again, he walked for some distance in the direction of the chapel, anxiously looking along the deserted way, in order to discover an unemployed soldier, who might serve to perform the menial offices of the absent sexton. He proceeded for some distance without success; for everything human seemed housed, even the number of lights in the windows beginning to decrease in a manner which denoted that the usual hour of rest had arrived. He had paused in the entrance of the Dock Square, uncertain where to apply for an assistant, when he caught a glimpse of the figure of a man, crouching under the walls of the old turreted warehouse, so often mentioned. Without hesitating an instant, he approached the spot, from which the figure neither moved, nor did it indeed betray any other evidence of a consciousness of his proximity. Notwithstanding the dimness of the moon, there was light enough to detect the extreme misery of the object before him. His tattered and thin attire sufficiently bespoke the motive of the stranger for seeking a shelter from the cutting winds behind an angle of the wall, while his physical wants were betrayed by the eager manner in which he gnawed at a bone that might well have been rejected from the mess of the meanest private, notwithstanding the extreme scarcity that prevailed in the garrison. Lionel forgot for a moment his present object, at this exhibition of human suffering, and with a kind voice he addressed the wretched being.

"You have a cold spot to eat your supper in, my friend," he said; "and it would seem, too, but a scanty meal."

Without ceasing to masticate his miserable nutriment, or even raising his eyes, the other said, in a growling voice,—

"The king could shut up the harbor, and keep out the ships; but he has n't the might to drive cold weather from Boston, in the month of March!"

"As I live, Job Pray! Come with me, boy, and I will give you a better meal, and a warmer place to enjoy it in; but first tell me, can you procure a lantern and a light from your mother?"

"You can't go in the ware'us' to-night," returned the lad, positively.

"Is there no place at hand, then, where such things might be purchased?"

"They keep them there," said Job, pointing sullenly to a low building on the opposite side of the square, through one of the windows of which a faint light was glimmering.

"Then take this money, and go buy them for me, without delay."

Job hesitated with ill-concealed reluctance.

"Go, fellow, I have instant need of them, and you can keep the change for your reward."

The young man no longer betrayed any indisposition to go, but answered with great promptitude, for one of his imbecile mind,—

"Job will go, if you will let him buy Nab some meat with the change."

"Certainly, buy what you will with it; and furthermore, I promise you, that neither your mother nor yourself shall want again for food or clothing."

"Job's a-hungry," said the simpleton; "but they say hunger don't come as craving upon a young stomach as upon an old one. Do you think the king knows what it is to be a-cold and hungry?"

"I know not, boy; but I know full well that if one suffering like you were before him, his heart would yearn to relieve him. Go, go, and buy yourself food too, if they have it."

In a very few minutes Lionel saw the simpleton issuing from the house to which he had run at his bidding, with the desired lantern.

"Did you get any food?" said Lionel, motioning to Job to precede him with the light; "I trust you did not entirely forget yourself in your haste to serve me."

"Job hopes he did n't catch the pestilence," returned the

lad, eating at the same time voraciously of a small roll of bread.

"Catch what? what is it you hope you did not catch?"

"The pestilence—they are full of the foul disorder in that house."

"Do you mean the small-pox, boy?"

"Yes; some call it small-pox, and some call it the foul disorder, and other some the pestilence. The king can keep out the trade, but he can't keep out the cold and the pestilence from Boston; but when the people get the town back, they 'll know what to do with it—they 'll send it all to the pest-housen!"

"I hope I have not exposed you unwittingly to danger, Job—it would have been better had I gone myself; for I was inoculated for the terrible disease in my infancy."

Job, who, in expressing the sense of the danger, had exhausted the stores of his feeble mind on the subject, made no reply, but continued walking through the square, until they reached its termination, when he turned, and inquired which way he was to go.

"To the church," said Lionel, "and swiftly, lad."

As they entered Cornhill, they encountered the fury of the wind, when Major Lincoln, bowing his head, and gathering his cloak about him, followed the light which flitted along the pavement in his front. Shut out in a manner from the world by this covering, his thoughts returned to their former channel, and in a few moments he forgot where he was, or whom he was following. He was soon awakened from his abstraction by perceiving that it was necessary for him to ascend a few steps, when, supposing he had reached the place of destination, he raised his head, and unthinkingly followed his conductor into the tower of a large edifice. Immediately perceiving his mistake, by the difference of the architecture from that of the King's Chapel, he reproved the lad for his folly, and demanded why he had brought him thither.

"This is what you call a church," said Job, "though I call it a meetin'us'. It 's no wonder you don't know it— for what the people built for a temple, the king has turned into a stable!"

18

"A stable!" exclaimed Lionel. Perceiving a strong smell of horses in the place, he advanced and threw open the inner door, when, to his amazement, he perceived that he stood in an area fitted for the exercises of the cavalry. There was no mistaking the place, nor its uses. The naked galleries, and many of the original ornaments, were standing ; but the accommodations below were destroyed, and in their places the floor had been covered with earth, for horses and their riders to practise in the cavesson. The abominations of the place even now offended his senses, as he stood on that spot where he remembered so often to have seen the grave and pious colonists assemble, in crowds, to worship. Seizing the lantern from Job, he hurried out of the building, with a disgust that even the unobservant simpleton had no difficulty in discovering. On reaching the street, his eyes fell upon the lights, and on the silent dignity of the Province House, and he was compelled to recollect, that this wanton violation of the feelings of the colonists had been practised directly under the windows of the royal governor.

"Fools, fools!" he muttered bitterly ; "when ye should have struck like men, ye have trifled as children ; and ye have forgotten your manhood, and even your God, to indulge your besotted spleen!"

"And now these very horses are starving for want of hay, as a judgment upon them!" said Job, who shuffled his way industriously at the other's side. "They had better have gone to meetin' themselves, and heard the expounding, than to set dumb beasts a-rioting in a place that the Lord used to visit so often!"

"Tell me, boy, of what other act of folly and madness has the army been guilty?"

"What! have n't you heard of the Old North! They 've made oven-wood of the grandest temple in the Bay! If they dared, they 'd lay their ungodly hands on old Funnel itself!"

Lionel made no reply. He had heard that the distresses of the garrison, heightened as they were by the ceaseless activity of the Americans, had compelled them to convert many houses, as well as the church in question, into fuel. But he saw in the act nothing more than the usual recourse of a common military exigency. It was free from that reckless contempt of a people's feelings, which was exhibited in the prostitution of the ancient walls of the sister edifice which was known throughout New England, with a species of veneration, as the "Old South." He continued his way gloomily along the silent streets, until he reached the more favored temple, in which the ritual of the English Church was observed, and whose roof was rendered doubly sacred, in the eyes of the garrison, by the accidental circumstance of bearing the title of their earthly monarch.

CHAPTER XXII.

"Thou art too like the spirit of Banquo; down!"

Macbeth.

AJOR LINCOLN found the King's Chapel differing in every particular from the venerable but prostituted building he had just quitted. As he entered, the light of his lantern played over the rich scarlet covering of many a pew, and glanced upon the glittering ornaments of the polished organ, which now slumbered in as chilled a silence as the dead, which lay in such multitudes within and without the massive walls. The labored columns, with their slender shafts and fretted capitals, threw shapeless shadows across the dim background, peopling the galleries and ceiling with imaginary phantoms of thin air. As this slight delusion passed away, he became sensible of the change in the temperature. The warmth was not yet dissipated, which had been maintained during the different services of the day; for, notwithstanding the wants of the town and garrison, the favored temple, where the representative of the sovereign was wont to worship, knew not the ordinary privations of the place. Job was directed to supply the dying embers of the stoves with fresh fuel, and as the simpleton well knew where to find the stores of the church, his office was performed with an alacrity that was not a little increased by his own sufferings.

When the bustle of preparation had subsided, Lionel drew a chair from the chancel, while Job crouched by the side of the quivering iron he had heated, in that attitude he was wont to assume, and which so touchingly expressed the secret consciousness he felt of his own inferiority. As the grateful warmth diffused itself over the half-naked frame of the simpleton, his head sunk upon his bosom, and he was fast falling into a slumber, like a worried hound that had at length found ease and shelter. A more active mind would have wished to learn the reasons that could induce his companion to seek such an asylum at that unseasonable hour. But Job was a stranger to curiosity ; nor did the occasional glimmerings of the mind often extend beyond those holy precepts which had been taught him with such care, before disease had sapped his faculties, or those popular principles of the time, that formed so essential a portion of the thoughts of every New Englandman.

Not so with Major Lincoln. His watch told him that many weary minutes must elapse before he could expect to receive his bride ; and he disposed himself to wait, with as much patience as comported with five-and-twenty, and the circumstances. In a short time the stillness of the chapel was restored, interrupted only by the passing gusts of the wind without, and the dull roaring of the furnace, by whose side Job slumbered in a state of happy oblivion.

Lionel endeavored to still his truant thoughts, and bring them in training for the solemn ceremony in which he was soon to be an actor. Finding the task too difficult, he arose, and approaching a window, looked out upon the solitude, and the whirlwinds of snow that drifted through the streets, eagerly listening for those sounds of approach, which his reason told him he ought not yet to expect. Again he seated himself and turned his eyes inquiringly about him, with a sort of inward apprehension that some one lay concealed, in the surrounding gloom, with a secret desire to mar his approaching happiness. There was so much of wild and feverish romance in the incidents of the day, that he found it difficult, at moments, to credit their reality, and had recourse to hasty glances at the alter, his attire, and even his insensible companion, to remove the delusion from his mind. Again he looked upward at the unsteady and huge shadows which wavered along the ceiling of the walls, and his former apprehensions of some hidden evil were revived with a vividness that amounted nearly to a presentiment. So uneasy did he become at length, under this impression, that he walked along the more distant aisles, scrupulously looking into the dark pews, and throwing a scrutinizing glance behind each column, and was rewarded for his trouble by hearing the hollow echoes of his own footsteps.

In returning from this round, he approached the stove, and yielded to a strong desire of listening to the voice of even Job, in a moment of such morbid excitement. Touching the simpleton lightly with his foot, the other awoke with that readiness which denoted the sudden and disturbed nature of his ordinary rest.

"You are unusually dull to-night, Job," said Lionel, endeavoring to hush his uneasiness in affected pleasantry, "or you would inquire the reason why I pay my visit to the church at this extraordinary hour."

"Boston folks love their meetin'us's," returned the obtuse simpleton.

"Ay! but they love their beds, too, fellow; and one half of them are now enjoying what you seem to covet so much."

"Job loves to eat, and be warm!"

"And to sleep too, if one may judge by your drowsiness."

"Yes, sleep is sweet; Job don't feel a-hungered when he's sleeping."

Lionel remained silent for several moments, under a keen perception of the suffering exhibited in the touching helplessness which marked the manner of the other, before he continued,—

"But I expect to be joined soon by the clergyman, and some ladies, and Captain Polwarth."

"Job likes Captain Polwarth—he keeps a grand sight of provisions!"

"Enough of this! can you think of nothing but your stomach, boy?"

"God made hunger," said Job, gloomily, "and he made food too; but the king keeps it for his rake-hellies!"

"Well, listen, and be attentive to what I tell you. One of the ladies who will come here is Miss Dynevor; you know Miss Dynevor, Job? the beautiful Miss Dynevor!"

The charms of Cecil had not, however, made their wonted impression on the dull eye of the idiot, who still regarded the speaker with his customary air of apathy.

"Surely, Job, you know Miss Dynevor!" repeated Lionel, with an irritability that, at any other time, he would have been the first to smile at; "she has often given you money and clothes."

"Yes; Ma'am Lechmere is her grandam!"

This was certainly one of the least recommendations his mistress possessed in the eyes of Lionel, who paused a moment, with inward vexation, before he added,—

"Let who will be her relatives, she is this night to become my wife. You will remain and witness the ceremony, and then you will extinguish the lights, and return the key of the church to Dr. Liturgy. In the morning, come to me for your reward."

The changeling arose with an air of singular importance, and answered,—

"To be sure. Major Lincoln is to be married, and he asks Job to the wedding! Now, Nab may preach her sarmons about pride and flaunty feelings as much as she will; but blood is blood, and flesh is flesh, for all her sayings!"

Struck by the expression of wild meaning that gleamed in the eyes of the simpleton, Major Lincoln demanded an explanation of his ambiguous language. But ere Job had leisure to reply, though his vacant look again denoted that his thoughts were already contracting themselves within their usually narrow limits, a sudden noise drew the attention of both to the entrance of the chapel. The door opened in the next instant, and the figure of the divine, powdered with drifted snow, and encased in various defences against the cold, was seen, moving with a becoming gravity, through the principal aisle. Lionel hastened to receive him, and to conduct him to the seat he had just occupied himself.

When Dr. Liturgy had uncloaked, and appeared in his robes of office, the benevolence of his smile, and the whole expression of his countenance, denoted that he was satisfied with the condition in which he found the preparations.

"There is no reason why a church should not be as comfortable as a man's library, Major Lincoln," he said, hitching his seat a little nearer to the stove. "It is a puritanical and a dissenting idea, that religion has anything forbidding or gloomy in its nature; and wherefore should we assemble amid pains and inconvenience to discharge its sacred offices?"

"Quite true, sir," returned Lionel, looking anxiously through one of the windows; "I have not yet heard the hour of ten strike, though my watch tells me it is time!"

"The weather renders the public clocks very irregular. There are so many unavoidable evils to which flesh is heir, that we should endeavor to be happy on all occasions— indeed it is a duty—"

"It 's not in the natur' of sin to make fallen man happy," said a low, growling voice from behind the stove.

"Ha! what! did you speak, Major Lincoln—a very singular sentiment for a bridegroom!" muttered the divine.

"'T is that weak young man, whom I have brought hither to assist with the fires, repeating some of the lore of his mother; nothing else, sir."

By this time Dr. Liturgy had caught a glimpse of the crouching Job, and comprehending the interruption, he fell back in his chair, smiling superciliously as he continued,—

"I know the lad, sir; I should know him. He is learned in the texts, and somewhat given to disputation in matters of religion. 'T is a pity the little intellect he has, had not been better managed in his infancy; but they have helped to crush his feeble mind with their subtilties. We—I mean we of the established church—often style him the Boston Calvin—ha, ha, ha! Old Cotton was not his equal in subtilty! But speaking of the establishment, do you not fancy that one of the consequences of this rebellion will be to extend its benefits to the colonies, and that we may look forward to the period when the true church shall possess its inheritance in these religious provinces?"

"O, most certainly!" said Lionel, again walking anxiously to the window; "would to God they had come!"

The divine, with whom weddings were matters of too frequent occurrence to awaken his sympathies, understood the impatient bridegroom literally, and replied accordingly—

"I am glad to hear you say it, Major Lincoln, and I hope, when the act of amnesty shall be passed, to find your vote on the side of such a condition."

At this instant Lionel caught a glimpse of the well-known sleigh, moving slowly along the deserted street, and, uttering a cry of pleasure, he rushed to the door to receive his bride. Dr. Liturgy finished his sentence to himself, and rising from his comfortable position, he took the light, and entered the chancel. The disposition of the candles having been previously made, when they were lighted, his book opened, his robes adjusted, and his features settled into a suitable degree of solemnity, he stood, waiting with becoming dignity the approach of those over whom he was to pronounce the nuptial benediction. Job placed himself within the shadows of the building, and stood regarding the attitude and imposing aspect of the priest, with a species of childish awe.

Then came a group, emerging from the obscurity of the distant part of the church, and moving slowly towards the altar. Cecil was in front, leaning on that arm which Lionel had given her, as much for support, as through courtesy. She had removed her outer and warmer garments in the vestibule of the sacred edifice, and now appeared, attired in a manner as well suited to the suddenness and privacy, as to the importance of the ceremony. A mantle of satin, trimmed with delicate furs, fell carelessly from her shoulders, partly concealing by its folds the exquisite proportions of her slender form. Beneath was a vestment of the same rich material, cut after the fashions of that period, in a manner to give the exact outlines of the bust. Across the stomacher were deep rows of fine lace, and wide borders of the same valuable texture followed the retiring edges of her robe, leaving the costly dress within partly exposed to the eye. But the beauty and simplicity of her attire (it was simple for that day) was lost, or rather it served to adorn, unnoticed, the melancholy beauty of her countenance.

As they approached the expecting priest, Cecil threw, by

a gentle movement, her mantle on the rails of the chancel, and accompanied Lionel with a firmer tread than before to the foot of the altar. Her cheeks were pale ; but it was rather with a compelled resolution than dread, while her eyes were full of tenderness and thought. Of the two devotees of Hymen, she exhibited, if not the most composure, certainly the most singleness of purpose, and intentness on the duty before them ; for while the looks of Lionel were stealing uneasily about the building, as if he expected some hidden object to start up out of the darkness, hers were riveted on the priest in sweet and earnest attention.

They paused in their allotted places ; and after a moment was allowed for Agnes and Polwarth, who alone followed, to enter the chancel, the low but deep tones of the minister were heard in the solemn stillness of the place.

Dr. Liturgy had borrowed a suitable degree of inspiration from the dreariness of the hour, and the solitude of the building where he was required to discharge his sacred functions. As he delivered the opening exhortation of the service, he made long and frequent pauses between the members of the sentences, giving to each injunction a distinct and impressive emphasis. But when he came to those closing words—

" *If any man can show just cause why they may not be lawfully joined together, let him now speak, or else, hereafter, forever hold his peace*"—

he lifted his voice, and raised his eyes to the more distant parts of the chapel, as though he addressed a multitude in the gloom. The faces of all present involuntarily followed the direction of his gaze, and a moment of deep expectation, which can only be explained by the singularly wild character of the scene, succeeded the reverberation of his tones. At that moment, when each had taken breath, and all were again turning to the altar, a huge shadow rose upon the gallery, and extended itself along the ceiling, until its gigantic proportions were seen hovering, like an evil spectre, nearly above them.

The clergyman suspended the half-uttered sentence. Cecil grasped the arm of Lionel convulsively, while a shudder passed through her frame, that seemed about to shake it to dissolution.

The shadowy image then slowly withdrew, not without, however, throwing out a fantastic gesture, with an arm which stretched itself across the vaulted roof, and down the walls, as if about to clutch its victims beneath.

"*If any man can show just cause why they may not be lawfully joined together, let him now speak, or else, hereafter, forever hold his peace,*" repeated the priest aloud, as if he would summon the universe at the challenge.

Again the shadow rose, presenting this time the strong and huge lineaments of a human face, which it was not difficult, at such a moment, to fancy possessed even expression and life. Its strongly marked features seemed to work with powerful emotion, and the lips moved as if the airy being was speaking to unearthly ears. Next came two arms, raised above the gazing group, with clasped hands, as in the act of benediction, after which the whole vanished, leaving the ceiling in its own dull white, and the building still as the graves which surrounded it.

Once more the excited minister uttered the summons; and again every eye was drawn, as by a secret impulse, to a spot which seemed to possess the form, without the substance, of a human being. But the shadow was seen no more. After waiting several moments in vain, Dr. Liturgy proceeded, with a voice in which a growing tremor was very perceptible; but no further interruption was experienced to the end of the service.

Cecil pronounced her vows, and plighted her troth, in tones of holy emotion; while Lionel, who was prepared for some strange calamity, went through the service to the end, with a forced calmness. They were married; and when the blessing was uttered, not a sound nor a whisper was heard in the party. Silently they all turned away from the spot, and prepared to leave the place. Cecil stood passively, and permitted Lionel to wrap her form in the folds of her mantle with tender care; and when she would have smiled her thanks for the attention she merely raised her anxious eyes to the ceiling, with an expression that could not be mistaken. Even Polwarth was mute; and Agnes forgot to offer those congratulations and good wishes, with which her heart had so recently been swelling.

The clergyman uttered a few words of caution to Job concerning the candles and the fire, and hurried after the retiring party with a quickness of step that he was willing to ascribe to the lateness of the hour, and with a total disregard to the safety of the edifice; leaving the chapel to the possession of the ill-gifted, but undisturbed son of Abigail Pray.

CHAPTER XXIII.

"Forbear to judge, for we are sinners all ;
Close up his eyes, and draw the curtain close ;
And let us all to meditation."

King Henry VI.

THE bridal party entered their little vehicle silent and thoughtful ; the voice of Polwarth being alone audible, as he gave a few low and hurried orders to the groom who was in waiting. Dr. Liturgy approached for a moment, and made his compliments, when the sleigh darted away from before the building, as swiftly as if the horses that drew it partook of the secret uneasiness of those it held. The movements of the divine, though less rapid, were equally diligent, and in less than a minute the winds whistled, and clouds of snow were driven through a street which everything possessing life appeared once more to have abandoned.

The instant Polwarth had discharged his load at the door of Mrs. Lechmere, he muttered something of "happiness and to-morrow," which his friend did not understand, and dashed through the gate of the courtyard, at the same mad rate that he had driven from the church. On entering the house, Agnes repaired to the room of her aunt, to report that the marriage knot was tied, while Lionel led his silent bride into the empty parlor.

Cecil stood, fixed and motionless as a statue, while her husband removed her cloak and mantle ; her cheeks pale, her eyes riveted on the floor, and her whole attitude and manner exhibiting the intensity of thought which had been created by the scene in which she had just been an actor. When he had relieved her light form from the load of garments in which it had been enveloped by his care, he impelled her gently to a seat by his side on the settee, and for the first time since she had uttered the final vow at the altar, she spoke,—

"Was it a fearful omen?" she whispered, as he folded her to his heart, "or was it no more than a horrid fancy?"

"'T was nothing, love—'t was a shadow— that of Job Pray, who was with me to light the fires."

"No, no, no!" said Cecil, speaking with the rapidity of high excitement, and in tones that gathered strength as she proceeded; "those were never the unmeaning features of the miserable simpleton! Know you, Lincoln, that in the haughty, the terrific outlines of those dreadful lineaments on the wall, I fancied a resemblance to the profile of our great-uncle, your father's predecessor in the title, Dark Sir Lionel, as he was called."

"It was easy to fancy anything, at such a time, and under such circumstances. Do not cloud the happiness of our bridal by these gloomy fancies."

"Am I gloomy or superstitious by habit, Lionel?" she asked, with a deprecating tenderness in her voice, that touched his inmost heart. "But it came at such a moment, and in such a shape, that I should be more than woman not to tremble at its terrible import!"

"What is your dread, Cecil? Are we not married; lawfully, solemnly united?"—the bride shuddered; but perceiving her unwilling, or unable to answer, he continued—"beyond the power of man to sever; and with the consent, nay, by the earnest wish, the command, of the only being who can have a right to express a wish, or have an opinion on the subject?"

"I believe—that is, I think, it is all as you say, Lionel," returned Cecil, still looking about her with a vacant and distressed air, that curdled his blood; "yes—yes, we are certainly married; and O! how ardently do I implore Him who sees and governs all things, that our union may be blessed! but—"

"But what, Cecil? will you let a thing of naught—a shadow—affect you in this manner?"

"''T was a shadow, as you say, Lincoln; but where was the substance?''

"Cecil, my sensible, my good, my pious Cecil, why do your faculties slumber in this unaccountable apathy? Ask your own excellent reason; can there be a shade where nothing obstructs the light?''

"I know not. I cannot reason—I have not reason. All things are possible to Him whose will is law and whose slightest wish shakes the universe. There was a shadow, a dark, a speaking, and a terrible shadow; but who can say where was the reality?''

"I had almost answered, with the phantom, only in your sensitive imagination, love. But arouse your slumbering powers, Cecil, and reflect how possible it was for some curious idler of the garrison to have watched my movements, and to have secreted himself in the chapel; perhaps from wanton mischief, perhaps without motive of any kind.''

"He then chose an awful moment in which to act his gambols!''

"It may have been one whose knowledge was just equal to giving a theatrical effect to his silly deception. But are we to be cheated of our happiness by such weak devices; or to be miserable because Boston contains a fool?''

"I may be weak, and silly, and even impious in this terror, Lincoln,'' she said, turning her softened looks upon his anxious face, and attempting to smile; "but it is assailing a woman in a point where she is most sensitive. You know that I have no reserve with you, now. Marriage with us is the tie that 'binds all charities in one,' and at the moment when the heart is full of its own security, is it not dreadful to have such mysterious presages, be they true, or be they false, answering to the awful appeal of the church!''

"Nor is the tie less binding, less important, or less dear, my own Cecil, to us. Believe me, whatever the pride of manhood may say of high destinies, and glorious deeds, the same affections are deeply seated in our nature, and must be soothed by those we love, and not by those who contribute to our vanity. Why then permit this chill to blight your best affections in their budding?''

There was so much that was soothing to the anxiety of a
bride, in his sentiments, and so much of tender interest in
his manner, that he at length succeeded, in a great degree,
in luring Cecil from her feverish apprehensions. As he
spoke, a mantling bloom diffused itself over her cold and
pallid cheeks, and when he had done, her eyes lighted
with the glow of a woman's confidence, and were turned on
his own in bright, but blushing pleasure. She repeated his
word "chill," with an emphasis and a smile that could
not be misconstrued, and in a few minutes he entirely succeeded in quelling the uneasy presentiments that had
gained a momentary ascendency over her clear and excellent
faculties.

But notwithstanding Major Lincoln reasoned well, and
with so much success, against the infirmity of his bride, he
was by no means equal to maintain as just an argument with
himself. The morbid sensibility of his mind had been
awakened in a most alarming manner by the occurrences of
the evening, though his warm interest in the happiness of
Cecil had enabled him to smother them, so long as he witnessed the extent and nature of her apprehensions. But,
exactly in the proportion as he persuaded her into forgetfulness of the past, his recollections became more vivid and
keen ; and, notwithstanding his art, he might not have been
able to conceal the workings of his troubled thoughts from
his companion, had not Agnes appeared, and announced
the desire of Mrs. Lechmere to receive the bride and bridegroom in her sick chamber.

"Come, Lincoln," said his lovely companion, rising at the
summons, "we have been selfish in forgetting how strongly
my grandmother sympathizes in our good or evil fortunes.
We should have discharged this duty without waiting to be
reminded of it."

Without making any other reply than a fond pressure of
the hand he held, Lionel drew her arm through his own, and
followed Agnes into the little hall which conducted to the
upper part of the dwelling.

"You know the way, Major Lincoln," said Miss Danforth ; "and should you not, my lady bride can show you.

I must go and cast a worldly eye on the little banquet I have
ordered, but which I fear will be labor thrown away, since
Captain Polwarth has disdained to exhibit his prowess at
the board. Truly, Major Lincoln, I marvel that a man of
so much substance as your friend, should be frightened from
his stomach by a shadow ! ''

Cecil even laughed, and in those sweet feminine tones that
are infectious, at the humor of her cousin ; but the dark and
anxious expression that gathered round the brow of her
husband as suddenly checked her mirth.

"Let us ascend, Lincoln," she said, instantly, "and leave
mad Agnes to her household cares, and her folly.''

"Ay, go," cried the other, turning away towards the
supper-room ; "eating and drinking is not ethereal enough
for your elevated happiness ; would I had a repast worthy of
such sentimental enjoyment ! Let me see—dew-drops, and
lovers' tears, in equal quantities, sweetened by Cupid's
smiles, with a dish of sighs, drawn by moonlight, for piquancy, as Polwarth would say, would flavor a bowl to their
tastes. The dew-drops might be difficult to procure, at this
inclement season, and in such a night ; but if sighs and tears
would serve alone, poor Boston is just now rich enough in
materials ! ''

Lionel, and his half-blushing, half-smiling companion,
heard the dying sounds of her voice, as she entered the distant apartment, expressing, by its tones, the mingled pleasantry and spleen of its mistress, and in the next instant they
forgot both Agnes and her humor, as they found themselves
in the presence of Mrs. Lechmere.

The first glance of his eye at their expecting relative,
brought a painful throb to the heart of Major Lincoln. Mrs.
Lechmere had caused herself to be raised in the bed, in which
she was seated nearly upright, supported by pillows. Her
wrinkled and emaciated cheeks were flushed with an unnatural color, that contrasted too violently with the marks
which age and strong passions had impressed, with their
indelible fingers, on the surrounding wreck of those haughty
features, which had once been distinguished for great, if not
attractive beauty. Her hard eyes had lost their ordinary

19

expression of worldly care, in a brightness which caused them rather to glare than to beam with flashes of unbridled satisfaction that could no longer be repressed. In short, her whole appearance brought a startling conviction to the mind of the young man, that whatever might have been the ardor of his own feelings in espousing her grandchild, he had at length realized the fondest desires of a being so worldly, so designing, and, as he was now made keenly to remember, of one also, who, he had much reason to apprehend, was so guilty. The invalid did not seem to think a concealment of her exultation any longer necessary; for stretching out her arms, she called to her child, in a voice raised above its natural tones, and which was dissonant and harsh from a sort of unholy triumph,—

"Come to my arms, my pride, my hope; my dutiful, my deserving daughter! Come, and receive a parent's blessing, that blessing which you so much deserve!"

Even Cecil, warm and consoling as was the language of her grandmother, hesitated an instant at the unnatural voice in which the summons was uttered, and advanced to meet her embrace with a manner less warm than was usual to her own ardent and unsuspecting nature. This secret restraint existed, however, but for a moment; for when she felt the encircling arms of Mrs. Lechmere pressing her warmly to her aged bosom, she looked up into the face of her grandmother, as if to thank her for so much affection, by her own guileless smiles and tears.

"Here, then, Major Lincoln, you possess my greatest, I had almost said my only treasure!" added Mrs. Lechmere. "She is a good, a gentle, and dutiful child; and Heaven will bless her for it, as I do." Leaning forward, she continued, in a less excited voice, "Kiss me, my Cecil, my bride, my Lady Lincoln! for by that loved title I may now call you, as yours, in the course of nature, it soon will be."

Cecil, greatly shocked at the unguarded exultation of her grandmother, gently withdrew herself from her arms, and with eyes bent to the floor in shame, and burning cheeks, she willingly moved aside, to allow Lionel to approach, and

receive his share of the congratulations. He stooped to
bestow the cold and reluctant kiss which the offered cheek
of Mrs. Lechmere invited, and muttered a few incoherent
words concerning his present happiness, and the obligation
she had conferred. Notwithstanding the high and disgust-
ing triumph which had broken through the usually cold and
cautious manner of the invalid, a powerful and unbidden
touch of nature mingled in her address to the bridegroom.
The fiery and unnatural glow of her eyes even softened with
a tear, as she spoke,—

"Lionel, my nephew, my son," she said, "I have endeavored to receive you in a manner worthy of the head of
an ancient and honorable name ; but were you a sovereign
prince, I have now done my last and best in your favor.
Cherish her, love her, be more than husband, be all of kin
to the precious child, for she merits all ! Now is my latest
wish fulfilled ! Now may I prepare myself for the last great
change, in the quiet of a long and tranquil evening to the
weary and troublesome day of life ! "

"Woman !" said a tremulous voice in the background,
"thou deceivest thyself ! "

"Who," exclaimed Mrs. Lechmere, raising her body with
a convulsive start, as if about to leap from the bed, "who
is it speaks ? "

"'T is I," returned the well-remembered tones of Ralph,
as he advanced from the door to the foot of her couch, "'t is
I, Priscilla Lechmere ; one who knows thy merits, and thy
doom ! "

The appalled woman fell back on her pillows, gasping for
breath, the flush of her cheeks giving place to their former
signs of age and disease, and her eye losing its high exultation in the glazed look of sudden terror. It would seem,
however, that a single moment of reflection was sufficient to
restore her spirit, and with it all her deep resentments. She
motioned the intruder away, by a violent gesture of the
hand, and after an effort to command her utterance, she
said, in a voice rendered doubly strong by overwhelming
passion,—

"Why am I braved, at such a moment, in the privacy of

my sick-chamber? Have that madman, or impostor, which-ever he may be, removed from my presence!"

She uttered her request to deadened ears. Lionel neither moved nor answered. His whole attention was given to Ralph, across whose hollow features a smile of calm indiffer-ence passed, which denoted how little he regarded the threat-ened violence. Even Cecil, who clung to the arm of Lionel, with all a woman's dependence on him she loved, was un-noticed by the latter, in the absorbing interest he took in the sudden reappearance of one whose singular and mysterious character had, long since, raised such hopes and fears in his own bosom.

"Your doors will shortly be open to all who may choose to visit here," the old man coldly answered. "Why should I be driven from a dwelling where heartless crowds shall so soon enter and depart at will? Am I not old enough; or do I not bear enough of the aspect of the grave, to become your companion? Priscilla Lechmere, you have lived till the bloom of your cheeks has given place to the color of the dead; your dimples have become furrowed and wrinkled lines, and the beams of your once bright eye have altered to the dull look of care—but you have not yet lived for repentance."

"What manner of language is this?" cried his wondering listener, inwardly shrinking before his steady, but glowing look. "Why am I singled from the world for this persecu-tion? Are my sins past bearing; or am I alone to be re-minded that sooner or later age and death will come? I have long known the infirmities of life, and may truly say that I am prepared for their final consequences."

"'T is well," returned the unmoved and apparently im-movable intruder. "Take, then, and read the solemn de-cree of thy God; and may He grant thee firmness to justify so much confidence."

As he spoke, he extended in his withered hand an open letter towards Mrs. Lechmere, which the quick glance of Lionel told him bore his own name in the superscription. Notwithstanding the gross invasion of his rights, the young man was passive under the detection of this second and gross interference of the other in his most secret matters, watching with eager interest the effect the strange communication would produce on his aunt.

Mrs. Lechmere took the letter from the stranger with a sort of charmed submission, which denoted how completely his solemn manner had bent her to his will. The instant her look fell on the contents, it became fixed and wild. The note was, however, short, and the scrutiny was soon ended. Still, she grasped it with an extended arm, though the vacant expression of her countenance betrayed that it was held before an insensible eye. A moment of silent and breathless wonder followed. It was succeeded by a shudder which passed through the whole frame of the invalid, her limbs shaking violently, until the rattling of the folds of the paper was audible in the most distant corner of the apartment.

"This bears my name," cried Lionel, shocked at her emotions, and taking the paper from her unresisting hands, "and should first have met my eye."

"Aloud, aloud, dear Lionel!" said a faint but earnest whisper at his elbow; "aloud, I implore you, aloud!"

It was not, perhaps, so much in compliance with this affecting appeal, in which the whole soul of Cecil seemed wrapped, as by yielding to the overwhelming flow of that excitement to which he had been aroused, that Major Lincoln was led to conform to her request. In a voice rendered desperately calm by his emotions, he uttered the fatal contents of the note, in tones so distinct that they sounded to his wife, in the stillness of the place, like the prophetic warnings of one from the dead :—

"The state of the town has prevented that close attention to the case of Mrs. Lechmere, which her injuries rendered necessary. An inward mortification has taken place, and her present ease is only the forerunner of her death. I feel it my duty to say, that though she may live many hours, it is not improbable that she will die to-night."

To this short but terrible annunciation, was placed the well-known signature of the attending physician. Here was a sudden change, indeed! All had thought that the disease had given way, when it seemed it had been preying insidiously on the vitals of the sick. Dropping the note, Lionel exclaimed aloud, in the suddenness of his surprise,—

"Die to-night! This is an unexpected summons indeed!"

The miserable woman, after the first nerveless moment of her dismay, turned her looks anxiously from face to face, and listened intently to the words of the note, as they fell from the lips of Lionel, like one eager to detect the glimmerings of hope, in the alarmed expression of their countenances. But the language of her physician was too plain, direct, and positive, to be misunderstood or perverted. Its very coldness gave it a terrific character of truth.

"Do you, then, credit it?" she asked, in a voice whose husky tones betrayed but too plainly her abject unwillingness to be assured. "You! Lionel Lincoln, whom I had thought my friend?"

Lionel turned away silently from the sad spectacle of her misery; but Cecil dropped on her knees at the bedside, and clasping her hands, she elevated them, looking like a beautiful picture of pious hope, as she murmured,—

"He is no friend, dearest grandmother, who would lay flattery to a parting soul! But there is a better and a safer dependence than all this world can offer!"

"And you, too!" cried the devoted woman, rousing herself with a strength and energy that would seem to put the professional knowledge of her medical attendant at defiance; "do you also abandon me? you, whom I have watched in infancy, nursed in suffering, fondled in happiness, ay! and reared in virtue—yes, that I can say boldly in the face of the universe!—you, whom I have brought to this honorable marriage—would you repay me for all, by black ingratitude?"

"My grandmother! my grandmother! talk not thus cruelly to your child!—but lean on the Rock of Ages for support, even as I have leaned on thee!"

"Away—away—weak, foolish child! Excess of happiness has maddened thee! Come hither, my son; let us speak of Ravenscliffe, the proud seat of our ancestors; and of those days we are yet to pass under its hospitable roofs. The silly girl thou hast wived would wish to frighten me!"

Lionel shuddered with inward horror while he listened to the forced and broken intonations of her voice, as she thus uttered the lingering wishes of her nature. He turned again from the view, and, for a moment, buried his face in his hands, as if to exclude the world and its wickedness, together, from his sight.

"My grandmother, look not so wildly at us!" continued the gasping Cecil; "you may have yet hours, nay, days, before you." She paused an instant to follow the unsettled and hopeless gaze of an eye that gleamed despairingly on the objects of the room, and then, with a meek dependence on her own purity, dropping her face between her hands, she cried aloud in her agony,—

"My mother's mother! would that I could die for thee!"

"Die!" echoed the same dissonant voice as before, from a throat that already began to rattle with the hastened approaches of death; "who would die amid the festivities of a bridal! Away—leave me! To thy closet, and thy knees, if thou wilt—but leave me!"

She watched, with bitter resentment, the retiring form of Cecil, who obeyed with the charitable and pious intention of complying literally with her grandmother's order, before she added,—

"The girl is not equal to the task I had set her! All of my race have been weak, but I—my daughter—my husband's niece—"

"What of that niece?" said the startling voice of Ralph, interrupting the diseased wanderings of her mind, "that wife of thy nephew—the mother of this youth? Speak, woman, while time and reason are granted thee."

Lionel now advanced to her bedside, under an impulse that he could no longer subdue, and addressed her solemnly,—

"If thou knowest aught of the dreadful calamity that has befallen my family," he said, "or in any manner hast been accessary to its cause, disburden thy soul, and die in peace. Sister of my grandfather! nay, more, mother of my wife, I conjure thee, speak—what of my injured mother?"

"Sister of thy grandfather—mother of thy wife," repeated Mrs. Lechmere, slowly, and in a manner that sufficiently indicated the unsettled state of her thoughts. "Yes, both are true!"

"Speak to me, then, of my mother, if you acknowledge the ties of blood—tell me of her dark fate!"

"She is in her grave — dead — rotten — yes — yes — her boasted beauty has been fed upon by beastly worms! What more would ye have, mad boy? Wouldst wish to see her bones in their winding-sheet?"

"The truth!" cried Ralph; "declare the truth, and thy own wicked agency in the deed!"

"Who speaks?" repeated Mrs. Lechmere, dropping her voice from its notes of high excitement again to the tremulous cadency of debility and age, and looking about her at the same time, as if a sudden remembrance had crossed her brain; "surely I heard sounds I should know!"

"Here; look on me; fix thy wandering eye, if it yet has power to see, on me," cried Ralph, aloud, as though he would command her attention at every hazard; "'t is I that speak to thee, Priscilla Lechmere."

"What wouldst thou have? My daughter? She is in her grave! Her child? She is wedded to another. Thou art too late! Thou art too late! Would to God thou hadst asked her of me in season— "

"The truth, the truth, the truth!" continued the old man, in a voice that rung through the apartment in wild and startling echoes; "the holy and undefiled truth? Give us that, and naught else."

This singular and solemn appeal awakened the latest energies of the despairing woman, whose inmost soul appeared to recoil before his cries. She made an effort to raise herself once more, and exclaimed,—

"Who says that I am dying? I am but seventy! and 't is only yesterday I was a child; a pure, and uncontaminated child! He lies, he lies! I have no mortification; I am strong, and have years to live and repent in."

In the pauses of her utterance, the voice of the old man was still heard shouting,—

"The truth—the truth; the holy, undefiled truth!"

"Let me rise and look upon the sun," continued the dying woman. "Where are ye all? Cecil, Lionel, my children, do ye desert me now? Why do ye darken the room? Give me light,—more light,—more light! for the sake of all in heaven and earth, abandon me not to this black and terrible darkness!"

Her aspect had become so hideously despairing, that the voice of even Ralph was stilled, and she continued uninterruptedly to shriek out the ravings of her soul.

"Why talk to such as I of death? My time has been too short! give me days,—give me hours,—give me moments! Cecil,—Agnes,—Abigail; where are ye? help me, or I fall!"

She raised herself, by a desperate effort, from the pillows, and clutched wildly at the empty air. Meeting the extended hand of Lionel, she caught it with a dying grasp, gave a ghastly smile, under the false security it imparted, and falling backward again, her mortal part settled, with a universal shudder, into a state of eternal rest.

As the horrid exclamations of the deceased ended, so deep a stillness succeeded in the apartment, that the passing gusts of the gale were heard sighing among the roofs of the town, and might easily be mistaken, at such a moment, for the moanings of unembodied spirits over so accursed an end.

CHAPTER XXIV.

" I wonder, sir, since wives are monstrous to you,
And that you fly them, as you swear them, lordship,
Yet, you desire to marry."

All's Well that Ends Well.

CECIL had left the room of her grandmother with the consciousness of sustaining a load of anguish, to which her young experience had hitherto left her a stranger. On her knees, and in the privacy of her closet, she poured out the aspirations of her pure spirit, in fervent petitions to that Power which she who most needed its support had so long braved, by the mockery of respect, and the seemliness of devotion. With her soul elevated by its recent communion with her God, and her feelings soothed even to calmness by the sacred glow that was shed around them, the youthful bride at length prepared to resume her post at the bedside of her aged relative.

In passing from her own room to that of Mrs. Lechmere, she heard the busy voice of Agnes below, together with the sounds of the preparations that were making to grace her own hasty bridal, and for a moment she paused, to assure herself that all which had so recently passed was more than the workings of a disturbed fancy. She gazed at the unusual, though modest ornaments of her attire ; shuddered as she remembered the awful omen of the shadow ; and then came to the dreadful reality with an overwhelming conviction of its truth. After laying her hand on the door, she paused, with secret terror, to catch the sounds that might issue from the chamber of the sick. After listening a moment, the bustle below was hushed, and she, too, heard the whistling of the wind, as its echoes died away among the chimneys and angles of the building. Encouraged by the death-like stillness of those within her grandmother's room, Cecil now opened the door, under the pleasing impression that she should find the resignation of a Christian, where she had so lately witnessed the incipient ravings of despair. Her entrance was timid ; for she dreaded to meet the hollow, but glaring eye of the nameless being who had borne the message of the physician, and of whose mien and language she retained a confused but fearful recollection. Her hesitation and her fears were, however, alike vain ; for the room was silent and tenantless. Casting one wondering look around, in quest of the form most dear to her, Cecil advanced with a light step to the bed, and raising the coverlet, discovered the fatal truth at a glance.

The lineaments of Mrs. Lechmere had already stiffened, and assumed that cadaverous and ghastly expression which marks the touch of death. The parting soul had left the impression of its agony on her features, exhibiting the wreck of those passions which caused her, even in death, to look backward on that world she was leaving forever, instead of forward to the unknown existence, towards which she was hurried. Perhaps the suddenness, and the very weight of the shock, sustained the cheerless bride in that moment of trial. She neither spoke nor moved for more than a minute ; but remained with her eyes riveted on the desolation of that countenance she had revered from her infancy, with a species of holy awe that was not entirely free from horror. Then came the recollection of the portentous omens of her wedding, and with it a dread that the heaviest of her misfortunes were yet in reserve. She dropped the covering on the pallid features of the dead, and quitted the apartment with a hurried step. The room of Lionel was on the same floor with that which she had just left, and before she had time for reflection, her hand was on its lock. Her brain was bewildered with the rush of circumstances. For a single instant she paused with maiden bashfulness, even recoiling in sensitive shame from the act she was about to commit, when all her fears, mingled with glimmerings of the truth, flashed again

across her mind, and she burst into the room, uttering the
name of him she sought, aloud.

The brands of a fallen fire had been carefully raked together, and were burning with a feeble and wavering flame.
The room seemed filled with a cold air, which, as she
encountered it, chilled the delicate person of Cecil ; and
flickering shadows were playing on the walls, with the uncertain movements imparted by the unsteady light. But,
like the apartment of the dead, the room was still and empty.
Perceiving that the door of the little dressing-room was
open, she rushed to its threshold, and the mystery of the
cold air, and the wavering fire was explained, when she felt
the gusts of wind rush by her from the open door at the foot
of the narrow stairs. If Cecil had ever been required to explain the feelings which induced her to descend, or the
manner in which it was effected, she would have been unable
to comply ; for, quick as thought, she stood on the threshold
of the outer door, nearly unconscious of her situation.

The moon was still wading among the driving clouds,
shedding just light enough to make the spectator sensible
of the stillness of the camp and town. The easterly wind
yet howled along the streets, occasionally lifting whirlwinds
of snow, and wrapping whole squares in its dim wreaths.
But neither man nor beast was visible amid the dreariness.

The bewildered bride shrunk from the dismal view, with
a keen perception of its wild consonance with the death of
her grandmother. In another moment she was again in
the room above, each part of which was examined with
maddening anxiety for the person of her husband. But her
powers, excited and unnatural as they had become, could
support her no longer. She was forced to yield to the impression that Lionel had deserted her in the most trying
moment, and it was not strange that she coupled the sin-
ister omens of the night with his mysterious absence.
The heart-stricken girl clasped her hands in anguish, and
shrieking the name of her cousin, sunk on the floor in total
insensibility.

Agnes was busily and happily employed with her domestics, in preparing such a display of the wealth of the Lech-

meres as should not disgrace her cousin in the eyes of her more wealthy lord and master. The piercing cry, however, notwithstanding the bustle of hurrying servants, and the clatter of knives and plates, penetrated to the supper-room stilling each movement, and blanching every cheek.

"'T is my name!" said Agnes; "who is it calls?"

"If it was *possible*," returned Meriton, with a suitable emphasis, "that Master Lionel's bride *could* scream so, I should say it was my lady's voice!"

"'T is Cecil—'t is Cecil!" cried Agnes, darting from the room. "O, I feared—I feared these hasty nuptials!"

There was a general rush of the menials into the chambers, when the fatal truth became immediately known to the whole family. The lifeless clay of Mrs. Lechmere was discovered in its ghastly deformity, and, to all but Agnes, it afforded a sufficient solution of the situation of the bride.

More than an hour passed before the utmost care of her attendants succeeded in restoring Cecil to a state in which questions might avail anything. Then her cousin took advantage of the temporary absence of her women, to mention the name of her husband. Cecil heard her with sudden joy; but looking about the room wildly, as if seeking him with her eyes, she pressed her hands upon her heart, and fell backward in that state of insensibility from which she had just been roused. No part of this expressive evidence of her grief was lost on the other, who left the room the instant her care had succeeded in bringing the sufferer once more to her recollection.

Agnes Danforth had never regarded her aunt with that confiding veneration and love which purified the affections of the granddaughter of the deceased. She had always possessed her more immediate relatives, from whom she derived her feelings and opinions, nor was she wanting in sufficient discernment to distinguish the cold and selfish traits that had so particularly marked the character of Mrs. Lechmere. She had, therefore, consented to mortify her own spirit, and submit to the privations and dangers of the siege, entirely from a disinterested attachment to her cousin, who, without her presence, would have found her solitude and situation irksome.

In consequence of this disposition of her mind, Agnes was more shocked than distressed by the unexpected death that had occurred. Perhaps, if her anxiety had been less roused in behalf of Cecil, she might have retired to weep over the departure of one she had known so long, and of one, also, that, in the sincerity of her heart, she believed so little prepared for the mighty change. As it was, however, she took her way calmly to the parlor, where she summoned Meriton to her presence.

When the valet made his entrance, she assumed the appearance of a composure that was far from her feelings, and desired him to seek his master, with a request that he would give Miss Danforth a short interview, without delay. During the time Meriton was absent on this errand, Agnes endeavored to collect her thoughts for any emergency.

Minute passed after minute, however, and the valet did not return. She arose, and stepping lightly to the door, listened, and thought she heard his footsteps moving about in the more distant parts of the building, with a quickness that proved he conducted the search in good faith. At length she heard them nigher, and it was soon certain he was on his return. Agnes seated herself, as before, and with an air that seemed as if she expected to receive the master instead of the man. Meriton, however, returned alone.

"Major Lincoln," she said, "you desired him to meet me here?"

The whole countenance of Meriton expressed his amazement, as he answered,—

"Lord! Miss Agnus, Master Lionel has gone out! gone out on *such* a night! and what is more remarkable, he has gone out without his mourning; though the dead of his own blood and connections lies unburied in the house!"

Agnes preserved her composure, and gladly led the valet on in the path his thoughts had taken, in order to come at the truth, without betraying her own apprehensions.

"How know you, Mr. Meriton, that your master has been so far forgetful of appearances?"

"As certain, ma'am, as I know that he wore his parade uniform this evening when he left the house the first time; though little did I dream his honor was going to get married! If he has n't gone out in the same dress, where is it? Besides, ma'am, his last mourning is under lock, and here is the key in my pocket."

"'T is singular he should choose such an hour, as well as the time of his marriage, to absent himself!"

Meriton had long learned to identify all his interests with those of his master, and he colored highly under the oblique imputation that he thought was no less cast on Lionel's gallantry, than on his sense of propriety in general.

"Why, Miss Agnus, you will please remember, ma'am," he answered, "as this wedding has n't been at all like an English wedding—nor can I say that it is altogether usual to die in England as suddenly as Ma'am Lechmere has been pleased—"

"Perhaps," interrupted Agnes, "some accident may have happened to him. Surely no man of common humanity would willingly be away at such a moment."

The feelings of Meriton now took another direction, and he unhesitatingly adopted the worst apprehensions of the young lady.

Agnes leaned her forehead on her hand for a minute in deep reflection before she spoke again, then, raising her eyes to the valet, she said,—

"Mr. Meriton, know you where Captain Polwarth sleeps?"

"Certainly, ma'am! He 's a gentleman as always sleeps in his own bed, unless the king's service calls him elsewhere. A considerate gentleman is Captain Polwarth, ma'am, in respect of himself."

Miss Danforth bit her lip, and her playful eye lighted for an instant, with a ray that banished its look of sadness; but in another moment her features became demure, if not melancholy, and she continued,—

"I believe, then,—'t is awkward and distressing, too, but nothing better can be done."

" Did you please to give me any orders, Miss Agnus ? "

"Yes, Meriton ; you will go to the lodgings of Captain Polwarth, and tell him Mrs. Lincoln desires his immediate presence here, in Tremont Street."

" My lady ! " repeated the amazed valet ; "why, Miss Agnus, the woman says as my lady is unconscionable, and does not know what is doing, or who speaks to her ! A mournful wedding, ma'am, for the heir of our house ! "

"Then tell him," said Agnes, as she arose to leave the room, " that Miss Danforth would be glad to see him."

Meriton waited no longer than was necessary to mutter his approbation of this alteration in the message, when he left the house, with a pace that was a good deal quickened by his growing fears on the subject of his master's safety. Notwithstanding his apprehensions, the valet was by no means insensible to the severity of the climate he was in, nor to the peculiar qualities of that night, in which he was so unexpectedly thrust abroad to encounter its fury. He soon succeeded, however, in making his way to the quarters of Polwarth, in the midst of the driving snow, and in defiance of the cold that chilled his very bones. Happily for the patience of the worthy valet, Shearflint, the semi-military attendant of the captain, was yet up, having just discharged his nightly duties about the person of his master, who had not deemed it prudent to seek his pillow without proving the consolations of the trencher. The door was opened at the first tap of Meriton, and when the other had expressed his surprise by the usual exclamations, the two attendants adjourned to the sitting-room, where the embers of a good wood fire were yet shedding a grateful heat in the apartment.

"What a shocking country is this America for cold, Mr. Shearflint ! " said Meriton, kicking the brands together with his boots, and rubbing his hands over the coals. " I does n't think as our English cold is at all like it. It 's a stronger and a better cold, is ours, but it does n't cut one like dull razors, as this here of America."

Shearflint, who fancied himself particularly liberal, and ever made it a point to show his magnanimity to his ene-

mies, never speaking of the colonists without a sort of protecting air, that he intended should reflect largely on his
own candor, briskly replied,—

"This is a new country, Mr. Meriton, and one should n't
be over-nice. When one goes abroad, one must learn to put
up with difficulties ; especially in the colonies, where it can't
be expected all things should be as comfortable as we has
'em at 'ome."

"Well, now, I call myself as little particular in respect of
weather," returned Meriton, "as any going. But give me
England for climate, if for nothing else. The water comes
down in that blessed country in good, honest drops, and not
in little frozen bits, which prick one's face like so many fine
needles !"

"You do look, Mr Meriton, a little as if you had been
shaking your master's powder puff about your own ears.
But I was just finishing the heel-tap of the captain's hot
toddy ; perhaps if you was to taste it, 't would help to thaw
out the idears."

"God bless me, Shearflint !" said Meriton, relinquishing
his grasp of the tankard, to take breath after a most vigorous draught ; "do you always stuff his night-cap so thick ?"

"No, no ; the captain can tell a mixture by his nose, and
it does n't do to make partial alterations in his glass," returned Shearflint, giving the tankard a circular motion to
stir its contents, while he spoke, and swallowing the trifle
that remained, apparently at a gulp. "Then, as I thinks
it a pity that anything should be wasted in these distressing
times, I generally drinks what 's left, after adding sum'at to
the water, just to mellow it down. But what brings you
abroad such a foul night, Mr. Meriton ?"

"Sure enough, my idears wanted thawing, as you insti-
gated, Shearflint ! Here have I been sent on a message of
life and death, and I was forgetting my errand like a raw
boy just hired from the country !"

"Something is stirring, then !" said the other, offering a
chair, which his companion received, without any words,
while Polwarth's man took another, with equal composure.
"I thought as much, from the captain's hungry appearance,

when he came home to-night, after dressing himself with so much care, to take his supper in Tremont Street."

"Something has been stirring, indeed ! For one thing, it is certain, Master Lionel was married to-night, in the King's Chapel ! "

"Married ! " echoed the other. "Well, thank Heaven, no such unavoidables has befallen us, though we have been amputrated. I could n't live with a married gentleman, no how, Mr. Meriton. A master in breeches is enough for me, without one in petticoats to set him on ! "

"That depends altogether on people's conditions, Shearflint," returned Meriton, with a sort of condescending air of condolence, as though he pitied the other's poverty. "It would be great folly for a captain of foot, that is nothing *but* a captain of foot, to unite in Hymen. But, as we say at Ravenscliffe and Soho, Cupid will listen to the siyths of the heir of a Devonshire baronet, with fifteen thousand a year."

"I never heard any one say it was more than ten," interrupted the other, with a strong taint of ill-humor in his manner.

"Not more than ten ! I can count ten myself, and I am sure there must be some that I does n't know of."

"Well, if it be twenty," cried Shearflint, rising, and kicking the brands among the ashes, in a manner to destroy all the cheerfulness of the little fire that remained, "it won't help you to do your errand. You should remember that us servants of poor captains have nobody to help us with our work, and want our natural rest. What 's your pleasure, Mr. Meriton ? "

"To see your master, Mister Shearflint."

"That 's impossibility ! he 's under five blankets, and I would n't lift the thinnest of them for a month's wages."

"Then I shall do it for you, because speak to him I must. Is he in this room ? "

"Ay, you 'll find him somewhere there, among the bed-clothes," returned Shearflint, throwing open the door of an adjoining apartment, secretly hoping Meriton would get his head broken for his trouble, as he removed himself out of harm's way, by returning to the fireplace.

Meriton was compelled to give the captain several rough shakes before he succeeded in rousing him, in the least, from his deep slumbers. Then, indeed, he overheard the sleeper muttering,—

"A damned foolish business, that! Had we made proper use of our limbs, we might have kept them. You take this man to be your husband,—better for worse,—richer or poorer,—ha! who are you rolling, dog? Have you no regard to digestion, to shake a man in this manner, just after eating?"

"It's I, sir—Meriton."

"And what the devil do you mean by this liberty, Mr. I, or Meriton, or whatever you call yourself?"

"I am sent for you in a great hurry, sir; awful things have happened to-night up in Tremont—"

"Happened!" repeated Polwarth, who by this time was thoroughly awake; "I know, fellow, that your master is married; I gave the bride away myself. I suppose nothing else, that is particularly extraordinary, has happened?"

"O! Lord, yes, sir: my lady is in fainting-fits, and Master Lionel has gone, God knows whither, and Madam Lechmere is dead!"

Meriton had not concluded, before Polwarth sprang from his bed in the best manner he was able, and began to dress himself, by a sort of instinct, though without any definite object. By the unfortunate arrangement of Meriton's intelligence, he supposed the death of Mrs. Lechmere to be in consequence of some strange and mysterious separation of the bride from her husband, and his busy thoughts did not fail to recall the singular interruption of the nuptials, so often mentioned.

"And Miss Danforth," he asked, "how does she bear it?"

"Like a woman, as she is, and a true lady. It is no small thing as puts Miss Agnus beside herself, sir!"

"No, that it is not! she is much more apt to drive others mad."

"'T was she, sir, as sent me to desire you to come up to Tremont Street without any delay."

"The devil it was! Hand me that boot, my good fellow. One boot, thank God, is sooner put on than two. The vest and stock next. You, Shearflint! where have you got to, sirrah? Bring me my leg this instant!"

As soon as his own man heard this order, he made his appearance; and as he was much more conversant with the mystery of his master's toilet than Meriton, the captain was soon equipped for his sudden expedition.

During the time he was dressing, he continued to put hasty questions to Meriton, concerning the cause of the disturbance in Tremont Street, the answers to which only served to throw him more upon the ocean of uncertainty than ever. The instant he was clad, he wrapped himself in his cloak, and, taking the arm of the valet, he essayed to find his way through the tempest to the spot where he was told Agnes Danforth awaited his appearance, with a chivalry that, in another age, and under different circumstances, would have made him a hero.

CHAPTER XXV.

"Proud lineage! now how little thou appearest!"

BLAIR.

NOTWITHSTANDING the unusual alacrity with which Polwarth obeyed the unexpected summons of the capricious being whose favor he had so long courted with so little apparent success, he lingered in his steps as he approached near enough to the house in Tremont Street to witness the glancing lights which flitted before the windows. On the threshold he stopped, and listened to the opening and shutting of doors, and all those marked and yet stifled sounds, which are wont to succeed a visit of the grim monarch to the dwellings of the sick. His rap was unanswered, and he was compelled to order Meriton to show him into the little parlor where he had so often been a guest, under more propitious circumstances. Here he found Agnes awaiting his appearance with a gravity, if not sadness of demeanor, that instantly put to flight certain complimentary effusions with which the captain had determined to open the interview, in order to follow up, in the true temper of a soldier, the small advantage he conceived he had obtained in the good opinion of his mistress. Altering the exulting expression of his features, with his first glance at the countenance of Miss Danforth, Polwarth paid his compliments in a manner better suited to the state of the family, and desired to know if in any manner he could contribute to their comfort or relief.

"Death has been among us, Captain Polwarth," said Agnes, "and his visit has, indeed, been sudden and unexpected. To add to our embarrassment, Major Lincoln is missing!"

As she concluded, Agnes fastened her eyes on the face of the other, as though she would require an explanation of the unaccountable absence of the bridegroom.

"Lionel Lincoln is not a man to fly because death approaches," returned the captain, musing; "and less should I suspect him of deserting, in her distress, one like the lovely creature he has married. Perhaps he has gone in quest of medical aid?"

"It cannot be. I have gathered from the broken sentences of Cecil, that he, and some third person to me unknown, were last with my aunt, and must have been present at her death; for the face was covered. I found the bride in the room which Lionel has lately occupied—the doors open, and with indications that he and his unknown companion had left the house by the private stairs which communicate with the western door. As my cousin speaks but little, all other clue to the movements of her husband is lost, unless this ornament, which I found glittering among the embers of the fire, may serve for such a purpose. It is, I believe a soldier's gorget."

"It is, indeed; and it would seem the wearer has been in some jeopardy, by this bullet-hole through its centre. By heavens!—'t is that of M'Fuse! Here is the 18th engraved; and I know these little marks, which the poor fellow was accustomed to make on it at every battle; for he never failed to wear the bauble. The last was the saddest record of them all!"

"In what manner, then, could it be conveyed into the apartment of Major Lincoln? Is it possible that—"

"In what manner, truly!" interrupted Polwarth, rising in his agitation, and beginning to pace the room, in the best manner his mutilated condition would allow. "Poor Dennis! that I should find such a relic of thy end at last! You did not know Dennis, I believe. He was a man, fair Agnes, every way adapted by nature for a soldier. His was the form of Hercules! the heart of a lion, and the digestion of an ostrich! But he could not master this cruel lead! He is dead, poor fellow, he is dead!"

"Still, you find no clue in the gorget by which to trace the living?" demanded Agnes.

"Ha!" exclaimed Polwarth, starting, "I think I begin to see into the mystery! The fellow who could slay the man with whom he had eaten and drunk, might easily rob the dead! You found the gorget near the fire of Major Lincoln's room, say you, fair Agnes?"

"In the embers, as if cast there for concealment, or dropped in some sudden strait."

"I have it—I have it!" returned Polwarth, striking his hands together, and speaking through his teeth,—"'t was that dog who murdered him, and justice shall now take its swing: fool or no fool, he shall be hung up like jerked beef, to dry in the winds of heaven!"

"Of whom speak you, Polwarth, with that threatening air?" inquired Agnes, in a soothing voice, of which, like the rest of her sex, she well knew not only the power, but when to exercise it.

"Of a canting, hypocritical miscreant, who is called Job Pray—a fellow with no more conscience than brains, nor any more brains than honesty. An ungainly villain; who will eat of your table to-day, and put the same knife that administered to his hunger to your throat to-morrow! It was such a dog that butchered the glory of Erin!"

"It must have been in open battle, then," said Agnes, "for though wanting in reason, Job has been reared in the knowledge of good and evil. The child must be strongly stamped with the wrath of God, indeed, for whom some effort is not made by a Boston mother, to recover his part in the great atonement."

"He, then is an exception; for surely no Christian will join you in the great natural pursuit of eating at one moment, and turn his fangs on a comrade at the next."

"But what has all this to do with the absent bridegroom?"

"It proves that Job Pray has been in his room since the fire was replenished, or some other than you would have found the gorget."

"It proves a singular association, truly, between Major Lincoln and the simpleton," said Agnes, musing; "but still it throws no light on his disappearance. 'T was an old man that my cousin mentioned in her unconnected sentences!"

"My life on it, fair Agnes, that if Major Lincoln has left the house mysteriously to-night, it is under the guidance of that wretch! I have known them together in council more than once, before this."

"Then, if he be weak enough to forsake such a woman as my cousin, at the instigation of a fool, he is unworthy of another thought!"

Agnes colored as she spoke, and turned the conversation with a manner that denoted how deeply she resented the slight to Cecil.

The peculiar situation of the town, and the absence of all her own male relatives, soon induced Miss Danforth to listen to the reiterated offers of service from the captain, and finally to accept them. Their conference was long and confidential; nor did Polwarth retire until his footsteps were assisted by the dull light of the approaching day. When he left the house to return to his own quarters, no tidings had been heard of Lionel, whose intentional absence was now so certain, that the captain proceeded to give his orders for the funeral of the deceased, without any further delay. He had canvassed with Agnes the propriety of every arrangement so fully, that he was at no loss how to conduct himself. It had been determined between them that the state of the siege, as well as certain indications of movements which were already making in the garrison, rendered it inexpedient to delay the obsequies a moment longer than was required by the unavoidable preparations.

Accordingly, the Lechmere vault, in the churchyard of the "King's Chapel," was directed to be opened, and the vain trappings, in which the dead are usually enshrouded, were provided. The same clergyman, who had so lately pronounced the nuptial benediction over the child, was now required to perform the last melancholy offices of the church over the parent, and the invitations to the few friends of the family who remained in the place were duly issued in suitable form.

By the time the sun had fallen near the amphitheatre of hills, along whose crests were, here and there, to be seen the works of the indefatigable men who held the place in leaguer, the brief preparations for the interment of the deceased were completed. The prophetical words of Ralph were now fulfilled, and, according to the custom of the province, the doors of one of its proudest dwellings were thrown open for all those who chose to enter and depart at will. The funeral train, though respectable, was far from extending to that display of solemn countenances which Boston, in its peace and pride, would not have failed to exhibit on any similar occasion. A few of the oldest and most respected of the inhabitants, who were distantly connected by blood or alliances with the deceased, attended; but there had been nothing in the cold and selfish character of Mrs. Lechmere to gather the poor and dependent in sorrowing groups around her funeral rites. The passage of the body, from its late dwelling to the tomb, was quiet, decent, and impressive, but entirely without any demonstrations of grief. Cecil had buried herself and her sorrows, together, in the privacy of her own room, and none of the more distant relatives who had collected, male or female, appeared to find it at all difficult to restrain their feelings within the bounds of the most rigid decorum.

Dr. Liturgy received the body, as usual, on the threshold of the sacred edifice and the same solemn and affecting language was uttered over the dead, as if she had departed soothed by the most cheerful visions of an assured faith. As the service proceeded, the citizens clustered about the coffin, in deep attention, in admiration of the unwonted tremor and solemnity that had crept into the voice of the priest.

Among this little collection of the inhabitants of the colony were interspersed a few men in the military dress, who, having known the family of the deceased in more settled times, had not forgotten to pay the last tribute to the memory of one of its dead.

When the short service was ended, the body was raised on the shoulders of the attendants, and borne into the yard, to its place of final rest. At such a funeral, where few mourned, and none wept, no unnecessary delay would be made in disposing of the melancholy relics of mortality. In a very few moments, the narrow tenement, which contained the festering remains of one who had so lately harbored such floods of human passion, was lowered from the light of day, and the body was left to moulder by the side of those who had gone before to the darkness of the tomb. Perhaps, of all who witnessed the descent of the coffin, Polwarth alone, through that chain of sympathies which bound him to the caprice of Agnes, felt any emotion at all in consonance with the solemn scene. The obsequies of the dead were, like the living character of the woman, cold, formal, and artificial. The sexton and his assistants had hardly commenced replacing the stone which covered the entrance of the vault, when a knot of elderly men set the example of desertion, by moving away in a body from the spot. As they picked their footsteps among the graves, and over the frozen ground of the churchyard, they discoursed idly together of the fortunes and age of the woman of whom they had now taken their leave forever. The curse of selfishness appeared even to have fallen on the warning which so sudden an end should have given to those who forgot they tottered on the brink of the grave. They spoke of the deceased as of one who had failed to awaken the charities of our nature, and though several ventured their conjectures as to the manner in which she had disposed of her worldly possessions, not one remembered to lament that she had continued no longer to enjoy them. From this theme they soon wandered to themselves, and the whole party quitted the churchyard joking each other on the inroads of time, each man attempting to ape the elastic tread of youth, in order not only to conceal from his companions the ravages of age, but with a vain desire to extend the artifice so far, if possible, as to deceive himself.

When the seniors of the party withdrew, the remainder of the spectators did not hesitate to follow ; and in a few min-

utes Polwarth found himself standing before the vault, with
only two others of all those who had attended the body.
The captain, who had been at no little expense of time and
trouble to maintain the decencies which became a near friend
of the family of the deceased stood a minute longer, to
permit these lingering followers to retire also, before he
turned his own back on the place of the dead. But perceiving they both maintained their posts, in silent attention, he
raised his eyes, more curiously, to examine who these loiterers might be.

The one nearest to himself was a man, whose dress and
air bespoke him to be of no very exalted rank in life, while
the other was a woman, of even an inferior condition, if an
opinion might be formed from the squalid misery that was
exhibited in her attire. A little fatigued with the arduous
labors of the day, and the duties of the unusual office he
had assumed, the worthy captain touched his hat with studied
decorum, and said,—

"I thank you, good people, for this mark of respect to
the memory of my deceased friend; but as we have performed all that can now be done in her behalf, we will
retire."

Apparently encouraged by the easy and courteous manner
of Polwarth, the man approached still nigher, and, after
bowing with much respect, ventured to say,—

"They tell me 't is the funeral of Madam Lechmere that
I have witnessed?"

"They tell you true, sir," returned the captain, beginning
slowly to pick his way towards the gate; "of Mrs. Priscilla,
the relict of Mr. John Lechmere—a lady of a creditable
descent, and I think it will not be denied that she has had
honorable interment."

"If it be the lady I suppose," continued the stranger, "she
is of an honorable descent, indeed. Her maiden name was
Lincoln, and she is aunt to the great Devonshire baronet of
that family."

"How! know you the Lincolns?" exclaimed Polwarth,
stopping short, and turning to examine the other with a
stricter eye. Perceiving, however, that the stranger was a

man of harsh and peculiarly forbidding features, in the vulgar dress already mentioned, he muttered, "You may have heard of them, friend, but I should doubt whether your intimacy could amount to such wholesome familiarities as eating and drinking."

"Stronger intimacies than that, sir, are sometimes brought about between men who were born to very different fortunes," returned the stranger, with a peculiarly sarcastic and ambiguous smile, which meant more than met the eye. "But all who know the Lincolns, sir, will allow their claims to distinction. If this lady was one of them, she had reason to be proud of her blood."

"Ay, you are not tainted, I see, with these revolutionary notions, my friend," returned Polwarth: "she was also connected with a very good sort of a family in this colony, called the Danforths—you know the Danforths?"

"Not at all, sir; I—"

"Not know the Danforths!" exclaimed Polwarth, once more stopping to bestow a freer scrutiny on his companion. After a short pause, however, he nodded his head, in approbation of his own conclusions, and added, "No, no—I am wrong—I see you could not have known much of the Danforths."

The stranger appeared quite willing to overlook the cavalier treatment he received, for he continued to attend the difficult footsteps of the maimed soldier, with the same respectful deference as before.

"I have no knowledge of the Danforths, it is true," he answered; "but I may boast of some intimacy with the family of Lincoln."

"Would to God, then," cried Polwarth, in a sort of soliloquy, which escaped him in the fulness of his heart, "you could tell us what has become of its heir!"

The stranger stopped short in his turn, and exclaimed,—

"Is he not serving with the army of the king, against this rebellion! Is he not here?"

"He is here, or he is there, or he is anywhere: I tell you he is lost."

"He is lost!" echoed the other.

"Lost!" repeated a humble female voice, at the very elbow of the captain.

The singular repetition of his own language aroused Polwarth from the abstraction into which he had suffered himself to fall. In his course from the vault to the churchyard gate, he had unconsciously approached the woman before mentioned, and when he turned at the sounds of her voice, his eyes fell full upon her anxious countenance. The very first glance was enough to tell the observant captain that, in the midst of her poverty and rags, he saw the broken remains of great female beauty. Her dark and intelligent eyes, set as they were in a sallow and sunken countenance, still retained much of the brightness, if not of the softness and peace, of youth. The contour of her face was also striking, though she might be said to resemble one whose loveliness had long since departed with her innocence. But the gallantry of Polwarth was proof even against the unequivocal signs of misery, if not of guilt, which were so easily to be traced in her appearance ; and he too much respected even the remnants of female charms which were yet visible amid such a mass of unseemliness, to regard them with an unfriendly eye. Apparently encouraged by the kind look of the captain, the woman ventured to add,—

"Did I hear aright, sir? Said you that Major Lincoln was lost?"

"I am afraid, good woman," returned the captain, leaning on the iron-shod stick, with which he was wont to protect his footsteps along the icy streets of Boston, "that this siege has, in your case, proved unusually severe. If I am not mistaken in a matter in which I profess to know much, nature is not supported as nature should be. You would ask for food, and God forbid that I should deny a fellow-creature a morsel of that which constitutes both the seed and the fruits of life. Here is money."

The muscles of the attenuated countenance of the woman worked with a sudden convulsive motion, and, for a moment, she glanced her eyes wistfully towards his silver, but a slight flush passing quickly over her pallid features, she answered,—

"Whatever may be my wants and my suffering, I thank my God that he has not levelled me with the beggar of the streets. Before that evil day shall come, may I find a place amongst these frozen hillocks where we stand ! But I beg pardon, sir : I thought I heard you speak of Major Lincoln."

"I did ; and what of him ? I said he was lost ; and it is true, if that be lost which cannot be found."

"And did Madam Lechmere take her leave before he was missing ? " asked the woman, advancing a step nearer to Polwarth, in her intense anxiety to be answered.

"Do you think, good woman, that a gentleman of Major Lincoln's notion of things would disappear after the decease of his relative, and leave a comparative stranger to fill the office of principal mourner ? "

"The Lord forgive us all our sins and wickedness ! " muttered the woman, drawing the shreds of her tattered cloak about her shivering form, and hastening silently away into the depths of the graveyard. Polwarth regarded her unceremonious departure for a moment in surprise, and then, turning to his remaining companion, he remarked,—

"That woman is unsettled in her reason, for the want of wholesome nutriment. It is just as impossible to retain the powers of the mind, and neglect the stomach, as it is to expect a truant boy will make a learned man." By this time the worthy captain had forgotten whom it was he addressed, and he continued, in his usual philosophic strain : "Children are sent to school to learn all useful inventions but that of eating ; for to eat—that is, to eat with judgment —is as much of an invention as any other discovery. Every mouthful a man swallows has to undergo four important operations, each of which may be called a crisis in the human constitution."

"Suffer me to help you over this grave," said the other, officiously offering his assistance.

"I thank you, sir, I thank you—'t is a sad commentary on my words ! " returned the captain, with a melancholy smile. "The time has been when I served in the light corps, but your men in unequal quantities are good for little else but garrisons ! As I was saying, there is first, the selection ; second, mastication ; third, deglutition ; and lastly, the digestion."

"Quite true, sir," said the stranger, a little abruptly; "thin diet and light meals are best for the brain."

"Thin diet and light meals, sir, are good for nothing but to rear dwarfs and idiots ! " returned the captain, with some heat ; "I repeat to you, sir—"

He was interrupted by the stranger, who suddenly smothered a dissertation on the connection between the material and immaterial, by asking,—

"If the heir of such a family be lost, is there none to see that he is found again ? "

Polwarth, finding himself thus checked in the very opening of his theme, stopped again, and stared the other full in the face for a moment, without making any reply. His kind feeling, however, got the better of his displeasure, and yielding to the interest he felt in the fate of Lionel, he answered,—

"I would go all lengths, and incur every hazard, to do him service."

"Then, sir, accident has brought those together who are willing to engage in the same undertaking. I, too, will do my utmost to discover him. I have heard he has friends in this province. Has he no connection to whom we may apply for intelligence ? "

"None nearer than a wife."

"A wife ! " repeated the other, in surprise. "Is he, then, married ?"

A long pause ensued, during which the stranger mused deeply, and Polwarth bestowed a still more searching scrutiny than ever on his companion. It would appear that the result was not satisfactory to the captain ; for, shaking his head, in no very equivocal manner, he resumed the task of picking his way among the graves, towards the gate, with renewed diligence. He was in the act of seating himself in the pung, when the stranger again stood at his elbow, and said,—

"If I knew where to find his wife, I would offer my services to the lady."

Polwarth pointed to the building of which Cecil was now
the mistress, and answered, somewhat superciliously, as he
drove away,—

"She is there, my good friend, but your application will
be useless."

The stranger received the direction in an understanding
manner, and smiled with satisfied confidence, while he took
the opposite route from that by which the busy equipage
of the captain had already disappeared.

CHAPTER XXVI.

"Up Fish Street ! down Saint Magnus' corner !
Kill and knock down ! Throw them into Thames !
What noise is this I hear ? Dare any be so bold to sound
Retreat or parley, when I command them kill ?"

King Henry IV.

IT was rarely, indeed, that the equal-minded Polwarth undertook an adventure with so fell an intent as was the disposition with which he directed the head of the hunter to be turned towards the Dock Square. He had long known the residence of Job Pray, and often, in passing from his lodgings near the common, into the more fashionable quarter of the town, the good-natured epicure had turned his head to bestow a nod and a smile on the unsophisticated admirer of his skill in the culinary art. But now, as the pung whirled out of Cornhill into the well-known area, his eye fell on the low and gloomy walls of the warehouse, with a far less amicable design.

From the time he was apprised of the disappearance of his friend, the captain had been industriously ruminating on the subject, in a vain wish to discover any probable reason that might induce a bridegroom to adopt so hasty, and, apparently, so unjustifiable a step, as the desertion of his bride, and that, too, under circumstances of such peculiar distress. But the more he reasoned, the more he found himself involved in the labyrinth of perplexity, until he was glad to seize on the slightest clue which offered, to lead him from his obscurity. It has already been seen in what manner he received the intelligence conveyed through the gorget of M'Fuse, and it now remains for us to show with what commendable ingenuity he improved the hint.

21

It had always been a matter of surprise to Polwarth, that a man like Lionel should tolerate so much of the society of the simpleton; nor had it escaped his observation, that the communications between the two were a little concealed under a shade of mystery. He had overheard the foolish boast of the lad, the preceding day, relative to the death of M'Fuse; and the battered ornament, in conjunction with the place where it was found, which accorded so well with his grovelling habits, had tended to confirm its truth. The love of Polwarth for the grenadier was second only to his attachment for his earlier friend. The one had avowedly fallen, and he soon began to suspect that the other had been strangely inveigled from his duty by the agency of this ill-gifted changeling. To conceive an opinion, and to become confirmed in its justice, were results generally produced by the same operation of the mind, with this disciple of animal philosophy. Whilst he stood near the tomb of the Lechmeres, in the important character of chief mourner, he had diligently revolved in his mind the brief arguments which he found necessary to this conclusion. The arrangement of his ideas might boast of the terseness of a syllogism. His proposition and inference were something as follows: Job murdered M'Fuse; some great evil has occurred to Lionel,—and therefore Job has been its author.

It is true, there was a good deal of intermediate argument to support this deduction, at which the captain cast an extremely cursory glance, but which the reader may easily conceive, if at all gifted in the way of imagination. It would require no undue belief of the connection between very natural effects and their causes, to show that Polwarth was not entirely unreasonable in suspecting the agency of the simpleton, nor in harboring the deep and bitter resentment that so much mischief, even though it were sustained from the hands of a fool, was likely to awaken. Be that as it may, by the time the pung had reached the point already mentioned, its rapid motion, which accelerated the ordinarily quiet circulation of his blood, together with the scene through which he had just passed, and the recollections which had been crowding on his mind, conspired

to wind up hi⸱ resolution to a very obstinate pitch of determination. Of all his schemes, embracing, as they did, com-
pulsion, confession, and punishment, Job Pray was, of
course, destined to be both the subject and the victim.

The shadows of evening were already thrown upon the
town, and the cold had long before driven the few dealers in
meats and vegetables, who continued to find daily employment around the ill-furnished shambles, to their several
homes. In their stead, there was only to be seen a meagre
and impoverished follower of the camp, stealing along the
shadows of the building, with her half-famished child, as
they searched among the offals of the market for some neglected morsel, to eke out the scanty meal of the night.
But while the common mart presented this appearance of
dulness and want, the lower² part of the square exhibited a
very different aspect.

The warehouse was surrounded by a body of men in
uniform, whose disorderly and rapid movements proclaimed
at once, to the experienced eye of the captain, that they
were engaged in a scene of lawless violence. Some were
rushing furiously into the building, armed with such weapons as the streets first offered to their hands, while others
returned, filling the air with their threats and outcries. A
constant current of eager soldiers was setting out of the
dark passages in the neighborhood towards the place, and
every window of the building was crowded with excited
witnesses, who clung to the walls, apparently animating
those within by their cheers and applause.

When Polwarth bade Shearflint pull the reins, he caught
the quick, half-formed sentences that burst from the rioters,
and even before he was able, in the duskiness of the evening,
to discover the facings of their uniform, his ear detected the
well-known dialect of the Royal Irish. The whole truth
now broke upon him at once, and throwing his obese person
from the sleigh, in the best manner he was able, he hobbled
into the throng, with a singular compound of feeling,
which owed its birth to the opposing impulses of a thirst for
vengeance, and the lingering influence of his natural kindness. Better men than the captain have, however, lost

sight of their humanity, under those fierce sympathies that are awakened in moments of tumult and violence. By the time he had forced his person into the large, dark apartment that formed the main building, he had, in a great degree suffered himself to be worked into a sternness of purpose, which comported very ill with his intelligence and rank. He even listened with unaccountable pleasure to the threats and denunciations which filled the building ; until he foresaw, from their savage nature, there was great danger that one half of his object, the discovery of Lionel, was likely to be frustrated by their fulfilment. Animated anew by this impression, he threw the rioters from him with prodigious energy, and succeeded in gaining a position where he might become a more efficient actor in the fray.

There is still light enough to discover Job Pray placed in the centre of the warehouse, on his miserable bed, in an attitude between lying and sitting. While his bodily condition seemed to require the former position, his fears had induced him to attempt the latter. The large, red blotches which covered his unmeaning countenance, and his flushed eyeballs, too plainly announced that the unfortunate young man, in addition to having become the object of the wrath of a lawless mob, was a prey to the ravages of that foul disorder which had long before lighted on the town. Around this squalid subject of poverty and disease, a few of the hardiest of the rioters, chiefly the surviving grenadiers of the 18th, had gathered ; while the less excited, or more timid among them, practised their means of annoyance at a greater distance from the malign atmosphere of the distemper. The bruised and bloody person of the simpleton manifested how much he had already suffered from the hands of his tormentors, who happily possessed no very fatal weapons, or the scene would have been much earlier terminated. Notwithstanding his great bodily debility, and the pressing dangers that beset him on every side, Job continued to face his assailants, with a sort of stupid endurance of the pains they inflicted.

At the sight of this revolting spectacle, the heart of Polwarth began greatly to relent, and he endeavored to make

himself heard in the clamor of fifty voices.   But his presence
was unheeded, for the remonstrances were uttered to ignorant
men, wildly bent on vengeance.

"Pul the baist from his rags!" cried one; "'tis no a
human man, but a divil's imp, in the shape of a fellow-
cratur!"

"For such as *him* to murder the flower of the British
army!" said another; "his small-pox is nothing but a foul
invintion of the ould one, to save him from his daisarrev-
ings!"

"Would any but a divil invint such a disorder at all?"
interrupted a third, who, even in his anger, could not forget
his humor. "Have a care, b'ys, he may give it to the
whole family the naat'ral way, to save the charges of the
inoculation?"

"Have done wid yer foolery, Terence," returned the first;
"would ye trifle about death, and *his* unrevenged? Put a
coal into his filth, b'ys, and burren *it* and him in the same
bonfire!"

"A coal! a coal!—a brand for the divil's burning!"
echoed twenty soldiers, eagerly listening, in the madness of
their fury, to the barbarous advice.

Polwarth again exerted himself, though unsuccessfully, to
be heard; nor was it until a dozen voices proclaimed, in disappointment, that the house contained neither fire nor fuel,
that the sudden commotion in the least subsided.

"Out of the way! out of the way wid ye!" roared one of
gigantic mould, whose heavy nature had, like an overcharged
volcano, been slowly wrought up to the eve of a fearful
eruption; "here is fire to destroy a salamander! Be he
divil or be he saint, he has great need of his prayers!"

As he spoke, the fellow levelled a musket, and another
instant would have decided the fate of Job, who cowered
before the danger with instinctive dread, had not Polwarth
beat up the piece with his cane, and interposed his body
between them.

"Hold your fire, brave grenadier," he said, warily adopting a middle course between the language of authority and
that of counsel. "This is hasty and unsoldier-like. I

knew and loved your late commander well ; let us obtain the confessions of the lad before we proceed to punishment, —there may be others more guilty than he."

The men regarded the unexpected intruder with such furious aspects as augured ill of their deference for his advice and station. "Blood for blood!" passed from mouth to mouth, in low, sullen mutterings; and the short pause which had succeeded his appearance was already broken by still less equivocal marks of hostility, when, happily for Polwarth, he was recognized, through the twilight, by a veteran of the grenadiers, as one of the former intimates of M'Fuse. The instant the soldier communicated this discovery to his fellows, the growing uproar again subsided, and the captain was relieved from no small bodily terror, by hearing his own name passing among them, coupled with such amicable additions as "*His* ould fri'nd!" "An offisher of the light troops!" "He that the ribbils massacred of a leg!" etc. As soon as this explanation was generally understood, his ears were greeted with a burst from every mouth, of—

"Hurrah for Captain Pollywarreth! *His* fri'nd! the brave Captain Pollywarreth!"

Pleased with his success, and secretly gratified by the commendations that were now freely lavished on himself, with characteristic liberality, the mediator improved the slight advantage he had obtained, by again addressing them.

"I thank you for your good opinion, my friends," he added, "and must acknowledge it is entirely mutual. I love the Royal Irish, on account of one that I well knew, and greatly esteemed, and who, I fear, was murdered in defiance of all the rules of war."

"Hear ye that, Dennis?—murdered!"

"Blood for blood!" muttered three or four surly voices at once.

"Let us deliberate, that we may be just, and just that our vengeance may be lawful," Polwarth quickly answered, fearful that if the torrent once more broke loose, it would exceed his powers to stay it. "A true soldier always awaits his orders ; and what regiment in the army can boast of its discipline, if it be not the 18th? Form yourselves in a circle around your prisoner, and listen, while I extract the truth from him. After that, should he prove guilty, I will consign him to your tenderest mercy.''

The rioters, who only saw, in the delay, a more methodical execution of their own violent purpose, received the proposition with another shout, and the name of Polwarth, pronounced in all the varieties of their barbarous idioms, rung loudly through the naked rafters of the building, while they disposed themselves to comply.

The captain, with a wish to gain time to command his thoughts, required that a light should be struck, in order, as he said, to study the workings of the countenance of the accused. As the night had now gathered about them in good earnest, the demand was too reasonable for objection, and with the same headlong eagerness that they had manifested a few minutes before, to shed the blood of Job, they turned their attention, with thoughtless versatility, to effect this harmless object. A brand had been brought, for a very different end, when the plan of burning was proposed, and it had been cast aside again with the change of purpose. A few of its sparks were now collected, and some bundles of oakum, which lay in a corner of the warehouse, were fired, and carefully fed in such a manner as to shed a strong light through every cranny of the gloomy edifice.

By the aid of this fitful glare, the captain succeeded once more in marshalling the rioters in such a manner that no covert injury could be offered to Job. The whole affair now assumed, in some measure, the character of a regular investigation. The curiosity of the men without overcame their fears of infection, and they crowded into the place, in earnest attention, until, in a very few moments, no other sound was audible but the difficult and oppressed respiration of their victim. When all the other noises had ceased, and Polwarth perceived by the eager and savage countenances, athwart which the bright glare of the burning hemp was gleaming, that delay might yet be dangerous, he proceeded at once in his inquiries.

''You may see, Job Pray, by the manner in which you are surrounded,'' he said, '' that judgment has at length overtaken you, and that your only hope for mercy lies in your truth. Answer, then, to such questions as I shall put, and keep the fear of God before your eyes."

The captain paused, to allow this exhortation to produce its desired effect. But Job, perceiving that his late tormentors were quiet, and to all appearances bent on no immediate mischief, sunk his head languidly upon his blankets, where he lay in silence, watching, with rolling and anxious eyes, the smallest movements of his enemies. Polwarth soon yielded to the impatience of his listeners, and continued,—

"You are acquainted with Major Lincoln?"

"Major Lincoln!" grumbled three or four of the grenadiers; "is it of *him* that we want to hear?"

"One moment, my worthy 18ths; I shall come at the whole truth the sooner, by taking this indirect course."

"Hurrah for Captain Pollywarreth!" shouted the rioters, "him that the ribbils massacred of a leg!"

"Thank you—thank you, my considerate friends: answer, fellow, without prevarication; you dare not deny to me your knowledge of Major Lincoln?"

After a momentary pause, a low voice was heard muttering among the blankets,—

"Job knows all the Boston people; and Major Lincoln is a Boston boy."

"But with Major Lincoln you had a more particular acquaintance. Restrain your impatience, men; these questions lead directly to the facts you wish to know." The rioters, who were profoundly ignorant of what sort of facts they were to be made acquainted with by this examination, looked at each other in uneasy doubt, but soon settled down again into their former deep silence. "You know him better than any other gentleman of the army?"

"He promised Job to keep off the grannies, and Job agreed to run his arr'nds."

"Such an arrangement betrays a greater intimacy than is usual between a wise man and a fool! If you are then so close in league with him, I demand what has become of your associate?"

The young man made no reply.

"You are thought to know the reasons why he has left his friends," returned Polwarth, "and I now demand that you declare them."

"Declare!" repeated the simpleton, in his most unmeaning and helpless manner; "Job was never good at his schooling."

"Nay, then, if you are obstinate, and will not answer, I must withdraw, and permit these brave grenadiers to work their will on you."

This threat served to induce Job to raise his head, and assume that attitude and look of instinctive watchfulness that he had so recently abandoned. A slight movement of the crowd followed, and the terrible words of "Blood for blood!" again passed among them in sullen murmurs. The helpless youth, whom we have been obliged to call an idiot, for want of a better term, and because his mental imbecility removed him without the pale of legal responsibility, now stared wildly about him, with an increasing expression of reason, that might be ascribed to the force of that inward fire which preyed upon his vitals, and which seemed to purify the spirit in proportion as it consumed the material dross of his existence.

"It 's agin the laws of the Bay to beat and torment a fellow-creature," he said, with a solemn earnestness in his voice, that would have melted hearts of ordinary softness; "and, what is more, it 's agin His holy book! If you had n't made oven-wood of the Old North, and a horse-stable of the Old South, you might have gone to hear such expounding as would have made the hair rise on your wicked heads!"

The cries of "Have done wid his foolery!" "The imp is playing his games on us!" "As if his wooden mockery was a church at all fit for a ra'al Christian!" were heard on every side, and they were succeeded by the often repeated and appalling threat of "Blood for blood!"

"Fall back, men, fall back!" cried Polwarth, flourishing his walking-stick in such a manner as effectually to enforce his orders; "wait for his confession before you judge.

Fellow, this is the last and trying appeal to your truth—your life most probably depends on the answer. You are known to have been in arms against the crown. Nay, I myself saw you in the field on that day when the troops a-a-a countermarched from Lexington; since when you are known to have joined the rebels while the army went out to storm the intrenchment on the heights of Charlestown;" at this point in the recapitulation of the offences of Job, the captain was suddenly appalled by a glimpse at the dark and threatening looks that encircled him, and he concluded with a laudable readiness; "on that glorious day when his majesty's troops scattered your provincial rabble like so many sheep driven from their pastures by dogs!"

The humane ingenuity of Polwarth was rewarded by a burst of loud and savage laughter. Encouraged by this evidence of his power over his auditors, the worthy captain proceeded with an increased confidence in his own eloquence.

"On that glorious day," he continued, gradually warming with his subject "many a gallant gentleman and hundreds of fearless privates met their fate. Some fell in open and manly fight, and according to the chances of regular warfare. Some—he-e-m—some have been mutilated; and will carry the marks of their glory with them to the grave." His voice grew a little thick and husky as he proceeded; but, shaking off his weakness, he ended with an energy that he intended should curdle the heart of the prisoner: "while, fellow, some have been murdered!"

"Blood for blood!" was heard again passing its fearful round. Without attempting any longer to repress the rising spirit of the rioters, Polwarth continued his interrogatories, entirely led away by the strength of his own feelings on this sensitive subject.

"Remember you such a man as Dennis M'Fuse?" he demanded in a voice of thunder: "he that was treacherously slain in your inmost trenches, after the day was won! Answer me, knave, were you not among the rabble, and did not your own vile hand the bloody deed?"

A few words were heard from Job, in a low muttering tone, of which only "the rake-hellies," and "the people will teach 'em the law !'' were sufficiently distinct to be understood.

"Murder him ! part him sowl from body !" exclaimed the fiercest of the grenadiers.

"Hold!" cried Polwarth; "but one moment more; I would relieve my mind from the debt I owe his memory. Speak, fellow ! what know you of the death of the commander of these brave grenadiers ?"

Job, who had listened to his words attentively, though his uneasy eyes still continued to watch the slightest movements of his foes, now turned to the speaker with a look of foolish triumph, and answered,—

"The 18th came up the hill, shouting like roaring lions ! but the Royal Irish had a death-howl, that evening, over their tallest man !"

Polwarth trembled with the violence of the passions that beset him ; but, while with one hand he motioned to the men to keep back, with other he produced the battered gorget from his pocket, and held it before the eyes of the simpleton.

"Know you this ?" he demanded; "who sent the bullet through this fatal hole ?"

Job took the ornament, and for a moment regarded it with an unconscious look. But his countenance gradually lighting with a ray of unusual meaning, he laughed in scornful exultation, as he answered,—

"Though Job is a fool, he can shoot !"

Polwarth started back aghast, while the fierce resentments of his ruder listeners broke through all restraint. They raised a loud and savage shout, as one man, filling the building with hoarse execrations and cries for vengeance. Twenty expedients to destroy their captive were named in a breath, and with all the characteristic vehemence of their nation. Most of them would have been irregularly adopted, had not the man who attended the burning hemp caught up a bundle of the flaming combustibles, and shouted aloud,—

"Smodder him in the fiery flames ! he's an imp of darkness ; burren him in his rags from before the face of man !

The barbarous proposition was received with a sort of frenzied joy, and in another moment a dozen handfuls of the oakum were impending above the devoted head of the helpless lad. Job made a feeble attempt to avert the dreadful fate that threatened him, but he could offer no other resistance than his own weakened arm, and the abject moanings of his impotent mind. He was enveloped in a cloud of black smoke, through which the forked flames had already begun to play, when a women burst into the throng, casting the fiery combustibles from her, on either side, as she advanced, with a strength that seemed supernatural. When she had reached the bed, she tore aside the smoking pile with hands that disregarded the heat, and placed herself before the victim, like a fierce lioness at bay, in defence of her whelps. In this attitude she stood an instant, regarding the rioters with a breast that heaved with passions too strong for utterance, when she found her tongue, and vented her emotions with all the fearlessness of a woman's indignation.

"Ye monsters in the shape of men; what is 't ye do !" she exclaimed in a voice that rose above the tumult, and had the effect to hush every mouth. "Have ye bodies without hearts ! the forms without the bowels of the creatures of God ! Who made you judges and punishers of sin ! Is there a father among you, let him come and view the anguish of a dying child ! Is there a son, let him draw near, and look upon a mother's sorrow ! O ! ye savages, worse than the beasts of the howling wilderness, who have mercy on their kinds, what is 't ye do ; what is 't ye do !"

The air of maternal intrepidity with which this burst from the heart was uttered, could not fail to awe the worst passions of the rioters, who gazed on each other in stupid wonder, as if uncertain how to act. The hushed and momentary stillness was, however, soon broken once more by the low, murmuring threat of "Blood for blood !"

"Cowards ! dastards ! soldiers in name, and demons in your deeds !" continued the undaunted Abigail ; "come ye here to taste of human blood? Go,—away with you to the hill ! and face the men of the Bay, who stand ready to meet you with arms in their hands, and come not hither to bruise the broken reed ! Poor, suffering, and stricken as he is, by a hand far mightier than yours, my child will meet you there, to your shame, in the cause of his country, and the law !''

This taunt was too bitter for the unnurtured tempers to which she appealed, and the dying spark of their resentment was at once kindled into a blaze by the galling gibe.

The rioters were again in motion, and the cry of ''Burn the hag and the imp together !'' was fiercely raised, when a man of a stout, muscular frame forced his way into the centre of the crowd, making room for the passage of a female, whose gait and attire, though her person was concealed by her mantle, announced her to be of a rank altogether superior to the usual guests of the warehouse. The unexpected appearance, and lofty, though gentle bearing of this unlooked-for visitor, served to quell the rising uproar, which was immediately succeeded by so deep a silence, that a whisper could have been heard in that throng, which so lately resounded with violent tumult and barbarous execrations.

CHAPTER XXVII.

"Ay, sir, you shall find me reasonable ; if it be so, I shall do that
that is reason."

SLENDER.

DURING the close of the foregoing scene, Polwarth
was in a bewildered state, that rendered him utterly
incapable of exertion, either to prevent or to assist
the evil intentions of the soldiery. His discretion
and all his better feelings were certainly on the side of humanity, but the idle vaunt of the simpleton had stirred anew
the natural thirst for vengeance. He recognized, at the first
glance, in the wan but speaking lineaments of the mother
of Job, those faded remnants of beauty that he had traced,
so lately, in the squalid female attendant who was seen lingering near the grave of Mrs. Lechmere. As she rushed before the men, with all the fearlessness of a mother who stood
in defence of her child, the brightness of her dark eyes,
aided as they were by the strong glare from the scattered
balls of fire, and the intense expression of maternal horror
that shone in every feature of her countenance, had imparted
to her appearance a dignity and interest that greatly served
to quell the unusual and dangerous passions that beset him.
He was on the point of aiding her appeal by his authority
and advice, when the second interruption to the brutal purpose of the men occurred, as just related. The effect of this
strange appearance, in such a place, and at such a time, was
not less instant on the captain than on the vulgar throng
who surrounded him. He remained a silent and an attentive spectator.

The first sensation of the lady in finding herself in the

centre of such a confused and unexpected throng, was unequivocally that of an alarmed and shrinking delicacy ; but,
forgetting her womanish apprehensions in the next moment,
she collected the powers of her mind, like one sustained by
high and laudable intentions, and dropping the silken folds
of her calash, exhibited the pale, but lovely countenance of
Cecil to the view of the wondering bystanders. After a
moment of profound silence, she spoke,—

"I know not why I find this fierce collection of faces
around the sick-bed of that unfortunate young man," she
said ; "but if it be with evil purpose, I charge you to relent, as you love the honor of your gallant profession, or
fear the power of your leaders. I boast myself a soldier's
wife, and promise you, in the name of one who has the ear
of Howe, pardon for what is past, or punishment for your
violence, as you conduct yourselves."

The rude listeners stared at each other in irresolute hesitation, seeming already to waver in their purpose, when
the old grenadier, whose fierceness had so nearly cost Job his
life, gruffly replied,—

"If you're an officer's lady, madam, you'll be knowing
how to feel for the fri'nds of him, that's dead and gone. I
put it to the face of your ladyship's reason, if it's not too
much for men to bear,—and they such men as the 18ths,
—to hear a fool boasting on the highways and through the
streets of the town, that he has been the death of the like
of Captain M'Fuse, of the grenadiers of that same radg'-
ment !"

"I believe I understand you, friend," returned Cecil,
"for I have heard it whispered that the young man was
believed to aid the Americans on the bloody day to which
you allude ; but if it is not lawful to kill in battle, what are
you, whose whole trade is war ? "

She was interrupted by half-a-dozen eager, though respectful voices, muttering, in the incoherent and vehement
manner of their country, "It's all a difference, my lady ! "
"Fair fighting isn't foul fighting, and foul fighting is murder !"—with many other similar half-formed and equally
intelligible remonstrances. When this burst was ended, the

same grenadier, who had before spoken, took on himself the office of explaining.

"If your ladyship spoke never a word again, ye 've said the truth this time," he answered, "though it is n't exactly the truth at all. When a man is kill't in the fair war, it 's a god-send ; and no true Irishman will gainsay the same : but skulking behind a dead body, and taking aim into the f'atures of a fellow-creature, is what we complain of against the bloody-minded rascal. Besides, was n't the day won? and even *his* death could n't give *them* the victory ! "

"I know not all these nice distinctions in your dreadful calling, friend," Cecil replied, "but I have heard that many fell after the troops mounted the works."

"That did they ; sure your ladyship is knowing all about it ! and it 's the more need that some should be punished for the murders ! It 's hard to tell when we 've got the day with men who make a fight of it after they are fairly baiten ! "

"That others suffered under similar circumstances," continued Cecil, with a quivering lip, and a tremulous motion of her eyelids, "I well know ; but never had supposed it more than the usual fortune of every war. But even if this youth has erred—look at him !—is he an object for the resentment of men, who pride themselves on meeting their enemies on equal terms? He has long been visited by a blow from a hand far mightier than yours, and even now is laboring, in addition to all other misfortunes, under that dangerous distemper, whose violence seldom spares those it seizes. Nay, you, in the blindness of your anger, expose yourselves to its attacks ; and when you think only of revenge, may become its victims ! "

The crowd insensibly fell back as she spoke, and a large circle was left around the bed of Job, while many in the rear stole silently from the building, with a haste that betrayed how completely apprehension had got the better of their more evil passions. Cecil paused but an instant, and pursued her advantage.

"Go," she said ; "leave this dangerous vicinity. I have business with this young man, touching the interests, if not the life of one dear, deservedly dear, to the whole army, and would be left alone with him and his mother. Here is money—retire to your own quarters, and endeavor to avert the danger you have so wantonly braved by care and regimen. Go ; all shall be forgotten and pardoned."

The reluctant grenadier took her gold, and, perceiving that he was already deserted by most of his companions, he made an awkward obeisance to the fair being before him, and withdrew, not without, however, casting many a savage and sullen glance at the miserable wretch who had been thus singularly rescued from his vengeance. Not a soldier now remained in the building ; and the noisy and rapid utterance of the retiring party, as each vehemently recounted his deeds, soon became inaudible in the distance.

Cecil then turned to those who remained, and cast a rapid glance at each individual of the party. The instant she encountered the wondering look of Polwarth the blood mantled her pale features once more, and her eyes fell, for an instant, in embarrassment to the floor.

"I trust we have been drawn here for a similar purpose, Captain Polwarth," she said, when the slight confusion had passed away—"the welfare of a common friend?"

"You have not done me injustice," he replied. "When the sad office, which your fair cousin charged me with, was ended, I hastened hither to follow a clue which, I have reason to believe, will conduct us to—"

"What we most desire to find," said Cecil, involuntarily glancing her anxious eyes towards the other spectators. "But our first duty is humanity. Cannot this miserable young man be reconveyed to his own apartment, and have his hurts examined?"

"It may be done now, or after our examination," returned the captain, with a cool indifference that caused Cecil to look up at him in surprise. Perceiving the unfavorable impression his apathy had produced, Polwarth turned carelessly to a couple of men who were still curious lookers-on, at the outer door of the building, and called to them—"Here, Shearflint, Meriton, remove the fellow into yonder room."

22

The servants in waiting, who had been hitherto wondering witnesses of all that passed, received this mandate with strong disgust. Meriton was loud in his murmurs, and approached the verge of disobedience before he consented to touch such an object of squalid misery. As Cecil, however, enforced the order by her wishes, the disagreeable duty was performed, and Job replaced on his pallet in the tower, from which he had been rudely dragged an hour before, by the soldiers.

At the moment when all danger of further violence disappeared, Abigail had sunk on some of the lumber of the apartment, where she remained during the removal of her child, in a sort of stupid apathy. When, however, she perceived that they were now surrounded by those who were bent on deeds of mercy rather than of anger, she slowly followed into the little room, and became an anxious observer of the succeeding events.

Polwarth seemed satisfied with what had been done for Job, and now stood aloof, in sullen attendance on the pleasure of Cecil. The latter, who had directed every movement with female tenderness and care, bade the servants retire into the outer room and wait her orders. When Abigail, therefore, took her place in silence near the bed of her child, there remained present, besides herself and the sick, only Cecil, the captain, and the unknown man, who had apparently led the former to the warehouse. In addition to the expiring flames of the oakum, the feeble light of a candle was shed though the room, merely rendering the gloomy misery of its tenants more striking.

Notwithstanding the high but calm resolution which Cecil had displayed in the foregoing scene with the rioters, and which still manifested itself in the earnest brightness of her intelligent eye, she appeared willing to profit by the duskiness of the apartment, to conceal her expressive features from the gaze of even the forlorn female. She placed herself in one of the shadows of the room, and partly raised the calash, by a graceful movement of one of her hands, while she addressed the simpleton.

"Though I have not come hither with any intent to punish, nor in any manner to intimidate you with threats, Job Pray," she said, with an earnestness that rendered the soft tones of her voice doubly impressive ; "yet have I come to question you on matters that it would be wrong, as well as cruel in you, to misrepresent, or in any manner to conceal—"

"You have little cause to fear that anything but the truth will be uttered by my child," interrupted Abigail. "The same power that destroyed his reason, has dealt tenderly with his heart ; the boy knows no guile ; would to God the same could be said of the sinful woman who bore him !"

" I hope the character you give your son will be supported by his conduct," replied Cecil ; "with this assurance of his integrity, I will directly question him. But that you may see I take no idle liberty with the young man, let me explain my motives." She hesitated a moment, and averted her face unconsciously, as she continued, " I should think, Abigail Pray, that my person must be known to you?"

"It is—it is," returned the impatient woman, who appeared to feel the feminine and polished elegance of the other a reproach to her own misery; "you are the happy and wealthy heiress of her whom I have seen this day laid in her vault. The grave will open for all alike,—the rich and and the poor, the happy as well as the wretched ! Yes, yes, I know you ! you are the bride of a rich man's son !"

Cecil shook back the dark tresses that had fallen about her countenance, and raised her face, tinged with its richest bloom, as she answered, with an air of matronly dignity,—

" If you then know of my marriage, you will at once perceive that I have the interest of a wife in Major Lincoln. I would wish to learn his movements of your son."

"Of my boy ! of Job ! from the poor despised child of poverty and disease, would you learn tidings of your husband?—no, no, young lady, you mock us ; he is not worthy to be in the secrets of one so great and happy !"

"Yet I am deceived if he is not. Has there not been one called Ralph, a frequent inmate of your dwelling, during the past year ; and has he not been concealed here within a very few hours?"

Abigail started at this question, though she did not hesitate to answer without prevarication,—

"It is true. If I am to be punished for harboring a being that comes I know not whence, and goes I know not whither, who can read the heart, and knows what man, by his own limited powers, could never know, I must submit. He was here yesterday; he may be here again to-night; for he comes and goes at will. Your generals and army may interfere, but such as I dare not forbid it."

"Who accompanied him when he departed last?" asked Cecil, in a voice so low that, but for the profound stillness of the place, it would have been inaudible.

"My child, my weak, unmeaning, miserable child!" said Abigail, with a reckless promptitude that seemed to court any termination to her misery, however sudden or adverse. "If it be treasonable to follow in the footsteps of that nameless man, Job has much to answer for!"

"You mistake my purpose; good, rather than evil, will attend your answers, should they be found true."

"True!" repeated the woman, ceasing the rocking motion of her body, and looking proudly up into the anxious face of Cecil; "but you are great and powerful, and are privileged to open the wounds of the unhappy!"

"If I have said anything to hurt the feelings of a child, I shall deeply regret the words," said Cecil, with gentle fervor; "I would rather be your friend than your oppressor, as you will learn when occasion offers."

"No—no—*you* can never be a friend to *me*!" exclaimed the woman, shuddering; "the wife of Major Lincoln ought never to serve the interests of Abigail Pray!"

The simpleton, who had apparently lain in dull indifference to what was passing, raised himself now from among his rags, and said, with foolish pride,—

"Major Lincoln's lady has come to see Job, because Job is a gentleman's son!"

"You are the child of sin and misery!" groaned Abigail, burying her head in her cloak; "would that you had never seen the light of day!"

"Tell me, then, Job, whether Major Lincoln himself has

paid you this compliment, as well as I," said Cecil, without regarding the conduct of the mother; "when did you see him last?"

"Perhaps I can put these questions in a more intelligible manner," said the stranger, with a meaning glance of his eye towards Cecil, that she appeared instantly to comprehend. He turned then to Job, whose countenance he studied closely, for several moments, before he continued,—"Boston must be a fine place for parades and shows, young man; do you ever go to see the soldiers exercise?"

"Job always keeps time in the marching," returned the simpleton; "'t is a grand sight to see the grannies treading it off to the awful sound of drums and trumpets!"

"And Ralph," said the other, soothingly, "does he march in their company too?"

"Ralph! he's a great warrior! he teaches the people their trainings, out on the hills; Job sees him there every time he goes for the major's provisions."

"This requires some explanation," said the stranger.

"'T is easily obtained," returned the observant Polwarth. "The young man has been the bearer of certain articles periodically, from the country into the town, during the last six months, under the favor of a flag."

The man mused a moment before he pursued the subject.

"When were you last among the rebels, Job?" he at length asked.

"You had best not call the people rebels," muttered the young man, sullenly, "for they won't put up with bitter names."

"I was wrong indeed," said the stranger. "But when went you last for provisions?"

"Job got in last Sabba'day morning; and that's only yesterday!"

"How happened it, fellow, that you did not bring the articles to me?" demanded Polwarth, with a good deal of impatient heat.

"He has unquestionably a sufficient reason for the apparent neglect," said the cautious and soothing stranger. "You brought them here, I suppose, for some good reason?"

" Ay ! to feed his own gluttony ! '' muttered the irritated captain.

The mother of the young man clasped her hands together convulsively, and made an effort to rise and speak ; but she sunk again into her humble posture, as if choked by emotions that were too strong for utterance.

This short, but impressive pantomime was unnoticed by the stranger, who continued his inquiries in the same cool and easy manner as before.

" Are they yet here ? '' he asked.

" Certain," said the unsuspecting simpleton ; " Job has hid them till Major Lincoln comes back. Both Ralph and Major Lincoln forgot to tell Job what to do with the provisions."

" In that case I am surprised you did not pursue them with your load."

" Everybody thinks Job's a fool," muttered the young man ; " but he knows too much to be lugging provisions out ag'in among the people. Why ! '' he continued, raising himself, and speaking, with a bright glare dancing across his eyes, that betrayed how much he prized the envied advantage ; " the Bay-men come down with cart-loads of things to eat, while the town is filled with hunger ! ''

"True; I had forgotten they were gone out among the Americans : of course they went under the flag that you bore in ? ''

" Job did n't bring any flag—insygns carry the flags ! He brought a turkey, a grand ham, and a little sa'ce—there was n't any flag among them."

At the sound of these eatables, the captain pricked up his ears, and he probably would have again violated the rigid rules of decorum, had not the stranger continued his questions.

" I see the truth of all you say, my sensible fellow," he observed. " It was easy for Ralph and Major Lincoln to go out by means of the same privilege that you used to enter."

" To be sure," muttered Job, who, tired of the questions, had already dropped his head again among his blankets— " Ralph knows the way—he 's Boston born ! ''

The stranger turned to the attentive bride, and bowed, as if he were satisfied with the result of his examination. Cecil understood the expression of his countenance, and made a movement towards the place where Abigail Pray was seated on a chest, betraying, by the renewed rocking of her body, and the low groans that from time to time escaped her, the agony of mind she endured.

"My first care," she said, speaking to the mother of Job, "shall be to provide for your wants; after which I may profit by what we have now gathered from your son."

"Care not for me and mine!" returned Abigail, in a tone of bitter resignation. "The last blow is struck, and it behooves such as we to bow our heads to it in submission. Riches and plenty could not save your grandmother from the tomb, and perhaps Death may take pity, ere long, on me. What do I say, sinner that I am! can I never bring my rebellious heart to wait his time!"

Shocked at the miserable despair that the other exhibited, and suddenly recollecting the similar evidences of a guilty life that the end of Mrs. Lechmere had revealed, Cecil continued silent, in sensitive distress. After a moment to collect her thoughts, she said, with the meekness of a Christian, united to the soothing gentleness of her sex,—

"We are surely permitted to administer to our earthly wants, whatever may have been our transgressions. At a proper time I will not be denied in my wish to serve you. Let us now go," she added, addressing her unknown companion. Then, observing Polwarth making an indication to advance to her assistance, she gently motioned him back, and anticipated his offer, by saying, "I thank you, sir—but I have Meriton, and this worthy man, besides my own maid without—I will not further interfere with your particular objects."

As she spoke, she bestowed a melancholy, though sweet smile on the captain, and left the tower and the building, before he could presume to dispute her pleasure. Notwithstanding Cecil and her companion had obtained from Job all that he could expect, or in fact had desired to know, Polwarth lingered in the room, making those preparations that should indicate an intention to depart. He found, at length, that his presence was entirely disregarded by both mother and child. The one was still sitting, with her head bowed to her bosom, abandoned to her own sorrows, while the other had sunk into his customary dull lethargy, giving no other signs of life than by his labored and audible breathing. The captain, for a moment, looked upon the misery of the apartment, which wore a still more dreary aspect under the dull light of the paltry candle, as well as at the disease and suffering which were too plainly exhibited in the persons of its abject tenants ; but the glance at neither served to turn him from his purpose. Temptation had beset the humble follower of Epicurus, in a form that never failed to subdue his most philosophic resolutions ; and, in this instance, it prevailed once more over his humanity. Approaching the pallet of the simpleton, he spoke to him in a sharp voice, saying,—

"You must reveal to me what you have done with the provisions with which Mr. Seth Sage has intrusted you, young man—I cannot overlook so gross a violation of duty, in a matter of such singular importance. Unless you wish to have the grannies of the 18th back upon you, speak at once, and speak truly."

Job continued obstinately silent, but Abigail raised her head, and answered for her child,—

"He has never failed to carry the things to the quarters of the major, whenever he got back. No, no—if my boy was so graceless as to steal, it would not be *him* that he would rob !"

"I hope so—I hope so, good woman ; but this is a sort of temptation to which men yield easily in times of scarcity," returned the impatient captain, who probably felt some inward tokens of his own frailty in such matters. "If they had been delivered, would not I have been consulted concerning their disposition ? The young man acknowledges that he quitted the American camp yesterday at an early hour."

"No, no," said Job ; "Ralph made him come away on Saturda'-night. He left the people without his dinner."

" And repaid his loss by eating the stores! Is this your honesty, fellow? "

" Ralph was in such a hurry that he would n't stop to eat. Ralph 's a proper warrior, but he does n't seem to know how sweet it is to eat! "

" Glutton! gormandizer! thou ostrich of a man! " exclaimed the angry Polwarth; " is it not enough that you have robbed me of my own, but you must make me more conscious of my loss by thy silly prating! "

" If you really suspect my child of doing wrong to his employer," said Abigail, " you know neither his temper now his breeding. I will answer for him, and with bitterness of heart do I say it, that nothing in the shape of food has entered his mouth for many long and weary hours. Hear you not his piteous longings for nourishment? God, who knows all hearts, will hear and believe his cry! "

" What say you, woman? " cried Polwarth, aghast with horror " not eaten, did you say? What, hast thou not, unnatural mother, provided for his wants?—why has he not shared in your meals? "

Abigail looked up into his face with eyes that gleamed with hopeless want, as she answered,—

" Would I willingly see the child of my body perish of hunger? The last crumb he had was all that was left me, and that came from the hands of one, who, in better justice, should have sent me poison! "

" Nab don't know of the bone that Job found before the barracks," said the young man, feebly; " I wonder if the king knows how sweet bones are? "

" And the provisions, the stores! " cried Polwarth, nearly choking—" foolish boy, what hast thou done with the provisions? "

" Job knew the grannies could n't find them under that oakum," said the simpleton, raising himself to point out their place of concealment, with silly exultation—" when Major Lincoln comes back, maybe he 'll give Nab and Job the bones to pick! "

Polwarth was no sooner made acquainted with the situation of the precious stores, than he tore them from their concealment, with the violence of a maniac. As he separated the articles with an unsteady hand, he rather panted than breathed ; and during the short operation, every feature in his honest face was working with extraordinary emotion. Now and then he muttered in an under-tone,— "No food!"—"Suffering of inanition!" or some such expressive exclamation, that sufficiently explained the current of his thoughts. When all was fairly exposed, he shouted in a tremendous voice,—

"Shearflint! thou rascal! Shearflint—where have you hidden yourself?"

The reluctant menial knew how dangerous it was to hesitate answering a summons uttered in such a voice, and while his master was yet repeating his cries, he appeared at the door of the little apartment, with a face expressive of the deepest attention.

"Light up the fire, thou prince of idlers!" Polwarth continued in the same high strain ; "here is food, and there is hunger! God be praised that I am the man who is permitted to bring the two acquainted! Here, throw on oakum—light up, light up!"

As these rapid orders were accompanied by a corresponding earnestness of action, the servant, who knew his master's humor, set himself most diligently at work to comply. A pile of the tarred combustible was placed on the dreary and empty hearth, and by a touch of the candle, it was lighted into a blaze. As the roar of the chimney and the bright glare were heard and seen, the mother and child both turned their longing eyes towards the busy actors in the scene. Polwarth threw aside his cane, and commenced slicing the ham with a dexterity that denoted great practice, as well as an eagerness that renewed the credit of his disgraced humanity.

"Bring wood—hand down that apology for a gridiron —make coals, make coals at once, rascal," he said, at short intervals : "God forgive me, that I should ever have meditated evil to one suffering under the heaviest of curses! D 'ye hear, thou Shearflint! bring more wood ; I shall be ready for the fire in a minute."

"'T is impossible, sir," said the worried domestic; "I have brought the smallest chip there is to be found—wood is too precious in Boston to be lying in the streets."

"Where do you keep your fuel, woman?" demanded the captain, unconscious that he addressed her in the same rough strain that he used to his menial—"I am ready to put down."

"You see it all! you see it all!" said Abigail, in the submissive tones of a stricken conscience; "the judgment of God has not fallen on me singly!"

"No wood! no provisions!" exclaimed Polwarth, speaking with difficulty; then, dashing his hand across his eyes, he continued to his man, in a voice whose hoarseness he intended should conceal his emotion,—"thou villain, Shearflint, come hither—unstrap my leg!"

The servant looked at him in wonder, but an impatient gesture hastened his compliance.

"Split it into ten thousand fragments; 't is seasoned and ready for the fire. The best of them,—they of flesh, I mean,—are but useless incumbrances, after all! A cook wants hands, eyes, nose, and palate, but I see no use for a leg!"

While he was speaking, the philosophic captain seated himself on the hearth with great indifference, and, by the aid of Shearflint, the culinary process was soon in a state of forwardness.

"There are people," resumed the diligent Polwarth, who did not neglect his avocation while speaking, "that eat but twice a day; and some who eat but once; though I never knew any man thrive who did not supply nature in four substantial and regular meals. These sieges are damnable visitations on humanity, and there should be plans invented to conduct a war without them. The moment you begin to starve a soldier, he grows tame and melancholy: feed him, and defy the devil! How is it, my worthy fellow? do you like your ham running or dry?"

The savory smell of the meat had caused the suffering invalid to raise his feverish body, and he sat watching, with greedy looks, every movement of his unexpected benefactor. His parched lips were already working with impatience, and every glance of his glassy eye betrayed the absolute dominion of physical want over his feeble mind. To this question he made the simple and touching reply of—

"Job is n't particular in his eating."

"Neither am I," returned the methodical gourmand, returning a piece of the meat to the fire, that Job had already devoured in imagination : " one would like to get it up well, notwithstanding the hurry. A single turn more, and it will be fit for the mouth of a prince. Bring hither that trencher, Shearflint—it is idle to be particular about crockery in so pressing a case. Greasy scoundrel, would you dish a ham in its gravy? What a nosegay it is, after all ! Come hither ; help me to the bed."

"May the Lord, who sees and notes each kind thought of his creatures, bless and reward you for this care of my forlorn boy ! " exclaimed Abigail, in the fulness of her heart. " But will it be prudent to give such strong nourishment to one in a burning fever ? "

"What else would you give, woman ? I doubt not he owes his disease to his wants. An empty stomach is like an empty pocket—a place for the devil to play his gambols in. 'T is your small doctor who prates of a meagre regimen. Hunger is a distemper of itself, and no reasonable man, who is above listening to quackery, will believe it can be a remedy. Food is the prop of life ; and eating, like a crutch to a maimed man. Shearflint, examine the ashes for the irons of my supporter, and then dish a bit of the meat for the poor woman. Eat away, my charming boy, eat away ! " he continued, rubbing his hands in honest delight, to see the avidity with which the famishing Job received his boon. "The second pleasure in life is to see a hungry man enjoy his meal ; the first being more deeply seated in human nature. This ham has the true Virginia flavor ! Have you such a thing as a spare trencher, Shearflint ? It is so near the usual hour, I may as well sup. It is rare, indeed, that a man enjoys two such luxuries at once ! "

The tongue of Polwarth ceased the instant Shearflint administered to his wants; the warehouse, into which he had so lately entered with such fell intent, exhibiting the strange spectacle of the captain, sharing, with social communion, in the humble repast of its hunted and miserable tenants.

CHAPTER XXVIII.

" Sir Thurio, give us leave, I pray, awhile ;
We have some secrets to confer about."
Two Gentlemen of Verona.

DURING the preceding exhibition of riot and degradation in the Dock Square, a very different state of things existed beneath the roof of a proud edifice that stood in an adjacent street. As was usual at that hour of the night, the windows of Province House were brilliant with lights, as if in mockery of the naked dreariness of the neighboring church ; and every approach to that privileged residence of the representative of royalty was closely guarded by the vigilance of armed men. Into this favored dwelling it now becomes necessary to remove the scene, in order to pursue the thread of our unpretending narrative.

Domestics, in rich military liveries, might be seen gliding from room to room, in the hurry of a banquet—some bearing vessels of the most generous wines into the apartment where Howe entertained the leaders of the royal army, and others returning with the remnants of a feast, which, though sumptuously served, having felt the scarcity of the times, had offered more to the eyes than to the appetites of the guests. Idlers, in the loose undress of their martial profession, loitered through the halls ; and many a wistful glance, or lingering look, followed the odorous scents, as humbler menials received the viands to transport them into the more secret recesses of the building. Notwithstanding the life and activity which prevailed, every movement was conducted in silence and regularity ; the whole of the lively scene affording a happy illustration of the virtues and harmony of order.

Within the walls of that apartment, to which every eye seemed directed as to a common centre, in anticipation of the slightest wish of those who revelled there, all was bright and cheerful. The hearth knew no want of fuel ; the coarser workmanship of the floor was hid beneath rich and ample carpets, while the windows were nearly lost within the sweeping folds of curtains of figured damask. Everything wore an air of exquisite comfort, blended with a species of careless elegance. Even the most minute article of the furniture had been transported from that distant country, which was then thought to monopolize all the cunning arts of handicraft, to administer to the pleasures of those who, however careless of themselves in moments of trial, courted the most luxurious indulgences in their hours of ease.

Along the centre of this gay apartment was spread the hospitable board of the entertainer. It was surrounded by men in the trappings of high military rank, though here and there might be seen a guest, whose plainer attire and dejected countenance betrayed the presence of one or two of those misjudging colonists, whose confidence in the resistless power of the crown began already to waver. The lieutenant of the king held his wonted place at the banquet, his dark visage expressing all the heartiness of a soldier's welcome, while he pointed out this or that favorite amongst an abundant collection of wines, that included the choicest liquors of Europe.

"For those who share the mess of a British general, you have encountered rude fare to-day, gentlemen," he cried ; "though, after all, 't is such as a British soldier knows how to fatten on, in the service of his master. Fill, gentlemen, fill in royal bumpers ; for we have neglected our allegiance."

Each glass now stood sparkling and overcharged with wine, when, after a short and solemn pause, the host pronounced aloud the magical words,—"The King." Every voice echoed the name, after which there literally succeeded a breathless pause ; when an old man, in the uniform of an officer of the fleet, first proving his loyalty by flourishing on high his inverted glass, added, with hearty will,—

"God bless him!"

"God bless him!" repeated the graceful leader, who has already been more than once named in these pages; "and grant him a long and glorious reign; and, should there be no treason in the wish, in death, a Grave like yourself, worthy admiral,—'Sepulcrum sine sordibus extrue.'"

"Like me!" echoed the blunt seaman, whose learning was somewhat impaired by hard and long service; "I am, it is true, none of your cabin-window gentry; but his majesty might stoop lower than by favoring a faithful servant, like me, with his gracious presence."

"Your pardon, sir; I should have included, 'permissum arbitrio.'"

The equivoque had barely excited a smile, when the sedate countenance of the commander-in-chief indicated that the subject was too serious for a jest. Nor did the naval chieftain appear to relish the unknown tongue; for, quite as much, if not a little more, offended with the liberty taken with his own name, than with the privileged person of the sovereign, he somewhat smartly retorted,—

"Permitted or not permitted, I command the fleet of his majesty in these waters, and it shall be noted as a cheerful day in our log-books, when you gentlemen of the army dismiss us to our duty again, on the high seas. A sailor will grow as tired of doing nothing, as ever a soldier did of work, and I should like 'elbow-room,' even in my coffin— ha, ha, ha!—what d'ye think of that, master wit? ha, ha, ha!—what d'ye say to that?"

"Quite fair, well deserved, and cuttingly severe, admiral," returned the undisturbed soldier, smiling with perfect self-possession, as he sipped his wine. "But as you find confinement and leisure so irksome, I will presume to advise your seizing some of these impudent Yankees, who look into the port so often, not only robbing us of our stores, but offending so many loyal eyes with their traitorous presence."

"I command a parley to be beaten," interrupted the commander-in chief, "and a truce to further hostilities. Where all have done their duty, and have done it so well, even wit must respect their conduct. Let me advise you to sound the contents of that dusty-looking bottle, Mr. Graves; I think you will approve the situation as an anchorage for the night."

The honest old seaman instantly drowned his displeasure in a glass of the generous liquor, and, smacking his lips after the potations, for he repeated the first on the moment, he exclaimed,—

"Ah! you are too stationary, by half, to stir up the soul of your liquors. Wine should never slumber on its lees until it has been well rolled in the trough of a sea for a few months; then, indeed, you may set it asleep, and yourself by the side of it, if you like a cat's nap."

"As orthodox a direction for the ripening of wine as was ever given by a bishop to his butler!" exclaimed his adversary. Another significant glance from his dark-looking superior again checked his wilful playfulness, when Howe profited by the silence, to say with the frank air of a liberal host,—

"As motion is, just now, denied us, the only means I can devise, to prevent my wine from slumbering on its lees, is to drink it."

"Besides which, we are threatened with a visit from Mr. Washington, and his thirsty followers, who may save us all trouble in the matter, unless we prove industrious. In such a dilemma, Mr. Graves will not hesitate to pledge me in a glass, though it should be only to disappoint the rebels!" added Burgoyne, making a graceful inclination to the half-offended seaman.

"Ay, ay, I would do much more disagreeable things to cheat the rascals of their plunder," returned the mollified admiral, good-naturedly nodding his head before he swallowed his bumper. "If there be any real danger of the loss of such liquid amber as this, 't would be as well to send it alongside my ship, and I will hoist it in, and find it a berth, though it shares my own cot. I believe I command a fortress which neither Yankee, Frenchman, nor Don, would like to besiege, unless at a respectful distance."

23

The officers around him looked exceedingly grave, exchanging glances of great meaning, though all continued silent, as if the common subject of their meditations was too delicate to be loudly uttered in such a presence. At length, the second in command, who still felt the coldness of his superior, and who had, hitherto, said nothing during the idle dialogue, ventured a remark, with the gravity and distance of a man who was not certain of his welcome.

" Our enemies grow bold as the season advances," he said, " and it is past a doubt that they will find us employment in the coming summer. It cannot be denied but they conduct themselves with great steadiness in all their batteries, especially in this last, at the water-side ; nor am I without apprehension that they will yet get upon the islands, and render the situation of the shipping hazardous."

"Get upon the islands ! drive the fleet from their anchors !" exclaimed the veteran sailor, in undisguised amazement. " I shall account it a happy day for England, when Washington and his rabble trust themselves within reach of our shot !"

"God grant us a chance at the rascals with the bayonet in the open field," cried Howe, " and an end of these winter-quarters ! I say winter-quarters, for I trust no gentleman can consider this army as besieged by a mob of armed peasants ! We hold the town, and they the country ; but when the proper time shall come—well, sir, your pleasure," he continued, interrupting himself to speak to an upper servant at his elbow.

The man, who had stood for more than a minute, in an attitude of respectful attention, anxious to catch the eye of his master, muttered his message in a low and hurried voice, as if unwilling to be heard by others, and at the same time conscious of the impropriety of whispering. Most of those around him turned their heads in polite indifference ; but the old sailor, who sat too near to be totally deaf, had caught the words, " a lady," which was quite enough to provoke all his merriment, after such a free indulgence of the bottle. Striking his hand smartly on the table, he exclaimed, with a freedom that no other present could have presumed to use,—

"A sail! a sail! by George, a sail! under what colors, friend? king's or rebels'? Here has been a blunder, with a vengeance! The cook has certainly been too late, or the lady is too early! ha, ha, ha!—O! you are wicked free livers in the army!"

The tough old tar enjoyed his joke exceedingly, chuckling with inward delight at his discovery. He was, however, alone in his merriment, none of the soldiers venturing to understand his allusions, any further than by exchanging a few stolen looks of unusual archness. Howe bit his lips with obvious vexation, and sternly ordered the man to repeat his errand in a voice that was more audible.

"A lady," said the trembling menial, "wishes to see your excellency, and she waits your pleasure, sir, in the library."

"Among his books, too!" shouted the admiral; "that would have better become you, my joking friend! I say, young man, is the girl young and handsome?"

"By the lightness of her step, sir, I should think her young; but her face was concealed under a hood."

"Ay! ay! the jade comes hooded into the house of the king! Damn me, Howe, but modesty is getting to be a rare virtue amongst you gentlemen on shore!"

"'T is a plain case against you, sir, for even the servant, as you find, has detected that she is light of carriage," said the smiling Burgoyne, making half a motion towards rising. "It is probably some applicant for relief, or for permission to depart the place. Suffer me to see her, and spare yourself the pain of a refusal."

"Not at all," said Howe, gaining his feet with an alacrity that anticipated the more deliberate movement of the other: "I should be unworthy of the trust I hold, could I not lend an occasional ear to a petition. Gentlemen, as there is a lady in the case, I presume to trespass on your indulgence. Admiral, I commend you to my butler, who is a worthy fellow, and can give you all the cruises of the bottle before you, since it left the island of Madeira."

He inclined his head to his guests, and passed from the room with a hurried step, that did not altogether consult appearances. As he proceeded through the hall, his ears were saluted by another burst from the hearty old seaman, who, however, enjoyed his humor alone, the rest of the party immediately turning to other subjects, with well-bred dulness. On entering the room already mentioned, Howe found himself in the presence of the female, who, notwithstanding their apparent indifference, was at that very moment occupying the thoughts, and exercising the ingenuity of every man he had left behind him. Advancing at once to the centre of the apartment, with the ease and freedom of a soldier who felt himself without a superior, he asked, with a politeness somewhat equivocal,—

"Why am I favored with this visit? and why has a lady, whose appearance shows she might command friends at any time, assumed this personal trouble?"

"Because I am a supplicant for a favor that might be denied to one who petitioned coldly," returned a soft, tremulous voice, deep within the covering of a silken calash. "As time is wanting to observe the usual forms of applications, I have presumed to come in person, to prevent delay."

"And surely, one like you can have little reason to dread a repulse," said Howe, with an attempt at gallantry, that would have better become the man who had offered to be his substitute. While speaking, he advanced a step nigher to the lady, and pointing to her hood, he continued: "Would it not be wise to aid your request with a view of a countenance that I am certain can speak better than any words? whom have I the honor to receive, and what may be the nature of her business?"

"A wife, who seeks her husband," returned the female, dropping the folds of her calash, and exposing to his steady eyes the commanding loveliness of the chaste countenance of Cecil. The sudden annunciation of her character was forced from the lips of the unclaimed bride, by the freedom of a gaze to which she was unused; but the instant she had spoken, her eyes fell on the floor in embarrassment, and she stood deeply blushing at the strength of her own language,

though preserving all the apparent composure and dignity
of female pride.   The English general regarded her beauty
for a moment, with a pleased, though doubting eye, before
he continued,—

"Is he whom you seek within or without the town?"

"I much fear without!"

"And you would follow him into the camp of the rebels?
This is a case that may require some deliberation.   I feel
assured I entertain a lady of great beauty; might I; in
addition, know how to address her?"

"For my name I can have no reason to blush," said
Cecil, proudly; "'t is noble in the land of our common ancestors, and may have reached the ears of Mr. Howe—I am
the child of the late Colonel Dynevor!"

"The niece of Lord Cardonnel!" exclaimed her auditor,
in amazement, instantly losing the equivocal freedom of his
manner in an air of deep respect: "I have long known that
Boston contained such a lady; nor do I forget that she is
accused of concealing herself from the attentions of the
army, like one of the most obdurate of our foes—attentions
which every man in the garrison would be happy to show
her, from myself down to the lowest ensign.   Do me the
honor to be seated."

Cecil bowed her acknowledgments, but continued standing.

"I have neither time nor spirits to defend myself from
such an imputation," she answered; "though, should my
own name prove no passport to your favor, I must claim it
in behalf of him I seek."

"Should he be the veriest rebel in the train of Washington, he has great reason to be proud of his fortune!"

"So far from ranking among the enemies of the king, he
has already been lavish of his blood in behalf of the crown,"
returned Cecil, unconsciously raising the calash again, with
maiden bashfulness, as she felt the moment was approaching
when she must declare the name of the man, whose influence
over her feelings she had already avowed.

"And he is called—"

The answer was given to this direct question in a low,
but distinct voice.   Howe started when he heard the well-

known name of an officer of so much consideration, though a meaning smile lighted his dark features, as he repeated her words in surprise,—

"Major Lincoln! his refusal to return to Europe, in search of health, is then satisfactorily explained! Without the town, did you say? There must be some error."

"I fear it is too true."

The harsh features of the leader contracted again into their sternest look, and it was apparent how much he was disturbed by the intelligence.

"This is presuming too far on his privilege," he muttered, in an under-tone. "Left the place, say you, without my knowledge and approbation, young lady?"

"But on no unworthy errand!" cried the almost breathless Cecil, instantly losing sight of herself in her anxiety for Lionel. "Private sorrows have driven him to an act that, at another time, he would be the first to condemn, as a soldier."

Howe maintained a cool, but threatening silence, that was far more appalling than any words could be. The alarmed wife gazed at his lowering face for a minute, as if to penetrate his secret thoughts; then yielding, with the sensitiveness of a woman, to her worst apprehensions, she cried,—

"O! you would not avail yourself of this confession to do him harm! Has he not bled for you—lingered for months on the verge of the grave, in defence of your cause —and will you now doubt him? Nay, sir, though chance and years may have subjected him, for a time, to your control, he is every way your equal, and will confront each charge before his royal master, let who may bring them against his spotless name!"

"'T will be necessary," the other coldly replied.

"Nay, hearken not to my weak, unmeaning words," continued Cecil, wringing her hands in doubting distress: "I know not what I say. He has your permission to hold intercourse with the country weekly?"

"For the purpose of obtaining the supplies necessary to his past condition."

"And may he not have gone on such an errand, and under favor of the flag you yourself have cheerfully accorded?"

"In such a case, would I not have been spared the pain of this interview?"

Cecil paused a moment, and seemed collecting her scattered faculties, and preparing her mind for some serious purpose. After a little time, she attempted a painful smile, saying, more calmly,—

"I had presumed too far on military indulgence, and was even weak enough to believe the request would be granted to my name and situation."

"No name, no situation, no circumstances, can ever render—"

"Speak not the cruel words, lest they once more drive me from my recollection," interrupted Cecil. "First, hear me, sir : listen to a wife and a daughter, and you will recall the cruel sentence."

Without waiting for a reply, she advanced with a firm and proud step to the door of the room, passing her astonished companion with an eye and a face beaming with the fulness of her object. In the outer passage, she beckoned from among the loiterers in the hall, to the stranger who had accompanied her in the visit to the warehouse ; and when he had approached, and entered the room, the door once more closed, leaving the spectators without wondering whence such a vision of purity could have made its way within the sullied walls of Province House.

Many long and impatient minutes were passed by the guests in the banqueting-room, during the continuance of this mysterious interview. The jests of the admiral began to flag, just as his companions were inclined to think they were most merited, and the conversation assumed that broken and disjointed character which betrays the wandering of the speakers' thoughts.

At length a bell rang, and orders came from the commander-in-chief to clear the hall of its curious idlers. When none were left but the regular domestics of the family, Howe appeared, supporting Cecil, closely hooded, to the conveyance that awaited her presence at the gate. The air of their master communicated a deep respect to the manners of the observant menials, who crowded about their persons, to aid the departure, with officious zeal. The amazed sentinels dropped their arms, with the usual regularity, to their chieftain, as he passed to the outer portal in honor of his unknown companion, and eyes met the expressive glances of eyes, as all who witnessed the termination of this visit sought, in the countenances of those around them, some solution of its object.

When Howe resumed his seat at the table, another attempt was made by the admiral to renew the subject; but it was received with an air so cold, and a look so pointedly severe, that even the careless son of the ocean forgot his humor under the impression of so dark a frown.

CHAPTER XXIX.

Nor martial shout, nor minstrel tone,
Announced their march."

SCOTT.

ECIL suffered the night to advance a little, before she left Tremont Street, to profit by the permission to leave the place her communication had obtained from the English general. It was, however, far from late when she took leave of Agnes, and commenced her expedition, still attended by Meriton and the unknown man, with whom she has already, more than once, made her appearance in our pages. At the lower part of the town she left her vehicle, and pursuing the route of several devious and retired streets, soon reached the margin of the water. The wharves were deserted and still. Indicating the course, by her own light and hurried footsteps, to her companions, the youthful bride moved unhesitatingly along the rough planks, until her progress was checked by a large basin between two of the ordinary wooden piers which line the shores of the place. Here she paused for a moment, in doubt, as if fearful there had been some mistake, when the figure of a boy was seen advancing out of the shadows of a neighboring storehouse.

"I fear you have lost your way," he said, when within a few feet of her, where he stood apparently examining the party with rigid scrutiny. "May I venture to ask whom or what you seek?"

"One who is sent hither on private duty, by orders from the commander-in-chief."

"I see but two," returned the lad, hesitating, "where is the third?"

"He lingers in the distance," said Cecil, pointing to Meriton, whose footsteps were much more guarded than those of his mistress. "Three is our number, and we are all present."

"I beg a thousand pardons," returned the youth, dropping the folds of a sailor's overcoat, under which he had concealed the distinguishing marks of a naval dress, and raising his hat at the same moment, with great respect; "my orders were to use the utmost precaution, ma'am, for, as you hear, the rebels sleep but little to-night."

"'Tis a dreadful scene I leave, truly, sir," returned Cecil, "and the sooner it will suit your convenience to transport us from it, the greater will be the obligation you are about to confer."

The youth once more bowed, in submission to her wishes, and requested the whole party to follow whither he should lead. A very few moments brought them to a pair of water-stairs, where, under cover of the duskiness thrown upon the basin from the wharf, a boat lay concealed, in perfect readiness to receive them.

"Be stirring, boys!" cried the youth, in a tone of authority: "ship your oars as silently as if stealing away from an enemy. Have the goodness, ma'am, to enter, and you shall have a quick and safe landing on the other shore, whatever may be the reception of the rebels."

Cecil and her two attendants complied without delay, when the boat glided into the stream with a velocity that promised a speedy verification of the words of the midshipman. The most profound stillness reigned among these nocturnal adventurers, and by the time they had rowed a short distance, the bride began to lose an immediate consciousness of her situation in contemplation of the scene.

The evening was already milder, and by one of those sudden changes, peculiar to the climate, it was rapidly becoming even bland and pleasant. The light of a clear moon fell upon the town and harbor, rendering the objects of both visible, in mellowed softness. The hugh black hulls of the vessels of war rested sullenly on the waters, like slumbering leviathans, without even a sail or a passing boat, except their own, to enliven the view in the direction of the port. On the other hand, the hills of the town rose, in beautiful relief, against the clear sky, with here and there a roof or a steeple reflecting the pale light of the moon. The bosom of the place was as quiet as if its inhabitants were buried in midnight sleep ; but behind the hills, in a circuit extending from the works on the heights of Charlestown, to the neck, which lay in open view of the boat, there existed all the evidences of furious warfare. During the few preceding nights the Americans had been more than commonly diligent in the use of their annoyances, but now they appeared to expend their utmost energies upon their enemies. Still they spared the town, directing the weight of their fire at the different batteries which protected the approaches to the place, as already described, along the western borders of the peninsula.

The ears of Cecil had long been accustomed to the uproar of arms, but this was the first occasion in which she was ever a witness of the mingled beauties and terrors of a cannonade at night. Suffering the calash to fall, she shook back the dark tresses from her face, and, leaning over the sides of the little vessel, listened to the bursts of the artillery, and gazed on the sudden flashes of vivid light that mocked the dimmer illumination of the planet, with an absorbed attention that momentarily lured her into forgetfulness. The men pulled their light boat with muffled oars, and so still was its progress, that there were instants when even the shot might be heard rattling among the ruins they had made.

" It 's amazement to me, madam," said Meriton, "that so many British generals, and brave gentlemen as there is in Boston, should stay in such a little spot to be shot at by a parcel of countrymen, when there is Lon'non, as still and as safe, at this blessed moment, as a parish churchyard at midnight ! "

Cecil raised her eyes at this interruption, and perceived the youth gazing at her countenance in undisguised admiration of its beauty. Blushing, and once more concealing her features beneath her calash, she turned away from the view of the conflict, in silence.

"The rebels are free with their gunpowder to-night!" said the midshipman. "Some of their cruisers have picked up another of our store-ships, I fancy, or Mr. Washington would not make such a noisy time of it, when all honest people should be thinking of their sleep. Don't you believe, ma'am, if the admiral would warp three or four of our heaviest ships up into the channel, back of the town, it would be a short method of lowering the conceit of these Yankees?"

"Really, sir, I am so little acquainted with military matters," returned Cecil, suffering her anxious features to relax into a smile, "that my opinion, should I venture to give one, would be utterly worthless."

"Why, young gentleman," said Meriton, "the rebels drove a galley out of the river, a night or two ago, as I can testify myself, having stood behind a large brick store, where I saw the whole affair most beautifully conducted!"

"A very fit place for one like you, no doubt, sir," returned the midshipman, without attempting to conceal his disgust at so impertinent an interruption. "Do you know what a galley is, ma'am? nothing but a small vessel cut down, with a few heavy guns, I do assure you. It would be a very different affair with a frigate or a two-decker. Do but observe what a charming thing our ship is, ma'am —I am sure so beautiful a lady must know how to admire a handsome ship!—she lies hereaway, nearly in a range with the second island."

To please the earnest youth, Cecil bent her head towards the quarter he wished, and murmured a few words in approbation of his taste. But the impatient boy had narrowly watched the direction of her eyes, and she was interrupted by his exclaiming, in manifest disappointment,—

"What! that shapeless hulk, just above the castle? She is an old Dutch prize, *en flûte*, ay, older than my grandmother, good old soul; and it would n't matter the value of a piece of junk, into which end you stepped her bowsprit! One of my school-fellows, Jack Willoughby, is a reefer on board her; and he says that they can just get six knots out of her, on her course in smooth water with a fresh breeze, allowing seven knots for leeway! Jack means to get rid of her the moment he can catch the admiral running large; for the Graveses live near the Willoughbys in town, and he knows all the soundings about the old man's humor. No, no, ma'am; Jack would give every shot in his lockers to swing a hammock between two of the beams of our ship. Do excuse me one moment,"—presuming to take one of the hands of Cecil, though with sufficient delicacy, as he pointed out his favorite vessel,—" there, ma'am, now you have her! she that's so taut rigged, with a flying-jib-boom, and all her top-gallant yards stopped to her lower rigging: we send them down every night at gun-fire, and cross them again next morning as regularly as the bell strikes eight. Is n't she a sweet thing, ma'am? for I see she has caught your eye at last, and I am sure you can't wish to look at any other ship in port."

Cecil could not refuse her commendations to this eloquent appeal, though at the next moment she would have been utterly at a loss to distinguish the much admired frigate from the despised store-ship.

"Ay, ay, madam, I knew you would like her when you got a fair glimpse at her proportions," continued the delighted boy; "though she is not half so beautiful on her broadside, as when you can catch her lasking, especially on her larboard bow. Pull long and strong, men, and with a light touch of the water: these Yankees have ears as long as borricoes, and we are getting in with the land. This set-down at Dorchester's neck will give you a long walk, ma'am, to Cambridge; but there was no possibility of touching the rebels anywhere else to-night, or, as you see, we should have gone right into the face of their cannon."

"Is it not a little remarkable," said Cecil, willing to pay the solicitude of the boy to amuse her, by some reply, "that the colonists, while they invest the town so closely on the north and west, should utterly neglect to assail it on the south? for I believe they have never occupied the hills in Dorchester at all ; and yet it is one of the points nearest to Boston."

"It is no mystery at all," returned the boy, shaking his head with all the sagacity of a veteran ; "it would bring another Bunker Hill about their ears ; for you see it is the same thing at this end of the place that Charlestown neck is at the other. A light touch, men, a light touch ! " he continued, dropping his voice, as they approached the shore. "Besides, ma'am, a fort on that hill could throw its shot directly on our decks, a thing the old man would never submit to ; and that would either bring on a regular hammering match, or a general clearing out of the fleet ; and then what would become of the army ? No, no—the Yankees would n't risk driving the cod-fish out of their bay, to try such an experiment. Lay on your oars, boys, while I take a squint along this shore, to see if there are any Jonathans cooling themselves near the beach, by moonlight."

The obedient seamen rested from their labors, while their youthful officer stood up in the boat, and directed a small night-glass over the intended place of landing. The examination proved entirely satisfactory, and, in a low, cautious voice, he ordered the men to pull into a place where the shadow of the hills might render the landing still less likely to be observed.

From this moment the most profound silence was observed, the boat advancing swiftly, though under perfect command, to the desired spot, where it was soon heard grazing upon the bottom, as it gradually lost its motion, and finally became stationary. Cecil was instantly assisted to the land, whither she was followed by the midshipman, who jumped upon the shore with great indifference, and approached the passenger, from whom he was now about to part.

"I only hope that those you next fall in with may know how to treat you as well as those you leave," said the boy, approaching, and offering his hand, with the frankness of an older seaman, to Cecil. "God bless you, my dear ma'am : I have two little sisters at home, nearly as handsome as yourself; and I never see a woman in want of assistance, but I think of the poor girls I 've left in old England. God bless you once more—I hope when we meet again, you will take a nearer view of the—"

"You are not likely to part so soon as you imagine," exclaimed a man, springing on his feet, from his place of concealment behind a rock, and advancing rapidly on the party; "offer the least resistance, and you are all dead."

"Shove off, men, shove off, and don't mind me!" cried the youth, with admirable presence of mind; "for God's sake, save the boat, if you die for it!"

The seamen obeyed with practised alacrity, when the boy darted after them with the lightness of his years, and, making a desperate leap, caught the gunwale of the barge, into which he was instantly drawn by the sailors. A dozen armed men had by this time reached the edge of the water, and as many muskets were pointed at the retreating party, when he who had first spoken, cried,—

"Not a trigger!—the boy has escaped us, and he deserves his fortune. Let us secure those who remain; but if a single gun be fired, it will only draw the attention of the fleet and castle."

His companions, who had acted with the hesitation of men that were not assured the course they took was correct, willingly dropped the muzzles of their pieces, and in another instant the boat was ploughing its way towards the much-admired frigate, at a distance which would probably have rendered their fire quite harmless. Cecil had hardly breathed during the short period of uncertainty; but when the sudden danger was passed, she prepared herself to receive their captors with the perfect confidence which an American woman seldom fails to feel in the mildness and reason of her countrymen. The whole party, who now approached her, were dressed in the ordinary habiliments of husbandmen, mingled, in a slight degree, with the more martial accoutrements of soldiers. They were armed with muskets only, which they wielded like men acquainted with all the uses of the weapon, at the same time that they were unaccustomed to the mere manual of the troops.

Every fibre of the body of Meriton, however, shook with fear, as he found this unexpected guard encircling their little party; nor did the unknown man who had accompanied them appear entirely free from apprehension. The bride still maintained her self-possession, supported either by her purpose, or her greater familiarity with the character of the people into whose hands she had fallen.

When the whole party were posted within a few feet of them, they dropped the butts of their muskets on the ground, and stood patient listeners to the ensuing examination. The leader of the party, who was only distinguished from his companions by a green cockade in his hat, which Cecil had heard was the symbol of a subaltern officer among the American troops, addressed her in a calm, but steady tone,—

"It is unpleasant to question a woman," he said, "and especially one of your appearance; but duty requires it of me. What brings you to this unfrequented point, in the boat of a king's ship, and at this unusual hour of the night?"

"I come with no intent to conceal my visit from any eyes," returned Cecil; "for my first wish is to be conducted to some officer of rank, to whom I will explain my object. There are many that I should know, who will not hesitate to believe my words."

"We none of us profess to doubt your truth; we only act with caution, because it is required by circumstances. Cannot the explanation be made to me? for I dislike the duty that causes trouble to a female."

"'T is impossible!" said Cecil, involuntarily shrinking within the folds of her mantle.

"You come at a most unfortunate moment," said the other, musing; "and I fear you will pass an uneasy night, in consequence. By your tongue I think you are an American?"

"I was born among those roofs, which you may see on the opposite peninsula."

"Then we are of the same town," returned the officer, stepping back in a vain attempt to get a glimpse of those features which were concealed beneath the hood. He made no attempt, however, to remove the silk ; nor did he in the slightest manner convey any wish of a nature that might be supposed to wound the delicacy of her sex; but finding himself unsuccessful, he turned away, as he added, "And I grow tired of remaining where I can see the smoke of my own chimneys, at the same time I know that strangers are seated around the hearths below !"

"None wish more fervently than I, that the moment had arrived when each might enjoy his own, in peace and quietness."

"Let the Parliament repeal their laws, and the king recall his troops," said one of the men, "and there will be an end of the struggle at once. We don't fight because we love to shed blood."

"He would do both, friend, if the counsel of one so insignificant as I could find weight in his royal mind."

"I believe there is not much difference between a royal mind and that of any other man, when the devil gets hold of it !" bluntly exclaimed another of the party. "I've a notion the imp is as mischievous with a king as with a cobbler."

"Whatever I may think of the conduct of his ministers," said Cecil, coldly, "'t is unpleasant to me to discuss the personal qualities of my sovereign."

"Why, I meant no offence ; though, when the truth is uppermost in a man's thoughts, he is apt to let it out," returned the soldier. After this uncouth apology, he continued silent, turning away like one who felt dissatisfied with himself for what he had done.

In the meantime, the leader had been consulting with one or two of his men aside. He now advanced again, and delivered the result of their united wisdom.

"Under all circumstances, I have concluded," he said, speaking in the first person, in deference to his rank, though in fact he had consented to change his own opinion at the instigation of his advisers, "to refer you for information to the nearest general officer, under the care of these two men, who will show you the way. They both know

24

the country, and there is not the least danger of their mistaking the road."

Cecil bowed in entire submission to this characteristic intimation of his pleasure, and declared her anxiety to proceed. The officer held another short consultation with the two guides, which soon terminated by his issuing orders to the rest of the detachment to prepare to depart. Before they separated, one of the guides, or, more properly, guards, approached Meriton, and said, with a deliberation that might easily be mistaken for doubt,—

"As we shall be only two to two, friend, will it not be as well to see what you have got secreted about your person, as it may prevent any hard words or difficulties hereafter? You will see the reason of the thing, I trust, and make no objection."

"Not at all, sir, not at all!" returned the trembling valet, producing his purse, without a moment's hesitation: "it is not heavy, but what there is in it, is of the best English gold, which I expect is much regarded among you, who see nothing but rebel paper."

"Much as we set store by it, we do not choose to rob for it," returned the soldier, with cool contempt. "I wish to look for weapons, and not for money."

"But, sir, as I unluckily have no weapons, had you not better take my money? There are ten good guineas, I do assure you; and not a light one among them all, 'pon honor! besides several pieces of silver.

"Come, Allen," said the other soldier, laughing, "it's no great matter whether that gentleman has arms or not, I believe. His comrade, here, who seems to know rather better what he is about, has none, at any rate; and for one of two men, I am willing to trust the other."

"I do assure you," said Cecil, "that our intentions are peaceable, and that your charge will prove in no manner difficult."

The men listened to the earnest tones of her sweet voice with much deference, and in a few moments the two parties separated, to proceed on their several ways. While the main body of the soldiers ascended the hill, the guides of Cecil took a direction which led them around its base.

Their route lay towards the low rock which connected the heights with the adjacent country, and their progress was both diligent and rapid. Cecil was often consulted as to her ability to endure the fatigue, and repeated offers were made to accommodate their speed to her wishes. In every other respect she was totally disregarded by the guides, who, however, paid much closer attention to her companions, each soldier attaching himself to one of her followers, whom he constantly regarded with a watchful and wary eye.

"You seem cold, friend," said Allen to Meriton ; "though I should call the night quite pleasant for the first week in March."

"Indeed, I'm starved to the bones !" returned the valet, with a shivering that would seem to verify his assertion. "It's a very chilly climate is this of America, especially of nights ! I never really felt such a remarkable dampness about the throat before, within memory, I do assure you."

"Here is another handkerchief," said the soldier, throwing him a common 'kerchief from his pocket : "wrap it round your neck, for it gives me an ague to hear your teeth knocking one another about so."

"I thank you, sir, a thousand times," said Meriton, producing his purse again, with an instinctive readiness ; "what may be the price ? "

The man pricked up his ears, and dropping his musket from the guarded position in which he had hitherto carried it, he drew closer to the side of his prisoner, in a very companionable way, as he replied,—

"I did not calculate on selling the article ; but if you have need of it, I wouldn't wish to be hard."

"Shall I give you one guinea, or two, Mr. Rebel?" asked Meriton, whose faculties were utterly confounded by his terror.

"My name is Allen, friend, and we like civil language in the Bay," said the soldier. "Two guineas for a pocket-handkerchief ! I couldn't think of imposing on any man so much ! "

"What shall it be, then—half a guinea, or four half-crown pieces ? "

"I did n't at all calculate to part with the handkerchief when I left home : it's quite new, as you can see by holding it up, in this manner, to the moon ; besides, you know, now there is no trade, these things come very high. Well, if you are disposed to buy, I don't wish to crowd ; you may take it, finally, for the two crowns."

Meriton dropped the money into his hands, without hesitation, and the soldier pocketed the price, perfectly satisfied with his bargain and himself, since he had sold his goods at a clear profit of about three hundred per cent. He soon took occasion to whisper to his comrade, that in his opinion "he had made a good trade"; and laying their heads together, they determined that the bargain was by no means a bad windfall. On the other hand, Meriton, who knew the difference in value between cotton and silk quite as well as his American protectors, was equally well satisfied with the arrangement ; though his contentment was derived from a very different manner of reasoning. From early habit, he had long been taught to believe that every civility, like patriotism in the opinion of Sir Robert Walpole, had its price ; and his fears had rendered him somewhat careless about the amount of the purchase money. He now considered himself as having a clear claim on the protection of his guard, and his apprehensions gradually subsided into security under the soothing impression.

By the time this satisfactory bargain was concluded, and each party was lawfully put in possession of his own, they had reached the low land already mentioned as the "neck." Suddenly the guard stopped, and bending forward, in the attitude of deep attention, they seemed to listen, intently, to some faint and distant sounds, that were, for moments, audible in the intervals of the cannonade.

"They are coming," said one to the other ; "shall we go on, or wait until they've passed ?"

The question was answered in a whisper, and, after a short consultation, they determined to proceed.

The attention of Cecil had been attracted by this conference, and the few words which had escaped her guides ; and, for the first time, she harbored some little dread as to her final destination. Full of the importance of her errand, the bride now devoted every faculty to detect the least circumstance that might have a tendency to defeat it. She trode so lightly on the faded herbage as to render her own footsteps inaudible, and more than once she was about to request the others to imitate her example, that no danger might approach them unexpectedly. At length her doubts were relieved, though her wonder was increased, by distinctly hearing the lumbering sounds of wheels on the frozen earth, as if innumerable groaning vehicles were advancing with slow and measured progress. In another instant her eyes assisted the organs of hearing, and by the aid of the moon her doubts, if not her apprehensions, were entirely removed.

Her guards now determined on a change of purpose, and withdrew with their prisoners within the shadow of an apple-tree that stood on the low land, but a few paces from the line of the route evidently taken by the approaching vehicles. In this position they remained for several minutes, attentive observers of what was passing around them.

"Our men have woke up the British by their fire," said one of the guards; "and all their eyes are turned to the batteries!"

"Yes, it's very well as it is," returned his comrade; "but if the old brass congress mortar had n't gi'n way yesterday, there would be a different sort of roaring. Did you ever see the old congress?"

"I can't say I ever saw the cannon itself, but I have seen the bombs fifty times; and pokerish-looking things they be, especially in a dark night—but hush! here they come."

A large body of men now approached, and moved swiftly past them, in deepest silence, defiling at the foot of the hills, and marching towards the shores of the peninsula. The whole of this party was attired and accoutred much in the fashion of those who had received Cecil. One or two who were mounted, and in more martial trappings, announced the presence of some officers of higher rank. At the very heels of this detachment of soldiers came a great number of carts, which took the route that led directly up to the neighboring heights. After these came another, and more numerous body of troops, who followed the teams, the whole moving in the profoundest stillness, and with the diligence of men who were engaged in the most important undertaking. In the rear of the whole, another collection of carts appeared, groaning under the weight of large bundles of hay, and other military preparations of defence. Before this latter division left the low land, immense numbers of the closely packed bundles were tumbled to the ground, and arranged with a quickness almost magical, in such a manner as to form a light breastwork across the low ground, which would otherwise have been completely exposed to be swept by the shot of the royal batteries; a situation of things that was believed to have led to the catastrophe of Breed's the preceding summer.

Among the last of those who crossed the neck, was an officer on horseback, whose eye was attracted by the group who stood as idle spectators under the tree. Pointing out the latter objects to those around him, he rode nigher to the party, and leaned forward in his saddle to examine their persons.

"How's this?" he exclaimed; "a woman and two men under the charge of sentinels! Have we then more spies among us? Cut away the tree, men; we have need of it, and let in the light of the moon upon them!"

The order was hardly given before it was executed, and the tree felled with a dispatch that, to any but an American, would appear incredible. Cecil stepped aside from the impending branches, and by moving into the light, betrayed the appearance of a gentlewoman by her mien and apparel.

"Here must be some mistake!" continued the officer; "why is the lady thus guarded?"

One of the soldiers, in a few words, explained the nature of her arrest, and in return received directions, anew, how to proceed. The mounted officer now put spurs to his horse, and galloped away, in eager pursuit of more pressing duties, though he still looked behind him, so long as the deceptive light enabled him to distinguish either form or features.

" 'T is advisable to go on the heights," said the soldier, " where we may find the commanding general."

"Anywhere," returned Cecil, confused with the activity and bustle that had passed before her eyes, " or anything, to be relieved from this distressing delay."

In a very few moments they reached the summit of the nearest of the two hills, where they paused just without the busy circle of men who labored there, while one of the soldiers went in quest of the officer in command. From the point where she now stood, Cecil had an open view of the port, the town, and most of the adjacent country. The vessels still reposed heavily on the waters, and she fancied that the youthful midshipman was already nestling safe in his own hammock, on board the frigate, whose tall and tapering spars rose against the sky in such beautiful and symmetrical lines. No evidences of alarm were manifested in the town ; but, on the contrary, the lights were gradually disappearing, notwithstanding the heavy cannonade which still roared along the western side of the peninsula ; and it was probable that Howe, and his unmoved companions, yet continued their revels, with the same security in which they had been left two short hours before. While, with the exception of the batteries, everything in the distance was still, and apparently slumbering, the near view was one of life and activity. Mounds of earth were already rising on the crest of the hill ; laborers were filling barrels with earth and sand ; fascines were tumbling about from place to place, as they were wanted ; and yet the stillness was only interrupted by the unremitting strokes of the pick, the low and earnest hum of voices, or the crashing of branches, as the pride of the neighboring orchards came crashing to the earth. The novelty of the scene beguiled Cecil of her anxiety, and many minutes passed unheeded by. Fifty times parties, or individuals amongst the laborers, approaching near her person, paused to gaze a moment at the speaking and sweet features that the placid light of the moon rendered even more than usually soft, and then pushed on in silence, endeavoring to repair, by renewed diligence, the transient forgetfulness of their urgent duties. At length the man returned, and announced the approach of the general who commanded on the hill. The latter was a soldier of middle age, of calm and collected deportment, roughly attired for the occasion, and bearing no other symbol of his rank than the distinctive crimson cockade, in one of the large military hats of the period.

"You find us in the midst of our labors," he pleasantly observed, as he approached ; "and will overlook the delay I have given you. It is reported you left the town this evening ? "

"Within the hour."

"And Howe,—dreams he of the manner in which we are likely to amuse him in the morning ? "

"It would be affectation in one like me," said Cecil, modestly, "to decline answering questions concerning the views of the royal general ; but still you will pardon me if I say, that in my present situation, I could wish to be spared the pain of even confessing my ignorance."

"I acknowledge my error," the officer unhesitatingly answered. After a short pause, in which he seemed to muse, he continued : "this is no ordinary night, young lady, and it becomes my duty to refer you to the general commanding this wing of the army. He possibly may think it necessary to communicate your detention to the commander-in-chief."

"It is he I seek, sir, and would most wish to meet."

He bowed, and, giving his orders to a subaltern in a low voice, walked away, and was soon lost in the busy crowd that came and went in constant employment, around the summit of the hill. Cecil lingered a single moment after her new conductor had declared his readiness to proceed, to cast another glance at the calm splendor of the sea and bay ; the distant and smoky roofs of the town ; the dim objects that moved about the adjacent eminence, equally and similarly employed with those around her ; and then raising her calash, and tightening the folds of her mantle, she descended the hill with the light and elastic steps of youth.

CHAPTER XXX.

"The rebel vales, the rebel dales,
        With rebel trees surrounded,
The distant woods, the hills and floods,
        With rebel echoes sounded."
                                The Battle of the Kegs.

THE enormous white cockade that covered nearly one side of the little hat of her present conductor, was the only symbol that told Cecil she was now committed to the care of one who held the rank of captain, among those who battled for the rights of the colonies. No other part of his attire was military, though a cut-and-thrust was buckled to his form, which from its silver guard and formidable dimensions, had probably been borne by some of his ancestors, in the former wars of the colonies. The disposition of its present wearer was, however, far from that belligerent nature that his weapon might be thought to indicate, for he tendered the nicest care and assiduity to the movements of his prisoner.

At the foot of the hill, a wagon, returning from the field, was put in requisition by this semi-military gallant; and, after a little suitable preparation, Cecil found herself seated on a rude bench by his side in the vehicle; while her own attendants, and the two private men, occupied its bottom in still more social affinity. At first their progress was slow and difficult, return carts, literally by hundreds, impeding the way; but when they had once passed the heavy-footed beasts who drew them, they proceeded in the direction of Roxbury, with greater rapidity. During the first mile, while they were extricating themselves from the apparently interminable line of carts, the officer directed his whole attention to this important and difficult manœuvre; but when their uneasy vessel might be said to be fairly sailing before the wind, he did not choose to neglect those services, which, from time immemorial, beautiful women in distress have had a right to claim of men in his profession.

"Now do not spare the whip," he said to the driver, at the moment of their deliverance; "but push on, for the credit of horse-flesh, and to the disgrace of all horned cattle. This near beast of yours should be a tory, by his gait and reluctance to pull in the traces for the common good—treat him as such, friend, and, in turn, you shall receive the treatment of a sound whig, when we make a halt. You have spent the winter in Boston, madam?"

Cecil bent her head in silent assent.

"The royal army will, doubtless, make a better figure in the eyes of a lady, than the troops of the colonies; though there are some among us who are thought not wholly wanting in military knowledge, and the certain air of a soldier," he continued, extricating the silver-headed legacy of his grandfather from its concealment under a fold of his companion's mantle: "you have balls and entertainments without number, I fancy, ma'am, from the gentlemen in the king's service."

"I believe that few hearts are to be found amongst the females in Boston, so light as to mingle in their amusements."

"God bless them for it!" exclaimed her escort; "I am sure every shot we throw into the town is like drawing blood from our own veins. I suppose the king's officers don't hold the colonists so cheap, since the small affair on Charlestown neck, as they did formerly?"

"None who had any interest at stake, in the events of that fatal day, will easily forget the impression it has made."

The young American was too much struck by the melancholy pathos in the voice of Cecil, not to fancy he had, in his own honest triumph, unwittingly probed a wound which time had not yet healed. They rode many minutes after this unsuccessful effort on his part to converse, in profound

silence; nor did he again speak until the trampling of
horses' hoofs was borne along by the evening air, unaccompanied by the lumbering sounds of wheels. At the next
turn of the road they met a small cavalcade of officers,
riding at a rapid rate in the direction of the place they had
so recently quitted. The leader of this party drew up when
he saw the wagon, which was also stopped in deference to
his obvious wish to speak with them.

There was something in the haughty, and yet easy air
of the gentleman who addressed her companion, that induced Cecil to attend to his remarks with more than the
interest that is usually excited by the commonplace dia-
logues of the road. His dress was neither civil, nor wholly
military, though his bearing had much of a soldier's manner. As he drew up, three or four dogs fawned upon him,
or passed with indulged impunity between the legs of his
high-blooded charger, apparently indifferent to the impatient repulses that were freely bestowed on their troublesome
familiarities.

"High discipline, by——!" exclaimed this singular specimen of the colonial chieftains; "I dare presume, gentlemen,
you are from the heights of Dorchester; and having walked
the whole distance thither from camp, are disposed to try the
virtues of a four-wheeled conveyance over the same ground,
in a retreat!"

The young man rose in his place, and lifted his hat, with
marked respect, as he answered,—

"We are returning from the hill, sir, it is true; but we
must see our enemy before we retreat!"

"A white cockade! As you hold such rank, sir, I presume you have authority for your movements? Down Juno
—down, slut!"

"This lady was landed an hour since on the Point, from
the town, by a boat from a king's ship, sir; and I am
ordered to see her in safety to the general of the right
wing."

"A lady!" repeated the other, with singular emphasis,
slowly passing his hand over his remarkably aquiline and
prominent features; "if there be a lady in the case, ease

must be indulged. Will you down, Juno!" Turning his head a little aside, to his nearest aid, he added, in a voice that was suppressed only by the action,—"Some trull of Howe's, sent out as the newest specimen of loyal modesty! In such a case, sir, you are quite right to use horses. I only marvel that you did not take six instead of two. But how come we on in the trenches? Down, you hussy, down! Thou shouldst go to court, Juno, and fawn upon his majesty's ministers, where thy sycophancy might purchase thee a ribbon! How come we on in the trenches?"

"We have broken ground, sir; and as the eyes of the royal troops are drawn upon the batteries, we shall make a work of it before the day shows them our occupation."

"Ah! we are certainly good at digging, if at no other part of our exercises. Miss Juno, thou puttest thy precious life in jeopardy!—you will? then take thy fate!" As he spoke, the impatient chief drew a pistol from his holster, and snapped it twice at the head of the dog, that still fawned upon him in unwitting fondness. Angry with himself, his weapon, and the animal at the same moment, he turned to his attendants, and added, with bitter deliberation, —"Gentlemen, if one of you will exterminate that quadruped, I promise him an honorable place in my first despatches to Congress, for the service!"

A groom in attendance whistled to the spaniel, and probably saved the life of the disgraced favorite.

The officer now addressed himself to the party he had detained, with a collected and dignified air, that showed he had recovered his self-possession, by saying,—

"I beg pardon, sir, for this trouble—let me not prevent you from proceeding; there may be serious work on the heights before morning, and you will doubtless wish to be there." He bowed with perfect ease and politeness, and the two parties were slowly passing each other, when, as if repenting of his condescension, he turned himself in his saddle, adding, with those sarcastic tones so peculiarly his own,—"Captain, I beseech thee have an especial care of *the lady!*"

With these words in his mouth, he clapped spurs to his

horse, and galloped onward, followed by all his train at the same impetuous rate.

Cecil had heard each syllable that fell from the lips of both in this short dialogue, and she felt a chill of disappointment gathering about her heart, as it proceeded. When they had parted, drawing a long, tremulous breath, she asked, in tones that betrayed all her feelings,—

"And is this Washington?"

"*That!*" exclaimed her companion, "no, no, madam, he is a very different sort of man! That is the great English officer, whom Congress has made a general in our army. He is thought to be as great in the field, as he is uncouth in the drawing-room—yes, I will acknowledge that much in his favor, though I never know how to understand him; he is so proud—so supercilious—and yet he is a great friend of liberty!"

Cecil permitted the officer to reconcile the seeming contradictions in the character of his superior, in his own way, feeling perfectly relieved when she understood it was not the man who could have any influence on her own destiny. The driver now appeared anxious to recover the lost time, and he urged his horses over the ground with increased rapidity. The remainder of their short drive to the vicinity of Roxbury, passed in silence. As the cannonading was still maintained with equal warmth by both parties, it was hazarding too much to place themselves in the line of the enemy's fire. The young man, therefore, after finding a secure spot among the uneven ground of the vicinity, where he might leave his charge in safety, proceeded by himself to the point where he had reason to believe he should find the officer he was ordered to seek. During his short absence, Cecil remained in the wagon an appalled listener, and a partial spectator of the neighboring contest.

The Americans had burst their only mortar of size, the preceding night; but they applied their cannon with unwearied diligence, not only in the face of the British entrenchments, but on the low land, across the estuary of the Charles; and still farther to the north, in front of the position which their enemies held on the well-known heights of

Charlestown. In retaliation for this attack, the batteries along the western side of the town were in a constant blaze of fire, while those of the eastern continued to slumber, in total unconsciousness of the coming danger.

When the officer returned, he reported that his search had been successful, and that he had been commanded to conduct his charge into the presence of the American commander-in-chief. This new arrangement imposed the necessity of driving a few miles farther; and as the youth began to regard his new duty with some impatience, he was in no humor for delay. The route was circuitous and safe, the roads good, and the driver diligent. In consequence, within the hour they passed the river, and Cecil found herself, after so long an absence, once more approaching the ancient provincial seat of learning.

The little village, though in the hands of friends, exhibited the infallible evidences of the presence of an irregular army. The buildings of the University were filled with troops, and the doors of the different inns were thronged with noisy soldiers, who were assembled for the inseparable purposes of revelry and folly. The officer drove to one of the most private of these haunts of the unthinking and idle, and declared his intentions to deposit his charge under its roof, until he could learn the pleasure of the American leader. Cecil heard his arrangements with little satisfaction; but, yielding to the necessity of the case, when the vehicle had stopped, she alighted without remonstrance. With her two attendants in her train, and preceded by the officer, she passed through the noisy crowd, not only without insult, but without molestation. The different declaimers in the throng, and they were many, even lowered their clamorous voices as she approached, the men giving way, in deference for her sex; and she entered the building without hearing but one remark applied to herself, though a low and curious buzz of voices followed her footsteps to its very threshold. This solitary remark was a sudden exclamation, in admiration of the grace of her movements; and, singular as it may seem, her companion thought it necessary to apologize for its rudeness, by whispering that it had proceeded from the lips of "one of the Southern riflemen; a corps as distinguished for its skill and bravery, as for its want of breeding!"

The inside of this inn presented a very different aspect from its exterior. The decent tradesman who kept it had so far yielded to the emergency of the times, and perhaps, also, to a certain propensity towards gain, as temporarily to adopt the profession he followed; but by a sort of implied compact with the crowd without, while he administered to their appetite for liquor, he preserved most of the privacy of his domestic arrangements. He had, however, been compelled to relinquish one apartment entirely to the service of the public, into which Cecil and her companions were shown, as a matter of course, without the smallest apology for its condition.

There might have been a dozen people in the common room; some of whom were quietly seated before its large fire, among whom were one or two females; some walking, and others distributed on chairs, as accident or inclination had placed them. A slight movement was made at the entrance of Cecil, but it soon subsided; though her rich mantle of fine cloth, and silken calash, did not fail to draw the eyes of the women upon her, with a ruder gaze than she had yet encountered from the other sex, during the hazardous adventures of the night. She took an offered seat near the bright and cheerful blaze on the hearth, which imparted all the light the room contained, and disposed herself to wait in patience the return of her conductor, who immediately took his departure for the neighboring quarters of the American chief.

"'Tis an awful time for women bodies to journey in!" said a middle-aged woman near her, who was busily engaged in knitting, though she also bore the marks of a traveller in her dress; "I'm sure if I had thought there'd ha' been such contentions, I would never have crossed the Connecticut; though I have an only child in camp!"

"To a mother, the distress must be great, indeed," said Cecil, "when she hears the report of a contest in which she knows her children are engaged."

" Yes, Royal is engaged as a six-months'-man, and he's partly agreed to stay till the king's troops conclude to give up the town."

" It seems to me," said a grave looking yeoman, who occupied the opposite corner of the fireplace, " your child has an unfitting name for one who fights against the crown ! "

" Ah, he was so called before the king wore his Scottish Boot! and what has once been solemnly named, in holy baptism, is not to be changed with the shift of the times ! They were twins, and I called one Prince and the other Royal; for they were born the day his present majesty came to man's estate. That, you know, was before his heart had changed, and when the people of the Bay loved him little less than they did their own flesh and blood."

" Why, Goody," said the yeoman, smiling good-humoredly, and rising to offer her a pinch of his real Scotch, in token of amity, while he made so free with her domestic matters, " you had then an heir to the throne in your own family ! The Prince Royal, they say, comes next to the king; and by your tell, one of them, at least, is a worthy fellow, who is not likely to sell his heritage for a mess of pottage ! If I understand you, Royal is here in service ? "

" He's at this blessed moment in one of the battering-rams in front of Boston neck," returned the woman ; " and the Lord, He knows, 'tis an awful calling, to be beating down the housen of people of the same religion and blood with ourselves ! but so it must be, to prevail over the wicked designs of such as would live in pomp and idleness, by the sweat and labor of their fellow-creatures."

The honest yeoman, who was somewhat more familiar with the terms of modern warfare than the woman, smiled at her mistake, while he pursued the conversation with a peculiar gravity, which rendered his humor doubly droll.

" ' T is to be hoped the boy will not weary at the weapon before the morning cometh. But why does Prince linger behind, in such a moment? Tarries he with his father, on the homestead, in safety, being the younger born ? "

" No, no," said the woman, shaking her head in sorrow ; " he dwells. I trust, with our common Father, in heaven !

Neither are you right in calling him the home-child. He was my first-born, and a comely youth he grew to be! When the cry that the reg'lars were out at Lexington, to kill and destroy, passed through the country, he shouldered his musket, and came down with the people, to know the reason the land was stained with American blood. He was young and full of ambition to be foremost among them who were willing to fight for their birthrights; and the last I ever heard of him was in the midst of the king's troops on Breed's. No, no; his body never came off the hill! The neighbors sent me up the clothes he left in camp, and 't is one of his socks that I 'm now footing for his twin-brother."

The woman delivered this simple explanation with perfect calmness; though, as she advanced in the subject, large tears started from her eyes, and, following each other down her cheeks, fell unheeded upon the humble garment of her dead son.

"This is the way our bravest striplings are cut off, fighting with the scum of Europe!" exclaimed the yeoman, with a warmth that showed how powerfully his feelings were touched. "I hope the boy who lives may find occasion to revenge his brother's death."

"God forbid! God forbid!" exclaimed the weeping mother,—"revenge is an evil passion; and least of all would I wish a child of mine to go into the field of blood with so foul a breast. God has given us this land to dwell in, and to rear up temples and worshippers of his holy name; and in giving it, He bestowed the right to defend it against all earthly oppression. If 't was right for Prince to come, 't was right for Royal to follow!"

"I believe I am reproved in justice," returned the man, looking around at the spectators with an eye that no longer teemed with a hidden meaning. "God bless you, my good woman, and deliver you, with your remaining boy, and all of us, from the scourge which has been inflicted on the country for our sins. I go west, into the mountains, with the sun; and if I can carry any word of comfort from you to the good man at home, it will not be a hill or two that shall hinder it."

25

"The same thanks to you for the offer, as if you did it, friend; my man would be right glad to see you at his settlement; but I sicken already with the noises and awful sights of warfare, and shall not tarry long after my son comes forth from the battle. I shall go down to Cragie's house in the morning, and look upon the blessed man whom the people have chosen from among themselves as a leader, and hurry back again; for I plainly see that this is not an abiding-place for such as I !"

"You will then have to follow him into the line of danger; for I saw him, within the hour, riding, with all his followers, towards the water-side; and I doubt not that this unusual waste of ammunition is intended for more than we of little wit can guess."

"Of whom speak you?" Cecil involuntarily asked.

"Of whom should he speak, but of Washington?" returned a deep, low voice at her elbow, whose remarkable sounds instantly recalled the tones of the aged messenger of death, who had appeared at the bedside of her grandmother. Cecil started from her chair, and recoiled several paces from the person of Ralph, who stood regarding her with a steady and searching look, heedless of the observation they attracted, as well as of the number and quality of the spectators.

"We are not strangers, young lady," continued the old man; "and you will excuse me if I add, that the face of an acquaintance must be grateful to one of your gentle sex, in a place so unsettled and disorderly as this."

"An acquaintance?" repeated the unprotected bride.

"I said an acquaintance; we know each other, surely," returned Ralph, with marked emphasis; "you will believe me when I add, that I have seen the two men in the guard-room, which is at hand."

Cecil cast a furtive glance behind her, and, with some alarm, perceived that she was separated from Meriton and the stranger. Before time was allowed for recollection, the old man approached her with a courtly breeding, that was rendered more striking by the coarseness as well as negligence of his attire.

"This is not a place for the niece of an English peer," he said; "but I have long been at home in this warlike village, and will conduct you to another residence, more suited to your sex and condition."

For an instant Cecil hesitated; but observing the wondering faces about her, and the intense curiosity with which all in the room suspended their several pursuits, to listen to each syllable, she timidly accepted his offered hand, suffering him to lead her, not only from the room, but the house, in profound silence. The door through which they left the building was opposite to that by which she had entered; and when they found themselves in the open air, it was in a different street, and a short distance removed from the crowd of revellers already mentioned.

"I have left two attendants behind me," she said, "without whom 't is impossible to proceed."

"As they are watched by armed men, you have no choice but to share their confinement, or to submit to the temporary separation," returned the other, calmly. "Should his keepers discover the character of him who led you hither, his fate would be certain!"

"His character!" repeated Cecil, again shrinking from the touch of the old man.

"Surely my words are plain! I said his character. Is he not the deadly, obstinate enemy of liberty? And think you these countrymen of ours so dull as to suffer one like him to go at large in their very camp? No, no," he muttered, with a low, but exulting laugh; "like a fool has he tempted his fate, and like a dog shall he meet it! Let us proceed; the house is but a step from this, and you may summon him to your presence if you will."

Cecil was rather impelled by her companion than induced to proceed, when, as he had said, they soon stopped before the door of a humble and retired building. An armed man paced along its front, while the lengthened shadow of another sentinel in the rear was every half-minute thrown far into the street, in confirmation of the watchfulness that was kept over those who dwelt within.

"Proceed," said Ralph, throwing open the outer door

without hesitation. Cecil complied, but started at encountering another man, trailing a musket, as he paced to and fro in the narrow passage that received her. Between this sentinel and Ralph there seemed to exist a good understanding, for the latter addressed him with perfect freedom,—

"Has no order been yet received from Washington?" he asked.

"None; and I rather conclude, by the delay, that nothing very favorable is to be expected."

The old man muttered to himself, but passed on, and throwing open another door, said,—

"Enter."

Again Cecil complied, the door closing on her at the instant; but before she had time to express either her wonder or her alarm, she was folded in the arms of her husband.

CHAPTER XXXI.

"Is she a Capulet?
O dear account! my life is my foe's debt."
Romeo and Juliet.

"AH! Lincoln! Lincoln!" cried the weeping bride, gently extricating herself from the long embrace of Lionel, "at what a moment did you desert me!"

"And how have I been punished, love! a night of frenzy, and a morrow of useless regrets! How early have I been made to feel the strength of those ties which unite us! unless, indeed, my own folly may have already severed them forever!"

"Truant! I know you! and shall hereafter weave a web, with woman's art, to keep you in my toils! If you love me, Lionel, as I would fain believe, let all the past be forgotten. I ask—I wish no explanation. You have been deceived, and that repentant eye assures me of your returning reason. Let us now speak only of yourself. Why do I find you thus guarded, more like a criminal than an officer of the crown?"

"They have, indeed, bestowed especial watchfulness on my safety."

"How came you in their power? and why do they abuse their advantage?"

"'T is easily explained. Presuming on the tempestuousness of the night—what a bridal was ours, Cecil!"

"'T was terrible!" she answered, shuddering; then, with a bright and instant smile, as if sedulous to chase every appearance of distrust or care from her countenance, she continued,—"but I have no longer faith in omens, Lincoln! or, if one has been given, is not the awful fulfilment already come? I know not how you value the benedictions of a parting soul, Lionel, but to me there is holy consolation in knowing that my dying parent left her blessing on our sudden union."

Disregarding the hand which, with gentle earnestness she had laid upon his shoulder, he walked gloomily away, into a distant corner of the apartment.

"Cecil, I do love you, as you would fain believe," he said, " and I listen readily to your wish to bury the past in oblivion. But I leave my tale unfinished. You know the night was such that none would choose, uselessly, to brave its fury: I attempted to profit by the storm, and availing myself of a flag, which is regularly granted to the simpleton, Job Pray, I left the town. Impatient—do I say, impatient? borne along rather by a tempest of passions that mocked the feebler elements, we ventured too much. Cecil, I was not alone!"

"I know it —I know it," she said, hurriedly, though speaking barely above her breath; "you ventured too much—"

"And encountered a picket that would not mistake a royal officer for an impoverished, though privileged idiot. In our anxiety we overlooked—believe me, dearest Cecil, that if you knew all—the scene I had witnessed—the motives which urged—they, at least, would justify this strange and seeming desertion."

"Did I doubt it, would I forget my condition, my recent loss and my sex, to follow in the footsteps of one unworthy of my solicitude!" returned the bride, coloring as much with innate modesty, as with the power of her emotions. "Think not I come, with girlish weakness, to reproach you with any fancied wrongs. I am your wife, Major Lincoln; and as such would I serve you, at a moment when I know all the tenderness of the tie will most be needed. At the altar, and in the presence of my God, have I acknowledged the sacred duty; and shall I hesitate to discharge it because the eyes of man are on me?"

"I shall go mad! I shall go mad!" cried Lionel, in un-governable mental anguish, as he paced the floor, in violent disorder. "There are moments when I think that the curse which destroyed the father, has already lighted on the son!"

"Lionel!" said the soft, soothing voice of his companion, at his elbow, "is this to render me more happy—the welcome you bestow on the confiding girl who has committed her happiness to your keeping? I see you relent, and will be more just to us both—more dutiful to your God! Now let us speak of your confinement. Surely, you are not suspected of any criminal designs in this rash visit to the camp of the Americans! 'T were easy to convince their leaders that you are innocent of so base a purpose."

"'T is difficult to evade the vigilance of those who struggle for liberty!" returned the low, calm voice of Ralph, who stood before them, unexpectedly. "Major Lincoln has too long listened to the counsels of tyrants and slaves, and forgotten the land of his birth. If he would be safe, let him retract the error, while yet he may, with honor."

"Honor!" repeated Lionel, with unconcealed disdain,—again pacing the room with swift and uneasy steps, without deigning any other notice of the unwelcome intruder. Cecil bowed her head, and, sinking in a chair, concealed her face in her small muff, as if to exclude some horrid and fearful sight from her view.

The momentary silence was broken by the sound of foot-steps and of voices in the passage, and at the next instant, the door of the room opening, Meriton was seen on its threshold. His appearance roused Cecil, who, springing on her feet, beckoned him away, with a sort of frenzied earnestness, exclaiming,—

"Not here! not here! For the love of Heaven, not here!"

The valet hesitated, but, catching a glimpse of his master, his attachment got the ascendency of his respect.

"God be praised for this blessed sight, Master Lionel!" he cried; "'t is the happiest hour I have seen since I lost the look at the shores of old England! If 't was only at Ravenscliffe, or in Soho, I should be the most contented fool in the three kingdoms! Ah, Master Lionel, let us get out of this province, into the country where there is no rebels; or anything worse than Kings, Lords, and Commons!"

"Enough now; for this time, worthy Meriton, enough!" interrupted Cecil, breathing with difficulty, in her eagerness to be heard. "Go—return to the inn—the colleges—anywhere—do but go!"

"Don't send a loyal subject, ma'am, again among the rebels, I desire to entreat of you. Such awful blasphemies, sir, as I heard while I was there! They spoke of his sacred majesty just as freely, sir, as if he had been a gentleman like yourself. Joyful was the news of my release!"

"And had it been a guard-room on the opposite shore," said Ralph, "the liberties they used with your earthly monarch would have been as freely taken with the King of kings!"

"You shall remain, then," said Cecil, probably mistaking the look of high disdain which Meriton bestowed on his aged fellow-voyager, for one of a very different meaning; "but not here. You have other apartments, Major Lincoln; let my attendants be received there—you surely would not admit the menials to our interview!"

"Why this sudden terror, love? Here, if not happy, you at least are safe. Go, Meriton, into the adjoining room; if wanted, there is admission through this door of communication."

The valet murmured some half-uttered sentences, of which only the emphatic word "genteel" was audible; while the direction of his discontented eye sufficiently betrayed that Ralph was the subject of his meditations. The old man followed his footsteps, and the door of the passage soon closed on both, leaving Cecil standing, like a beautiful statue, in an attitude of absorbed thought. When the noise of her attendants, as they quietly entered the adjoining room, was heard, she breathed again, with a tremulous sigh, that seemed to raise a weight of apprehension from her heart.

"Fear not for me, Cecil, and least of all for yourself," said Lionel, drawing her to his bosom with fond solicitude: "my headlong rashness, or rather that fatal bane to the happiness of my house, the distempered feeling which you must have often seen and deplored, has indeed led me into a seeming danger. But I have a reason for my conduct, which, avowed, shall lull the suspicions of even our enemies to sleep."

"I have no suspicions—no knowledge of any imperfections—no regrets, Lionel; nothing but the most ardent wishes for your peace of mind; and, if I might explain!— yes, now is a time—Lionel, kind, but truant Lionel—"

Her words were interrupted by Ralph, who appeared again in the room, with that noiseless step, which, in conjunction with his great age and attenuated frame, sometimes gave to his movements and aspect the character of a being superior to the attributes of humanity. On his arm he bore an overcoat and a hat, both of which Cecil recognized, at a glance, as the property of the unknown man who had attended her person throughout all the vicissitudes of that eventful night.

"See!" said Ralph, exhibiting his spoils with a ghastly, but meaning smile, "see in how many forms Liberty appears to aid her votaries! Here is the guise in which she will now be courted! Wear them, young man, and be free!"

"Believe him not—listen not," whispered Cecil, while she shrunk from his approach in undisguised terror; "nay, do listen, but act with caution!"

"Dost thou delay to receive the blessed boon of freedom, when offered?" demanded Ralph. "Wouldst thou remain, and brave the angry justice of the American chief, and make thy wife, of a day, a widow for an age?"

"In what manner am I to profit by this dress?" said Lionel. "To submit to the degradation of a disguise, success should be certain."

"Turn thy haughty eyes, young man, on the picture of innocence and terror at thy side. For the sake of her whose fate is wrapped in thine, if not for your own, consult thy safety, and fly—another minute may be too late."

"O! hesitate not a moment longer, Lincoln," cried Cecil, with a change of purpose as sudden as the impulse was powerful; "fly—leave me; my sex and station will be—"

"Never," said Lionel, casting the garment from him, in cool disdain. "Once, when death was busy, did I abandon thee; but, ere I do it again, his blow must fall on me!"

"I will follow—I will join you."

"You shall not part," said Ralph, once more raising the rejected coat, and lending his aid to envelope the form of Lionel, who stood passive under the united efforts of his bride and her aged assistant. "Remain here," the latter added, when their brief task was ended, "and await the summons to freedom. And thou, sweet flower of innocence and love, follow and share in the honor of liberating him who has enslaved thee!"

Cecil blushed with virgin shame, at the strength of his expressions, but bowed her head in silent acquiescence to his will. Proceeding to the door, he beckoned her to approach, indicating by an expressive gesture to Lionel, that he was to remain stationary. When Cecil had complied, and they were in the narrow passage of the building, Ralph, instead of betraying any apprehension of the sentinel who paced its length, fearlessly approached, and addressed him with the confidence of a known friend,—

"See!" he said, removing the calash from before the pale features of his companion, "how terror for the fate of her husband has caused the good child to weep! She quits him now, friend, with one of her attendants, while the other tarries to administer to his master's wants. Look at her; is 't not a sweet, though mourning partner, to smooth the path of a soldier's life?"

The man seemed awkwardly sensible of the unusual charms that Ralph so unceremoniously exhibited to his view; and while he stood in admiring embarrassment, ashamed to gaze, and yet unwilling to retire, Cecil traced the light footsteps of the old man entering the room occupied by Meriton and the stranger. She was still in the act of veiling her features from the eyes of the sentinel, when Ralph reappeared, attended by a figure muffled in the well-known overcoat. Notwithstanding the flopped hat, and studied concealment of his gait, the keen eyes of the wife penetrated the disguise of her husband; and recollecting, at the same instant, the door of communication between the two apartments, the whole artifice was at once revealed. With trembling eagerness she glided past the sentinel, and pressed to the side of Lionel, with a dependence that might have betrayed the deception to one more accustomed to the forms of life, than was the honest countryman who had so recently thrown aside the flail to carry a musket.

Ralph allowed the sentinel no time to deliberate; but waving his hand in token of adieu, he led the way into the street with his accustomed activity. Here they found themselves in the presence of the other soldier, who moved to and fro, along the allotted ground in front of the building, rendering the watchfulness by which they were environed, doubly embarrassing. Following the example of their aged conductor, Lionel and his trembling companion walked with apparent indifference towards this man, who, as it proved, was better deserving of his trust than his fellow within doors. Dropping his musket across their path, in a manner which announced an intention to inquire into their movements, before he suffered them to proceed, he roughly demanded,—

"How's this, old gentleman? you come out of the prisoners' rooms by squads! one, two, three; our English gallant might be among you, and there would still be two left! Come, come, old father, render some account of yourself, and of your command. For, to be plain with you, there are those who think you are no better than a spy of Howe's, notwithstanding you are left to run up and down the camp as you please. In plain Yankee dialect, and that's intelligible English, you have been caught in bad company of late, and there has been hard talk about shutting you up, as well as your comrade."

"Hear ye that?" said Ralph, calmly smiling, and addressing himself to his companions, instead of the man whose interrogatories he was expected to answer; "think you the hirelings of the crown are thus alert? Would not the slaves be sleeping the moment the eyes of their tyrants are turned on their own lawless pleasures? Thus it is with liberty. The sacred spirit hallows its meanest votaries, and elevates the private to all the virtues of the proudest captain!"

"Come, come," returned the flattered sentinel, throwing his musket back to his shoulder again, "I believe a man gains nothing by battling you with words. I should have spent a year or two inside yonder colleges to dive at all your meaning. Though I can guess you are more than half right in one thing ; for if a poor fellow, who loves his country, and the good cause, finds it so hard to keep his eyes open on post, what must it be to a half-starved devil on sixpence a day ! Go along, go along, old father ; there is one less of you than went in, and if there was anything wrong, the man in the house should know it !"

As he concluded, the sentinel continued his walk, humming a verse of Yankee Doodle, in excellent favor with himself and all mankind, with the sweeping exception of his country's enemies. To say that this was not the first instance of well-meaning integrity being cajoled by the jargon of liberty, might be an assertion too hazardous ; but that it has been the last, we conscientiously believe, though no immediate example may present itself to quote in support of such heretical credulity.

Ralph appeared, however, perfectly innocent of intending to utter more than the spirit of the times justified ; for, when left to his own pleasure, he pursued his way, muttering rapidly to himself, and with an earnestness that attested his sincerity. When they had turned a corner, at a little distance from any pressing danger, he relaxed in his movements, and, suffering his eager companions to approach, he stole to the side of Lionel, and, clenching his hand fiercely, he whispered, in a voice half choked by inward exultation,—

"I have him now ; he is no longer dangerous ! Ay—ay—I have him closely watched by the vigilance of three incorruptible patriots !"

"Of whom speak you ?" demanded Lionel—"what is his offence, and where is your captive ?"

"A dog ! a man in form, but a tiger in heart ! Ay ! but I have him !" the old man continued, with a hollow laugh, that seemed to heave up from his inmost soul—"a dog ; a veritable dog ! I have him, and God grant that he may drink the cup of slavery to its dregs ! ''

"Old man," said Lionel, firmly, "that I have followed you thus far on no unworthy errand, you best may testify : I have forgotten the oath which, at the altar, I had sworn to, to cherish this sweet and spotless being at my side, at your instigation, aided by the maddening circumstances of a moment ; but the delusion has already passed away ! Here we part forever, unless your solemn and often-repeated promises are on the instant redeemed.''

The high exultation, which had so lately rendered the emaciated countenance of Ralph hideously ghastly, disappeared like a passing shadow ; and he listened to the words of Lionel with calm and settled attention. But when he would have answered, he was interrupted by Cecil, who uttered, in a voice nearly suppressed by her fears,—

"O ! delay not a moment ! Let us proceed anywhere, or anyhow even : now the pursuers may be on our track. I am strong, dearest Lionel, and will follow to the ends of the earth, so you but lead ! ''

"Lionel Lincoln, I have not deceived thee !'' said the old man, solemnly. "Providence has already led us on our way, and a few minutes will bring us to our goal— suffer, then, that gentler trembler to return into the village, and follow ! ''

"Not an inch !'' returned Lionel, pressing Cecil still closer to his side ; "here we part, or your promises are fulfilled.''

"Nay, go with him—go," again whispered the being who clung to him in trembling dependence. "This very controversy may prove your ruin—did I not say I would accompany you, Lincoln ? ''

"Lead on, then," said her husband, motioning Ralph to proceed ; "once again will I confide in you ; but use the trust with discretion, for my guardian spirit is at hand ; and remember, thou no longer leadest a lunatic ! ''

The moon fell upon the wan features of the old man, and exhibited their contented smile, as he silently turned away, and resumed his progress with his wonted rapid and noiseless tread. Their route still lay towards the skirts of the village. While the buildings of the University were yet in the near view, and the loud laugh of the idlers about the inn, with the frequent challenges of the sentinels, were still distinctly audible, their conductor bent his way beneath the walls of a church, that rose in solemn solitude in the deceptive light of the evening. Pointing upward at its somewhat unusual, because regular architecture, Ralph muttered, as he passed,—

"Here, at least, God possesses his own, without insult!"

Lionel and Cecil slightly glanced their eyes at the silent walls, and followed into a small inclosure, through a gap in its humble and dilapidated fence. Here the former again paused, and spoke,—

"I will go no further," he said, unconsciously strengthening the declaration by placing his foot firmly on a mound of frozen earth, in an attitude of resistance; "'t is time to cease thinking of self, and to listen to the weakness of her whom I support!"

"Think not of me, dearest Lincoln—"

Cecil was interrupted by the voice of the old man, who, raising his hat, and baring his gray locks to the mild rays of the planet, answered with tremulous emotion—

"Thy task is already ended! Thou hast reached the spot, where moulder the bones of one who long supported thee. Unthinking boy, that sacrilegious foot treads on thy mother's grave!"

CHAPTER XXXII.

"O, age has weary days,
And nights o' sleepless pain!
Thou golden time o' youthful prime!
Why com'st thou not again?"

BURNS.

THE stillness that succeeded this unexpected annunciation was like the cold silence of those who
slumbered on every side of them. Lionel recoiled a pace, in horror; then, imitating the
action of the old man, he uncovered his head, in pious
reverence of the parent whose form floated dimly in his
imagination, like the earliest recollections of infancy, or
the imperfect fancies of some dream. When time was
given for these sudden emotions to subside, he turned to
Ralph, and said,—

"And was it here that you would bring me, to listen to
the sorrows of my family?"

An expression of piteous anguish crossed the features of
the other, as he answered, in a voice which was subdued to
softness,—

"Even here—here, in the presence of thy mother's grave,
shalt thou hear the tale!"

"Then let it be here!" said Lionel, whose eye was
already kindling with a wild and disordered meaning, that
curdled the blood of the anxious Cecil, who watched its
expression with a woman's solicitude. "Here, on this hallowed spot, will I listen, and swear the vengeance that is
due, if all thy previous intimations should be just—"

"No, no, no—listen not—tarry not!" said Cecil, clinging to his side in undisguised alarm : "Lincoln, you are not equal to the scene ! "

" I am equal to anything in such a cause."

"Nay, Lionel, you overrate your powers ! Think only of your safety, now ; at another, and happier moment, you shall know all—yes—I—Cecil—thy bride, thy wife, promise that all shall be revealed—"

" Thou ! "

" It is the descendant of the widow of John Lechmere who speaks, and thy ears will not refuse the sounds," said Ralph, with a smile that acted like a taunt on the awakened impulses of the young man. "Go—thou art fitter for a bridal than a churchyard ! "

" I have told you that I am equal to anything," sternly answered Lionel ; " here will I sit, on this humble tablet, to hear all that you can utter, though the rebel legions encircle me to my death ! "

"What! dar'st brave the averted eye of one so dear to thy heart ? "

" All, or anything," exclaimed the excited youth, "with so pious an object."

" Bravely answered ! and thy reward is nigh—nay, look not on the siren, or thou wilt relent."

" My wife ! " said Lionel, extending his hand, kindly, towards the shrinking form of Cecil.

" Thy mother ! " interrupted Ralph, pointing with his emaciated hand to the cold residence of the dead.

Lionel sunk on the dilapidated grave-stone to which he had just alluded, and gathering his coat about him, he rested an arm upon his knee, while his hand supported his quivering chin, as if he were desperately bent on his gloomy purpose. The old man smiled with his usually ghastly expression, as he witnessed this proof of his success, and he took a similar seat on the opposite side of the grave, which seemed the focus of their common interest. Here he dropped his face between his hands, and appeared to muse, like one who was collecting his thoughts for the coming emergency. During this short and impressive pause, Lionel felt the trembling form of Cecil drawing to his side ; and before his aged companion spoke, her unveiled and pallid countenance was once more watching the changes of his own features, in submissive, but anxious attention.

"Thou knowest already, Lionel Lincoln," commenced Ralph, slowly raising his body to an upright attitude, "how in past ages, thy family sought these colonies, to find religious quiet, and the peace of the just. And thou also knowest,—for often did we beguile the long watches of the night in discoursing of these things, while the never-tiring ocean was rolling its waters unheeded around,—how Death came into its elder branch, which still dwelt amid the luxury and corruption of the English court, and left thy father the heir of all its riches and honors."

"How much of this is unknown to the meanest gossip in the province of Massachusetts Bay?" interrupted the impatient Lionel.

"But they do not know, that, for years before this accumulation of fortune actually occurred, it was deemed to be inevitable by the decrees of Providence; they do not know how much more value the orphan son of the unprovided soldier found in the eyes of those even of his own blood, by the expectation; nor do they know how the worldly-minded Priscilla Lechmere, thy father's aunt, would have compassed heaven and earth, to have seen that wealth, and those honors, to which it was her greatest boast to claim alliance, descend in the line of her own body."

"But 't was impossible! She was of the female branch; neither had she a son!"

"Nothing seems impossible to those on whose peace of mind the worm of ambition feeds; thou knowest well she left a grandchild; had not that child a mother?"

Lionel felt a painful conviction of the connection, as the trembling object of these remarks sunk her head in shame and sorrow on his bosom, keenly alive to the justice of the character drawn of her deceased relative, by the mysterious being who had just spoken.

"God forbid, that I, a Christian, and a gentleman," continued the old man, a little proudly, "should utter a syllable to taint the spotless name of one so free from blemish as

26

she of whom I speak. The sweet child who clings to thee, in dread, Lionel, was not more pure and innocent than she who bore her. And long before ambition had wove its toils for the miserable Priscilla, the heart of her daughter was the property of the gallant and honorable Englishman, to whom in later years she was wedded.''

As Cecil heard this soothing commendation of her more immediate parents, she again raised her face into the light of the moon, and remained, where she was already kneeling, at the side of Lionel, no longer an uneasy, but a deeply interested listener to what followed.

"As the wishes of my unhappy aunt were not realized,'' said Major Lincoln, "in what manner could they affect the fortunes of my father?''

"Thou shalt hear. In the same dwelling lived another, even fairer, and, to the eye, as pure as the daughter of Priscilla. She was the relative, the god-child, and the ward of that miserable woman. The beauty, and seeming virtues of this apparent angel in human form, caught the young eye of thy father, and, in defiance of arts and schemes, before the long-expected title and fortune came, they were wedded, and thou wert born, Lionel, to render the boon of Fate doubly welcome.''

"And then—''

"And then thy father hastened to the land of his ancestors, to claim his own, and to prepare the way for the reception of yourself, and his beloved Priscilla,—for then there were two Priscillas; and now both sleep with the dead! All having life and nature can claim the quiet of the grave, but I,'' continued the old man, glancing his hollow eye upwards, with a look of hopeless misery,—"I, who have seen ages pass since the blood of youth has been chilled, and generation after generation swept away, must still linger in the haunts of men! but 't is to aid in the great work which commences here, but which shall not end until a continent be regenerated.''

Lionel suffered a minute to pass without a question, in deference to this burst of feeling; but soon, making an impatient movement, it drew the eyes of Ralph once more upon him, and the old man continued,—

"Month after month, for two long and tedious years, did thy father linger in England, struggling for his own. At length he prevailed. He then hastened hither; but there was no wife,—no fond and loving Priscilla, like that tender flower that reposes in thy bosom, to welcome his return."

"I know it," said Lionel, nearly choked by his pious recollections; "she was dead."

"She was more," returned Ralph, in a voice so deep, that it sounded like one speaking from the grave: "she was dishonored!"

"'T is false!"

"'T is true!—true as that holy gospel which comes to men through the inspired ministers of God!"

"'T is false!" repeated Lionel, fiercely; "blacker than the darkest thoughts of the foul spirit of evil!"

"I say, rash boy, 't is true! She died in giving birth to the fruits of her infamy. When Priscilla Lechmere met thy heart-stricken parent with the damning tale, he read in her exulting eye the treason of her mind, and, like thee, he dared to call Heaven to witness that thy mother was defamed. But there was one known to him, under circumstances that forbade the thoughts of deceit, who swore— ay, took the blessed name of Him who reads all hearts, for warranty of her truth! and she confirmed it."

"The infamous seducer!" said Lionel, hoarsely, his body turning unconsciously away from Cecil; "does he yet live? Give him to my vengeance, old man, and I will yet bless you for your accursed history!"

"Lionel, Lionel," said the soothing voice of his bride, "do you credit him?"

"Credit him!" said Ralph, with a horrid, inward laugh, as if he would deride the idea of incredulity; "all this must he believe, and more! Once again, weak girl, did thy grandmother throw out her lures for the wealthy baronet, and when he would not become her son, then did she league with the spirits of hell to compass his ruin. Revenge took place of ambition, and thy husband's father was the victim!"

"Say on!" cried Lionel, nearly ceasing to breathe in the intensity of his interest.

"The blow had cut him to the heart ; and, for a time, his reason was crushed beneath its weight. Yet 't was but for an hour, compared to the eternity a man is doomed to live ! They profited by the temporary derangement, and when his wandering faculties were lulled to quiet, he found himself the tenant of a madhouse, where, for twenty long years, was he herded with the defaced images of his Maker, by the arts of the base widow of John Lechmere."

"Can this be true? Can this be true?" cried Lionel, clasping his hands wildly, and springing to his feet, with a violence that cast the tender form that still clung to him, aside, like a worthless toy. "Can this be proved? How knowest thou these facts?"

The calm, but melancholy smile that was wont to light the wan features of the old man, when he alluded to his own existence, was once more visible, as he answered,—

"There is but little hid from the knowledge acquired by length of days. Besides, have I not secret means of intelligence that are unknown to thee? Remember what, in our frequent interviews, I have revealed ; recall the death-bed scene of Priscilla Lechmere, and ask thyself if there be not truth in thy aged friend."

"Give me all ! hold not back a tittle of thy accursed tale —give me all—or take back each syllable thou hast uttered ! "

"Thou shalt have all thou askest, Lionel Lincoln, and more," returned Ralph, throwing into his manner and voice its utmost powers of solemnity and persuasion ; "provided thou wilt swear eternal hatred to that country and those laws, by which an innocent and unoffending man can be levelled with the beasts of the field, and be made to rave even at his Maker, in the bitterness of his sufferings."

"More than that—ten thousand times more than that, will I swear ; I will league with this rebellion—"

"Lionel, Lionel, what is 't you do?" interrupted the heart-stricken Cecil.

But her voice was stilled by loud and busy cries, which broke out of the village, above the hum of revelry, and was instantly succeeded by the trampling of footsteps, as men rushed over the frozen ground, apparently by hundreds, and with headlong rapidity. Ralph, who was not less quick to hear these sounds than the timid bride, glided from the grave, and approached the highway, whither he was slowly followed by his companions ; Lionel utterly indifferent whither he proceeded, and Cecil trembling in every limb with terror for the safety of him who so little regarded his own danger.

"They are abroad and think to find an enemy," said the old man, raising his hand with a gesture to command attention ; "but he has sworn to join their standards, and gladly will they receive any of his name and family !"

"No, no, he has pledged himself to no dishonor," cried Cecil. "Fly, Lincoln, while you are free, and leave me to meet the pursuers ; they will respect my weakness."

Fortunately, the allusion to herself awakened Lionel from the dull forgetfulness into which his faculties had fallen. Encircling her slight figure with his arm, he turned swiftly from the spot, saying, as he urged her forward,—

"Old man, when this precious charge is in safety, thy truth or falsehood shall be proved."

But Ralph, whose unincumbered person and iron frame, which seemed to mock the ravages of time, gave a vast superiority over the impeded progress of the other, moved swiftly ahead, waving his hand on high, as if to indicate his intention to join in the flight, while he led the way into the fields adjacent to the churchyard they had quitted.

The noise of the pursuers soon became more distinct, and, in the intervals of the distant cannonade, the cries and directions of those who conducted the chase were distinctly audible. Notwithstanding the vigorous arm of her supporter, Cecil was soon sensible that her delicate frame was unequal to continue the exertions necessary to insure their safety. They had entered another road, which lay at no great distance from the first, when she paused, and reluctantly declared her inability to proceed.

"Then, here will we wait our captors," said Lionel, with forced composure : " let the rebels beware how they abuse their slight advantage !"

The words were scarcely uttered, when a cart, drawn by

a double team, turned an angle in the highway near them, and its driver appeared within a few feet of the spot where they stood. He was a man far advanced in years, but still wielded his long goad with a dexterity which had been imparted by the practice of more than half a century. The sight of this man, alone, and removed from immediate aid, suggested a desperate thought for self-preservation to Lionel. Quitting the side of his exhausted companion, he advanced upon him with an air so fierce, that it might have created alarm in one who had the smallest reason to apprehend any danger.

"Whither go you with that cart?" sternly demanded the young man on the instant.

"To the Point," was the ready answer. "Yes, yes—old and young—big and little—men and cre'turs—four-wheels and two-wheels—everything goes to the Point to-night, as you can guess, fri'nd! Why," he continued, dropping one end of his goad on the ground, and supporting himself by grasping it with both his hands; "I was eighty-three the fourteenth of the last March, and I hope, God willing, that when the next birthday comes, there won't be a red-coat left in the town of Boston. To my notion, fri'nd, they have held the place long enough, and it's time to quit. My boys are in the camp, soldiering a turn; the old woman has been as busy as a bee, sin' sun-down, helping me to load up what you see, and I am carrying it over to Dorchester, and not a farthing shall it ever cost the Congress!"

"And are you going to Dorchester Neck with your bundles of hay?" said Lionel, eying both him and his passing team, in hesitation whether to attempt violence on one so infirm and helpless.

"Anan! you must speak up, soldier-fashion, as you did at first, for I am a little deaf," returned the carter. "Yes, yes, they spared me in the press, for they said I had done enough; but I say a man has never done enough for his own country, when anything is left to be done. I'm told they are carrying over fashines, as they call 'em, and pressed hay, for their forts. As hay is more in my fashion than any other fashion, I've bundled up a stout pile on't here;

and if that won't do, why, let Washington come ; he is welcome to the barn, stacks and all ! ''

"While you are so liberal to the Congress, can you help a female in distress, who would wish to go in the direction of your route, but is too feeble to walk?"

"With all my heart," said the other, turning round in quest of her whom he was desired to assist. "I hope she is handy ; for the night wears on, and I should n't like to have the English send a bullet at our people on Dorchester hills, before my hay gets there, to help stop it."

"She shall not detain you an instant," said Lionel, springing to the place where Cecil stood, partly concealed by the fence, and supporting her to the side of the rude vehicle ; "you shall be amply rewarded for this service."

"Reward ! Perhaps she is the wife or daughter of a soldier, in which case she should be drawn in her coach and four, instead of a cart and double team."

"Yes, yes—you are right, she is both—the wife of one, and the daughter of another soldier."

"Ay ! God bless her ! I warrant me old Put was more than half right, when he said the women would stop the two ridgments, that the proud parliamenter boasted could march through the colonies, from Hampshire to Georgi'. Well, fri'nds, are ye situated?"

"Perfectly," said Lionel, who had been preparing seats for himself and Cecil, among the bundles of hay, and assisting his companion into her place during the dialogue ; "we will detain you no longer."

The carter, who was no less than the owner of a hundred acres of good land in the vicinity, signified his readiness ; and sweeping through the air with his goad, he brought his cattle to the proper direction, and slowly moved on. During this hurried scene, Ralph had continued hid by the shadows of the fence. When the cart proceeded, he waved his hand, and gliding across the road, was soon lost to the eye in the misty distance, with which his gray apparel blended, like a spectre vanishing in air.

In the meantime the pursuers had not been idle. Voices were heard in different directions, and dim forms were to be seen rushing through the fields, by the aid of the deceptive light of the moon. To add to the embarrassment of their situation, Lionel found, when too late, that the route to Dorchester lay directly through the village of Cambridge. When he perceived they were approaching the streets, he would have left the cart, had not the experiment been too dangerous, in the midst of the disturbed soldiery, who now flew by on every side of them. In such a strait, his safest course was to continue motionless and silent, secreting his own form, and that of Cecil, as much as possible, among the bundles of hay. Contrary to all the just expectations which the impatient patriotism of the old yeoman had excited, instead of driving steadily through the place, he turned his cattle a little from the direct route, and stopped in front of the very inn where Cecil had so lately been conducted by her guide from the Point.

Here the same noisy and thoughtless revelry existed as before. The arrival of such an equipage at once drew a crowd to the spot, and the uneasy pair on the top of the load became unwilling listeners to the conversation.

"What, old one, hard at it for Congress!" cried a man approaching with a mug in his hand; "come, wet your throat, my venerable Father of Liberty, for you are too old to be a son!"

"Yes, yes," answered the exulting farmer, "I am father and son, too! I have four boys in camp, and seven grand-'uns in the bargain; and that would be eleven good triggers in one family, if five good muskets had so many locks— but the youngest men have got a ducking-gun, and a double-barrel atween them, howsomever; and Aaron the boy carries as good a horse-pistol, I calculate, as any there is going in the Bay! But what an easy time you have on 't to-night! There 's more powder spent in mocking thunder, than would fight old Bunker over again, at 'white o' the eye' distance!"

"'T is the way of war, old man; and we want to keep the reg'lars from looking at Dorchester."

"If they did, they could n't see far to-night. But, now, do tell me; I am an old man, and have a grain of cur'osity in the flesh ; my woman says that Howe casts out his carcasses at you ; which I hold to be an irreligious deception.''

"As true as the gospel.''

"Well, there is no calculating on the wastefulness of an ungodly spirit ! '' said the worthy yeoman, shaking his head, "I could believe any wickedness in him but that ! As cre'-turs must be getting scarce in the town, I conclude he makes use of his own slain ? ''

"Certain,'' answered the soldier, winking at his companions : "Breed's hill has kept him in ammunition all winter.''

"'T is awful, awful ! to see a fellow-cre'tur flying though the air, after the spirit has departed to judgment ! War is a dreadful calling ; but, then, what is a man without liberty ! ''

"Hark ye, old gentleman, talking of flying, have you seen anything of two men and a woman, flying up the road as you came in ? ''

"Anan ! I 'm a little hard o' hearing—women, too ! do they shoot their Jezebels into our camp ? There is no wickedness the king's ministers won't attempt, to circumvent our weak naturs ! ''

"Did you see two men and a woman, running away as you came down the road ? '' bawled the fellow, in his ear.

"Two ! did you say two ? '' asked the yeoman, turning his head a little on one side, in an attitude of sagacious musing.

"Yes, two men.''

"No, I did n't see two. Running out of town, did you say ? ''

"Ay, running, as if the devil was after them.''

"No ; I did n't see two, nor anybody running away—it 's a sartain sign of guilt to run away—is there any reward offered ? '' said the old man, suddenly interrupting himself, and again communing with his own thoughts.

"Not yet—they 've just escaped.''

"The surest way to catch a thief is to offer a smart reward : no—I did n't see two men ; you are sartain there was two ? ''

"Push on with that cart! drive on, drive on," cried a mounted officer of the quartermaster's department, who came scouring through the street at that moment, awakening all the slumbering ideas of haste, which the old farmer had suffered to lie dormant so long. Once more flourishing his goad, he put his team in motion, wishing the revellers good night as he proceeded. It was, however, long after he had left the village, and crossed the Charles, before he ceased to make frequent and sudden halts in the highway, as if doubtful whether to continue his route, or to return. At length he stopped the cart, and, clambering up on the hay, he took a seat, where with one eye he could regulate his cattle, and with the other examine his companions. This investigation continued another hour, neither party uttering a syllable, when the teamster appeared satisfied that his suspicions were unjust, and abandoned them. Perhaps the difficulties of the road assisted in dissipating his doubts ; for as they proceeded, return carts were met, at every few rods, rendering his undivided attention to his own team indispensable.

Lionel, whose gloomy thoughts had been chased from his mind by the constant excitement of the foregoing scenes, now felt relieved from any immediate apprehensions. He whispered his soothing hopes of a final escape to Cecil, and folding her in his coat, to shield her from the night-air, he was pleased to find, ere long, by her gentle breathing, that, overcome by fatigue, she was slumbering in forgetfulness on his bosom.

Midnight had long passed when they came in sight of the eminences beyond Dorchester Neck. Cecil had awoke, and Lionel was already devising some plausible excuse for quitting the cart, without reviving the suspicions of the teamster. At length a favorable spot occurred, where they were alone, and the formation of the ground was adapted to such a purpose. Lionel was on the point of speaking, when the cattle stopped, and Ralph suddenly appeared in the highway, at their heads.

"Make room, fri'nd, for the oxen," said the farmer,— "dumb beasts won't pass in the face of man."

"Alight!" said Ralph, seconding his words with a wide sweep of his arm towards the fields.

Lionel quickly obeyed, and, by the time the driver had descended also, the whole party stood together in the road.

"You have conferred a greater obligation than you are aware of," said Lionel to the driver. "Here are five guineas."

"For what? for riding on a load of hay a few miles?—no, no; kindness is no such boughten article in the Bay, that a man need pay for it. But fri'nd, money seems plenty with you for these difficult days!"

"Then thanks, a thousand times—I can stay to offer you no more."

He was yet speaking, when, obedient to an impatient gesture from Ralph, he lifted Cecil over the fence, and in a moment they disappeared from the eyes of the astonished farmer.

"Halloo, fri'nd!" cried the worthy advocate for his country, running after them as fast as old age would allow, "were there three of you, when I took ye up?"

The fugitives heard the call of the simple and garrulous old man, but, as easily will be imagined, did not deem it prudent to stop and discuss the point in question between them. Before they had gone far, the furious cry of "Take care of that team!" with the rattling of wheels, announced that their pursuer was recalled to his duty, by an arrival of empty wagons; and, before the distance rendered sounds unintelligible, they heard the noisy explanation, which their late companion was giving to the others, of the whole transaction. They were not, however, pursued; the teamsters having more pressing objects in view than the detection of thieves, or even of pocketing a reward.

Ralph led his companions, after a brief explanation, by a long and circuitous path to the shores of the bay. Here they found, hid in the rushes of a shallow inlet, a small boat, that Lionel recognized as the little vessel in which Job Pray was wont to pursue his usual avocation of a fisherman. Entering it without delay, he seized the oars, and aided by a flowing tide, he industriously urged it towards the distant spires of Boston.

The parting shades of the night were yet struggling with the advance of day, when a powerful flash of light illumi-nated the hazy horizon, and the roar of cannon, which had ceased towards morning, was again heard. But this time the sounds came from the water, and a cloud rose above the smoking harbor, announcing that the ships were again en-listed in the contest. This sudden cannonade induced Lionel to steer his boat between the islands; for the castle, and southern batteries of the town, were all soon united in pour-ing out their vengeance on the laborers, who still occupied the heights of Dorchester. As the little vessel glided by a tall frigate, Cecil saw the boy, who had been her first escort in the wanderings of the preceding night, standing on its taffrail, rubbing his eyes with wonder, and staring at those hills, whose possession he had prophesied would lead to such bloody results. In short, while he labored at the oars, Lionel witnessed the opening scene of Breed's acted anew, as battery after battery, and ship after ship, brought their guns to bear on their hardy countrymen, who had once more hastened a crisis by their daring enterprise. Their boat passed unheeded, in the excitement and bustle of the moment, and the mists of the morning had not yet dissi-pated, when it shot by the wharves of Boston, and, turning into the narrow entrance of the town Dock, it touched the land, near the warehouse, where it had so often been moored, in more peaceable times, by its simple master.

CHAPTER XXXIII.

" Now cracks a noble heart ; good-night,
Sweet prince."

Hamlet.

LIONEL, assisted Cecil to ascend the difficult water-stairs, and, still attended by their aged companion, they soon stood on the drawbridge that connected the piers which formed the mouth of the narrow basin.

"Here we again part," he said, addressing himself to Ralph ; " at another opportunity let us resume your melancholy tale."

"None so fitting as the present : the time, the place, and the state of the town are all favorable."

Lionel cast his eyes around on the dull misery which pervaded the neglected area. A few half-dressed soldiers and alarmed townsmen were seen, by the gray light of the morning, rushing across the square towards the point whence the sounds of cannon proceeded. In the hurry of the moment, their own arrival was not noted.

"The place—the time ! " he slowly repeated.

"Ay, both. At what moment can the friend of liberty pass more unheeded amongst these miscreant hirelings than now, when fear has broken their slumbers ! Yon is the place," he said, pointing to the warehouse, " where all that I have uttered will find its confirmation."

Major Lincoln communed momentarily with his thoughts.

It is probable that, in the rapid glances of his mind, he traced the mysterious connection between the abject tenant of the adjacent building and the deceased grandmother of his bride, whose active agency in producing the calamities of his family had now been openly acknowledged. It was soon apparent that he wavered in his purpose; nor was he slow to declare it.

"I will attend you," he said; "for who can say what the hardihood of the rebels may next attempt; and future occasions may be wanting. I will first see this gentle charge of mine—"

"Lincoln, I cannot—must not leave you," interrupted Cecil, with earnest fervor: "go, listen, and learn all; surely there can be nothing that a wife may not know!"

Without waiting for further objection, Ralph made a hurried gesture of compliance, and, turning, he led the way with his usual swift footsteps, into the low and dark tenement of Abigail Pray. The commotion of the town had not yet reached this despised and neglected building, which was even more than ordinarily gloomy and still. As they picked their way, however, among the scattered hemp, across the scene of the preceding night's riot, a few stifled groans proceeded from one of the towers, and directed them where to seek its abused and suffering inmates. On opening the door of this little apartment, not only Lionel and Cecil paused, but even the immovable old man appeared to hesitate in wonder.

The heart-stricken mother of the simpleton was seated on her humble stool, busied in repairing some mean and worthless garments, which had, seemingly, been exposed to the wasteful carelessness of her reckless child. But while her fingers performed their functions with mechanical skill, her contracted brow, working muscles, and hard, dry eyes, betrayed the force of the mental suffering that she struggled to conceal. Job still lay stretched on his abject pallet, though his breathing was louder and more labored than when we last left him, while his sunken features indicated the slow, but encroaching advances of the disease. Polwarth was seated at his side, holding a pulse, with an air of medical deliberation; and attempting, every few moments, to confirm his hopes or fears, as each preponderated in turn, by examining the glazed eyes of the subject of his care.

Upon a party thus occupied, and with feelings so much engrossed, even the sudden entrance of the intruders was not likely to make any very sensible impression. The languid and unmeaning look of Job wandered momentarily towards the door, and then became again fixed on vacancy. A gleam of joy shot into the honest visage of the captain, when he first beheld Lionel, accompanied by Cecil, but it was instantly chased away by the settled meaning of care, which had gotten the mastery of his usually contented expression. The greatest alteration was produced in the aspect of the woman, who bowed her head to her bosom, with a universal shudder of her frame, as Ralph stood unexpectedly before her. But from her, also, the sudden emotion passed speedily away, her hands resuming their humble occupation, with the same mechanical and involuntary movements as before.

"Explain this scene of silent sorrow!" said Lionel to his friend; "how came you in this haunt of wretchedness? and who has harmed the lad?"

"Your question conveys its own answer, Major Lincoln," returned Polwarth, with a manner so deliberate, that he refused to raise his steady look from the face of the sufferer, "I am here, because they are wretched!"

"The motive is commendable; but what aileth the youth?"

"The functions of nature seem suspended by some remarkable calamity. I found him suffering from inanition, and notwithstanding I applied as hearty and nutritious a meal as the strongest man in the garrison could require, the symptoms, as you see, are strangely threatening!"

"He has taken the contagion of the town, and you have fed him, when his fever was at the highest!"

"Is small-pox to be considered more than a symptom, when a man has the damnable disease of starvation! Go to—go to, Leo; you read the Latin poets so much at the schools, that no leisure is left to bestow on the philosophy of nature. There is an inward monitor, that teaches every child the remedy for hunger."

Lionel felt no disposition to contend with his friend on a

point where the other's opinions were dogmatical, but, turning to the woman, he said,—

"The experience of a professional nurse should have taught you, at least, more care."

"Can experience steel a mother to the yearnings of her offspring for food?" returned the forlorn Abigail. "No, no—the ear cannot be deaf to such a moaning, and wisdom is as folly when the heart bleeds."

"Lincoln, you chide unkindly," said Cecil; "let us rather attempt to avert the danger, than quarrel with its cause."

"It is too late—it is too late!" returned the disconsolate mother; "his hours are already numbered, and death is on him. I can now only pray, that God will lighten his curse, and suffer the parting spirit to know his Almighty power."

"Throw aside these worthless rags," said Cecil, gently attempting to take the clothes, "nor fatigue yourself longer, at such a sacred moment, with unnecessary labor."

"Young lady, you little know a mother's longings; may you never know her sorrows! I have been doing for the child these seven-and-twenty years; rob me not of the pleasure, now that so little remains to be done."

"Is he, then, so old!" exclaimed Lionel, in surprise.

"Old as he is, 'tis young for a child to die! He wants the look of reason; Heaven, in its mercy, grant that he may be found to have a face of innocence!"

Hitherto Ralph had remained where he first stood, as if riveted to the floor, with his eyes fastened on the countenance of the sufferer. He now turned to Lionel, and, in a voice rendered even plaintive by his deep emotion, he asked the simple question,

"Will he die?"

"I fear it—that look is not easily to be mistaken."

With a step so light that it was inaudible, the old man moved to the bed, and seated himself on the side opposite to Polwarth. Without regarding the wondering look of the captain, he waved his hand on high, as if to exhort to silence, and then gazing on the features of the sick, with melancholy interest, he said,—

"Here, then, is death again! None are so young as to be unheeded; 't is only the old that cannot die. Tell me, Job, what seest thou in the visions of thy mind,—the unknown places of the damned, or the brightness of such as stand in presence of their God?"

At the well-known sound of his voice, the glazed eye of the simpleton lighted with a ray of reason, and was turned towards the speaker, once more, teeming with a look of meek assurance. The rattling in his throat, for a moment, increased, and then ceased entirely; when a voice so deep, that it appeared to issue from the depths of his chest, was heard, saying,—

"The Lord won't harm him who never harmed the creatures of the Lord!"

"Emperors and kings, yea, the great of the earth, might envy thee thy lot, thou unknown child of wretchedness!" returned Ralph. "Not yet thirty years of probation, and already thou throwest aside the clay! Like thee did I grow to manhood, and learn how hard it is to live; but like thee I cannot die! Tell me, boy, dost thou enjoy the freedom of the spirit, or hast thou still pain and pleasure in the flesh? Dost see beyond the tomb, and trace thy route through the pathless air, or is all yet hid in the darkness of the grave?"

"Job is going where the Lord has hid his reason," answered the same hollow voice as before: "his prayers won't be foolish any longer."

"Pray, then, for one aged and forlorn; who has borne the burden of life till Death has forgotten him, and who wearies of the things of earth, where all is treachery and sin. But stay; depart not till thy spirit can bear the signs of repentance from yon sinful woman into the regions of day."

Abigail groaned aloud; her hands again refused their occupation, and her head once more sunk on her bosom in abject misery. From this posture of self-abasement and grief, the woman raised herself to her feet, and, putting aside the careless tresses of dark hair, which, though here and there streaked with gray, retained much of their youthful gloss,

27

she looked about her with a face so haggard, and eyes so full of meaning, that the common attention was instantly attracted to her movements.

"The time has come, and neither fear nor shame shall longer tie my tongue," she said. "The hand of Providence is too manifest in this assemblage around the death-bed of that boy, to be unheeded. Major Lincoln, in that stricken and helpless child, you see one who shares your blood, though he has ever been a stranger to your happiness. Job is your brother!"

"Grief has maddened her!" exclaimed the anxious Cecil; "she knows not what she utters."

"'T is true!" said the calm tones of Ralph.

"Listen," continued Abigail; "a terrible witness, sent hither by Heaven, speaks to attest I tell no lie. The secret of my transgression is known to him, when I had thought it buried in the affection of one only who owed me everything."

"Woman!" said Lionel, "in attempting to deceive me, you deceive yourself. Though a voice from Heaven should declare the truth of thy damnable tale, still would I deny that foul object being the child of my beauteous mother."

"Foul and wretched as you see him, he is the offspring of one not less fair, though far less fortunate, than thy own boasted parent, proud child of prosperity! Call on Heaven as thou wilt, with that blasphemous tongue, he is no less thy brother, and the elder born."

"'T is true—'t is true—'t is most solemnly a truth!" repeated the unmoved and aged stranger.

"It cannot be!" cried Cecil. "Lincoln, credit them not; they contradict themselves."

"Out of thy own mouth will I find reasons to convince you," said Abigail. "Hast thou not owned the influence of the son at the altar? Why should one vain, ignorant, and young as I was, be insensible to the seductions of the father?"

"The child is, then, thine!" exclaimed Lionel, once more breathing with freedom. "Proceed with thy tale; you confide it to friends."

"Yes—yes," cried Abigail, clasping her hands, and speaking with bitter emphasis, "you have all the consolation of proving the difference between the guilt of woman and that of man! Major Lincoln, accursed and polluted as you see me, thy own mother was not more innocent nor fair, when my youthful beauty caught thy father's eye. He was great and powerful, and I unknown and frail; yon miserable proof of our transgression did not appear, until he had met your happier mother."

"Can this be so?"

"The holy Gospels are not more true!" murmured Ralph.

"And my father! did he—could he desert thee in thy need?"

"Shame came when virtue and pride had been long forgotten. I was a dependant of his own proud race, and opportunities were not wanting to mark his wandering looks and growing love for the chaste Priscilla. He never knew my state. While I was stricken to the earth by the fruits of guilt, he proved how easy it is for us to forget, in the days of prosperity, the companions of our shame. At length, you were born; and, unknown to him, I received his new-born heir from the hands of his jealous aunt. What accursed thoughts beset me at that bitter moment! But, praised be God in heaven, they passed away, and I was spared the sin of murder!"

"Murder?"

"Even of murder. You know not the desperate thoughts the wretched harbor for relief! But opportunity was not long wanting, and I enjoyed the momentary, hellish pleasure of revenge. Your father went in quest of his rights, and disease attacked his beloved wife. Yes, foul and unseemly as is my wretched child, the beauty of thy mother was changed to a look still more hideous! Such as Job now seems, was the injured woman on her death-bed. I feel all thy justice, Lord of power, and bow before thy will!"

"Injured woman!" repeated Lionel, "say on, and I will bless thee!"

Abigail gave a groan, so deep and hollow, that, for a moment, the listeners believed it was the parting struggle of the spirit of her son, and she sunk helplessly into her seat, again concealing her features in her dress.

"Injured woman!" slowly repeated Ralph, with the most taunting contempt in his accents, "what punishment does not a wanton merit?"

"Ay, injured!" cried the awakened son; "my life on it, thy tale at least, is false."

The old man was silent, but his lips moved rapidly, as if he muttered an incredulous reply to himself, while a scornful smile cast its bright and peculiar meaning across the wasted lineaments of his face.

"I know not what you may have heard from others," continued Abigail, speaking so low that her words were nearly lost in the difficult and measured breathing of Job, "but I call Heaven to witness, that you now shall hear no lie. The laws of the province commanded that the victims of the foul distemper should be kept apart, and your mother was placed at the mercy of myself, and one other, who loved her still less than I."

"Just Providence! you did no violence?"

"The disease spared us such a crime. She died in her new deformity, while I remained a looker-on, if not in the beauty of my innocence, still free from the withering touch of scorn and want. Yes, I found a sinful but flattering consolation in that thought! Vain, weak, and foolish as I had been, never did I regard my own fresh beauty with half the inward pleasure that I looked upon the foulness of my rival. Your aunt, too—she was not without the instigations of the worker of mischief."

"Speak only of my mother," interrupted the impatient Lionel; "of my aunt I already know the whole."

"Unmoved and calculating as she was, how little did she understand good from evil! She even thought to crack the heart-strings, and render whole, by her weak inventions, that which the power of God could only create. The gentle spirit of thy mother had hardly departed, before a vile plot was hatched to destroy the purity of her fame. Blind fools that we were! She thought to lead by her soothing arts, aided by his wounded affections, the husband to the feet of her own daughter, the innocent mother of her who stands beside thee; and I was so vain as to hope, that, in time, justice and my boy might plead with the father and seducer, and raise me to the envied station of her whom I hated."

"And this foul calumny you repeated, with all its basest coloring, to my abused father?"

"We did—we did; yes, God, he knows we did! and when he hesitated to believe, I took the holy evangelists as witnesses of my truth!"

"And he," said Lionel, nearly choked by his emotions,— "he believed it!"

"When he heard the solemn oath of one, whose whole guilt, he thought, lay in her weakness to himself, he did. As we listened to his terrible denunciations, and saw the frown which darkened his manly beauty, we both thought we had succeeded. But how little did we know the difference between rooted passion and passing inclination! The heart we thought to alienate from its dead partner, we destroyed; and the reason we conspired to deceive, was maddened!"

When her voice ceased, so profound a silence reigned in the place, that the roar of the distant cannonade sounded close at hand, and even the low murmurs of the excited town swept by like the whisperings of the wind. Job suddenly ceased to breathe, as though his spirit had only lingered to hear the confession of his mother; and Polwarth dropped the arm of the dead simpleton, unconscious of the interest he had so lately taken in his fate. In the midst of this deathlike stillness, the old man stole from the side of the body, and stood before the self-condemned Abigail, whose form was writhing under her mental anguish. Crouching more like a tiger than a man, he sprang upon her, with a cry so sudden, so wild, and so horrid, that it caused all within its hearing to shudder with instant dread.

"Beldame!" he shouted, "I have thee now! Bring hither the book! the blessed, holy word of God! Let her swear, let her swear! Let her damn her perjured soul, in impious oaths!"

" Monster ! release the woman ! " cried Lionel, advancing to the assistance of the struggling penitent ; " thou too, hoary-headed wretch, hast deceived me ! "

"Lincoln ! Lincoln ! " shrieked Cecil, "stay that unnatural hand ! you raise it on thy father ! "

Lionel staggered back to the wall, where he stood motionless, and gasping for breath. Left to work his own frantic will, the maniac would speedily have terminated the sorrows of the wretched woman, had not the door been burst open with a crash, and the stranger, who was left, by the cunning of the madman, in the custody of the Americans, rushed to the rescue.

" I know your yell, my gentle baronet ! " cried the aroused keeper, for such in truth he was, "and I have a mark for your malice, which would have gladly had me hung ! But I have not followed you from kingdom to kingdom—from Europe to America—to be cheated by a lunatic ! "

It was apparent, by the lowering look of the fellow, how deeply he resented the danger he had just escaped, as he sprang forward to seize his prisoner. Ralph abandoned his hold the instant this hated object appeared, and he darted upon the breast of the other with the undaunted fury that a lion, at bay, would turn upon its foe. The struggle was fierce and obstinate. Hoarse oaths, and the most savage execrations, burst from the incensed keeper, and were blended with the wildest ravings of madness from Ralph. The excited powers of the maniac at length prevailed, and his antagonist fell under their irresistible impulse. Quicker than thought, Ralph was seen hovering on the chest of his victim, while he grasped his throat with fingers of iron.

"Vengeance is holy ! " cried the maniac, bursting into a shout of horrid laughter, at his triumph, and shaking his gray locks till they flowed in wild confusion around his glowing eyeballs ; " Urim and Thummim are the words of glory ! Liberty is the shout ! Die, damned dog ! die like the fiends in darkness, and leave freedom to the air ! "

By a mighty effort, the gasping man released his throat a little from the gripe that nearly throttled him, and cried, with difficulty,—

"For the love of heavenly justice, come to my aid!—will you see a man thus murdered?"

But he addressed himself to the sympathies of the listeners in vain. The females had hid their faces, in natural horror; the maimed Polwarth was yet without his artificial limb; and Lionel still looked upon the savage fray with a vacant eye. At this moment of despair, the hand of the keeper, was seen plunging with violence into the side of Ralph who sprang upon his feet at the third blow, laughing immoderately, but with sounds so wild and deep, that they seemed to shake his inmost soul. His antagonist profited by the occasion, and darted from the room with the head-long precipitation of guilt.

The countenance of the maniac, as he now stood, struggling between life and death, changed with each fleeting impulse. The blood flowed freely from the wounds in his side, and, as the fatal tide ebbed away, a ray of passing reason lighted his pallid and ghastly features. His inward laugh entirely ceased. The glaring eyeballs became stationary; and his look, gradually softening, settled on the appalled pair who took the deepest interest in his welfare. A calm and decent expression possessed those lineaments which had just exhibited the deepest marks of the wrath of God. His lips moved in a vain effort to speak; and, stretching forth his arms in the attitude of benediction, like the mysterious shadow of the chapel, he fell backward on the body of the lifeless and long-neglected Job, himself perfectly dead.

CHAPTER XXXIV.

"I saw an aged man upon his bier,
 His hair was thin and white, and on his brow
 A record of the cares of many a year;
 Cares that were ended and forgotten now,
 And there was sadness round, and faces bowed,
 And woman's tears fell fast, and children wailed aloud."
BRYANT.

AS the day advanced, the garrison of Boston was put in motion. The same bustle, the same activity, the same gallant bearing in some, and dread reluctance in others were exhibited, as on the morning of the fight of the preceding summer. The haughty temper of the royal commander could ill brook the bold enterprise of the colonists; and, at an early hour, orders were issued to prepare to dislodge them. Every gun that could be brought to bear upon the hills, was employed to molest the Americans, who calmly continued their labors, while shot were whistling around them on every side. Towards evening a large force was embarked, and conveyed to the castle. Washington appeared on the heights, in person, and every military evidence of the intention of a resolute attack on one part, and of a stout resistance on the other became apparent.

But the fatal experience of Breed's had taught a lesson that was still remembered. The same leaders were to be the principal actors in the coming scene, and it was necessary to use the remnants of many of the very regiments which had bled so freely on the former occasion. The half-trained husbandmen of the colonies were no longer despised; and the bold operations of the past winter had

taught the English generals that, as subordination increased
among their foes, their movements were conducted with a
more vigorous direction of their numbers. The day was
accordingly wasted in preparations. Thousands of men
slept on their arms that night, in either army, in the expectation of rising, on the following morning, to be led to the
field of slaughter.

It is not improbable, from the tardiness of their movements, that a large majority of the royal forces did not
regret the providential interposition, which certainly saved
them torrents of blood, and, not improbably, the ignominy
of a defeat. One of the sudden tempests of the climate
arose in the darkness, driving before it men and beasts, to
seek protection, in their imbecility, from the more powerful
warring of the elements. The golden moments were lost ;
and after enduring so many privations, and expending so
many lives in vain, Howe sullenly commenced his arrangements to abandon a town, on which the English ministry
had, for years, lavished their indignation, with all the acri-
mony, and, as it now seemed, with the impotency of a blind
revenge.

To carry into effect this sudden and necessary determination, was not the work of an hour. As it was the desire
of the Americans, however, to receive their town back
again as little injured as possible, they forbore to push the
advantage they possessed, by occupying those heights,
which, in a great measure, commanded the anchorage, as
well as a new and vulnerable face of the defences of the
king's army. While the semblance of hostilities was maintained by an irregular and impotent cannonade, conducted
with so little spirit as to wear the appearance of being intended only to amuse, one side was diligently occupied in
preparing to depart, and the other was passively awaiting
the moment when they might peaceably repossess their own.
It is unnecessary to remind the reader that the entire command of the sea, by the British, would have rendered any
serious attempt to arrest their movements perfectly futile.

In this manner a week was passed after the tempest had
abated—the place exhibiting, throughout this period, all

the hurry and bustle, the joy and distress, that such an un-looked-for event was likely to create.

Towards the close of one of those busy and stirring days, a short funeral train was seen issuing from a building, which had long been known as the residence of one of the proudest families in the province. Above the outer door of the mansion was suspended a gloomy hatchment, charged with the "courant" deer of Lincoln, encircled by the usual mementoes of mortality, and bearing the rare symbol of the "bloody hand." This emblem of heraldic grief, which was never adopted in the provinces, except at the death of one of high importance, a custom that has long since disappeared with the usages of the monarchy, had caught the eyes of a few idle boys, who alone were sufficiently unoccupied, at that pressing moment, to note its exhibition. With the addition of these truant urchins, the melancholy procession took its way towards the neighboring churchyard of the King's Chapel.

The large bier was covered by a pall so ample, that it swept the stones of the threshold, while entering into the body of the church. Here it was met by the divine we have had occasion to mention more than once, who gazed, with a look of strange interest, at the solitary and youthful mourner that followed in his dark weeds. The ceremony, however, proceeded with the usual solemnity, and the attendants slowly moved deeper into the sacred edifice. Next to the young man came the well-known persons of the British commander-in-chief, and of his quick-witted and favorite lieutenant. Between them walked an officer of inferior rank, who, notwithstanding his maimed condition, had been able, by the deliberation of the march, to beguile the ears of his companions, to the very moment of meeting the clergy-man, with some tale of no little interest, and great apparent mystery. The remainder of the train, which consisted only of the family of the two generals and a few menials, came last, if we except the idlers, who stole curiously in their footsteps.

When the service was ended, the same private communication was resumed between the two chieftains and their companion, and continued until they arrived at the open vault, in a distant corner of the inclosure. Here the low conversation ended ; and the eye of Howe, which had hitherto been riveted in deep attention on the speaker, began to wander in the direction of the dangerous hills occupied by his enemies. The interruption seemed to have broken the charm of the secret conversation ; and the anxious countenances of both the leaders betrayed how soon their thoughts had wandered from a tale of great private distress, to their own heavier cares and duties.

The bier was placed before the opening, and the assistants of the sexton advanced to perform their office. When the pall was removed, to the evident amazement of most of the spectators, two coffins were exposed to view. One was clothed in black velvet, studded with silver nails, and ornamented after the richest fashions of human pride, while the other lay in the simple nakedness of the clouded wood. On the breast of the first rose a heavy silver plate, bearing a long inscription, and decorated with the usual devices of heraldry ; and on the latter were simply carved on the lid the two initial letters J. P.

The impatient looks of the English generals intimated to Dr. Liturgy the value of every moment, and in less time than we consume in relating it, the bodies of the high-descended man of wealth, and of his nameless companion, were lowered into the vault, and left to decay, in silent contact with that of the woman who, in life, had been so severe a scourge to both. After a hesitation of a single moment, in deference to the young mourner, the gentlemen present, perceiving that he manifested a wish to remain, quitted the place in a body, with the exception of the maimed officer, already mentioned, whom the reader has at once recognized to be Polwarth. When the men had replaced the stone above the mouth of the vault, securing it by a stout bar of iron, and a heavy lock, they delivered the key to the principal actor in the scene. He received it in silence, and, dropping gold into their hands, motioned to them to depart.

In another instant, a careless observer would have thought that Lionel and his friend were the only living possessors of the churchyard. But under the adjoining wall, partly hid from observation by the numerous head-stones, was the form of a woman, bowed to the earth, while her figure was concealed by the cloak she had gathered shapelessly about her. As soon as the gentlemen perceived they were alone, they slowly advanced to the side of this desolate being.

Their approaching footsteps were not unheeded, though, instead of facing those who so evidently wished to address her, she turned to the wall, and began to trace, with un-conscious fingers, the letters of a tablet in slate, which was let into the brick-work, to mark the position of the tomb of the Lechmeres.

"We can do no more," said the young mourner; "all now rests with a mightier hand than any of earth."

The squalid limb, that was thrust from beneath the red garment, trembled, but it still continued its unmeaning em-ployment.

"Sir Lionel Lincoln speaks to you," said Polwarth, on whose arm the youthful baronet leaned.

"Who?" shrieked Abigail Pray, casting aside her covering, and baring those sunken features, on which misery had made terrible additional inroads within a few days: "I had forgotten—I had forgotten! the son suc-ceeds the father; but the mother must follow her child to the grave!"

"He is honorably interred with those of his blood, and by the side of one who loved his simple integrity."

"Yes, he is better lodged in death than he was in life! Thank God! he can never know cold nor hunger more."

"You will find that I have made a provision for your future comfort; and I trust that the close of your life will be happier than its prime."

"I am alone," said the woman hoarsely. "The old will avoid me, and the young will look upon me in scorn! Perjury and revenge lie heavy on my soul!"

The young baronet was silent, but Polwarth assumed the right to reply,—

"I will not pretend to assert," said the worthy captain, "that these are not both wicked companions; but I have no doubt you will find, somewhere in the Bible, a suitable consolation for each particular offence. Let me recommend to you a hearty diet, and I 'll answer for an easy conscience. I never knew the prescription fail. Look about you in the world—does your well-fed villain feel remorse? No; it's only when his stomach is empty, that he begins to think of his errors! I would also suggest the expediency of commencing soon, with something substantial, as you show altogether too much bone at present, for a thriving condition. I would not wish to say anything distressing, but we both of us may remember a case, where the nourishment came too late."

"Yes, yes, it came too late!" murmured the conscience-stricken woman; "all comes too late! even the penitence, I fear!"

"Say not so," observed Lionel; "you do outrage to the promises of one who never spoke false!"

Abigail stole a fearful glance at him, which expressed all the secret terror of her soul, as she half whispered,—

"Who witnessed the end of Madam Lechmere? did her spirit pass in peace?"

Sir Lionel again remained profoundly silent.

"I thought it," she continued. "'T is not a sin to be forgotten on a death-bed! To plot evil, and call on God aloud, to look upon it! Ay! and to madden a brain, and strip a soul like his to nakedness! Go," she added, beckoning them away with earnestness: "ye are young and happy; why should ye linger near the grave! Leave me, that I may pray among the tombs! If anything can smooth the bitter moment it is prayer."

Lionel dropped the key he held in his hand at her feet, and said, before he left her,—

"Yon vault is closed forever, unless, at your request, it should be opened, at some future time, to place you by the side of your son. The children of those who built it are already gathered there with the exception of two, who go to the other hemisphere to leave their bones. Take it, and may Heaven forgive you, as I do."

He let fall a heavy purse by the side of the key, and

without uttering more, he again took the arm of Polwarth, and together they left the place.

As they turned through the gateway into the street, each stole a glance at the distant woman. She had risen to her knees; her hands had grasped a headstone, and her face was bowed nearly to the earth, while, by the writhing of her form, and the humility of her attitude, it was apparent that her spirit struggled powerfully with the Lord for mercy.

Three days afterwards, the Americans entered, triumphantly, on the retiring footsteps of the royal army. The first among them who hastened to visit the graves of their fathers, found the body of a woman, who had seemingly died under the severity of the season. She had unlocked the vault, in a vain effort to reach her child, and there her strength had failed her. Her limbs were decently stretched on the faded grass, while her features were composed, exhibiting in death the bland traces of that remarkable beauty which had distinguished and betrayed her youth. The gold still lay neglected, where it had fallen.

The amazed townsmen avoided this spectacle with horror, rushing into other places to gaze at the changes and the destruction of their beloved birthplace. But a follower of the royal army, who had lingered to plunder, and who had witnessed the interview between the officers and Abigail, shortly succeeded them. He lifted the flag, and, lowering the body, closed the vault; then hurling away the key, he seized the money, and departed.

The slate has long since mouldered from the wall; the sod has covered the stone, and few are left who can designate the spot where the proud families of Lechmere and Lincoln were wont to inter their dead.

So Lionel and Polwarth proceeded, in the deepest silence, to the Long Wharf, where a boat received them. They were rowed to the much-admired frigate, that was standing off-and-on, under easy sail, waiting their arrival. On her deck they met Agnes Danforth, with her eyes softened by tears, though a rich flush mantled on her cheeks, at witnessing the compelled departure of those invaders she had never loved.

"I have only remained to give you a parting kiss, cousin Lionel," said the frank girl, affectionately saluting him, "and now shall take my leave, without repeating those wishes that you know are so often conveyed in my prayers."

"You will, then, leave us?" said the young baronet, smiling for the first time in many a day. "You know that this cruelty—"

He was interrupted by a loud hem from Polwarth, who advanced, and, taking the hand of the lady, repeated his wish to retain it forever, for at least the fiftieth time. She heard him, in silence, and with much apparent respect, though an arch smile stole upon her gravity, before he had ended. She then thanked him with suitable grace, and gave a final and decided refusal. The captain sustained the repulse like one who had seen much similar service, and politely lent his assistance to help the obdurate girl into her boat. Here she was received by a young man, who was apparelled like an American officer. Sir Lionel thought the bloom on her cheek deepened, as her companion assiduously drew a cloak around her form to protect her from the chill of the water. Instead of returning to the town, the boat, which bore a flag, pulled directly for the shore occupied by the Americans. The following week, Agnes was united to this gentleman, in the bosom of her own family. They soon after took quiet possession of the house in Tremont Street, and of all the large real estate left by Mrs. Lechmere, which had been previously bestowed on her, by Cecil, as a dowry.

As soon as his passengers appeared, the captain of the frigate communicated with his admiral, by signal, and received, in return, the expected order to proceed in the execution of his trust. In a few minutes the swift vessel was gliding by the heights of Dorchester, training her guns on the adverse hills, and hurriedly spreading her canvas as she passed. The Americans, however, looked on in sullen silence, and she was suffered to gain the open ocean, unmolested, when she made the best of her way to England, with the important intelligence of the intended evacuation.

She was speedily followed by the fleet, since which period

the long-oppressed and devoted town of Boston has never been visited by an armed enemy.

During their passage to England, sufficient time was allowed Lionel and his gentle companion to reflect on all that had occurred. Together, and in the fullest confidence, they traced the wanderings of intellect which had so closely and mysteriously connected the deranged father with his impotent child; and, as they reasoned, by descending to the secret springs of his disordered impulses, they were easily enabled to divest the incidents we have endeavored to relate, of all their obscurity and doubt.

The keeper, who had been sent in quest of the fugitive madman, never returned to his native land. No offers of forgiveness could induce the unwilling agent in the death of the baronet to trust his person, again, within the influence of the British laws. Perhaps he was conscious of a motive, that none but an inward monitor might detect. Lionel, tired at length with importuning without success, commissioned the husband of Agnes to place him in a situation where, by industry, his future comfort was amply secured.

Polwarth died quite lately. Notwithstanding his maimed limb, he contrived, by the assistance of his friend, to ascend the ladder of promotion, by regular gradations, nearly to its summit. At the close of his long life, he wrote Gen., Bart., and M. P. after his name. When England was threatened with the French invasion, the garrison he commanded was distinguished for being better provisioned than any other in the realm, and no doubt it would have made a resistance equal to its resources. In Parliament, where he sat for one of the Lincoln boroughs, he was chiefly distinguished for the patience with which he listened to the debates, and for the remarkable cordiality of the "Ay" that he pronounced on every vote for supplies. To the day of his death, he was a strenuous advocate for the virtues of a rich diet, in all cases of physical suffering, "especially," as he would add, with an obstinacy that fed itself, "in instances of debility from febrile symptoms."

Within a year of their arrival, the uncle of Cecil died,

having shortly before followed an only son to the grave. By this unlooked-for event, Lady Lincoln became the possessor of his large estates, as well as of an ancient barony, that descended to the heirs general. From this time until the eruption of the French Revolution, Sir Lionel Lincoln, and Lady Cardonnell, as Cecil was now styled, lived together in sweetest concord ; the gentle influence of her affection moulding and bending the feverish temperament of her husband, at will. The heirloom of the family, that distempered feeling so often mentioned, was forgotten, in the even tenor of their happiness. When the heaviest pressure on the British Constitution was apprehended, and it became the policy of the minister to enlist the wealth and talent of his nation in its support, by propping the existing administration, the rich baronet received a peerage in his own person. Before the end of the century, he was further advanced to a dormant earldom, that had, in former ages, been one of the honors of an elder branch of his family.

Of all the principal actors in the foregoing tale, not one is now living. Even the roses of Cecil and Agnes have long since ceased to bloom, and Death has gathered them, in peace and innocence, with all that had gone before. The historical facts of our legend are beginning to be obscured by time ; and it is more than probable that the prosperous and affluent English peer, who now enjoys the honors of the house of Lincoln, never knew the secret history of his family, while it sojourned in a remote province of the British empire.

28

THE END.

9 781410 104007